MASK OF THE BLOOD QUEEN

Book Three of the World of Ruin

Erik Scott de Bie

MASK OF THE BLOOD QUEEN

"The World of Ruin:
A dying world—an inevitable end.
Much and many have been lost,
All must pass to Ruin."

Mask of the Blood Queen

Map created by Cory Gelnett

ISBN 13 978-1-98825661-0

www.dragonmoonpress.com

To Gabrielle, for believing in this story as much as I do,
and for all the nicknames she thinks up for Mask

Dear Reader

The World of Ruin series was originally going to be three books. Then, when I was halfway through writing book 2, *Shield of the Summer Prince*, I realized I was telling two entirely different stories: one about Ovelia, Garin, and Davargorn, and one about Regel and Semana. Two tales crammed together, and each of them would be the length of a novel when fully fleshed out. Rather than publish a half-measure, and tell each story halfway, my esteemed editor Gabrielle Harbowy suggested I break Regel and Semana's story into a third book, and then write a fourth to wrap everything up. Thus, this book, *Mask of the Blood Queen*, which you hold in your hands, which gives a full accounting of the harrowing journey of the ferocious winter princess and her deadly warder, Regel Oathbreaker.

Shield of the Summer Prince and *Mask of the Blood Queen* take place at roughly the same time, so they can be read in either order. Do bear in mind, however, that the epilogue of *Mask of the Blood Queen* takes place after the events in *Shield of the Summer Prince*, so if you want to preserve the revelations in that book, do make sure you've read it before you finish this one.

And there will be a fourth novel to conclude the series. And just as each of the first three bears its name in honor of one of the principal characters fate has chosen to tell this tale, so too will that novel take its name from an important figure in the World of Ruin. One whose chance for glory has yet to come, but will not be denied.

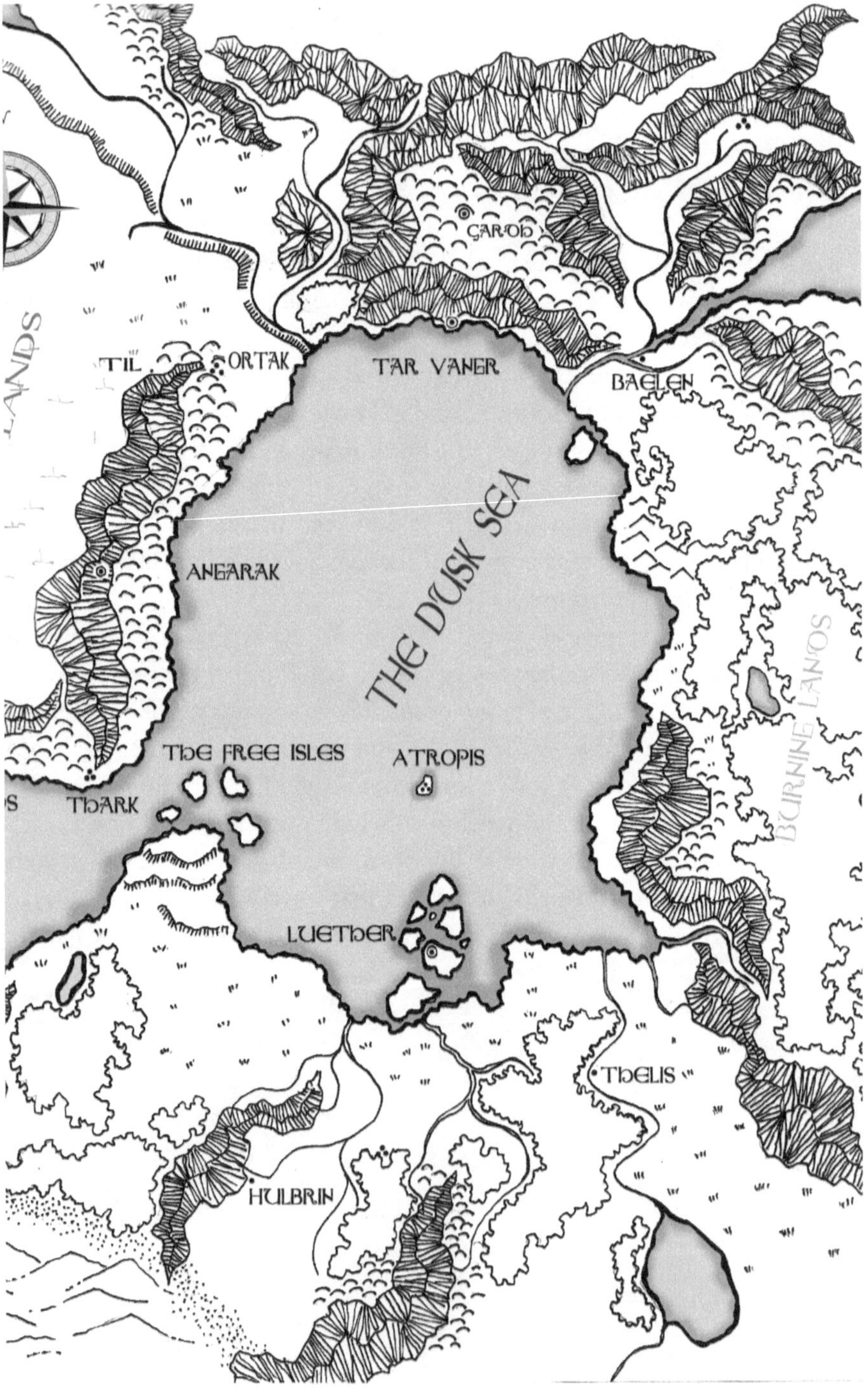
GAR'OTH
LANDS
TIL
ORTAK
TAR VANER
BAELEN
THE DUSK SEA
ANGARAK
BURNING LANDS
THE FREE ISLES
ATROPIS
THARK
LUETHER
THELIS
HULBRIN

PROLOGUE

The Winter Wilds—982 Sorcerus Annis

"You return with the Oathbreaker and the masked…*thing*," Lan Ravalis had said, "or you don't return at all."

Most of them had done exactly that. All but Loris.

Ten had set out from Tar Vangr on the Summer King's orders, and the snow-burned northland had claimed nine. And what he with his single sword could do against a sorcerer and his pet slayer, Loris did not know, but to go back was death. So he pushed on through the swirling blizzard, trying to comfort himself with vague memories of warmth.

Beneath the snow, the lands under Tar Vangr's aegis promised nothing but death to the unwary. Dizzying precipices, sheer cliffs, and forests of rock that could rend the flesh from an unwary traveler forbade all but the hardiest of pilgrims. The snow hid these dangers beneath a veneer of peaceful white, but the sense of security was illusory. A single false step could break through to a half-frozen river or a fathomless drop into darkness. Their guide had warned them to avoid snow that took on a ruddy cast, and anything that looked too white and pure. Such drifts contained burning acid or poisons of Ruin's wrath, awaiting contact with a man's skin that it might burn and ravage.

The priests of Loris's youth had spoken of an eternity of torment that awaited every man after death. But after nine days in the snow, he knew they had been wrong. He could imagine no landscape more forbidding than the one that greeted his every step, and no pain more terrible than the one that clutched at his chest with every breath.

Rhogas, their boisterous captain with his meticulous golden goatee, had been the first to go. When the cold air killed the ornithopter's engines and grounded the pursuit on the second day, Rhogas had made the decision to continue on foot. Not an hour later, a careless step took him on a shattering fall into a ravine. He dropped without a sound over the howling wind. That had put Loris in command, a task he had not savored then and bitterly regretted now.

The difficult landscape Loris might have borne, were it not for the persistent chill. It had started with a tingle in his skin and itching beneath, and after that first night it had settled in his bones like an uninvited guest who would not leave. However many skins he might don or however close to the fire he crept by night, he went to his blankets cold and awoke colder still.

Four days in, after most of them had lost toes and fingers to frostbite, Loris could hardly blame his fellows for the mutiny. He'd shot one man for desertion, but that didn't stop two others melting away during the bitter night that followed. That put their number at six, but scalding flurries, a foot cracked against an unseen root, and snow madness turned bloody reduced their band to two over the next three days. Before this quest, Loris had not imagined a man could die of three smashed toes, but poor Aeschius could do little more than scream as they left him behind, unable to stop lest they all collapse from the sheer cold.

The Winterborn guide had stuck it out better than any of the others, seeming to shrug off flurries that threatened to put summerblooded Loris down into a dreamless slumber. Few men amongst the Luethaar would trust a woman to don a soldier's uniform much less guide such a quest, but her sheer drive had instilled a healthy respect in Loris.

He had never known her name, he realized: Selya? Silka? He didn't remember.

A deadfall had claimed her two days back, and as he pulled her broken corpse from the rubble, all he could think—too late—is that he'd have liked to keep warm with her one of these bitter nights. He might have left her body in the ravine for the dead winter gods, but he had needed her furs to keep warm. That and the caster she'd carried. He'd already gone through four of the weapons, breaking down their mechanisms so he could press their fire-ensorcelled foci to his naked chest and belly under his furs. Were it not for the Thaumaturgy meant to slay their quarry, he would have succumbed to the winter long ago.

By the time Loris saw the campfire, his last reserves of strength had almost gone. The breath steaming in front of his face seemed thinner than it had an hour before and he could no longer feel his feet or hands. Down a rise beyond, Loris saw the snowy spikes of a forest he'd been approaching for days. Perhaps his quarry would have hid there, though he couldn't imagine how he'd find them, much less capture them, and even less likely return to Tar Vangr with them in tow.

One thing at a time.

Swaddled in the furs of half a dozen dead warriors and barely walking on legs like icicles, he thought the speck of light some kindly mirage for his winter-ruined mind. The little fire looked so tempting, though, that his heart broke at the thought it might not be real. He staggered a few more steps in the calf-deep snow, twice-gloved hand raised to shield his eyes from the drift. Sure enough, he saw the fire more clearly and could feel his skin prickle as it shook itself from an icy stupor. The flames drew him like a dumb brute, his mind sluggish and only instinct guiding his steps.

A dozen paces out, Loris summoned the presence of mind to slow to a wary approach. This could be a trap, his training told him. He drew his own caster—the last one, unused as yet—from its oiled pouch, beseeching it silently to function despite the chill. He'd taken care not to get the weapon wet, as damp could disrupt its Thaumaturgical function. He could feel the warm magic radiating within—dimmed but not gone. The snowflakes evaporating from its warm haft reassured and comforted him.

A lone figure hunkered beside the fire, an old man whose gray beard dripped with snowmelt. He'd laid camp seemingly out in the open, but when Loris approached, the wind vanished behind a low rise and he found himself entering a circle of pleasant warmth. Clearly the old man knew the bitter weather well. The snow had melted near the fire, revealing rough stones and dirt. A long walking stick leaned against the stump upon which the old man sat, and a beaten leather pack sat at his feet. He'd bared his face to the weather, but a leather mask with goggles hung from his belt where he could don it quickly.

To occupy himself, the old man was carving something from a block of light wood. Whatever he was roasting on the two spits over the fire smelled amazing, and Loris's stomach lurched.

"Be welcome, traveler." The old man spoke without looking up from his carving. He hardly seemed to notice Loris's drawn caster. "Share my fire and warm yourself."

It was a friendly greeting, but Loris was a soldier, not a fool. He hadn't the least idea who the old man might be or how he had come to this place that was so intolerant of life. "Are you alone, graybeard?"

"No." The old man adjusted the spits. "You are here as well, syr."

"So I am." Loris huffed. The old man had some wit to him, then. "Are you a loyal King's man?"

The old man looked up at Loris with eyes of such deep blue they seemed black. "Beyond death."

Loris suppressed a shiver at the cold words. The wind howled beyond the bounds of the camp, reminding him of what awaited. All around them stretched empty fields of snow and rock back up into the mountains. They seemed quite alone. Loris saw no weapon or real threat, and he needed the warmth of that fire and shelter from the cutting wind.

"Good enough." Loris slid his caster back into its sheath. "I'll share your fire, then."

The old man nodded to a second weathered stump, and Loris sat gladly. The winds all but vanished and he felt genuine warmth for the first time in days. He breathed deep of the enticing roast—two rabbits, he realized—and his mouth started to dampen. His chapped lips hurt.

Without being asked, the old man took one of the rabbits from the fire and offered it across. Loris opened his mouth, but the old man talked over him. "I have little, but please, eat of my food and be my guest," he said. "Out of loyalty to the true King of Tar Vangr."

So speaking, he thrust the point of the spit into the icy ground between them. Loris, who had eaten nothing but mostly frozen biscuits and tough salt jerky for days, accepted gladly. He snatched up the rabbit and bit in greedily, a shudder of pleasure rushing through him as the hot juices seared his tongue. He relished the pain. The rabbit was good and eased the gnawing ache in his belly.

The old man watched him eat without comment and even offered the second rabbit, then one of the blackened potatoes sizzling among the coals. This treasure Loris hadn't even imagined, and he ate that too, cracking open the ash-coated skin for the soft flesh beneath. The old man even uncorked a flask of whiskey and shared it, though he himself drank only little. Through it all, he said and asked nothing but only sat in companionable silence as Loris restored himself.

And somehow, Loris found himself talking. He spoke of his mission, his dead companions, even about himself.

He told the old man about Dell and Delwa, brother and sister and both stronger than three men, who had gone mad in the blur of the winter wind and hacked each other to pieces, bellowing all the while. Perhaps they'd really thought the other was their quarry, or perhaps—deep down—they'd just wanted to be warm again. He spoke about Captain Rhogas and about their winterborn guide—Skilla, he was certain now—and how he had grown to respect her. The old man listened to all without comment.

They became like old friends—Loris and the old man—though they had never met, and the weary hunter felt entirely at ease. He could not credit the feeling, but it seemed entirely natural that he would talk. The old man's lined face had a demeanor that encouraged confidence—eyes that had seen much and ears that had heard more. It was not until Loris had spoken for nearly an hour that it occurred to him that he should stop before he said the wrong thing or said too much.

And just at that moment, the old man finally asked a question. He adjusted his coat sleeve, which had revealed the edge of a leather bracer. "These fugitives," he said. "What of them?"

A warning sounded dully in Loris's whiskey-soaked mind. "What business is it of yours?"

The old man shrugged. "Perhaps I have seen them, and even if not, perhaps I will in the future. I would not wish to invite dangerous folk to my fire."

"No, perhaps not." Loris grinned. "They are deadly indeed, if the tales are to be believed. A terrible sorcerer clad in black leather, whose gaze melts men's flesh. A mighty warrior who accompanies him—warder and guide both. Certainly you would know them if you saw them."

He might have stopped there, but his befuddled mind could not quite control his tongue.

"Traitors and assassins, if you'd know the truth of it," he continued. "Slew a king and fled into Ruin's Night. Cowards." He took a long pull of the flask. "It doesn't surprise me. A withered wretch, rotten within and without, and a broken husk of a would-be bloodbreaker. Neither a man worthy of…"

Belatedly, Loris realized he'd trailed off, his mouth suddenly full of a thick wetness. He tried to swallow, but his stomach heaved up more, and he spat something black and sizzling into the snow.

The old man was looking back over his shoulder, expression disapproving.

"What?" Loris asked of no one. He lurched halfway to his feet before his legs failed and he slumped into the snow. Poison?

The old man was on his feet, facing away toward the low rise that miraculously blocked the wind. He was shouting, but Loris could not catch the words in the sudden flurry. It was as though whatever protection they had enjoyed had vanished.

Trap, Loris thought. The old man had set a trap for him. Loris closed shivering fingers around his caster but they slipped off and the weapon dropped it in the snow. He scrambled to pick it up again, and its energies flared to hot life. If he was going to die, he would not die alone. Loris raised the weapon to aim at the old man's back.

Then the air shimmered and he felt a gust of wind so cold it *burned.* The fire magic coursing through the caster evaporated into cold mist, and frost shot up Loris's arm, leaving numb emptiness in its wake. The limb was just gone, no longer flesh at all. At his feet, the flames of the campfire dimmed and froze, turned instantly into thin sheets of sharp ice.

A black-swathed figure stepped out of the snowy mist, blue fire coursing around its limbs. It wore black leather strapped across every inch of its thin body, including a black mask that allowed only thin slits for eyes and nose.

Tendrils of twisting green and black magic snaked from the sorcerer's mask, shifting in the air like living things. A mass of a dozen or so of the strands connected the mask to Loris himself, and wherever they touched, he felt his body growing sore, weak, and…*rotten*. Dying.

"You were half right," the creature in a broken mess of a voice. "Only one of us is a man."

Then it drew off the mask, breaking the connection, and revealed its face. *Her* face: a sallow but unmistakably striking visage, from proud nose to hazel eyes flecked with red to silver-blonde hair that fell to her shoulders. She pulled thin lips back from sharp teeth in a smile that looked too predatory for a young woman's face. Loris suddenly remembered a portrait he had seen once of a long-dead winter princess, daughter of the Winter King and heir of Blood Denerre, and he thought this woman looked like her, but for the red in her eyes, the warmer skin, and the fury on her face.

"The other of us is not a man," she said, "but a monster."

She raised her left hand, which was cloaked in a silver mesh of rings, but the old man seized her arm and stepped between her and Loris. "Semana," he said. "Enough."

She turned her burning gaze on him. "Unhand me, Oathbreaker."

A lesser man would have quailed, but the old man stood firm. "This man is our guest. You will not dishonor us by striking him."

"He is a summerblood," Semana said. "He is a stooge of the Ravalis. He is our enemy."

Loris fumbled to draw his sword in his off-hand, since he couldn't feel the other. The plague magic had ceased for a moment, and the old man's interruption had bought him a breath. Their argument was his chance.

Awkwardly, he rose and steadied his sword over his frozen gauntlet for a thrust. He could cut out the witch's throat in her distraction, and then it would be just the old man. Loris struck.

The old man reacted faster than Loris could have expected, moving before he saw the attack coming—before Loris had so much as launched it. The old man grasped the staff leaning against the stump, whirled, and knocked the sword ringing from the hunter's fingers. He seemed much younger in that moment, and unstoppable.

The blow carried through and struck his frozen arm, which shattered under the force, sending shards of red ice cascading into the snow. It didn't hurt—Loris hardly felt it at all—but it was the horror of watching himself maimed that made the scream batter against his teeth. Gasping and cursing, Loris stumbled only to find himself face-to-face with the one called Semana. Her eyes were big and bright on his, and she pressed her silver gloved hand to his chest. Caught in her bewitching hazel eyes, Loris wondered at the trick of the light that had made them seem red. In that moment, she became beautiful and delicate, like an impossibly blooming flower in winter.

"Enemy," she said.

Then magic flared, her eyes gleamed red once more, and she was a monster again. Loris smelled the reek of magic sparking to life. From her silver gauntlet came a mighty blow that struck him not only in the chest but swept in all directions like ripples in a pool. He heard more than felt his bones shattering in a hot storm, ripping out through his flesh, and then the wave reached his head.

Cloak stirring in the cutting wind, Regel the Oathbreaker stood over the bloody mess in the snow. Without the silver gauntlet's magic, the invisible wall that had shielded him before had loosed the storm like a broken dam. He held up one hand to shield his eyes and pulled his cowl lower. "Semana," he said.

The princess stood, arms outstretched as though to embrace the storm. Snow swirled around her like a tide of tiny white blades that could not bite into her skin. The cold never seemed to touch her.

"Semana," he said again.

Finally she seemed to notice him and sighed. Semana waved her hand, and magic flared from the silver gauntlet to shield them from the blizzard's onslaught. Regel looked up at the invisible walls where the snow broke like waves.

"That was not necessary."

"Was it not? He was a villain and our enemy." The princess averted her eyes, chin raised against the blizzard as though toward the sun. "And I am Mask, the greatest slayer this world has ever known."

Regel let that pass without comment. He knelt down in the snow beside the twitching body, and listened as the last gasps of life inexorably fled its broken frame. "He could have told us much and more about the forces arrayed behind us. The hunters."

"Then go back and find out for yourself," Semana said. "I'll go on alone."

They stared at one another, neither moving or speaking. Both knew that would never happen.

"We've been dodging and ducking hunters for half a season now." Semana shrugged and closed her eyes. "That one told us all he knew. He was less useful than a corpse. At least now there is quiet."

"You should not be so quick to kill," Regel said.

"Why, because I am so pure and sweet?" Semana asked. "That part of me died long ago."

"Because he was a living man," Regel said. "He had a story of his own. Purpose. Dreams. He had a home. A family."

She looked over her shoulder at him, and her golden eyes held no mercy. "So did I."

Regel met her gaze briefly, then nodded. He noted, however, that Semana pointedly did not look down at her handiwork. She was not so hard as she pretended.

"We should move on," he said.

Semana held the gaze levelly. "I trust there is some purpose to all this wandering and moralizing, or do you merely intend us to kill slayers for the rest of our short, bitterly cold lives?"

"Yes."

"Yes to the purpose, or yes to the wandering?"

"We should move on," Regel said again. "Unless you think Lan Ravalis would have sent only a single hunting party."

That made Semana's icy visage crack into a smile. "I am surprised he still lives, after what the Bloodbreaker did to him. Almost a shame she's dead." Regel hesitated, just for half a breath, and Semana narrowed her eyes. "What. You don't agree?"

"She had her uses." The Oathbreaker stuffed their gear in his pack. "I would give much to have her beside us."

"No doubt you would." The princess's look of uncertainty became one of disgust. "She was worse than any of them. A Ravalis mongrel of dirty summerblood. She failed to save my mother, she seduced my father, and she killed my greatfather." Her chin rose. "I won't mourn the death of that traitor."

"You should learn to tell your foes from your friends," Regel said.

"Oh, I have. I know just how to see the monsters." Semana looked at him sidelong. "Do you?"

She turned and strode into the snow, leaving Regel uneasy. The wind howled, and the cold seemed to cut straight through his furs deep into the flesh beneath. He glanced back to the south, where the dark rise of Tar Vangr could just be seen on the misty horizon, through the swirling snow. He drew up his hood against the chill and followed his princess across the snow-swept plain.

BOOK ONE: FUGITIVES

Five Years Previous—Tar Vangr—Ruin's Eve, 976 Sorcerus Annis

Ashes wafted down from the sky where snow should have fallen, the desiccated corpses of exploded fireworks. They burned at a touch, leaving a sticky brown residue on her putrid black leathers. What was another layer of grime to add to the filth of so many years of atrocities? It might have been decades, or centuries even. How long had that monster worn these leathers, never losing a battle?

Semana Denerre nô Ravalis, last Princess of Winter, had worn them less than an hour, and she had already failed. She had watched the treacherous Ovelia Dracaris murder her greatfather, and for all the power Mask had offered, she could not stop it.

Buoyant upon the magic of her boots, she darted through the night sky over Tar Vangr, narrowly eluding trailing streamers of burning paper and phosphorous. Silently, she willed one of them to strike her from the sky, that she might die along with the rest of her family. All the ones who mattered, at least.

Her mother Lenalin, long dead. Her brother Darak, exiled and lost. Her greatfather Orbrin murdered this night. And a slayer had come for her as well.

She, in her thirteenth winter, was the last of her Blood.

Narrowly, Semana dodged a blackened smokestack with a sharp gasp of greasy air. She spun madly through the rising smoke and only narrowly righted herself to float up into the sky. Even if she had the full focus to pay attention, Semana could only barely control her weightless travel. Even the most subtle shifts of her feet propelled her in unexpected directions, and keeping her balance had become a constant struggle. Even now, she flew higher and higher into the skies over Tar Vangr, twisting around ashy plumes and through drifts of burning snow.

The tainted air of the World of Ruin infected the clouds above, making the rain burn like acid and the snow tingle on exposed skin. Mask's leathers protected every inch of Semana's flesh, from face to boot, and she shut her eyes by reflex against the haze as she floated through it. She felt the burning on her eyelids and almost opened her eyes to let it in. But even in the depths of her helpless anguish, the familiar spark of pragmatism that had never left her kept her from blinding herself.

She would have vengeance in many ways, and the first would be by surviving this. She swore it.

In the skies over Tar Vangr, Semana righted herself and worked to stabilize her course. She'd only worn the boots perhaps an hour now, but she was coming to learn how they functioned. The trick was to move her feet only slightly, sometimes just by tensing or relaxing her calves. It reminded her of learning to walk all over again, but Semana had always been a fast learner. How else could she have achieved the relative miracle of not only escaping the sinking Heiress but also flying across half of Tar Vangr to land on the palace balcony?

The palace, where she'd watched—

Distracted, Semana found herself falling in an uncontrolled spiral, one of her legs thrust out to propel her around and around at dizzying speeds. She tried to steady herself with her hands, but there was no magic in those. She tumbled from the sky like a broken black bird, tattered cloak flailing like ruined wings behind her. The smoke of her magic marked her path like footprints in the air.

She crashed through a tower window thrown open to the fireworks of Ruin's Night, prompting screams from the Vangryur huddled inside. Hands jerked and words flew and screams vibrated through the air in a cacophony of colors and swirling snow. Semana experienced the episode in a dizzy blur, as her feet ended up under her and the boots launched her out an opposite window from the elevated room. This one stood only half open, and she smashed the shutters outward against the snowy night with a stinging rush that left her coughing and sputtering as she flew on.

Finally, despite the pain and dizziness, Semana managed to calm herself and straighten out to fly sideways, rather than down. She realized she'd lost perhaps a hundred paces of altitude. She now skimmed the domed rooftops of Tar Vangr, her wake stirring the banners of ice-stiffened fabric that hung otherwise undisturbed in the snowy night. By moving her feet and legs, she could change her trajectory radically to change course and avoid obvious obstacles. She could avoid smashing wholly into a wall, perhaps, but she needed to learn to steer more subtly to avoid unforeseen obstacles, like—

A spire loomed out of the darkness, and Semana caught her breath. By instinct, she threw her left hand forward as though to catch herself, and unseen magic exploded out to knock her spinning. Her right arm cracked against the stone with numbing force. Mask's barbed war gauntlet—the one that expelled fire at her will—hung loosely at her side, barely affixed to her now useless arm.

Gritting her teeth against the pain, Semana forced herself to think. That'd been bad, but at least she'd learned something. She'd lashed out blindly before, but now that she knew what was coming, she could control it. The glove on her left hand had magic of its own, and she would learn to control it.

Semana opened herself to the silver glove, awakened its magic, and shoved out with invisible force. The bricks of a nearby tower shifted slightly, and she found herself floating in the opposite direction. She sent out multiple gentle pulses, more refined with experience. Between the boots and the silver glove, she managed to float steadily among the spires. It would take more practice, but Semana would master flying with Mask's relics in time.

Semana felt so alone. She was a tiny bird flying above the sprawling mage-city below, with its two platter-like tiers. Above, the powerful and named dwelled in a city built upon mage-glass: limpid crystal stronger than steel. Below, the nameless smallborn masses eked out a living that grew harder and harder each year among the dregs and runoff from high-city. Semana drifted amongst Tar Vangr's reaching spires, blending in with the night sky and illumined only incidentally when a stray firework exploded near her. The celebrations of Ruin's Night had mostly ended, and a new year had begun. The city as a whole didn't yet know its king lay dead, which would shroud this new year in chaos.

The relative calm left her alone with her thoughts. She pushed the grief aside and looked at the world with an icy calm. Who had done it? Who had sent Mask to slay her? She'd stumbled upon a conspiracy to slay the Blood of Winter, and she had almost no idea who had taken part or why. When she'd confronted the Frostburn, his confusion had proved he was not part of it, but who was? Before tonight, she'd have trusted Ovelia Dracaris with her life, but she'd just watched the woman slay her greatfather. Who could she trust? She had Tithian, but in what possible world would he be enough?

Her father. Paeter would know what to do. And he would be the king. He could protect her.

She'd have to approach him cautiously. For all she knew, he was part of the conspiracy. They'd never got on particularly well, but he was her best chance. Her only chance, perhaps.

She turned in the air and looked back to the top of the palace, with its great black glass dome rising above Tar Vangr. As a child, she'd thought it the top of the world itself—certainly the top of *her* world. Gazing at it now, she wondered if she would ever see it again after this night.

"Yes," she said, her voice soft.

She closed her hands into fists.

When she spoke again, Semana's voice came out cold and ragged.

"Yes," she said.

The Twisted Tower was a popular tavern in high-city: a common house that had taken over one of the lesser holdings of a Blood that had died out two centuries past. Its greatest claim to infamy was an apocryphal legend that the original founder of the Tower had broken that Blood herself and poured the first bowl of wine over the corpse of the Blood's last heir. As a child, Semana had thrilled to that particular story, but as she had grown, she'd realized that such a thing was not likely. Of all the monsters the World of Ruin had to offer, Bloodbreakers were one of the most hated. Were their crimes known, they could not own property in Tar Vangr, let alone seize the holdings of those they had destroyed. In the tale, the Tower's first owner would have been chased out of the city if not slain out of hand.

As she circled the tower, trying to determine the correct angle of approach, Semana wondered idly if Ovelia Dracaris would be named a Bloodbreaker now, if she was thought dead. By revealing herself as alive, would Semana not do a service to the treacherous woman? Ovelia might have slain a king, but at least she had not ended a Blood tracing back over a thousand years.

A churning panic was building in Semana, but she couldn't give it voice. She had to think clearly. She had to, or she would surely scream. Focus, she told herself. Careful—

She saw it. A window at the top of the Twisted Tower, which had been left open despite the chill, per instructions. Tithian had proved useful in that, at least. Semana turned her boots toward the high window, using her glove to make small adjustments as she approached. Her right arm still ached badly from when she'd slammed it against the spire, so she clenched her teeth, hoping she wouldn't hit it again. As the window grew larger—but not nearly large enough for her peace of mind—Semana tried hard not to visualize loosing an arrow through the eye of a needle.

She might have learned to fly well enough, but landing proved quite a bit more complicated.

Semana came in entirely too fast, whistling through the window before smashing through hanging curtains and overturning a standing wardrobe, which sent her into a crazy spin into the far wall. She managed to slow enough that she didn't shatter her bones when she hit, but the resulting crash sent aches all over as she slumped moaning against the wall. Papers and the remains of fabric swirled all around her, and burning snow wafted in through the open window.

A figure shuffled through the semi-darkness to crouch beside her. One luminous white eye gleamed at her. "Princess—" Tithian said.

"No!" she said, her voice breaking. "The window, you fool!"

Tithian's good eye widened, and he hurried to close the window through which she had come. She could tell he was shivering in the cold, but she didn't feel it. That pain, at least, she didn't have to endure. He came back to her then, this time bringing the dripping candle from the table. In its flickering light, his drawn face looked tighter than usual.

"I'm well," Semana said, interpreting his anxiety as concern for her.

"That—that's good," he said, looking a little confused. "Princess, I have to tell you—"

"None of that," she said. "I'm not your princess, nor Semana—not until we find out what is happening." A shudder passed through her, and she gritted her teeth against the fear and unreasoning panic. She had no time for hysterics. Her life—Tithian's life—all of it depended on her control. "My greatfather—Orbrin, the Winter King—lies dead."

Tithian shuddered as though Semana had punched him in the stomach. "No," he said.

"Yes." Semana set her teeth. "Murdered by Ovelia Dracaris."

"The King's Shield?" Tithian's face grew pale indeed. "Surely there's been some mistake—"

Semana shook her head firmly. "It happened. I saw it with my own eyes," she said. "Ravalis blades took her—maybe killed her. The Frostburn was there, too."

"He was her ally?" Tithian asked.

Semana considered that, then shook her head. "He was as surprised as I was."

Trembling with growing fear, Tithian put his hands up to his head as though to contain it from bursting. Semana could veritably feel the terrified panic rising up in him, threatening to break his mind. Strange, to watch him lose control while she, who had suffered far more directly, was able to hold herself together. She should have lost control as surely as he did, but somehow it all seemed far away—behind an icy wall she had built within herself. The horror raged against it like a tidal wave crashing against the rocks below a tower. She could watch it safely from the battlements, untouched by madness and loss.

In any case, Tithian looked like a child on the verge of a screaming fit, and she couldn't have that. She grasped his head tightly and held his forehead against hers.

"Tithian," she said softly, her voice a scant whisper. "I need you. Do not leave me."

The words sent a fresh shudder through him, but then his body calmed. His mismatched eyes opened and searched her face. "What would you have of me, master?" he asked.

"I need you to hold yourself fast, at least long enough to find my father," she said. "The prince will need to know what has befallen this night. The throne is his now, and he will be able to help. Or perhaps he might be against us, but that we need to know. Either way—what?"

Again Tithian recoiled as though she had struck him.

"What?" Semana asked, irked at his inability to remain calm. "You disagree?"

"That's just it," Tithian said. "Your father, he—" He shook his head. "Prince Paeter is dead."

"You—what?" Semana furrowed her brow. "No. That's not true. That doesn't make any sense."

Her denial fell on deaf ears. Tithian shook his head. "It passed," he said. "This night, in low-city, a slayer cut down Prince Paeter."

She knew he wasn't lying to her. "But why? This night was about slaying the last of Denerre," she said, her mind racing. "If the Ravalis were behind it, why would they slay their own? And if they weren't, why would someone kill the king and prince and princess all? Who would remain to claim power? Who could possibly want—?"

Tithian put his arms around Semana. "I'm sorry," he said. "I'm so sorry."

Semana didn't know what to say. She stared over Tithian's shoulder.

And then, as though something had broken inside her, it finally became too much to ignore. The pain and loss rose up and bloomed inside her, awakening a thousand burning hurts just under her skin. The armor was suddenly stifling, closing around her like iron shackles, and she couldn't breathe. She shoved Tithian away, gasping and choking, and reached up with shaking hands to the clasps of her mask. She fumbled at the catches, desperately trying to pull it free. Tithian started to return, but she snarled at him and drove him back with one stiff arm. Her pounding heart felt like it would burst from her chest.

Tithian approached once more, hands up. "Let me help you," he said.

"Get it off," Semana said. "Get it off! Get it off!"

As she knelt, taut and shivering, his fingers worked at the clasps of her mask. She moaned, a deep rumble of horror from the pit of her gut, and finally the mask came loose. She ripped it off, uncaring for threads of her hair caught in the leather, and hurled the horrid thing against the wall. She vomited, but she could bring up nothing but dry heaves. Semana turned to trying to open the leather cuirass, at which she partly succeeded before her hands went entirely numb and all she could do was sit there and weep.

Her entire Blood, drained away. Her enemies, unknown and powerful. Her resources, diminished.

And all she wanted was her mother, who'd been dead almost her entire life.

Tithian put his arms around Semana anew. She tried to pull away, but she had no strength for it. Instead, she relaxed into his embrace and wept bitter tears for the horrid jest it all seemed. He held her for a time as she railed against the world, unable to understand how it could go so wrong and unwilling to try.

For his part, Tithian spoke to her, offering soothing words she did not bother trying to understand. Instead, Semana listened mostly to the tone of his voice rather than its content. She wondered if he knew the effect his voice had upon her—that she clung to it like a line cast to a drowning woman. Even if everyone else had abandoned her, at least he remained: a warm and solid bulwark in her life.

For all her resolve—all her brave self-assurance that vengeance was not only possible but within her grasp—Semana thought she might have gone mad without her last friend there to reassure her.

After a long, long time, during which Tithian held Semana in her trembling, at length the world seemed less awful. All the same tragedy remained, but it seemed less onerous somehow. And it would feel less the next day, and the next. She drew away, and at first he tried to hold on. Semana would not indulge herself in more comfort than she required, however, so she pushed him gently but firmly aside.

"What do we do now?" Tithian asked.

Semana considered. She knew she could not go back. At best, one of the Ravalis would claim her as a prisoner to secure his crown. At worst, the conspiracy was theirs, and her blood would stain the palace floor. And even if the Ravalis were not behind the slayings, how long would she last as the only Blood of Winter amongst the refuse of Summer?

Semana Denerre was no one's toy, and she would not be a victim.

"We do as I said on the *Heiress*," she said.

Tithian looked at her with obvious confusion, and she shook her head. No wonder he needed to hear it again. It had seemed like years ago, while in truth it had all come to pass not an hour before.

"We go forward as though Mask succeeded," she said. "I am he, and you are his apprentice. In this way, we will use his contacts, identify his allies, and find who enlisted him to kill me."

"How can we do that?" Tithian asked. "We don't even know where to start."

Semana shook her head. "We do as a mage slayer would," she said. "Slay."

ONE

The Winter Wilds

The Bloodbreaker's dark face floated before her, wreathed in crimson curls, and they breathed together in the semi-darkness of the hall. Light flashed over the woman's golden skin, illumining the tightly knotted jaw and the dark blood trickling from between her lips. Deep crevasses of worried shadow traced the eyes. There was pain there—behind those golden-hazel eyes—but there was victory too.

Slowly, the face relaxed, and the lips spread into a smile.

Then one black-gloved hand rose between them, fingers curled like talons. Mask's hand. It reached toward the Bloodbreaker's blissful face.

Then green fire flared between them, and the Bloodbreaker sailed away to slam into the opposite wall. Mask's magic held her in place, contorted in agony, screaming soundlessly. Her clothes burned, and the fire lanced into her over and over. Her face was on fire, her eyes smoldering in their sockets. All the while, she did not look away.

The Bloodbreaker collapsed to the floor, a smoking ruin, her crimson hair half burned away, the remainder crackling like burned straw. Ashes floated like searing snowflakes from Ruin. Her chest heaved one last time, and she spoke even though she should have been dead.

Her words vanished in the howl of the wind and flame.

Semana awoke sitting bolt-upright, shoulders heaving. Cold moisture drenched her face and neck, and she thought for one horrible moment it might be blood. But she wiped it away, and her fingers came away clear with sweat. Frozen tears burned on her cheeks, and she flicked them away.

She looked around, heart thudding, but there was no reaving green fire, no throne room, no dying Bloodbreaker. Instead, she saw canvas walls flapping in the winter breeze. Cold light filtered through the tarred edges of the ratty tent, offering only a little warmth where it touched Semana's bare skin. She looked again at her bare fingers, and her bare arm, then down at herself. A thick blanket covered her lower half, but she wore only a thin shift above the waist. She shivered for a reason that had nothing to do with the cold she could not feel.

She felt weak without her armor—lonely and vulnerable.

Mask's leathers lay beside her bedroll, sagging without flesh not unlike a shriveled corpse. She'd arranged them the night before as though they were a person, and the illusion was enough to make her shiver. The armor smelled like old blood and unwashed, dead flesh. The black mask glared up at her reproachfully, as if to condemn her for removing it in the first place. She hadn't wanted to, but her companion insisted that sleeping in the armor would weary her.

Semana made a face. "Burn you, Regel."

She threw off the blanket and immediately pulled the leather breeches over her slender legs and cinched her storing belt. The leathers' tight fit reassured her: as though death embraced her and made her its own. She buckled on the cuirass without bothering to bind her breasts first, but it fit well enough. Her body had never put on much flesh. The armor wouldn't allow it. Her *task* wouldn't.

Semana cast about for her gloves. After a heartbeat, she remembered that she had lost her fire-throwing gauntlet in the clash in the throne room, despite having just wielded the magic in her dream. She felt the loss anew like a knife to the bowels. She'd worn that gauntlet every day for five years—learned its secrets, used its powers, kept herself and Tithian alive on particularly cold nights. And now that it was gone, she felt like a piece of herself had gone with it. Her bare right hand seemed so burning *useless*: little more than sinew and bones.

Insanely, she had the impulse to hack off the pointless appendage, and she reached for her silver mesh relic to do just that. It was not, however, near to hand. Her head growing warm, Semana fumbled about the tent, throwing their meager stores of gear and clothes aside, but she could not find it.

Regel. He must have taken it.

Semana tore open the tent and stepped barefoot into the snowy bowl in which they'd laid camp. The object of her vehemence sat on a stump, tending a surprisingly healthy fire considering the deep snow. Silvery flakes drifted on the breeze, and she instinctively flinched from their burning touch. Ten days out from Tar Vangr, though, the weather wasn't quite as caustic. The smell of cooking meat filled her nostrils, and her watering mouth undercut some of her righteous fury.

"Morn." Regel turned a spit over the fire, upon which sizzled and spat the corpse of some woodland animal. Two potatoes bubbled amongst the coals. "Hungry?"

Semana crossed her arms and willed her stomach not to growl. "My glove?"

Regel nodded to the spindly tree in the middle of their camp, where the silver mesh hung from a branch. "It used up its magic before dawn, but the worst of the storm was past."

Semana's mind put it together easily enough. Against her better judgment, she'd showed Regel how to set up barrier wards against the snow with the relic. He must have taken it from the tent after she fell asleep, then left the glove secured in place to maintain the effect. She stomped over to it, where it hung in a blackened, soot-stained circle. The tree upon which Regel had mounted the relic drooped noticeably, its vibrancy leeched by the glove's magic, and it smelled like rot. The branch cracked and crumbled away under the slightest pressure.

"Wonderful." Semana slid the glove onto her left hand as Regel watched dubiously. She sensed immediately that it was all but drained. She could perhaps move a feather, but that was all. "And now it won't rebuild its charge until the eve. Did you mean to leave me powerless?"

Regel offered no answer to that, which infuriated her. Instead, he held out the meat. "Rabbit," he said. "It's easy enough to find their hideaways, if you know where to look."

"Not hungry." She flopped down onto the other stump by the fire.

"As you will. I caught two." Regel took a bite of the cooked flesh, then drew out one of his falcata to spear a potato. One of their last, Semana thought. He glanced at her feet. "Boots?"

Semana looked down at her bare feet, which were darker than the snow, but obviously made pale in the cold. In her haste, she hadn't even thought to put them on. "I don't feel it."

That made Regel pause in devouring his meal. After a moment, he bit into his potato.

"The magic of your Blood," he said. "Frostfire."

"As you say." Semana ran her fingers over the silver mesh, tracing the cords and rings. "I'll put my trust in relics I can touch. In magic I know."

Regel nodded, but she could tell he didn't understand. How could he? He was just a lowborn slayer—just an old man, for all the legends that surrounded him. He knew nothing of magic. So why was she bothering to follow him? Because he was her father?

"I'm done with sleep," she said finally. "Ready for another day on the endless road into the snowy wilderness. When are we leaving?"

"Soon." Regel took a bite of his potato and chewed thoughtfully. He put it back in the firepit. "These are not quite ready."

They sat in silence. Regel didn't seem to look at Semana—at her bare feet and hand—but she felt his scrutiny. She made a show of ignoring her hunger, but the potatoes gave off an enticing smell. She used the silver glove's invisible hand to edge the potato out of the coals before it got too black. She didn't like her food burned. If Regel noticed the thin plume of smoke rising from her hand, he said nothing of it.

"I want to move," Semana said. "I want to fight. I want to do something."

Regel glanced over his shoulder toward a ridge of mountains far in the distance. "An hour yet before it's warm enough," he said. "But if you want to fight—" In two long, smooth motions he drew one of his falcata, reversed it, and extended it toward Semana. "Then we fight."

That, at least, made her smile slightly. "Sword play," she said. "Me."

"Where is it written a sorcerer cannot swing a sword?" he asked. "Or a princess?"

Semana took the proffered blade. For years, she'd had Tithian to swing a sword but also eyes to watch him, so she had a basic concept of how this was done. She took a two-handed grip on the handle of Regel's falcat—both hands fit, thanks to their relative smallness—and stepped back into what she hoped was a decent approximation of a warrior's pose. She wondered idly if she'd ever see Tithian again, and whether she even wanted to. Just thinking of him squeezed her guts in all sorts of unpleasant contortions: guilt, shame, anger, indignation. She flexed her left hand in the silver glove, the power barely whispering around her fingers.

"If you insist on using my weapon to make us more comfortable, Syr Shadow, then I may as well learn to use yours to do the opposite." Semana held the sword pointed at Regel's face. "Teach me, then."

Regel adjusted his stance gracefully, albeit not quite as smoothly as she remembered him moving when they'd met the previous year. Ruin's Night had left its mark, and Regel favored the leg that had taken a casterbolt at close range. All this walking couldn't have been good for the healing process.

Regel had made a massive sacrifice for her in this regard. Not that she had asked him to.

With an impassive expression, Regel stepped around Semana to scrutinize her at various angles, then made an unimpressed sound. "We need to fix your stance."

"I'm sure that's an exaggeration," Semana said. "Show me—"

Regel stepped into her range, pushing her off balance without even trying, and twisted the blade from her hand in one smooth motion. It rang against a stray boulder and slid into the snow. Regel's scabbarded falcat ended up at Semana's throat.

"Point taken," she said. "I'll listen patiently."

Silently, Regel tapped Semana's leg until she moved it into the position he wanted: her feet about shoulder width apart and only a little uneven, her arms up. Her muscles quivered in the unusual pose.

He laid his hands on her shoulders. "Relax," he said. "Do not expend your energy while at rest."

"You relax," Semana said. "This position comes naturally to you."

"Only with practice," he said.

She raised the blade. "Show me again."

Over the next hour or so, Regel showed her simple footwork: how to move forward and back, side to side, around in a circle without taking her focus from her opponent. He taught her to use her weight and leverage and how to strike with the muscles of her legs more than those of her arms, so that she wouldn't tire herself out swinging the blade. Only when what seemed like an hour had passed did he collect his second sword from the snow and put it in her hand. He showed her an easy one-handed grip, with her other hand poised lightly on the pommel of the sword for leverage. The grip felt simultaneously more comfortable and also unwieldy, at least until Regel showed her how to pull the pommel as she cut to create additional force. Then it felt powerful.

By the fifth time Regel had put Semana on her backside in the snow, her cocksure attitude had melted like the snow into grim frustration.

"Balance." Regel swiped his sword through the air twice to stretch. "Where you step is more important than how to strike."

Surging up with a growl, Semana scraped the sword up off the ground and smashed into Regel's defense. She took some satisfaction in making him strain to block her assault, then fumbled to get into the proper position he had demonstrated for her stance.

"Better," he said. "But keep your anger under control. You need to know the fundamentals before you start throwing yourself into battle."

"I know them" Not entirely true. If only this came as easily as did magic, Semana would have overpowered and outfought Regel some time ago.

With a dubious expression, Regel looked up the length of the sword to her face. "Five years a slayer, and you never wielded a blade?" His expression grew shrewd. "You had Tithian for that."

"You need not mention him again." Her former friend was a sour subject indeed.

"Keep the blade up," Regel said.

Semana gave him a wry grimace. "Yes, my Lord Wit."

They practiced while the potatoes finished cooking and the sun rose slightly higher in the sky. He'd set the spitted rabbit off to the side to cool slightly, waiting during their training session. The coals had burned down to almost nothing, but Regel didn't seem to need the warmth. The physical exertion seemed to be helping him, and Semana thought he had even started to ignore his limp.

They kept sparring, and Regel showed Semana a few more forms. Mostly he taught her defensive postures: high guard and low guard, how to anticipate and step around attacks, and how to keep the enemy far away. When she eventually lost her composure and tried to catch him off guard with a surprise attack, Regel put her flat on her back without obvious effort. Patience had never been Semana's strength, but she exercised it now as best she could. She wanted to learn, after all.

And he *was* brilliant: as good with a sword as Semana was with her magic. She'd watched Tithian and thought him very proficient, but there was an eloquence to Regel's movements and strikes—a skill and understated ferocity that enriched her respect for him as a warrior. She could learn quiet well, and she would learn only from the best.

Of course, it was easier to state such a claim aloud than to actually make it so.

Finally, when Regel had attempted to show her the same block five times, Semana threw down her sword in frustration. "We shouldn't even be out here," she said. "We should have struck when the Ravalis were weak. Mayhap then—" Regel tensed and Semana cut off instantly. Somewhere off in the distance, she heard a rumble. She pitched her voice lower. "What is that?"

"Ornithopter, far away." He seemed calm, but Semana saw his fingers had gone white on the hilt of his falcat. "The Ravalis were never weak. *We* were weak—as you made us."

Semana shifted uncomfortably. "I suppose there is some truth in that. If I had reveled myself 'ere we went to the palace—"

"We wouldn't have gone at all," Regel said.

"Exactly."

Regel gazed at her for a long time. Finally, he nodded. "Very well."

That, Semana had not expected. "*Very well?* You are content? That I deceived you?"

"I understand what you did and why." Regel stooped to pick up Semana's sword. "In your boots, I might have done much the same."

"Why, then, do you constantly cross me?" Semana asked. "Why did you refuse my commands in the palace? Why did you try to stop me from killing

Demetrus? Why did you whisk me out of Tar Vangr like a coward?"

Regel sheathed both swords, one by one. "We cannot win—not then, and certainly not now," he said. "Not with Lan yet living and a dozen more Ravalis heirs besides. The people do not know you."

"And they will know me better after a few weeks wandering the chill tundra, will they?" Semana threw her arms wide. "Oh glorious vision, Regel! Well and truly planned!"

"I know what I'm about."

"Well *I* don't what you're about," Semana said. "I don't understand you at all."

She looked away, letting her anger seethe. She stared out over the valley, with its snow-crusted treetops and rocky slopes. The northland was beautiful and terrible and hers by right. But alas, she was the only one who would fight for it—if anyone would give her a chance.

"These should be ready." Regel indicated the potatoes in the firepit with his boot.

"I'm not—" Semana's stomach rumbled, and she finally gave up trying to pretend she wasn't hungry. She called upon the silver glove, and one of the potatoes floated out of the coals toward her. It made it only halfway, and she had to pull it out of the air herself. The magic of the relic would take hours to recharge.

With his blade, Regel pulled the other potato from the fire. Wordlessly, he extended the speared rabbit to her. Semana accepted it without acknowledgement. They ate in silence for a few breaths more.

"Where are we going, Regel?" she asked between bites.

"Somewhere safe."

"Safe." Semana spat the word. "You say that as though it's what I want."

"Not want, but need."

She looked at him, her hunger momentarily stayed. "What I *need* is an army, the better to recapture my kingdom. *Our* kingdom." She let the potato fall into the snow. "I'm going back."

That caught his attention. "Back."

"Back." Semana stood tall. "I have a duty. The Ravalis murdered my mother and greatfather and sent my brother into exile, which is the same thing. And I could have avenged them all, but for you."

Regel pushed himself to his feet. "Come. We should go, else our blood will freeze."

Semana would not let him ignore her. She looked him straight in the eye. "We already know the cold will not harm me. Winter is in my Blood, or have you forgotten already?" She pointedly shrugged off her outer cloak and unbuttoned the front of Mask's armor, revealing her pale skin. Cold air scythed through, but she felt liberated. Her heart pounded. "Hear me, *Father*—if so you are. I am not weak, and I will not break. If you'll not walk my path beside me—"

"We *are* walking your path, Highness," Regel said, his voice level. "We all do as we must, even if we have to retreat to move forward."

"No." Semana closed her hands into fists. "I am sick of fleeing. I am going back to reclaim my throne, whether you come with me or no."

"Semana—"

"How dare you." She turned back to him, her breath emerging sharply. "You have no right to address me in that way. I am not my mother, burn the gods—whatever you may think, I am not her."

Regel's eyes were cold. "I know that."

"I know that, *Highness,*" she said.

Regel nodded. "I know that, Highness."

Semana was about to retort—to add another rebuke against this sullen, insubordinate man, but she saw the agony on his face and realized its source. She had mentioned Lenalin, and that caused Regel as much pain as leaving behind Tar Vangr caused her. She had dreamed of redeeming her city for the last five years—how long had Regel dreamed of his own unattainable goal?

"Very well." She realized she was cold—that perhaps her frostfire wasn't as powerful as she claimed—and she redid the buttons on her armor. "Let's get on with your endless quest." When he didn't follow, she looked back. "Was there something else?"

"It's not your fault," he said. "What happened to Ovelia."

Her dream flashed through her memory. He must have heard her cry out.

"I know that," she said, keeping her voice cool and level. "Why would you say that?"

"I noticed you weren't wearing the mask," Regel said. "And I can tell you've been crying."

Semana clenched her hands and cut back a retort, letting it froth inside her. To rise to the bait would empower him more than she already had. Instead, she strode away to the tent and shut the flap behind her. The interior was a cluttered mess, but she easily found her boots and pulled them on. She snatched up the leather mask but hesitated to don it.

"So foolish," she said to herself.

She pressed the leather to her face, and it adhered with a warm, greasy kiss.

TWO

THEY LEFT THE MOUNTAINS and took shelter amongst the thick pines and cedars that marked the valley north of Tar Vangr. The tedious days had been brisk at best and bone-chilling at worst, and the winter showed no signs of abating. It would not let up for months, Regel had explained, and even then the thaw would last only a few fortnights before snows began to fall once more. Untouched by the cold herself, nonetheless Semana watched Regel grow slower and shiver more frequently. Toward midday, she wordlessly gave him her cloak despite his objections. She felt only a little cooler without it.

They frequently hid, taking shelter in hollowed out trees or caves Semana hadn't seen. They saw no sign of Ravalis patrols, but Regel warned of greater threats that lurked in the snowy shadows. As wolves and deadlier predators howled outside, they huddled for warmth while Regel melted snow for tea with the searing plate he'd brought with him. The sickly smoke of its operation made Semana's stomach knot, but her tea soothed her. She caught him staring at her tin once, and she silently shook some of the leaves into his cup. He tried it, made a face, and dumped it out while Semana smiled in satisfaction.

When they reached the edge of the wood, Regel diverted their course to head deeper in. They rested only as much as Regel dared. After the long journey over the tundra on foot, Semana hardly minded leaving the scouring wind, but she wondered why they had changed direction. Curious.

When they camped, Regel drew his two swords, handed Semana one, and they practiced again.

For all her inexperience, Semana learned quickly. She'd always been good at picking things up, be they as simple but significant as Mask's gravel-shredded voice or as complex as sowing fear. She pondered, not for the first time, if it was this same facility that had come to her aid in the palace of Tar Vangr, when she had used Vhaerynn the Necromancer's blood sorcery against him. Never had she even considered that she could do such a thing, and yet it had come so naturally to her.

Other personas, swordplay, and even magic—what else could she learn?

Regel's quiet patience allowed Semana's mind to wander, but every so often he demanded her attention once more with an unexpected move that caught her unawares. Just then, he slipped under her guard and twisted her sword wide, then lay his falcat across her chest. It was the tenth time he'd demonstrated a killing move, and Semana demanded he repeat it more than once to that she could understand. Only once was truly necessary for her to remember what it looked like, but by the third demonstration her body could perform a less graceful variant of the attack.

She could sense Regel growing more and more comfortable with their sparring, doing more complicated things and exerting more force behind his strikes. It was something she could use. The more at ease he felt, the more information she could get from him.

If Semana was honest with herself, she had begun to feel more comfortable with him as well. But at least she was aware of it, and could avoid making misjudgments.

Her opportunity came when they took a break. The cold air made for difficult but refreshing breath. She stretched her tired arms and legs. Apparently perfectly at ease despite an hour of hard work—other than his leg—Regel returned to the fire, which had started burning in earnest while they practiced.

"Why have we changed course?" Semana asked, seemingly out of idle curiosity. "Is death in the woods greater than death on the open plain?"

"We were not moving as fast as I wanted." He stoked the coals with a blackened stick.

"Marching too slowly into death, you mean," Semana said. "I don't know why the Ravalis bother to pursue us. At this rate, we'll deal our own deaths before their slayers catch us."

Regel continued stoking the coals. He opened their pack, revealing the last two spindly potatoes that remained of the stash they'd taken from the Burned Man, as well as a few strips of hardened deer meat. He'd stepped away twice today to hunt hibernating wildlife but returned with nothing, forcing them to rely on their packed supplies. He started a fire going.

"I take it we're out of food," Semana said. "You hope game will be more plentiful in the woods?"

"Perhaps."

He wedged the last potatoes amongst the coals of the fire, where they would cook for at least an hour before they could eat them. He'd used such a mundane action to avoid answering her before—almost every day along their journey—and she'd had just about all of it she could take.

"I grow weary of this way of yours," Semana said. "Deflecting my questions like casterbolts. Yes, I trust you. Fine." She unbuckled and drew off her mask, which came away from her skin with a sucking sound. "Can you not answer me one thing?"

He considered, then nodded.

"And you will answer honestly, without any attempt to deceive or obfuscate?"

He nodded again, still without looking at her.

Semana blew out a slow, steady breath and centered herself. All the things she could ask him—about her mother, about her greatfather, about Tar Vangr and their quest…She would start with something simple. Earn the other answers. There would be time.

"Where does this path of ours lead?" she asked.

He paused in stirring the flames. "You won't believe me."

"You know me so well, do you?"

He raised his dark eyes under a brooding brow. "Necthana," he said.

Confusion swept over Semana. The name sounded so very familiar, and yet… Suddenly, she realized where she had heard the word before. "The Deathless City?" she asked, unable to keep a note of disbelief from the question. "But that is a fancy tale for bards and children. Surely it is not a real place."

"As I said." Regel shrugged.

They sat in silence for a moment, Semana simmering with thwarted anger, Regel cold and unreadable. After days on the road, she had learned to loathe his reticence.

Finally, when she could stand it no more, Semana stood up abruptly. "I'm going for more firewood. I'll be careful."

Regel nodded without looking up.

Semana stomped off into the trees, caring nothing for the snow crunching underfoot or the twigs rustling in her wake. Her thoughts lingered on Regel, and they were not pleasant ones. He did not trust her, and why should he? As Mask, she had manipulated him almost unto death, along the same path that had killed Ovelia and driven Tithian from her side. How different this journey would be with Tithian Davargorn as her companion, rather than Regel. Him, she could control, but her father…

Father. When had she begun thinking of him thus? It made her vaguely sick.

Regel might be her ally, but he was not her friend—not by any stretch. He constantly thwarted her every action, it seemed. He tried to stop her from dealing with their enemies, he sought to deprive her of her sources of magic, one by one. She felt like a thrashing viper strangling in his left hand, while with his right he calmly wrenched out her fangs, one by one. She felt trapped and powerless to resist.

As Mask, she had never been powerless. Heavy use drained her relics, but she had always made a point to let them recharge before she went back out into the field. Now, her fire gauntlet was gone, her silver glove daily exhausted, and only her mask remained to her as a means of attack. The plaguefire was an uncertain weapon, and one that extracted a cost from her. It briefly occurred to her how grieved he would be if something did happen to her, but it was a petulant fantasy. Far better to persevere despite his efforts to hold her back, and thus prove to him the depth of his foolishness.

Whatever assurances she had made Regel, Semana wandered aimlessly through the trees, hardly aware of her path in the midst of her dark thoughts. If a predator or hunter came upon her during her reverie, she would have no defense to offer. The thought of her vulnerability made her both uneasy and angry. What right had that man to reduce her to this, meandering like a lost doe through the woods?

It was at that moment she became aware of the dark shape standing against the snow just ahead of her, and she stopped cold. It was a buck, and a mighty one at that. The light of Ruin's rising moon danced off the silvery rack of horns with at least twelve points, and its six muscular legs clashed with the snow underfoot. It stared at her, unmoving, its eyes bright yellow in the moonlight. The world seemed to fall silent around them, such that she could hear the drifting snowflakes sizzling into the ground and onto her hood and exposed skin. She shut out the tingling burn and blew out a slow breath.

All that mattered was the magnificent creature before her.

The buck turned slightly, and she saw its second head—that of a goat with curled, barbed horns. Its blood-shot eyes glared at her hungrily—viciously. Its lips drew back from sharp, yellow teeth. It was a mutant creature, twisted by the roving magic that tainted the World of Ruin. No simple prey, this, but a predator.

Immediately, warning rose in Semana, and she instinctively fell into communion with the leather mask she grasped so tightly in her right hand. She would rot the creature to bone and gore where it stood, no matter the consequences. Slowly, she raised the mask toward her face.

A hand clapped around her mouth from behind, and another seized her wrist. She went taut as a wire, startled into hesitation by the sudden assault, and her captor hauled her backward. It was not until they were behind a fallen log that Semana managed to struggle, fighting and kicking at her attacker for a heartbeat until she recognized Regel. His eyes were up and gazing into the clearing at the two-headed beast, which had begun to walk cautiously toward them, hackles raised. She could tell from Regel's face that he didn't want her to move, and as much as she wanted to scream around his hand, she listened to her intuition. She could barely see through a snow-choked bush into the clearing.

The creature took another step, and abruptly an arrow appeared, sticking out of the buck's left eye. The beast collapsed to its knees, and the goat head loosed a keening wail that rippled amongst the trees and made Semana's bones grind. She saw rather than heard a pair of white winter birds take flight, wings flapping crazily in their haste to escape. Regel's cloak enveloped them against the snowy earth.

The bleating screams droned on, diminishing in volume, as a figure seemingly clad in snow-dappled branches strode out of the trees into the clearing. She slung the bow around her shoulder, drew a forward-curved knife—not unlike one of Regel's falcata—and slashed the goat's throat. The cries became a burbling gush of blood on the fresh snow, and the creature thrashed for a heartbeat and died.

The hunter wiped the knife on its carcass and sheathed it once more. She unslung the bow from around her shoulder, calmly set an arrow to the string, lowered herself into a ready posture and looked around the clearing. Semana realized the chimerical beast's behavior must have seemed suspicious, and the woman with the bow was checking for other movement.

When the hunter looked in the other direction, Semana closed her fingers around Regel's hand on her mouth. She nodded slightly, and he took his hand away to put on the hilt of one of his falcata. She pressed the mask into place on her face, its leather embrace both welcoming and vaguely uncomfortable. She looked back to the hunter through reddening vision, ready for a fight.

The woman looked back around, and narrowed her eyes in their direction. She stepped toward them, bow raised, arrow covering every shadow. Semana could feel Regel's tension, muscles tightly coiled and ready to spring. They had no caster or bow of their own: the hunter would have to be close, and even then, it would be a near thing. How far could they continue if one of them was wounded?

Snow crunched under the hunter's feet not five paces from their hiding place, and the woman crouched lower to peer through the brush. Beneath her winter forest cloak, she looked rough and ruin-scarred, but not like one of the Children. Just a woman—not a monster. She held the arrow ready to draw, and at this distance Semana could see its wicked barbs and the waxy sheen across the head. Poison. Semana held her breath. They were not moving—she would not see them. Unless…

The hunter's nose twitched as a foul odor wafted through the air, and Semana realized it was the result of the mask's gathering magic. She was so used to its stench that she hadn't even thought of it. The relic felt warm against her face, simmering with barely contained death, and she could feel it starting to reach its tendrils into her. Its power was polluting the air, and a grayish haze appeared around her eyes. Regel was staring at her, eyes wide, unable to speak lest he give them away.

The hunter must have smelled the corruption, for she came toward them, ready to loose.

Against every impulse in her to rise up and attack—to mete out her festering rage upon the mere mortal woman with the bow—Semana put her hands on either side of the mask and pulled it off. It stuck to her face, but only enough to let her know it wanted to remain. It came away with a slick sound, and the magic abruptly vanished. The stench dissipated into the chill night.

The hunter peered about for another moment, then stood up and eased the bowstring back. She slid the barbed arrow back into her leather quiver. She returned to the beast she had shot, hefted it over her shoulders in an impressive display of strength, and hauled it back the way she had come.

Semana counted silently to a hundred after the hunter had faded from sight before Regel finally moved. He whispered, "I'll see," and detached from her like a shadow peeling from a stone.

He moved quickly and silently, similar to how Tithian had learned to comport himself but obviously with decades more practice. She couldn't deny a tingle of admiration for such skill and grace—despite his age, Regel moved better than any man she had ever seen.

While she waited, Semana found that Regel had brought their packs from the camp and secreted them behind a boulder nearby, as if in preparation for heading out. Sigh. Did the man think of everything?

She realized, of a sudden, that there was something else—a presence watching her. She looked around, but she saw nothing. Only the empty, dark forest, the shadows turning to haze as a cloud passed over the moon. Semana wondered.

Regel returned after a moment, his face grim. "One hunter, moving slowly with her burden."

"You don't sound surprised," Semana said. "You planned to find someone. Why?"

He nodded. "We can follow her to Gardh and thus find a safe approach."

"Gardh?" Semana asked. "I think I've heard of that place, but I thought Ruin had claimed the northland since the Winter King…" She paused, readjusting. She was not accustomed to speaking as Semana. "Since my greatfather's death."

"Not entirely," Regel said.

"I see." Semana's jaw ground tight. As she spoke, her voice dropped lower. "And you would go there. To this not-so-abandoned city." She clenched her fists. "Without consulting me."

"We need supplies," Regel said. "You should trust my judgment."

"I am your liege," she said.

"And I am your father."

"And what does that mean to me?" Semana asked. "You bedded my mother, true, but that is all. You did not raise me and have no hold over me. You were never a father to me—you were barely a shadow. Why should I grant your claim now?"

They stood silent in the grove, a light snow just beginning to fall around them. Though the chill did not bother her, Semana felt the gray-white flakes tingling on her skin. She knew the exposure would burn her, but she did not care. The unease on Regel's face was worth a little discomfort.

"I did not—" Regel hesitated. "My apologies, Highness. I do trust your judgment."

Semana crossed her arms, jaw set against the niggling pain. "Gardh is our best option?"

"Yes, but it is not ideal," Regel said. "I would not lead you to death, though I cannot promise that a warm welcome awaits us if we go to Gardh. I found little such when last I passed through, and no doubt they remember. Otherwise, we can attempt to press on our own, albeit with diminished supplies." He started away, then stopped to look back at where she stood waiting. "What say you?"

Semana thought about the moment she had looked upon the buck in the clearing, and realized she had not felt quite as at peace since that moment in her mother's garden, back in Tar Vangr. There she had stood, safe in Regel's arms, with the burning rain falling and a thousand foes around them. It had seemed like madness, but for the voice in her heart that reassured her. She had never failed to listen to that voice. Not when it said to take Mask's armor, to coerce the Bloodbreaker and manipulate the Lord of Tears, to abandon Tithian...It had led her this far, and it would lead her on.

She still needed Regel, but she would not *always* need him.

She drew on her hood against the snow. "To Gardh, last Knight of Winter," she said. "Lead on."

For now, she added silently.

THREE

Gardh, Deep in the Winter Wilds

Semana's voice rasped against the leather of her mask. "That's it, then?"

Regel nodded. "It is."

He edged up to peer closer over the fallen log at the frost-encrusted gate. The icy bastion shut out the surrounding wilderness with walls thrice the height of a man and wrought of stout, iron-reinforced timber. Sharpened stakes adorned the top, serving both as a deterrent for would-be invaders and a stark warning. Regel could make out three pitch-blackened heads atop those spikes even now, the frost well preserving their features. Six outposts stood at the corners of the wall, and Regel could see archers manning at least two, including the one nearest the main entrance. And if he remembered correctly, there would be plenty of armed men and women inside.

"Amazing," Semana said. "No one's heard from these people in years. And yet they're still here—still alive." She sniffed. "Some of them, anyway."

Regel nodded. "King Orbrin—your greatfather—he was always kind to the folk of Gardh, and regular envoys passed between the mage-city and this place during his reign. But Demetrus abandoned them to Ruin when he ascended."

"So they've lived her alone for five years? I suspect they won't be so welcoming of their queen," Semana said. "You've been here more recently, have you not?"

He nodded again, though his expression was solemn. That was not a happy memory.

Getting to Gardh was not so difficult. Approaching the city *safely* was another matter altogether, but their chance encounter with the hunter had proved fortuitous. On foot, they'd followed the hunter's trail until the early hours, around the defensive traps and two parties of armed warders, until finally they'd come to the forest outpost as the distant horizon was starting to lighten behind the mountains. Dawn would not come for hours yet. The weather remained clear, but Regel had felt a subtle shift in the heaviness of the air that spoke of an incoming storm. Now that they beheld Gardh—so heavily defended and seemingly impenetrable—he despaired of finding shelter here. He'd made the mistake of holding out hope, only to see it broken as they stood on the threshold. Why had he expected anything different?

Semana picked up on his concern. "We need to get inside," she said. "I'm not spending another night out here freezing near to death, and waking just to eat those two potatoes we have left."

"I'll scout the perimeter," Regel said. "Find a way around."

"This *is* our way," the princess said.

And without warning, she rose and walked toward Gardh, snow crunching under her black boots. Regel cursed and reached for her, but she was too fast.

Bows shot up as soon as Semana came within two dozen paces. The two guards at the gate—grizzled men with danger written on their faces—were instantly on the alert, as were at least two more Regel saw in the outpost above the wall. Only the hunter with the deformed deer slung across her shoulders did not draw a weapon, but merely stared at them.

As though she did not notice the threat, Semana threw back her hood and put her hands up wide and spoke in a trembling voice like that of a scared child. "Help!" she called. "Please!"

Regel stopped a few steps from her, because a sudden movement might make the men loose their arrows. He raised his hands as well, palming a throwing blade from his sleeve.

"Please, please help us!" Again ignoring the immediate threat, Semana reached up slowly and put her fingers on the clasps of her mask. Gradually, so as not to provoke sudden violence, she drew off the mask and gazed up at them, her eyes wet with tears of fright. "My father and I...we are travelers from Tar Vangr! Please! Grant us succor!"

That was the moment, Regel knew—the moment they should have died—but for some reason the arrows didn't descend. Semana's wild protestations had bought them a moment. She'd mentioned Tar Vangr, and these folk had heard no word of the City of Steel in years. Why had he not thought of it?

The two guards at the gates seemed taken in at once, their body language relaxed and trusting, but the hunter they'd followed narrowed her eyes in suspicion. No one had moved, and that meant Semana still had the advantage. "Summer outlanders now rule Tar Vangr," she told them. "They held us both as slaves, and forced me to do unspeakable, *demeaning* things."

Here she put in a little bit of a shudder, to clutch at their sympathy. It worked.

Regel stopped listening to Semana's words and instead evaluated her technique. He watched her shift from fabricating details to forcing empathy. They were exiles, forced out and abandoned. Not unlike the people of Gardh themselves—though this went unspoken, of course. Now that he knew what to look for, it seemed obvious. Semana—*Mask*—was a master of manipulation.

"Please." Semana looked desperate. "We too have been cast out of the mage-city, abandoned. We heard word of this place, and barely dared hope we might find it. Please—we must stand together, all of us that the great and powerful have sent away."

The guards glanced at the hunter, who gave a tiny nod and stepped inside the gates, unattended. Then they moved to either side of Semana and Regel, lowering their bows but not putting them away.

"Come, lass," one said. He had a pudgy face and a thick nose. "It passes well—"

He laid a rough hand on Semana's arm, and she threw her arms around him. "Thank the Fire," she said, weeping real tears. "Oh thank you, thank you!"

The soldier seemed genuinely touched by her act, allowing himself a faint smile despite the seriousness of the moment. "Be welcome."

The one escorting Regel did nothing of the sort. His left eye was swollen half shut by an ugly scar across his brow. "Move," he said, accompanying the command with a thrust of his head toward the gate.

Regel and Semana found themselves escorted together into Gardh, squeezed so close through the narrow gates that their heads touched. Semana smirked at him. "You said we would find no welcome here," she said. "You are not always right, Lord of Tears."

From the mistrustful glances of the soldiers flanking them, and their forbidding grasp on their arms, Regel could not entirely agree.

Gardh had changed little in the years since Regel's last visit. The lean faces and suspicious stares that followed him down the snowy road seemed familiar, though they were fewer now. Thick winter snows hid many of the log and stone houses beneath heavy drifts, but smoke emerging from a series of drifts spoke to the number of concealed dwellings. He estimated the town's population at around a thousand, a little less than half of what he remembered.

The guards led Regel and Semana through the streets, and all eyes fell upon them. Dark-furred hounds on leather leashes growled and snapped, but otherwise the people of Gardh regarded them with silence. Regel suspected these folk had not seen an outsider in some time. They clutched their mundane weapons tightly: spears, knives, axes, and bows, mostly. Not a caster or thaumaturgic device among them. Regel looked for a friendly expression, but all he saw was stony indifference. No one wanted anything to do with them, but all wanted to know their story.

They made their way to the largest building in the fort—a composite structure built up to three floors, raised on the site of Gardh's original holdfast. Upon a foundation of blistered, cracked stone stood dowdy walls of thick, pitch-sealed pine, cut with arrow-slit windows. The first rays of the rising sun glinted off arrows held at the ready for any false move, and Regel could see more archers at the top of the squat tower. The place seemed big enough to fit most if not all the people of Gardh into it, at need.

Someone was watching out for these people, Regel knew.

The guards deposited them in a tower bedroom that had not seen guests in some time. Candles smoked on the table in the middle of the floor, smelling strongly of animal fat. In the corner squatted a single bed, wide enough for a single occupant and covered with a thin layer of dust. Ratty towels sat folded on a shelf, dusty and stiff with neglect. Snow swirled outside a narrow window, mostly fogged over, with a dully flickering glow toward its base. The place smelled of old wood and mildew, and Regel detected the whiff of dried blood. He'd always been able to feel out a room the instant he entered, and this one did not reassure him.

"Wait here," the big-nosed guard said.

Semana fell to her knees and grasped his calves, in the traditional manner of supplication. "Water, goodsyr? And food?" She looked up at him with big eyes. "My father and I haven't eaten in days."

He looked confused, then smiled again, wider this time. "I'll have something brought to you. But stay here. You're safe."

"Oh, thank you." Semana seized his hand and kissed it. "Bless the Nar for you."

The squinting one didn't take his one-and-a-half eyes off them until the door shut.

As soon as they were alone, Semana dropped the look of dazed appreciation in favor of something more contemptuous. "That passed well."

Regel drew a shard of wood from an inside pocket and focused upon it, letting his senses expand. He took in the room, with its smells hidden under years of dust, and searched the walls for spy holes. When he had contented himself, he put the statue back in his pocket. Semana was watching him steadily. She knew of his talent, and the interest she paid him was both satisfying and unsettling. Her way of looking at him—as though cataloguing his every word and action for consumption later—made him a bit uneasy. He nodded to reassure her they were alone and unobserved.

"You wove a thick tale," he said.

She shrugged. "I got us inside, didn't I? And they haven't killed us yet."

"How could they?" Regel gestured toward the door. "One of those guards is half in love with you already. Is this how you turned Tithian into your personal slayer?"

Her eyes flashed red, and for an instant she gave him a look of such venom Regel could scarce credit it. Then the anger was gone from her face, and she smiled carelessly. "You worry too much."

The door unlatched and swung open to admit a dark-haired woman Regel found familiar. She had a tightly muscled body and dark eyes set into a hard face, and her assertive stance brooked no nonsense. Slung over her arm was a dark cloak, stained with greasy snow. She was the hunter from the woods, Regel realized, but he thought he had seen her before as well.

"I am Phend." Her almost black eyes regarded them evenly and without fear. "Let us be clear: you live yet at my bidding."

"Are you the ruler of this place?" Semana asked.

The woman shook her head. "Gardh has no master, and never will," she said, pulling out her shirt to hang over her belt. In so doing, she laid her hand on the hilt of her one visible weapon—a wide blade the length of a man's forearm, balanced for chopping. "You might instead call me its protector."

"You have not been Gardh's protector long," Regel said.

She nodded. "You may not remember me, Regel Winter, but I remember you." She deliberately drew her thick-bladed knife, let it sparkle in the candlelight, then set it on the table. "I had no name when you were here last, but I took one from the old protector, Jeht. His ill-conceived mercy in sheltering you and letting you free proved his undoing."

Regel nodded. "He was a fair man."

"Perhaps." Phend's grimace hardened, but he saw a touch of regret in her eyes.

He did remember her then, from his last visit years ago: a gangly girl, all bones and gawky glances, then about as old as Semana was now. She'd borne no name, which had not surprised him. Folk her age often had not earned names. If he recalled correctly, she and Serris had shared a night together in this place. He had never asked Jeht, but it was clear from their shared features that Phend had been a child of the man's blood. If so, it had not stopped her betraying Jeht to his death.

To her credit, Semana didn't show the tiniest hesitation in the wake of the revelation that their host not only knew Regel, but was potentially their enemy. It hardly seemed to surprise her, much less disrupt her plan. Any touch of the sweetling in distress that she had played for the warders vanished, and she looked at Phend levelly and without artifice. "So what happens now?" she asked, her voice smooth.

Phend's narrowed eyes registered Semana as a factor for the first time. "I suspected any woman traveling with the shadow of the Winter King would be something more than a babbling idiot," she said. "I know him. I do not know *you*. I imagine he is not really your father, yes?"

Regel cast Semana a warning glance, but she ignored him. "I am Semana Denerre nô Ravalis," she said. "Last scion of Orbrin Denerre and last true heir to the throne of Tar Vangr."

Whatever answer Phend had suspected, that one caught her by surprise. Her eyes widened slightly. "That cannot be," she said, her words faintly confused. "Last we heard from Tar Vangr, all of Denerre was dead and dust."

"Not all of us," Semana said. "This Ruin's Night was my awakening revel. I slew two would-be kings that night, including the usurper Demetrus Ravalis."

Regel caught her eye and bid her silently to still herself, but the damage had been done.

"And why is my lady come to Gardh in the dark of night, dressed as a common bandit?" Phend asked. "Surely your palace is far warmer a place than this."

"I am your majesty, not your lady, but it makes no great matter," Semana said. "I wished to inspect my ancestral holdings, and my greatfather's court slayer has escorted me. Our ornithopter broke down a day's journey to the east, and we covered the rest of the distance on foot. Your holdfast has not sent an envoy to Tar Vangr in years, and I wanted to see if it yet stood. Imagine my surprise to find not only the crumbling fort, but people as well." She offered a dismissive wave. "Don't concern yourself with bowing. I care little for ceremony."

Awkward silence lingered in the room as the two women stared at one another. Phend searched Semana for a lie, while Semana dared her to question her words.

"That is...quite a story," Phend said. "I shall have to consider what you have said."

"Of course." Semana's manner was affable, but her hazel eyes flecked with crimson motes were dangerous. "I would be disappointed if you took me at my word. I could, after all, be anyone. Far too many false mage-kings draw breath these days. Well"—she smiled thinly—"fewer now than last year."

Phend nodded warily, visibly shaken. "You shall remain my guests for the time being, *Majesty*," she said. "I will have food and mulled wine brought for your meal this morn." She picked up her long knife once more. "I must request you not leave the tower without my escort or that of my men. For your own protection, you understand."

She sheathed the blade with the hiss of steel on oiled leather and then a click, sending a very different message.

"Naturally." Semana stretched her arms and shoulders with an audible series of pops. "A day to the east. Silver ornithopter with crimson trim and my house's colors emblazoned on the shield. You'll find it wedged into a crevasse and half-covered with snow, to keep anyone from spotting it easily. Regel hid it quite well." Her easy smile widened. "Best of luck."

Phend gave Regel a cold nod and a warning look, then took her leave. Regel took out his sculpture to do a quick sweep of the room, but detected no one listening in.

"She seems perfectly well, for an ice-hearted slayer," Semana said. "Seems like your ilk. I gather you'll rut her before we go?"

Regel ignored the question. "Phend will dispatch a search party, if she hasn't already."

"Obviously," Semana said. "But it will take at least a day, and we will be long quit of this awful place. We can enjoy it for now, though." She slumped down on the bed with a sigh. "Like paradise."

She was asleep within moments, not having bothered to remove even part of her stinking leathers.

Regel sat at the table, his mind unable to relax so easily. He looked at Semana, her arms and legs stretched at odd angles out from her body, and wondered that she could find rest when they were in such obvious danger. Perhaps that was more of her magic.

He drew out his small carving knife and the little sculpture he'd been working on since Ruin's Night and began to cut. As he worked, his mind fell away and his senses expanded. He tasted the smoke on the air, even through the window, and heard the sounds of Gardh waking for the day. He listened to the guards outside their room—their converse and their breathing. One was the man Semana had charmed, and Regel suspected that might be as much problem as blessing. The other was a new one he did not know: a woman, thick as a tree by the way the floor creaked beneath her and probably just as dense. Their guards were capable warriors, and Regel worried for a moment that they might assert themselves over them at any moment.

After a time, Regel realized Semana was staring at him. She hardly moved and her lungs breathed but narrowly. She might as well have been asleep as far as he could tell, even through his focused senses, but her eyes were open.

"You worry for me," she said. "You shouldn't. Worry instead for that treacherous girl and anyone else who dares open that door."

So speaking, she raised her left hand with the silver gauntlet, humming with a nearly full charge, and set her mask upon her face. It molded expertly to her cheekbones as though fitted just for her.

FOUR

THE MORNING DAWNED BITTER in Gardh, brightening a little as the storm let up for a brief respite. They ate small bowls of boiled oats, hard boiled eggs, and some sort of root vegetable, topped with cream of a tangy sort that Semana attested was the finest she'd ever tasted. Regel could understand the sentiment: after so many days on the road away from a decent meal, elk's milk wouldn't seem strange. Regel didn't feel the need to tell Semana the truth and make her queasy.

He'd just been glad the food that previous night was not poisoned, and he detected none this morning either. They were Phend's guests in Gardh, but the ancient laws and customs of hospitality held less sway these days than they once had. He'd tasted the food before Semana and bade her wait to see if he suffered any ill effect. A request she argued quite vehemently.

"Poison?" she asked, taking her bowl. "I've killed for coin for five years now. You don't think I can smell poison ere I taste it?"

Regel gave her a nod of neutral acknowledgement, while in truth he wasn't sure whether to be proud or unnerved.

"What is it?" Semana asked.

He shook his head. She'd taken her mask off to eat, and for that moment, seeing her so unabashedly happy to have the meal, Regel had seen the lost princess he had dreamed of. Then the sardonic façade returned—the reminder of the dark thing she had become to survive—and the morning felt just a little darker and colder.

"I have arranged a tour of Gardh," Regel said. "Can I trust you not to compromise us?"

Semana's smile was probably meant to be reassuring. "Again, you worry too much."

"In my experience," Regel said. "Such a thing is not possible."

An hour later, Semana accompanied Regel out into the open air of the fortress city of Gardh. The passing storm had left them in a strange lull, where the blazing sun to the east gave the world a strange, orange tinge. The rosy glow made Gardh seem comforting and entirely too welcoming. Nothing felt quite real, but Regel knew not to let a trick of the light fool his perceptions.

He glanced at Semana. The princess still wore the leathers of Mask, but she'd draped a brown cloak over the fearsome armor. With the relatively innocuous cloak and her hair growing out, she almost looked like any nameless girl of her age, and not like Mask at all. The illusion was truly uncanny.

"Such a lovely morning walk," Semana said in Regel's ear. "So glad to see our hosts trust us."

Half a dozen warriors surrounded them as they walked, breathing out silver clouds as they tried not to be too obvious about watching their ostensible guests. They wore coats of metal rings and leather, carried spears, and wore swords at their belts. None of them looked more than passable with those weapons, but they had the numbers, and Regel wasn't a young man anymore. Not to mention that their escorts had taken Regel's swords and any other weapons they could find.

Perhaps with her magic, Semana could have slain them quickly enough, but as a terrified young woman in distress, she made no aggressive movements of any kind. No doubt she realized how much that irked him, based on the way she kept glancing over and smiling. Anyone else he'd have thought wasn't taking the situation seriously, but Semana? He wondered what mischief she intended.

The princess had certainly built a strong foundation for some sort of trickery. Such was the strength of her presence that all eyes seemed to fall upon her wherever they went. It was something deeper than her looks: something about her drew attention and enflamed the onlooker, just as it had with all the Blood of Denerre. These folk sensed the power in her blood, and it gave them hope.

By contrast, Regel lacked Semana's glow of power and importance, and it made walking with her feel like flitting through the shadows while she held aloft a brightly glowing lantern. He slowly faded into the gray background, and unless he spoke, no one seemed to notice him. Should that comfort him or make him uneasy?

The storm had passed for the time being, and by the clarity of day, Gardh looked significantly less threatening than it had the previous night. He recognized familiar brick and thatch buildings, somewhat more scarred and pitted than when he had seen them last, and the layout of the place came back to him as they walked the streets. It hardly seemed like home, of course. Quite the opposite. He'd killed a few men and women here on his last visit—not by choice—and he found that he remembered their faces far better than the town itself.

Regel's actions had begun to haunt him more and more over the years, and his time in Gardh had not ranked among the proudest episodes in his life.

At least his service to the former Protector of Gardh hadn't depopulated the entire fort. As they made their way through the streets, Regel though his initial estimate of a thousand was far too high. He saw perhaps a hundred folk out in the streets taking advantage of the lull, while the others kept to their boarded-over cottages. It was more than he had initially expected, but fewer than he had seen on his previous visit just five years ago. The cold winters had not treated Gardh well, and he suspected that the five years of isolation from Tar Vangr hadn't helped.

They passed the Victorious Hunter, a stout building that served as Gardh's sole common house. In his time at the fort, the Hunter had served as the center of government and commerce in the fort. It would be little more than a hunting lodge in another city, but in Gardh it was one of the more impressive buildings. He understood why Phend had moved her quarters to the old tower at the center of Gardh. The Hunter must have carried dark memories of Phend's treacherous rise to power.

Near the center of Gardh, they found a small market of sorts, in which stood two dozen or so people with weathered faces. He didn't imagine the people of Gardh saw many travelers, and he doubted those who had witnessed their arrival had spoken well of them in the interim. Semana drew plenty of attention, with many of the menfolk giving her curious, admiring glances, while some of the women looked upon her with something like envy. Those few who noticed Regel at all tended to grimace at him or look away quickly.

"I'm surprised anyone could dwell out here," Semana said. "Cut off from trade, frozen half the year." She scanned the swaddled faces of passersby. "None too friendly."

Regel shook his head. They were not, at that.

A livestock yard near the market boasted a number of elk, sheltered under snowy boughs or crouched in the snow to form their own hulking drifts to shelter young ones. Behind a rusted metal wall, he heard the grumble of pigs mucking through half-frozen mud. He could almost taste the slight acidity of the mud through his enhanced senses. The sign hanging over the door to an attached building showed a cleaver bisecting an animal: a pig on its back on one side, and a haunch of meat on the other.

Semana turned up her nose at the acrid stench. "Smells like home," she said. "But better."

At first, Regel thought of Tar Vangr—itself filled with the greasy smell of smoke and steel—but realized Semana meant Luether. She had lived there more than five years: the entirety of her prematurely adult life. He could hardly think of a worse place for a child to grow to majority, except perhaps

Gardh. Snow had started to fall once more, dulling the stench.

Regel searched everywhere for the scent of an alchemic lab or thaumaturgical forge, but Gardh had neither of these things. Isolation had reduced them to living off the land in a more mundane fashion, and Regel found something pure in that. Even in the shadow of Tar Vangr's creeping contamination, the air tasted sweeter in Gardh, rid of the sulfur, ammonia, and the pungent fumes of industry. Unlike the snow in Tar Vangr, the stuff here had a faint gray tinge and produced only a faint tingle against the skin rather than an acidic burn. The relative cleanliness reminded him of the last place he had been happy, though his stay had been only a passing dream before the bitterness of the mundane world intruded.

Phend appeared at the end of the road and headed toward them, walking smoothly and with a purpose. Regel reached for Semana's wrist, but she was moving before he could touch her. She broke away from their escort, seemingly heedless of their startled cries, and hurried toward her. Even Phend was surprised, her eyes going wide and her hand too slow to reach for a weapon before Semana reached her and fell to one knee in the snow. She took the woman's hand and pressed it to her lips.

"Thank you, good lady," Semana said. "A thousand thanks for your hospitality."

The warders escorting Regel hurried toward the Protector, but she held up a hand to stay them.

"Of course." Phend's stricken expression melted into something softer for a moment. "You and your father—"

Semana rose and embraced Phend, putting her mouth close to her ear. Sharp as he'd honed his senses, Regel could not hear the words that passed between the two women. He could only judge from Phend's face, which hardened once more into the pragmatic mask she always seemed to wear.

"Yes," she said. "I have come to collect you and your father. The storm is gathering once more at the bounds of Gardh's lands, and will resume its onslaught. Best to have you indoors."

During their tour of Guard, Regel had paid more attention to the defenses and layout than to the weather, but now that Phend said that, it rang true. A cold wind swept along the snow, and the pressure in the air had dipped, presaging coming precipitation.

"Of course," Semana said. "I'd hate to be out in that cold again."

She feigned a shiver to accentuate the point. Phend's grimace suggested she was not fooled, but Semana's act stirred the compassion of their escorts. Regel heard more than one murmured word that suggested as much. The princess had proved entirely too charming. Her current play might just succeed.

Semana threaded her arm under Phend's, beaming up at her. "Wherever you'll take me, lady."

After Semana had won the hearts of her people, Phend had no choice but to accept. She nodded curtly and they started away, along with their former escorts. Snow started to fall heavily, and folk scattered into the surrounding houses for shelter. The wind began to howl, and Regel pulled his cowl low.

His escorts' attention seemed to be on Semana, and Regel realized he had his chance to slip away. As they headed toward the tower at the center of Gardh, he seized the opportunity to slip out between two buildings. He did not linger to see if the warders had noticed. Voices went up belatedly, but by then Regel had worked his way around back toward the market and took shelter behind a stack of frost-hardened barrels. From the ground, he plucked up a withered apple that someone had left in their rush to take shelter, and focused on it to let his senses expand.

He waited.

They returned to the tower before anyone realized Regel had disappeared. That, Semana took as a victory: she'd let Regel slip away and kept their escorts distracted all the way back. She permitted herself a small, self-satisfied smile as they stood in the entry hall, hot and dripping, arguing about who to blame for losing him. Such fools.

With the storm descending, shelter became everyone's priority, and none of the warders seemed to care particularly about an old man who had lost his way in the flurry. Phend, on the other hand, would have none of it. Her cheeks flushing bright red with growing anger, she ordered two of her warders back out into the storm. Semana watched, bemused, as she barked the instructions in sharp, clipped phrases.

"You go and find him," Phend said. "Bring him here, or you stay and watch him. Do you understand?"

The two men hesitated by the billowing portal, giving the whirling snow a wide berth. A flurry was not a pleasant atmosphere to wade through, and could become dangerous if the clouds carried fire within. Phend's anger seemed to carry just as much threat as the inclement weather. They headed out, and Semana couldn't help but note that the Protector of Gardh had only four other blades left to ward her.

Whatever Phend might lack as a ruler, one could never accuse her of being imperceptive. She noted Semana's appraising glance and bit her lip. If Regel could so easily defy her, it made her vulnerable: not the best trait for a ruler. If she hadn't seen the two travelers as a threat before, she'd have to be a fool not to do so now.

"You should wait out the storm in your room, young one," Phend said tightly.

"All by myself?" Semana asked, feigning innocence. "Whatever shall I do—?"

She let the question hang without speculation, and Phend picked up on the implication. Regel was a known quantity to her, or at least she had some sense of his capabilities. Semana, on the other hand, was a stranger, and now, without even Regel to keep her in check, who could say what she might get up to?

"Very well. You." Phend looked to one of their escorts—a plain, stocky man Semana vaguely remembered as one of their welcome party the day before. "Wait upon our guest, and satisfy her every desire." She gave Semana a warning look. "This is sufficient?"

"I suppose." Semana spared her would-be warder no more than a single dismissive glance. She had eyes and a smile only for Phend. The air pulsed between them, and Semana could feel the blood coursing a bit faster in Phend's body. There was heat between them, and Semana could use it. "Unless you wish to keep me company yourself."

"You mean—" The suggestion surprised Phend, but she regained her composure quickly. After a heartbeat, her face might as well have been carved of stone. "I shall call upon you when the storm passes. Doubtless you can behave until then."

"Doubtless." Semana's heart thundered between her ears.

The moment passed, and Phend walked away, her steps a little rough.

Semana recognized the signs. No doubt, the Protector of Gardh could see through the empty flirtation and shifting pressure, and so she would prove invulnerable to Semana's attempts to manipulate her. Phend had an undeniably strong force of will. Pity. Alluring her would have been useful.

"Lady?" the warder asked. "Shall we?"

Semana smiled at him. She could feel the blood in his veins, responding to the unfulfilled heat left with Phend's refusal. He did not have her power or strength, but he would do for now. She was, after all, just learning.

"Lead the way," Semana said.

He showed Semana back to her room, where she and Regel had spent the previous night. Things looked slightly disheveled, as though someone had been through in their absence. Phend's servants, no doubt. She stepped out of the damp cloak and let it puddle on the floor around her ankles. Fully aware of his scrutiny, Semana stretched, slender and hard as though wrought of metal.

The warder lingered at the door, his eyes hard on her body. Obviously he wanted her, and that was a new sensation—to be wanted. The last five years, she had tried hard to make herself a creature that attracted no man or woman. This reminded her why. She found it more than vaguely repulsive. If not for the hot blood soaring in his body—the taste of it thick and rich on her tongue—she might have sent him away or struck him. She supposed she could tolerate his leering in exchange for that taste.

"You want me, do you?" Semana asked.

He nodded dumbly, his bulky body trembling with repressed desire. Grotesque.

"You think you know what I want?" Semana asked.

A lascivious grin spread across the man's face. "Since I first saw you," he said. "I—"

He came toward her, but she casually stopped him with a rising left hand, catching him in the magic of her silver glove. He floated off the floor, eyes going wide in shock. The beating of his blood drove her more than a little out of her head. She reached into him and pulled, and he went rigid, every muscle swollen. The man gasped and drooled. He could barely breathe, much less speak.

When she'd used blood magic in the palace at Tar Vangr, Semana done so by reflex, barely knowing what she was doing. She still didn't quite know how she'd managed it, but the power was there, waiting. Now she had time and space to test its limits—to learn. And she had a subject.

"You're right," she said. "This *is* what I want."

Her eyes burned, and she saw them reflected in the warder's wide eyes as burning red coals.

Over many years as a slayer and then an avenger, Regel had well learned the value of patience.

At length, two figures appeared out of the snow, hands raised to hold their hoods closed against the snow. The gray-white haze cut visibility significantly, so there was little to no chance they would find him. Regel waited, listening to them breathe and trade hurried whispers. They weren't certain if they had missed him, or perhaps he had found his way into another shelter. Whether they truly thought such or they simply made justifications for their failure to keep Regel under their control. He could not say for certain, though he suspected the latter.

Soon enough, they turned back toward the tower, and Regel found himself once again at liberty.

The snow swirled around him, bathing the fort in a sheet of corrupted white. The snow set his exposed flesh to tingling, but Regel was accustomed to the pain. He turned toward the east, away from Tar Vangr, and saw the light of the sun barely diffused through the clouds in the distance. It was beautiful and hopeful, but he knew what lay what lay at the end of that path.

Now he went east for the third time in his life, and for the same reason as before: escape. But this time, it was not his own need that drove him forward, but that of his charge. She'd let Semana believe an army awaited them in Necthana, but when she discovered the truth, would she see it through? The hunger for vengeance had driven her into madness and murder for five years. If they even reached their destination, he could hardly guess what she would ultimately choose.

Was this the right path?

Regel realized he had been standing in the street unmoving for a moment, and he was not alone. How the man had come upon him unawares while he focused on his sculpture, he could not say, but it put him on his guard immediately. The snow swirled around him as densely as a wall, making his eyes all but useless, but he caught glimpses of the man perhaps a dozen paces away on the street. He wore a snowy white cloak, rendering him all but invisible to the naked senses, but Regel could just barely sense him: the faint whiff of oiled leather, the flash of bright green eyes. He was there, waiting.

Slowly, Regel dropped his hand to the hilt of his falcat.

Just like that, he lost his sense of the man in the storm. Calmly, Regel fell deeper into his focus. Sure enough, the man in the snow had moved away, and was even now rapidly cutting through the gale the other way up the street. Regel gave chase, one hand holding up his cloak to shield against the wind and the other on the hilt of his sword. He moved slowly but surely toward his white-clad pursuer.

They went north for a time, then the man ducked around a corner toward the center of Gardh. Regel traced his quarry through smell and instinct, until finally he caught a better glimpse of him, sheltering under the eaves of a common house. There was something familiar about the way the man moved, and his sense of confidence. His stance held no fear or surprise at Regel's skill in finding him, as though he had expected no less. They shared a moment, and then the man retreated into the snow.

He wanted to be followed, Regel realized. As to why, he could not say.

Figures pushed through the snow, clad in gray cloaks. They moved with purpose, their torches flickering in the driving snow. Regel ducked behind cover anew, though he suspected he could have stood in the flurry without them seeing. They headed up the steps to the Victorious Hunter, where the leader of the group pounded on the door. The bolt drew open and permitted them entrance, and the door shut after they entered.

Regel climbed onto the porch of the common house, where the wind howled a little less. He was about to move around the building when voices inside caught his focus. He heard the name "Semana," and it resounded inside him like a blast from a heavy caster. All thoughts of pursuit immediately left him, and leaned against the wall near the window through which the voices faintly emanated.

"Can you be certain?" The speaker had a big and boisterous voice, and the emphasis on the sound "be" made Regel think him rather fat. "The Winter Princess died five years ago, when her skyship broke up over Tar Vangr harbor. We heard the stories."

"We heard lies, it seems." This voice was thick with phlegm. The speaker coughed and spat into some sort of metal pot, making a ringing sound. "I seen Semana Denerre when she was a child, and this one has the look. The airs of a Denerre and the conceit of a rutting Ravalis."

Regel looked about to make sure there was no one nearby. He pressed closer to the window.

"I don't believe it, Hiesk," said the fat man. "I just don't—"

"Ruin claim what you believe, Tsarn." This third speaker was a woman, her voice deep and powerful. Dangerous. "Now the question is, do we believe her?"

"We do not, Nys," said a fourth conspirator—a woman of even temper whose words were all the more dangerous for it. "We do not."

This voice Regel knew, and it made his eyes narrow.

"The real question is," Phend said to her fellow conspirators. "What do we do with them?"

He wanted to burst in through the window and kill them all where they sat, but something warned him to wait. Instead, he focused his senses upon the converse.

"Why has this supposed princess come to Gardh?" asked the one with the broken voice: Hiesk. "And with only the Frostburn. Formidable as he is, the Winter King's shadow is an old man now."

"I agree," said the woman, Nys. "If her story were true, she would have come with a more substantial royal escort. Her family is dead. Why risk herself in this way? It makes no sense."

"So she's on the run," Hiesk said. "Is there any point in sending a squad to investigate her story? Find this broken down ornithopter?"

"Not in this storm," the fat man—Tsarn—said. "We use it. It gives us time."

"Obviously." Regel could hear the derision in Nys's voice. "We should kill them now and bury their corpses in the snow. Let the corpse-wolves eat them after thaw."

"Not yet," Phend said. "We—wait. Did you hear that?"

A caster *cracked* and the window exploded outward, showering glass out into the blizzard. Within two heartbeats, the door slammed open and Phend emerged onto the porch, arrow on the string, her keen eyes searching for a target. A barbed arrowhead shimmering with venom traced a line across the open air.

Regel stood a dozen paces away, hidden behind a spindly tree, letting the storm rage around him. With so much snow choking his cloak, he might as well have been a ghost in the white. They stared at each other—Regel, hardly able to sense her through his statue, Phend seemingly blinded. In truth, though, he was not focusing upon her, but searching instead for his own phantom: the white-cloaked man who had led him to just this spot, at just this time.

After a ten-count, Phend went back inside, drawn by the voices of her co-conspirators.

Regel was gone.

FIVE

SLIPPING BACK INTO THE tower was not difficult. Two warders patrolled the halls, securing it against the weather and watching for anything or anyone not in the proper place. No doubt this would include aging slayers trying to pursue a new path in life, but Regel hardly saw cause for concern. These sentries could do nothing but train and sharpen their senses for another ten years at least and still stand no chance of detecting him.

One of the searchers—a woman of about thirty winters or so—paced along the inner, circular passage of the tower, her boots squelching faintly on the damp floor. She wore thick furs matted and dripping with melting snow, and she rested her hand on the handle of a hatchet at her belt. The broken nose and twin scars on her pockmarked face spoke of a history of violence. A faint sound caught her attention—leather scuffing on stone—and she paused. She followed the sound into a darkened alcove around a shuttered window to the outside. The latch wasn't fully set, so the wood shook and buckled against the storm.

Pressed against the wall in the shadows not a pace away, Regel kept his face turned to the stone so it would not catch the light and give him away. She had come closer than most to finding him. Eyes closed, he slowly inhaled the musk of the warder's furs—the smell of sweat and the mild acid of the rain. He heard the leather squeezing against the polished haft of her axe.

If he'd wanted to, Regel could have killed her before she even got a chance to pull that weapon from its loop. He could slip around and cut her throat with the small knife he'd secreted out of the tower that morn. It might serve their escape to have one fewer warder standing between them and freedom.

Twenty years ago, he would have done it—even as recently as five years ago, he might have.

Instead, he waited until the warder adjusted the window, coughed twice in the lingering cold, and went on her way.

Regel slipped through the passage and up the stairs until he came to their room. No warders by the door—not a good sign. Raising one hand with the knife, he pressed his ear at hip height against the door, and heard Mask's guttural voice. Also, there was a faint hum, as of the very air crackling. Perhaps she was working magic to some purpose?

Regel pushed through the door. "Gather your things," he said. "We're—"

He trailed off and took in the startling scene. The big-nosed guard knelt in the middle of the room, his every muscle stretched taut like those of a hooked fish, veins popping through his thick flesh like cords in a mariner's net. He had torn away much of his clothing, baring his skin to the tense heat of the chamber. His body radiated pain in every direction, but upon his face was a look of pure rapture. Fully clad in her leathers, Semana floated above him, slowly circling, her feet just a hand's breadth from the ground. She held a hand above his head, fingers splayed, and her face was turned up toward the ceiling. Magic flowed between the guard and her palm, coiling crimson and putrid greens—the magic of Plaguefire mingled with something else Regel did not recognize. She did not seem to see him.

"Semana." Regel choked on the thick smoke in the room. Too much magic. "We have to go."

She gazed down at the helpless warder like an avenging angel, wholly insensible to the world around her. She was looking, Regel realized, not at the shivering guard but upon the flowing energies that connected them. He knew little of the ways of magic, but the sheer force of her concentration warned him that whatever she was attempting was no simple matter, and that it took all of her focus to maintain it.

Unfortunately, they had no time to wait.

"Semana," he said again. His voice rasped. "*Mask.*"

The princess looked to him, her eyes glowing bright red in the depths of her magic. Silver-blue lines shot through the crimson, like lightning crackling amidst a firestorm. The magic surged, demanding her attention, but she closed her fist and it dissipated, flames licking off into smoke around her. Then it was over, and the pungent smoke of relics and magic filled the room around them. The guard slumped, unmoving, to the floor.

"What?" The cracked voice that emerged from Semana made Regel shiver. She coughed and waved away greasy smoke from her face. "What passes?"

"We need to go." Regel saw that Semana's bag was already packed. Good. "Phend—"

"Has betrayed us. Or she will. So we need to go." Mask's rasping voice emerged from Semana's throat, but it climbed as she spoke until finally it was her own voice. "Can we go out in this storm?"

"With that." Regel nodded to her silver gauntlet, which she wore. Likely, it had a full charge, as it had not been the source of the magic she had used on the guard. That sorcery was something far darker.

He became aware of footsteps—another warder coming down the passage. "Hold—"

"Let's away then," Semana said.

With that, she strode right out of the room, thrusting open the door with a jolt of invisible magic. The approaching warder opened his mouth to shout, but she waved him away and he hurtled down the corridor. Casually, she looked both ways, then followed after where the man had flown.

The dismissive, almost contemptuous nature of her assault should have startled Regel, but it was nothing compared to what she had been doing when he entered the room. He had not liked the look of that magic, nor the expression on Semana's face: one of power and of ecstasy.

He knelt over the guard, who lay senseless upon the floor. The man took shallow breaths and his body trembled, as though he had run all day and night. Upon his face was such a look of absolute contentment mingled with the tiniest bit of something else. Awe, perhaps—or terror.

Regel put his hand on the man's forehead and shut his eyes. To him, the guard became an object—one of infinitely more complexity than one of his carvings. Rather than expand to encompass the room, his senses focused upon the guard, who became Regel's world. The blood ran sluggish in his veins and arteries, his lungs swelled and emptied haltingly, and his muscles twitched between tight and slack. His flesh stretched across his bones, bound to one another and to joints by sinews. Regel could feel every inch of the man's body as though it were his own—taste the raw flesh, breathe the ragged breaths, and feel every bit of pain. The guard felt diminished, as though the magic had reached in and torn out something irreplaceable inside him.

Regel concentrated on the man and himself, thinking of them as two parts of the same whole. Power flowed between them, and a bright light shone out for just a heartbeat.

Semana appeared in the doorway, magic-born smoke swirling around her. "Coming, father?"

He left the guard—breathing but exhausted—and joined her.

Giddy on surging magic, Semana strode out into the depths of the storm, heedless of the stinging chill. The storm embraced her like an old friend. It was a constant companion upon their journey, rather than the threat it posed to more mundane creatures.

She felt revitalized after her encounter with the warder. She'd tasted his blood and drank of his life, and it gave her new, fresh strength. She almost bounced off the ground with very step, and she had to restrain herself to keep from punching holes in doors or walls when she touched them. Already she could feel the stolen vitality start to ebb as her body burned it up, but just at the moment, she felt unstoppable.

"Semana, wait!" Regel called from behind, but the storm swallowed his words.

She headed from the tower straight toward the entrance to Gardh, magic crackling around her in a haze of heat and smoke. The snow near her turned it to slush as she walked. The storm seemed drawn to her: either to lash against the source of warmth in its midst or called to her magic, she could not say. She suspected Regel was following somewhere, probably being stealthy. But if he had meant them to slip out of Gardh quietly, Semana would do the opposite, simply because she could.

An arrow whizzed past Semana's masked head and stuck into the snow. Ten paces away, Semana saw Phend sheltering under the eaves of one of the buildings off the main road through the fort, a second arrow already nocked on her hunting bow. She shouted something—a warning, perhaps—but Semana didn't care. She could feel the Protector's pulsing blood on her tongue, and it tasted so much better than that of the warder back in the tower. She wanted it. She *needed* it.

Semana reached out with her magic, making Phend stiffen. She sensed the woman's confusion and rising terror as she fought in vain to move. Semana well remembered what it had felt like to lose control of her own body against a blood sorcerer. Not that empathy stayed her, obviously. A scream wrenched itself from Phend's pulsing throat, cutting through the howl of the wind.

Regel appeared out of the snow at her side and touched her arm. "Semana. Stop this."

"Stop it?" Anger, hot and powerful, rose up in her gut. "Stop trying to control me, Oathbreaker."

A pair of warriors rushed out of the building across from Phend, and Semana seized their blood as well. They stood on their toes, arms and weapons outstretched, and could not move. A burst of plaguefire from the mask rotted the supports of the porch, and the eaves came collapsing down atop the two, removing them from the battle. The magic danced and spat like a living thing in the air, noxious and glowing putrid green.

"This is who I am!" Semana screamed at Regel. "This is *what* I am!"

A woman with an axe rushed at them out of a nearby alley, uttering a mad cry, and Semana extended her left hand to smash her away with a burst of unseen magic in a wave that wiped the snow from the sky. The warrior flew backward as though struck by a rolling boulder and rolled across the ground to collapse in a boneless heap. Wordless triumph filled Semana.

"You cannot control me!" Semana cried.

Semana felt her focus waver, and that was the only warning she got before

Phend finally managed to loose the arrow she'd been holding. It smashed into Semana's leather breastplate but bounced off the shimmering blue-white magic it projected to shield her. The useless arrow spun off into the snow.

"You cannot touch me!" Semana roared.

Rage setting her body to thrumming like a live wire, Semana turned back to Phend and her fellows and raised her right hand, which curled into a claw. The Protector of Gardh gasped in pain and fear as the blood magic wrenched her to her knees. Blood welled in her eyes like tears and streamed down her face, and she babbled nonsense words.

"I am your queen!" Semana screamed. "I am—"

Then she felt cold steel at her throat, and realized Regel had pressed his knife to her skin, under the mask. She looked at him with first confusion, then simmering rage.

"How dare you," she said. "I am the Winter Queen. I—"

Regel lowered the knife. "You are not this."

He inclined his head to indicate the plaza, which had filled with people huddled against the storm. The snow had let up enough that she could make out their chapped, blistered features, and she beheld the chorus of their fear as they watched. Half a hundred souls bore witness to her rage, all of them terrified beyond measure. This should have filled Semana with pride. Such power she wielded over them. Mask would have been overjoyed to be so feared. But why did she feel only emptiness? Sorrow?

A small figure detached itself from the warding arms of someone at the edge of the plaza and ran across the snow. Semana turned, raising the silver gauntlet to ward off any threat, but it was only a child, perhaps six or seven winters of age. The youth stopped over the crumpled body of the axe-woman she had put down earlier and wept openly, tears freezing on its rose-red cheeks.

And she felt the child's delicious blood beating fiercely in its little body, inviting her to seize it.

"No," Semana said. "I didn't mean—"

Everyone flinched at her words, and they uttered a collective gasp when she took a step toward the child and its mother. This was not power. This was not majesty. It was horror.

Semana opened her mouth to speak, but the words wouldn't come.

Regel had gone over to the woman and child, and was making soothing noises at the little creature. Semana wanted to go help him, but she hadn't the least idea what to say. Everyone was staring at her, waiting for some sign of her intentions, and she couldn't do anything.

She had never intended this. It was the magic. The seductive lure of the power. The blood. The magic was more than she could resist, and the price had been more than she could bear.

It was the mask.

"Out." Free of the magic, Phend struggled up and spoke the hoarse and ragged word. Her voice sounded almost as haunted and broken as Mask's had. "Get out. Never return."

Semana's pride wanted to argue, but all she could do was hang her head.

Once they were outside the gates of Gardh and out of range of bow or caster, Semana could take it no longer. She wrenched the mask from her face and stared at it. Her eyes welled.

She had told Regel she was Mask, over and over. Perhaps it was even true. She certainly did not deserve to be anything else.

Regel put his arms around Semana as she wept.

BOOK TWO: EXILES

Ten years previous—The Palace of Tar Vangr—Winter 972 Sorcerus Annis

"COME, DARAK!" THE GIRL beamed, a look of pure joy on her face. "Come play with me!"

From the shadows, Regel watched as the boy—who'd seen all of three winters more than his sister's eight—lowered his book and looked down at her after the manner of a man grown.

"I've no time for silly games, Semana," he said. "Go and play with yourself."

Semana looked up at him with a childishly defiant look. She held a down-stuffed leather ball, around which she closed her hands very tightly. "For certain you won't catch the ball," she said.

"Yes," Darak said. "Now run along and—"

The ball plunked off the side of his head, where Semana had lobbed it. She hadn't thrown it hard, but in his surprise, Darak fell off the little parapet where he'd been sitting and into the dirt, book fluttering to the ground. He came up with a shocked face to confront a beaming Semana, who shrugged.

"I had to make sure," she said.

The retort died on Darak's lips, swallowed up by Semana's simple charm. Then he was chasing her, both of them screaming as they circled Lenalin's garden in the palace courtyard. They finally ended up rolling in the grass by the pond at the center of the garden, where lilies floated and crystals hung above them, glittering with small Thaumaturgical enchantments.

Regel let out a relieved breath as he crouched atop the wall over the garden. With his senses extended, he noted the location of the warders and searched for any details on the fringes of the scene. A maid passed along one of the walkways just below the garden, carrying a basket of fruit from the high-city market. He smelled fresh citrus and could almost taste the bright red persimmons. He let his focus linger on her bundle long enough to make sure there was no threat, then searched for other watchers. He found no one, aside from the expected Ravalis warders. Their presence could not be helped.

He'd watched the children in this way for years—whenever the Winter King left him at leisure. After what happened to Lenalin five years before, he could not trust Paeter or any other Ravalis. At least the Crown Prince had little enough use for his children, especially not Semana. The youngest of the Winter blood might as well not exist as far as he was concerned, and that suited Regel just fine.

Ovelia Dracaris, the King's Shield, usually visited the children whenever Orbrin could part with her, as he did increasingly rarely these past years. She loved Semana like her own child, and Regel well understood the connection. She'd been Lenalin's closest friend—almost her sister—and that made Semana almost her own child. For her part, Semana had seen only three or four winters when Lenalin died, so Regel suspected that to her, Ovelia must seem like Blood. There'd always been a distance between the King's Shield and Darak, however, and that Regel understood as well. He'd never heard the entire tale of the dark day of the prince's birth, but he'd found the child barely alive in a warzone, seemingly abandoned by Ovelia and Lenalin both. He was not sure he could trust Ovelia with the children either, but at least she seemed to care deeply for them.

For many reasons, Regel did not always make the best decisions where Ovelia was concerned.

A new observation broke Regel from his reverie. He heard boots and the clink of metal rings. Soldiers approached, and he could tell by their determined pace that they meant nothing good. He became very aware of the cold weight of Frostburn at his belt, but he would not draw it until he knew for sure that he needed it. Instead, he drew his handcaster, which unfolded once it cleared the holster.

Two Ravalis soldiers stepped out into the garden, fully armed and clad in crimson-plated ringmail with blue sashes under cloaks of gray. The cloaks marked them as Dustblades: eElite knights of the Summerblood. The children, scrambling in the dirt and laughing at the far end of the garden, hadn't seen them. Regel tensed, ready to interrupt their would-be slayers. The first he'd fell with a casterbolt—between the eyes—and the second he'd fall upon like a bolt of lightning. They stepped forward—

"Stop."

Ovelia Dracaris stormed out of the door behind the soldiers, Draca burning naked in her hand. Blood-red smoke rose from the blade, filling the air over the garden. Dimly, Regel could make out figures in the smoke, but only because he knew to look for them. They told the near future, for those who knew how to read them. She raised Draca at the two dusters, one of whom staggered back a step, while the other visibly winced. They knew that sword, or at least they'd heard enough stories of Ovelia's prowess to fear it. Regel knew she could slay them both without even sweating—he'd taught her how.

He looked to the children, who had ceased their play upon the arrival of Ovelia and now stood watching the drama unfold. Darak stood tall, trying to appear brave, while Semana took shelter behind him. Even at a distance, Regel could hear her asking her brother "what passes?" over and over, but he said nothing. Though Darak's body trembled, his face was cold and unsurprised. He recognized what had come to pass and would face it unafraid.

A strong baritone voice rolled out of the tower behind them. "Stand down, Dragon's Daughter."

Lan Ravalis appeared, every muscular line of his body from his cocky stance to his haughty sneer writ large in the language of supercilious contempt. Between the flaming hair of the Blood of Summer, the deep brown complexion to match, and his dazzling golden armor that threatened to blind onlookers even in the weak winter sun, he could not have looked more out of place in Tar Vangr had he tried. He took in Ovelia in one lewd glance and dismissed her just as quickly.

If his impressive physicality and presence didn't command obedience, the half dozen Ravalis soldiers behind him did.

"These are your brother's blood." Ovelia shifted her stance so that she could watch all the soldiers at once. "I am sworn to protect them."

Lan spoke over Ovelia in the direction of the children. "Darak Ravalis nô Denerre," he said. "You are to accompany us, offering no resistance." He spread his hands. "I think you know why."

Regel watched Ovelia's mouth and brow purse in confusion—no recognition there—but a quick glance at Darak confirmed his suspicions. Semana's gaze flicked wildly among the soldiers to Ovelia and Lan, full of uncertainty and mounting anxiety. Darak, on the other hand, wore an expression of cool understanding on his deep brown face. The boy knew exactly why Lan had come for him, and his expression suggested he wasn't even much surprised.

The young prince had gone through with it. *Damn.*

The two forward dusters moved toward the children again, but Ovelia interposed herself, halting them once more. This time, the shadows of her sword danced around the face of one of the knights, wreathing his cheeks in echoes of a world yet to be. Regel suspected the shadows promised the man's bloody death if he pressed the issue. The other soldiers trained their armed casters on her.

"You will not touch them," she said.

Regel's heart lurched. If he did not intercede, Ovelia would have a fight on her hands, but most of those soldiers did not even realize he existed. If he suddenly appeared from above, chaos would erupt and plenty of blood would spill in the garden that day. He wouldn't be saving anyone.

Lan spoke up from behind the ranks of the soldiers with the casters. "You would do well not to stay these knights," he said. "They act on orders from that very Blood you invoke."

"Whose orders?" Ovelia asked. "Yours?"

No, Regel realized. They were—

"Mine."

Paeter Ravalis pushed his way through the ranks of the castermen, and all eyes fell upon him. Unlike the assembled warriors, the Elder Prince of Tar Vangr opted for a much more comfortable red robe, which fell open down half his hairy chest. Once, he'd more than matched any sword in Tar Vangr in strength and skill, but five years of drink and debauchery had not treated his body kindly. His tightly corded muscles had started to relax into fat, like those of an old mouser after gelding. Though he and Regel were of an age, more or less, he seemed significantly older.

Though Regel saw the man very little—entirely by choice—he had no need to wonder what demons hounded Paeter. He'd put a debilitating fear into the Elder Prince five years ago, after what had passed with Lenalin, and he considered that a very gentle price to pay for his crimes. Regel may have chosen to honor Lenalin's wishes and spare Paeter, but he took no small delight in seeing the prince suffer. Five years ago, he'd not have thought the man capable of guilt and fear, but he knew otherwise now. Neither failing excused what Paeter had taken from this city and its people.

Paeter's arrival defused the tension in the garden, at least enough to prevent an imminent battle. Lessened as his body had become, he still wore his personality around him like a cloak made of lightning and thunder. The gathered warriors snapped to attention and inclined their heads in deference to the Elder Prince, though Regel saw a few of their expressions tended toward something like disgust. Lan had never proven adept at hiding his feelings or—particularly—concealing his jealousy for his brother. The glare he gave Paeter's back could have stabbed a lesser man to death.

"Mine, Syr Dracaris," Paeter said. "The orders were mine. And well founded."

He stepped up to Ovelia, heedless of her burning sword, and touched her chin with his fingers. Seeing him touch her like that—demeaning her into a stubborn child at a single careless stroke—made Regel furious. Ovelia was a warrior: proud and strong and deserving of far better treatment than to be pawed at by a broken wretch that used to be a man. At that moment, Regel wanted to kill Paeter, Lan, and the rest, but he held himself back. His muscles ached and burned at the strain of holding himself unmoving, especially when he wanted so badly to leap upon them. Dust trickled down the wall from the edge of the roof, but the moment was too tense for anyone to note it.

"Darak stands accused of high treason against the Winter Throne." Paeter shot a glance to the children. "If you would have my recite the charges in hearing of the Princess—"

The reminder of Semana's presence cut Ovelia's strings, and Regel could see the strength rush out of her. She even seemed to tremble under Paeter's touch. "You wouldn't," she said.

"He won't." Darak stepped away from Semana, who reached for him but did not follow. He raised his chin haughtily, looking rather like his father in that moment. "I will go with them willingly. You are dismissed, Syr Dracaris. Watch over my sister, as you are loyal."

Ovelia looked at him askance, as though she might argue, but Darak had delivered the order with a firm confidence that belied his age. She stepped back, out of Paeter's reach, and bowed her head. She eased herself toward Semana in a protective posture. If any of them made a move toward the princess, no forceful words or implied threat would stop her.

The two Ravalis warders who had first appeared—young people Regel did not know, one man and one woman—moved past her and flanked the prince. Darak shook off their hands, proud enough to walk on his own rather than under their control. Paeter led the way back into the tower. The Ravalis closed ranks behind them, lowering their casters but keeping them ready. Lan gave Ovelia a last smirk, then followed.

Paeter may have stopped Ovelia with ease, but not Regel. He skittered across the acid-pitted rooftop like a spider and swung down through a near window into a small servant's cell just below the roof. He shot past the open door of the chamber like a shadow, only distantly noting the surprised noises of two footmen passing by in the corridor. By the time they came into the room to investigate, he had closed the false shelf behind him and vanished into the hidden passages of the palace.

These passages were his kingdom. He'd spent more time walking them than the palace proper.

He followed alongside the party escorting Darak down into the bowels of the palace, working his way around curving passages and down steep steps to parallel their progress. He could track them every so often through one of the many strategically-cut spyholes that allowed warders to do so. Infuriatingly, they'd put a black sack over Darak's head, as much to conceal his identity as to disorient him. Regel could have shot them all dead with his caster more than once had he desired it, but a brawl in the corridors would serve none but his own anger. Instead, Regel would bide his time and wait for his moment.

He guessed their course easily enough: toward the dungeons beneath the palace, which bored like worm trails through the mountain at the heart of Tar Vangr. He got ahead of them before they descended and then followed their path closely, lingering always at the edge of their light. He could perceive them without seeing, and even had he not known his way intimately, his freed senses would have guided him. They let him dodge warders patrolling the corridors, giving him time to blend into the shadows like another part of the rough hewn stone.

The dungeons were ancient indeed, carved and occupied and abandoned even before the line of Denerre emerged from the scarred stone a thousand years ago to fulfill the Prophecy of Return. Ancient pipes corroded almost to dust studded the walls like veins, running to and from hatches that led to cramped rooms of long forgotten purpose. Some of these chambers could still be entered, and some of the devices in the caverns even powered on if one knew how to work them—usually by blood or body heat.

As he entered the antechamber of a suite used for torture, Regel found his ideal waiting place. Chains dangled from the ceiling and manacles studded the walls, and a distinctive yeasty smell of rot and despair floated on the air. The odors of rust and old blood wafted from rooms deeper within, including the three small chambers off this room. It was not all so inhospitable: a table and a pair of chairs were there to host warders, complete with a number of cards from a game in progress. Whoever had been playing, Regel suspected they'd received orders to take a respite this hour specifically.

Thaumaturgic candles set in the near wall sputtered to life at his proximity, taking some of his warmth to power themselves, but when he put his hand on Frostburn, the sword blocked the exchange of energy and the candles flickered out. The icy blue steel consumed all the life he had to offer.

As he waited, the cold seeping up his arm, a memory rose unbidden.

"What is this?" he had asked, marveling at the luminous blue steel—more like glass than metal.

"He is death." The woman with the rosy eyes had smiled. "His hunger will not be quenched."

Regel shook the conversation away as voices approached, and he released the sword with a crinkle of rimefrost that had built up around his fingers.

Most of his arm was numb and the cold had seeped into his chest. Frostburn's chill had almost turned him into a standing corpse in just those few breaths where he had let his mind drift. The speed and efficacy of the sword's leeching power unnerved him, but it also spoke to a deep, dark void within himself that hungered for the same thing Frostburn did.

They came around the corner then: Paeter, Darak, and the two Ravalis escorts. The whole group hadn't followed, which made sense if Paeter intended to keep this matter private. Regel waited until they drew close enough for their own life force to activate the candles, in the light of which they could finally see him. He felt them shudder and heard them gasp with surprise—all but Paeter, who seemed unaffected.

"Oathbreaker," the Elder Prince said.

Wordlessly, Regel pushed aside the fringe of his cloak, revealing Frostburn at his hip, and he put his hand once more on its hilt. He felt its chill suffuse him, blotting out all other thoughts or feelings. He was a creature of cold fury. The fae blade thirsted for the warmth of living flesh—a driving need that grew stronger the longer he left it unsated. He knew that if he drew the blade now, he could not sheathe it again until it bathed in hot blood. As many as he could kill, and that would be all of them.

The soldiers might not have recognized him, but they knew that sword from whispers over too many bowls of wine in rooms lit with crackling embers. He could smell the man voiding himself and almost taste the fear sweating off the woman. These things he noticed but attached no passion to them. He was a creature of the icy world beyond.

Darak stood masked and unseeing, his body clenched in uncertainty. He didn't know what was happening. To him, the Frostburn was likely just a story.

"Leave us," Paeter said to the soldiers.

The man stared at him in bewilderment, while the woman stuttered an argument. "But Your Highness—"

Paeter turned on her with a snarl and raised his hand as though to strike her. Good that she recoiled, for if he had struck her, Regel would have cut the life from him in an instant. He would not tolerate seeing Paeter harm anyone ever again, least of all a woman.

"Leave us," Paeter said. "I would speak with this man alone."

The guards took their leave. Paeter and Regel gazed at one another, Darak between them. Paeter put his hands on his son's shoulders, but the prince shrugged them off and tore his hood free, blinking in the sudden light. A smile spread across his face, and he looked up at Regel with smug satisfaction.

"I knew it," Darak said. "I knew you were real."

Regel stared at him without reply. He and the prince had met before on several occasions, but no one had told Darak who or what Regel was. Apparently, the lad had figured it out, or perhaps he'd paid good coin for the secrets. Regardless.

"This is right," Darak said. "I imagine you thought you would stop me, Father. But in truth, all you've done is hasten my plans."

"Have I." Paeter spoke very levelly without obvious emotion.

The droll tone did nothing to stop Darak. He was a showman like his father, and they two were his audience.

"You were right, of course, Father." Darak stepped into the center of the antechamber as he spoke, every bit as arrogant as his father and as eloquent as his mother ever was. He moved around the space, brushing his fingers along dusty chairs and tables, claiming it all for himself. "I have indeed been employing men to sabotage and frustrate your efforts. Paying servants to spread rumors of your liaisons. Making friends on the Council who will oppose you. When the time comes."

"All these things I would expect. Ambition is in your blood." Paeter scowled. "But you reach too far. The visits to Gardh? The secret messages planning a coup? Did you think I would not find them?"

"I knew you would," Darak said. "And they have led us here. To this moment. I had to do something to force your hand, and you danced as I directed. Courteous as a pageboy." He smirked. "You would make a move against me, and the Winter King's Shadow would intervene, to your death. I win."

Paeter sighed. "I did not raise you this way."

"You did not raise me at all." Darak's eyes flashed with sudden rage, but just as quickly he buried his outburst under icy command. "You are not fit to rule this city, and I will succeed where you cannot. Once you are gone."

"You are the Crown Prince." Paeter shook his head. "You already stand closer to the throne than I. Did you think I would slay my own child?"

Darak gestured around the torture chamber. "We are here, are we not?"

"That we are." Paeter shrugged. "I see I cannot sway you."

Darak turned to Regel, who had watched all this without speaking.

"I knew my greatfather kept a slayer," Darak said. "I'd heard the stories, but that was not what convinced me. No." He clenched his hands into fists and set one hard on the table. "I remember that day, when my mother died. I remember a man more shadow than flesh. You. The Frostburn of legend."

He turned, leaned back on the table, and crossed his arms.

"You are a loyal blade of the Blood of Winter, are you not?" Darak asked.

Regel nodded. "Beyond death," he said.

"What are you waiting for?" Darak beamed widely and pointed at Paeter. "Kill him."

The moment stretched in the chamber, as Darak indicated his father and gazed upon Regel with perfect confidence that he would obey. As heartbeats passed, though, his confidence waned.

Finally, Paeter chuckled ruefully. "You poor, poor idiot boy."

"What passes?" Darak asked finally. "Is this some sort of jest?"

Regel could see the anger coiling inside the prince, darkening his face and filling his eyes with silver-hot rage. He had the touch of Frostfire himself, like his greatfather before him. How rare that spark of true magic had become, and how terrible that it would now be extinguished.

"Well?" Darak said, the word almost a growl. "Why do you stand, Frostburn? I gave you a direct order. Protect your prince. Slay the Usurper. Avenge my mother."

Regel almost did it.

He could picture drawing the blue steel and slashing Paeter's head from his shoulders, carving through that smug expression even as it became stupefied. He would have hacked and stabbed and cut into Paeter Ravalis's body until there was no more warmth or blood for Frostburn to feed upon, and then he would have ground whatever remained into the stone beneath his boots.

But in the end, he stayed his hand—going so far as to remove it from Frostburn entirely.

Ironically, it was the sword's cold focus that did it. It drowned out all his hot rage and impossible hatred and allowed him to assess the situation free of emotion.

"He cannot," Paeter said. "You see, I call him Oathbreaker, but he keeps a different oath—an oath he swore to your mother." He turned Darak to face him, and the boy's eyes were wide and wild. "He swore to honor her wishes, and she never wanted me dead. She made him swear not to kill me."

"But—" Darak goggled. "That makes no sense. You killed her. You killed my mother."

Paeter nodded. "But I am the reason your sister lives," he said. "If I die, she dies. The Frostburn knows this, and he—" He shook his head. "He has decided whose life he values more."

Darak whirled back toward Regel, his widening features writ with betrayal and heartbreak. "I—"

He did not see Paeter extend a lightning prod toward his back, and strike him down with a Thaumaturgical charge. Sparks danced briefly in the corridor, and Darak's body went rigid. His eyes rolled back and he slumped to the floor, twitching senselessly.

The two men stood over him as though ready for a duel. The same one they had been fighting for years. Regel felt so very tired.

"What now?" he asked.

"There are other conspirators." Paeter ran his fingers almost casually through Darak's hair. "We will get the names from him. Their heads will adorn the gate."

"You didn't answer my question," Regel said. "What of *him*, now?"

Paeter sighed. The way he was looking at Darak almost approached affection. "Exile," he said. "I will not slay my own blood. I would never do that." He looked back up at Regel. "This is not a victory for me. Now—" He sighed and shook his head. "Now my fool brother will have the throne one day, no doubt. A disaster for us all."

The Elder Prince—soon to be the Crown Prince once again—regarded Darak one last time, then stood, his bones crackling at the effort to hoist his increasing bulk. He looked as though he had aged ten years in the space of a moment.

"Have you had your revenge, Oathbreaker?" Paeter asked. "Does it please you to see me struggle? To see my life collapse season by season, in this horrid waste of a world?" He indicated Darak with a derisive scoff. "This boy was my legacy: that my name might live on in the annals of Ruin's history. Now I have nothing."

"You have another child," Regel said.

"Do I." Paeter's eyes glittered in the candlelight. "Warders."

The two dusters returned and scooped up the limp Darak under the armpits. Out of healthy fear, they did their best not to look at Regel as they hauled the boy deeper into the dungeons. Paeter gave him a final nod before he too retreated into the darkness.

Footsteps from the other direction caught his attention, and Regel realized Ovelia was approaching. He recognized the crimson light of Draca, which danced violently across the wavy steel. It told the future, and while he could not make out the images, he saw plenty of pain there. Ovelia came to him and reached for his arm.

At her touch, Regel felt as though a spell had broken upon him, and all the hate and rage he'd pushed down so that he could deal with Paeter and Darak swept over him anew. His body tensed to rush after them—to paint the crypts of old Tar Vangr with their blood—and place Darak safe on the throne.

And as though she knew his mind—as she always seemed to—Ovelia stopped him.

"Regel." Ovelia's hazel eyes seemed to glow in the blue candlelight. "This must pass."

"I will kill him this time," Regel said. "This time—"

"Semana," Ovelia said.

Just the one name, but it stopped Regel like a blow to the stomach.

Paeter stood third in line for the throne, behind his own children in order of their birth: first Darak, then Semana. Here in Tar Vangr, kings and queens could expect equal respect and acknowledgement, but among the Ravalis, only men could sit a throne or wield any real power. With his son removed from succession, Paeter could make a claim on the throne, and he would not consider Semana a threat to his ascension. She would be safe.

Why hadn't he seen it? Ovelia had always had an especial love for the girl, and she would choose Semana over Darak in a heartbeat. She already had.

"Yes," Regel said at length. Just the one word, but it held so much pain and anguish as a thousand words could not capture. He betrayed Lenalin every day.

"Regel." Ovelia laid her hand on his bicep. "We—"

He shook her off and strode away.

Regel made his way back through the bowels of the palace in a daze, careless as to his direction. The maze of cavernous tunnels became once again the impossible warren he'd discovered as a child, and he could not remember where more than half the passages led. For the first time he felt old, his five and thirty winters of battle weighing heavily on his shoulders and back and legs. The walls felt hot to the touch, compared to the sucking cold deep in his core. He felt he would never be warm again.

He finally found his way out through one of the secret passages and out into the hall of Queen Denes, the first of the Winterborn to answer the Prophecy of Return and rise from the depths nearly a thousand years ago. He paused to look up at the statue, and found breath hard to come by. The great Denes, legendary warrior and avenging angel, looked just like Lenalin standing there above him, her bare feet scant inches from his face. In one hand, she grasped a scepter that could have been a war mace, and her other hand extended toward him, palm out, offering him peace. Her face of marble wore a beatific expression, one that Regel suspected the real Queen Denes had never used in real life.

He reached out to touch one of the stone feet, but stopped short, overcome with a rising dread that he could not name or face. Lenalin was gone, and now her son as well.

How badly he had failed the woman he loved—five years ago and again this night.

How long he stood at the statue's feet, Regel didn't notice. He only knew that a significant amount of time had passed before he became aware of another presence in the darkness behind him.

"Hail."

The voice filled Regel with dread, however tiny it seemed. He turned, and there she stood: Semana Denerre nô Ravalis, the last of the Winter Blood, the last princess of Tar Vangr.

"Hail," she said again. "Do you know, syr, where's my brother? I can't find him anywhere."

He couldn't say if Semana knew him. The last time Regel had allowed the child to see him—five years ago, the day her mother had died—she'd been much younger than she was now. What whispers she might have heard, or what words one of her Summerblooded kin might have put in her ears, he could not say. But he saw no fear on her face or in her eyes. Even after the loss that had touched her, she still maintained her simple innocence to the darker, harsher truths of the world.

In that moment, he wanted so badly to see her keep that innocence. Let her be the good, perfect child she had always been, for as long as possible if not forever. Let her be safe. Let her grow up to be a wonderful, powerful woman. No matter what action he needed to take or sacrifice he needed to make, he would have gladly done it for her sake. But he knew it would not last.

All things pass to Ruin.

Regel knelt to put their faces on the same level. He looked into Semana's eyes, and she into his. He could not lie to her. "Your brother is gone," he said.

Semana frowned. "Will he come back?"

Regel shook his head.

"Ever?"

He could tell she knew the answer to that without having to ask. The knowledge was in her eyes.

They needed no more words. They regarded one another for a moment, and then Semana stepped toward Regel and put her little arms around him. It was what she had done the first time they'd met, five years before. Regel hadn't known what to do that time, and he barely knew now. He put his arms around her in turn and comforted her as she wept softly.

It was not the first time Ruin had visited Semana's life, and it would not be the last. But he would protect her. He would always be there to keep Ruin's claws from her face.

Because she was his daughter—a secret he could never tell anyone—and because she was herself.

SIX

The Winter Wilds

CHILL WATER DRIPPED FROM the ceiling and ran down the walls of the tunnel before and around them, slipping from fragile icicles to run down matching stalagmites.

With a sickly *squelch*, Semana's bare right hand sank deep into moss of such a deep green that it appeared black. Its fronds felt soft going in, but when she tried to pull away it tugged back like a trap. With a bit of effort, she extricated herself, but the experience left her hand covered in green and brown muck. She wiped her hand on her leather and made a concerted effort to avoid touching the stone wall. Her boots made an unpleasant sound all their own, and she pointedly did not look down.

"You had better be right about sleeping in this cave," Semana said.

Ahead of her, Regel pushed a dripping fall of moss aside and ducked past. "You will see."

"You keep saying that." Semana grimaced. She glanced down at one of her boots, thankful the black leather hid the muck. "I could fly. Just hover a hand off the ground. Just for a while."

"If you want to smother us." Regel gestured forward with the alchemical torch.

She sighed. He was right, of course. Rarely before had she considered the fumes her various relics exuded when she used them, but several times over the past twenty days she had done so out of necessity. First the stench that almost gave them away to Phend the hunter, then trying to keep a tent warm during a blizzard, and now this. Sometimes she wondered if Regel purposefully led her into these situations where her magic was a hindrance rather than a help.

That child's eyes in Gardh… She shivered.

As they climbed deeper, they found less and less damp stone until the rock became vaguely warm to the touch. Semana thought this strange, with the winter come in earnest in the world above. Then, when they broke through into a chamber at the heart of the cave, she gasped aloud. Here, the air grew warm, even balmy—akin to an autumnal day in Luether—and wisps of steam rose from the pool of dark water illumined in the blue light of Regel's torch. A waterfall fed the natural pool, and silvery light flickered where it fell into the water. Other than a few large rock formations and stalagmites, the cavern seemed remarkably smooth and almost perfectly spherical, like a bubble of open air in the mass of stone beneath the earth. Semana realized she was standing not on blank stone or blackened moss but something akin to grass. Greenery blanketed the entire chamber, from the soft beds beneath her feet to the mushrooms growing to knee or even waist height on the floor and walls.

"This is a flamewell," Regel said. "In places such as this, the Narfire draws close to the surface of Ruin and creates…a pocket, of sorts, where living things thrive." He took off his pack and set it against a boulder covered with moss and tiny purple flowers. He shed his cloak and unbuttoned the shirt beneath against the heat. "We'll be safe here for a time."

Semana could feel the radiant warmth of the water calling to her with an irresistible allure, and it made her reach for the buckles of her leathers. She hesitated, though, remembering the last time Regel had seen her without her armor. Over her shoulder, she saw his much-scarred back, sinuously muscled and dusted with gray. The humidity of the chamber made sweat break out on her forehead.

"The road has been long," Semana said. "Give me a moment."

Regel paused and glanced at her, his expression uneasy at the prospect of leaving her alone. He'd watched her every moment of every day since Gardh, and she could hardly blame him for it.

"I've come with you this far," she said. "You can leave me alone for an hour."

Eyes on the tunnel through which they had come, Regel touched the hilt of his sword.

"You aren't worried I'll leave you," Semana said. "There's something else."

Regel shrugged back into his coat. He nodded.

A thrill ran through Semana, and her muscles stiffened. "Someone is following us."

"I underestimated you," Regel said. "I had not thought you so astute."

"I take that from my father, no doubt." Semana flexed her hands open and closed, then purposefully balled them into fists at her sides. "All my looks come from my mother, however."

"Indeed." That made Regel smile, but the expression faded within a heartbeat. Semana saw concern written upon his face, and it disgusted her. "No fear," he said. "It will only give us away."

"Fear?" Semana crossed her arms. "You know I have nothing to fear."

Nothing but herself, anyway.

"This is something new," Regel said. "Something different."

That piqued her curiosity. "What?"

"Something I expected, but not yet," Regel said. "Not until we had drawn closer."

"Closer to—the Deathless City?" In that moment, Semana found breath hard to come by. "You think a *fae* is following us."

"No," Regel said. "I *know* it's a *fae*."

Warmth rose in Semana's core. Rather than fear, she felt a sort of excitement. The Deathless *fae* were creatures from children's tales—the greatest warriors in the world, immortal, blessed with powers she could scarce imagine. She had thought Regel a daft old man when he promised to take her to Necthana, the Deathless City, but now the truth seemed so close. Did it truly exist?

She would know soon enough.

Semana clutched her fingers into fists. She struggled hard to keep her voice under control. "Does he mean us harm?"

"Perhaps." Regel shook his head. "Perhaps he is only here to watch."

"Well." With a smile, Semana began to unbuckle her armor. "I suppose you should keep him from doing that."

Regel understood her meaning and averted his eyes. "I will ward us."

"Tell yourself whatever you like. We both know I'm the more powerful force in this cave." Semana realized her error, however, when he reached down to pick up the alchemical torch left to spark and sputter on the ground. "You're not taking our only light."

Regel gave her the sly little smile he reserved for when he knew an answer but would not say. "I'll not spoil the surprise." He nodded and was gone, leaving Semana alone in the steaming cavern.

Darkness closed around her like a shroud, and for a moment she saw absolutely nothing. Her eyes adjusted after a few quick heartbeats, and she perceived a faint glow whistling through the water—traces of silver-blue light that shot past with no apparent source. It emanated primarily from the waterfall, but Semana saw no device there. Hardly enough to see by, but at least the light marked the water for her.

"Burn you, Regel." Semana grimaced. How was she supposed to bathe without light?

Flecks of light shot through the water again, and she knelt down to get a better look. The light followed no set path but instead danced back and forth, like a maddened insect thrashing just beneath the surface. It appeared, traced an unpredictable trail of light, then vanished out of existence. She reached out her bare right hand to touch where she thought the light would appear.

Radiance bloomed around her fingers in a dozen streaks that snaked out in all directions, so bright and sudden it took Semana's breath away. She drew her hand out of the pool, and the light flickered and died away. At a second touch, it appeared once more, swirling around each spot where he fingers disturbed the water. A wave of her hand sent ripples of silver-blue racing to the far edges of the pool.

Magic, but not her own—and not any kind that caused harm. It occurred in nature and existed only to create beauty. What a wondrous thing.

"Well," she said.

The air stung her naked skin as Semana shed her black leathers, piece by piece, until she stood nude on the warm stone. She hadn't taken off more than a piece or two since that horrible night back in Tar Vangr, and she'd almost forgotten the sensation. Disrobing felt like flensing herself—peeling away her skin to reveal naked, bleeding muscle beneath. She felt raw and lighter and frail, such that she had to flex her muscles to remind herself of her own body's strength. Her sun-deprived skin stretched over her arms like wrought iron and her legs tightened to finely sculpted pistons like those of a crafted mechanic.

"*Magic you may have, but strength you have to earn*," Tithian had told her often, as she grunted and sweated through grueling exercises. She had argued and whined and threatened but in the end, she'd known him to speak truth. He'd always wanted her to put on more muscle, but what she had was strong.

How long since she had last thought of her lost companion?

Semana let the question subside as she slipped into the warm water. It lit up all around her, as though her skin began to glow on contact. Silver-blue light danced like a corona around her, and she became the only bright spot in a world of darkness. It was so beautiful and wondrous she could not help but laugh. Life surrounded her, and she didn't even feel the desire to absorb it. The blood magic that had welled up in Gardh seemed far away.

And yet, magic still spiraled inside her. Not the petty artifice contained in her armor and relics, but the Frostfire in her blood. It still felt foreign to her, this power that was her birthright as an heir of Blood Denerre, but in this place it flowed naturally. The water warmed or cooled at her touch as she willed it, matching the temperature she had not known consciously she wanted.

"Let us see," she said.

She focused on controlling the Frostfire, and it slipped from her grasp to work its own will. Silvery trails of rimefrost cut across the water around her, then raced over to the waterfall. As she watched, it froze from the bottom up until a sheet of silver hung over the pool where the water had been. Semana gaped at the distorted reflection in the icy mirror, which melted apart once more in a ten count, allowing the water to flow. The Frostfire eluded her will once more, and she abandoned attempting to control it. She threw herself fully into the pool, letting the light dance from every part of her.

The water soothed her sore muscles. Regel had been drilling her in swordplay seemingly non-stop since Gardh, wearing down her body but allowing her mind to release the memory of what transpired there. The warmth of the pool felt like a gentle radiating massage all over.

Fully immersed now, Semana lifted handfuls of liquid light and let them spill over her face and into the crevasses of her neck and collarbone. She waded out to the middle of the pool, where the water reached almost to her shoulders, and dug her toes into the soft moss that grew on the rocks underfoot. The light bathed the chamber in shifting silvery shadows, and specks of silvery light like stars appeared on the walls and ceiling. She dipped her head back into the water, then kicked up her feet to float. Her ears half underwater, the dripping sound of the cavern vanished into the peaceful, lapping ripples.

Regel had chosen rightly in letting her discover the secret of the pool on her own. Drifting in a sea of warm brightness, embraced by the Narfire, she felt—for the first time in years—almost at peace. She felt happy with her magic. Not angry. Not hateful. *Happy*.

And into that blissful solitude, Semana felt a shadow creep.

Her eyes snapped open and she bobbled out of her float, exposing only her head out of the water. She could not say how long the man had been there, watching from the darkness, nor could she say exactly how she had seen him. She did not have Regel's uncanny perception or the precognitive flames of Draca to guide her. Even now Semana could not see the thing in the shadows, but she knew he was there.

"You are not the Oathbreaker," she said into the darkness.

"No."

Soft but powerful, the fae's husky voice reverberated throughout the cavern, making the water stir. Semana could not see its source, but she could feel him faintly. Close. She drew up to her full height, rising half out of the water. One hand she stretched toward the shore of the pool, while she held the other back near her face. Frostfire swirled around her hands and arms, ready to answer any threat to its mistress.

"Come into the light," Semana said. "Or are you afraid?"

The silence stood in judgment, considering her. The intruder made no reply with words, but Semana thought she could feel his bemusement. Anger rose, and cut through her hesitation. She let the Frostfire burn away and focused on the darkness within her. Blood quickened in her veins and she heard it beating in her head.

Semana channeled the magic she had stolen from Vhaerynn the Necromancer and tasted the fae's blood: metal and of cinnamon, which she had not expected. She could sense him now—feel the strange blood coursing sluggishly through his veins. His heart…it beat only once every few breaths. How could that be possible? She tried to focus on his blood, but it was like trying to pick out a single cricket against the cacophony that was her own racing heartbeat. She had been fortunate to hear him at all.

"Daughter of Winter." He spoke behind her. "This is not your power."

That truth struck her like a hammer to the chest. She'd sworn not to call upon the Blood magic after Gardh, but she hadn't even hesitated to use it again. Despite the iron will she took such pride in, she had failed this particular test. She tried to banish the blood magic, but it dripped out of her much more slowly than it had answered her call. Her heartbeat grew softer gradually, but no less fast.

"Your powers frighten you," he said. "You need fear no judgment from me."

"I fear nothing," Semana said.

She wondered who she meant to convince.

The fae said something in a language she did not understand, and Semana shivered in the cold wind swept through the cavern. Her skin prickled as the darkness grew chill but the water remained warm. He meant to distract her, and it would not work. The light dimmed in the water around her, so she ran her hands through it to stir up more radiance. Her bones had begun to glow, visible through her skin as necromancy flowed through her. The effect was both beautiful and eerie.

"Step into the light," she said, trying to sound brave. "Show yourself."

A figure unfolded from one of the boulders at the back of the cavern, shrouded in stout fabric that fell in waves from a deep cowl. So perfectly had his cloak matched the stone around him that Semana wondered at first if he had been part of it the whole while. In that moment, the world seemed to thin, as though the veneer of what one could see stretched near to breaking over what truly was. Her mind grated open just a crack, and it excited her as much as frightened her.

She spread her hands and bared her breasts to him. "Have you enjoyed your show?"

The fae abruptly vanished, as though the darkness of the cave had swallowed him. It took Semana a heartbeat to confirm that he no longer stood there, and it was only when she felt his heart beating behind her did she turn to see him perched atop the waterfall, more like a hunting falcon than a man. A stretch of finely muscled chest showed through the fold in his cloak. She had caught sight of the fae, she realized, by the white marks that gleamed on his otherwise night-black face. Now his dark eyes bore down into her like pools of night that flickered as the light played across them.

Semana wrestled down a thrill and turned her crimson-glowing hands toward her stalker. "I would not see you if you did not wish it," she said. "You *want* me to see you. Do not deny it."

"Perhaps."

The fae gazed at her levelly. Then he vanished once more, boiling away into the darkness as though a part of it. When Semana saw him again, he stood at the edge of the pool not three paces distant. His cloak fell around him like a mountain of night, hardly separate from the surrounding darkness.

Semana realized how absurd she must seem—unarmed, naked, half-submerged—threatening this nigh mythical creature that veteran warriors spoke of in hushed tones. A man who seemed to go where he wanted with little more than a thought. She stood up to her full height, heedless of her vulnerability, and held up one hand through which the bones burned. She did not know if she could control him with Blood magic—or if she trusted herself to try—but she would show no fear. No weakness.

"Away with your mantle," she said. "I would see your face."

After one long heartbeat, he did as she asked, stripping the garment with one smooth pull of a drawstring. It slipped from his body and slithered to the floor, a pool of fabric the color of the stone. Beneath, he wore only a loose pair of gray hose, tattered where they ended at his ankles. Nothing else: no shirt, gloves, or shoes. He stood on the bank, a tall shard of night in the form of a man. Semana could not say for certain what she had expected, but he defied her preconceived notions. His skin was dark as pitch, shadows flowing across it like mottling that danced upon the flesh. His body was perfect, glistening in the humid chamber with corded muscle in tight rows like soldiers before a march.

"That too." She nodded to his last covering. When he looked dubious, she shrugged. "Out of fairness. You've seen all of me."

Semana could not say for certain, but a faint smile seemed to play at his lips. Perhaps it was just her imagination. His white teeth gleamed. "As you wish, Daughter of Winter."

As instructed, he reached down and loosened the drawstring of his hose. They slid off his muscular legs as easily as his cloak had slipped his shoulders. He *was* beautiful. Perfect, even.

"You look like a man to me." Semana raised one eyebrow. "Not some creature out of legend."

"I am Deathless," he said. "Born of the flesh but heir to the darkness at the end of the world."

"Still a man." Semana let her magic die away and raised her chin. "I see, however, that you are not pleased to look upon me." She gestured to his flaccid member. "Do you not find me beautiful?"

"I do." Stars whirled in the Deathless's eyes to match the markings on his face. "Many things I have found beautiful, but they have no hold over me. What intrigues me, however…" He stepped into the water, and Semana sucked in a breath when no light erupted around his bare foot. The pool parted to either side of his black flesh as around a lifeless stone. "A beautiful thing so afraid and yet so purposeful."

Semana stiffened. "I am not afraid."

She cupped a handful of glowing water and hurled it to strike him in the chest. The radiance vanished as soon as it struck him, and the dark water ran into the hollows around his muscles and dripped over his impressive belly. Wonderful. She'd only made him *more* attractive.

Semana had found herself drawn to men at times, of course, but none who captivated her. She'd always kept herself carefully aloof. The great mage-slayer Mask was a sexless weapon, and as such had no use for the desires of the flesh. Seeing this fae creature before her now, though, Semana questioned that resolve. Perhaps it was the storm of magic in Gardh that had breached her icy wall of resolve. Perhaps it was the taste of his blood in her mouth—the way it called to her like a bright spot of warmth in a freezing fog. The attraction was not a sexual one, but the power inside him wouldn't let her look away.

She wondered if the fae could sense her thoughts. Some of the stories claimed they could do that. He moved with such self-assurance, gaze fixed upon her face, that she would have believed it of him.

He stepped to within arm's reach but came no closer, and they stood together like opposing forces, the light swimming around her and fading to darkness around him. At this distance, Semana could feel the cold of his body like a palpable thing, drinking in the warmth of the water and that of her body. His eyes were the starry midnight sky: a man's eyes but with irises of pure black with hundreds of shimmering lights that wheeled and danced as she watched.

She reached out and brushed his stomach lightly with her fingertips: it felt like cool stone, the muscles hardened to perfection through years of training and suffering. Her nakedness had not aroused him before, but she could see that her touch was another matter. It amused her, and she wondered what it would be like to be aroused in such a way. How would it feel? She wondered.

Semana looked up into the fae's starry eyes. "Do you have a name?"

"Yes, and I will give it," the fae said. "What will you give me in return?"

"Oh?" She gave him a smug smile and ticked her fingers down his perfect belly. "What would you have of me?"

He hesitated, and that made her heart pick up its beat. She felt giddy and struggled to remain in control. "A name should suffice," he said. "Out of fairness."

She was about to answer, but checked herself. "I have two names. That would not be a fair trade."

"Tell me the name that is your own." He put his hand over his heart. "The name that is here."

She opened her mouth to reply, but suddenly she wasn't sure what to say. She was Mask. Princess Semana Denerre nô Ravalis had perished on Ruin's Night five years ago. And yet, she had spent so long in Regel's company, speaking only to him, hearing the name her mother had given her upon his lips every hour. When had she begun to think of herself by that old name?

The man's attention shifted from her toward the entrance to the chamber, where blue light flared. The alchemical torch rolled down the boulders to sputter and burn against the stone. Water splashed around her, and abruptly the fae stood once more upon the shore of the pool, drawing up his hose and reclaiming his cloak. Semana wondered what she had done.

"I see now." His expression grew stormy. "Your beauty is a lure."

"What?" Semana furrowed her brow. "I didn't—"

"I did." Regel stepped out from behind a stone between the fae and the exit. He extended his drawn sword across the fae's shoulder, so that a tiny movement of his wrist would open the man's throat.

"Silver Fire!" Semana ducked mostly under the water to hide herself, her cheeks hot with anger and shame. Had she her mask, she'd have glared Regel to death. As it passed, she waded toward the boulder where she had heaped her armor.

Regel and the fae stared at one another, dueling with their eyes rather than their swords. Of the two of them, the old man moved first, raising his sword at a more threatening angle so that the edge almost touched the sculpted black chin.

"I do not know you," Regel said. "But you know me."

"The great Frostburn—I am honored." Wary of the steel, the fae affected half a bow, extending one empty hand out to the side in a respectful gesture. Regel's sword followed him throughout the motion. "I underestimated you both. It will not happen again."

"No."

Regel lifted the sword so that it barely touched the fae's neck, and the fae flinched away as though scalded by super heated metal. Semana thought, for one terrible moment, that Regel had cut the fae's throat. Blisters appeared under his jaw where the steel had touched him. She understood: most stories of the fae claimed their flesh burned at the touch of iron. That legend, at least, seemed to hold true.

"You will speak only when I speak to you," Regel said. "Do you understand?"

Wincing in what was obviously great pain, the fae nodded. "Know that if you kill me, it will be my great honor to join your dark path."

"I'm sure." Regel nodded, and the fae put out his arms, opening himself for inspection. Regel searched him for a weapon Semana knew he would not find, then stepped back out of reach. The sword remained hovering at the fae's throat. "Now. What will you? Why have you followed us?"

"There exists an inequity between us," the fae said. "This cannot pass."

Semana, pulling on her leather breeches, realized what the fae meant. *He knows your name, but you do not know his.* She slid into her cuirass and secured the first buckle.

"You will answer what I ask." Regel's face might have been chiseled of ice. "Nothing else."

The fae nodded slightly.

"What will you?" Regel asked. "Have you come to do us harm?"

"You draw close to the borders of Necthana." The fae shrugged. "What sense lies in blindness?"

"A scout, then."

The fae offered the same subtle nod as before. "I have that honor."

"And what says the Rose of our approach?"

To that, the fae only stared at Regel.

"She does not know," Regel said. "Interesting." He turned the sword over to gleam in the blue light the pool radiated. "Tell me then, Deathless, why I should not end your second life."

Semana raised one glowing hand. "Because I won't let you."

Regel's body tensed, but his arm would not obey his commands. It was hers now. Semana felt his blood thundering back and forth through his body, and she focused particularly on his arm. The blood listened to her, as though the limb had attached itself to her body instead of his.

She stepped near to him, her armor half-donned, her mask in one hand. Her cuirass hung awkwardly, one arm threaded through and buckled loosely at the back, and she'd managed to slip the silvery mesh onto her left hand.

The magic of the invisible hand flared within the device, and she lifted Regel away. The stench of expended magic seemed choking in the enclosed space. Regel struggled against her will, but that only made him roll over and over where he hung suspended and weightless.

The Deathless stared at her, his expression difficult to read. Curiosity, she saw, and also a sort of hunger that she rather liked. "I am called Mask," she said. "Let us part as friends, not enemies."

He nodded to her. "I am called Gilt, for that which I prized most highly in a life that is gone."

"Guilt?" Semana asked. "Guilt for what?"

He smiled slightly, the bemused expression of one accustomed to jesting. "You have not earned that story, Daughter of Winter—*Mask*," the fae said. "Perhaps in time you might." Gilt inclined his head to the floating Regel. "You shall walk in safety from the Deathless, Frostburn. May your dark path lead to wisdom." He turned toward the tunnel.

"What wisdom?" Semana asked.

Gilt looked back over his shoulder. "That death walks never before or behind, but always beside."

Then he was gone, melting into the darkness as abruptly as he had appeared. Semana strained to see him go, but his power exceeded her mortal senses. She could no longer taste his blood: he'd slipped away like a lover in the night. She inhaled deeply, trying to catch the last of his scent, but she found only the reek of burning magic. Her silver glove glowed hot as it held Regel floating above the pool. He'd stopped struggling and now stared at her in that judgmental way of his.

Well, he *had* told her not to use magic.

Semana banished the magic, dropping Regel with a great splash into the pool. It instantly lit in blue-silver all around him, the light racing outward to the edges. To his credit, he struggled only a little to put his head above the surface, spat water, then glared at her.

"You were starting to smell," she said with a shrug. "Your clothes too."

Regel wasn't laughing. He unbuckled his coat. "He is dangerous."

"So am I." Semana ran her fingers over her silver glove, still warm from the expenditure of power. "Beneath his darkness, he is only a man."

"You think so." Regel hoisted his drenched coat out of the pool onto the stone. "The Deathless take the name of those things they most loved, to kill their old lives."

"Now I understand," Semana said. "Necthana is where you trained. That is how you move as you do—faster than any man should." She crossed her arms. "Is that the source of your name, as well? Have you surrendered regality, knowing you could never rule at my mother's side?"

His eyes glowed bright and angry in the pool's radiance. "He is a slayer and nothing more."

"That's what I thought about you."

To that, Regel had no answer. He stripped the rest of his sopping clothes, and Semana turned away. How tempting it was to leave—to walk out of the cave and continue on alone. By the time Regel dried his clothes and could venture into the winter without dying on the spot, she could be leagues away. Between her Frostfire, Blood Magic, and the power in Mask's relics, what need had she for Regel?

Somehow, she could not go. Perhaps she still needed something from him.

"Who was this Rose you spoke of?" Semana asked. "Some manner of queen, perhaps? My slayer-warder has left yet another heart broken in his wake, I think."

She'd meant it as a barb, but Regel did not rise to the occasion. Another secret of his she would unravel in time. He had never failed to yield to her yet.

"You left matters unequal," Regel said. "The Deathless seek balance in all things."

"You mean regarding my name," Semana said. "Oh yes. He'll be back."

"We leave within the hour," Regel said. "This place is safe no longer."

"With that, I can agree." Semana shrugged and adjusted her armor.

Perhaps she had seen Regel's plan in the wrong light. She had thought him beyond insane for bringing her to the mythical Deathless City, but she'd had no other choice but to follow him. Now, she had seen a fae—touched him with her own fingers—and knew the legends were true. Let Regel bring her to safety in Necthana—she would welcome it.

But she would not stay there. Not if she could muster an army of Deathless. With a thousand like Gilt at her side, Tar Vangr would fall within days, not weeks.

Her mind roiled.

SEVEN

SHORTLY AFTER DAWN, FIVE days past the flamewell where they'd met the fae, Regel grew tense enough to light a tinder on his cheek. Semana had noted his rising anxiety over the previous days, seemingly fueled by minor observations: broken branches, furrows in trees, scratches on boulders. She'd seen a few of these, but assumed they indicated mundane animal activity. Between Regel's steel and her magic, Semana couldn't imagine a creature of the natural world posed them any genuine threat.

She could no longer fool herself, however, when they found a whole section of the forest...*crushed.* It resembled a ditch more than a grove—a canal of broken branches and pulverized trees. Red-white flesh leaked around the yellowed spines of shattered trunks. The sheer strength and violence expended in that place made her teeth rattle and her legs shake.

"You know what caused this," she said as Regel knelt amongst the devastation, examining the broken ground.

Regel rose, rubbing his hands clean. "A dragon."

Semana stared at him. "First Deathless fae, then dragons?" she asked.

Regel grimaced. "The beast's territory has expanded in the years since I passed this place," he said. "These marks are fresh. Three days, perhaps."

"So you're not kindling me," Semana said. "I thought dragons only myth."

Regel nodded gravely. "Shelter first," he said.

They backtracked from the devastation to a small stand of trees they'd passed a few moments before, where the shadows stretched long even as the sun rose high. Semana remembered a sense of tranquility as she passed among the trees, glancing up at the light filtering through the dripping canopy high overhead. Now it felt vaguely sinister: part of the hunting grounds of a creature Semana had not thought existed, much less expected to encounter.

Her mind ran through all the stories about dragons and the heroes who slew them, protecting villages or rescuing kidnapped royalty or all the other silly quests that such tales chronicled. Born of powerful spells gone awry, the tales claimed that dragons grew to the size of skyships and propelled themselves through the murky sky on massive wings and powerful magic within. They were relics of an age long past: weapons of the World of Wonder before Ruin fell and mankind took shelter in its tombs. But as with most of the things from that world that had thrilled her as a child, Semana as an adult had convinced herself they no longer existed. And yet, here was the evidence, right before her eyes. Mask's relics were real enough, why not dragons?

"Tell me," she said to Regel.

"I have passed this way many times before," Regel said, "and only twice have I seen her."

"Her?" Semana asked.

He nodded. "Once, I came upon her nest, and found a dozen eggs," he said. "Dragons lay as birds do, but this dragon has no male to fertilize her clutch. They were massive, these eggs." He held his hands wide to demonstrate a size matching that of his well muscled torso.

"That would make quite a feast." Semana had attempted to lighten the moment with her mirth, but Regel just stared at her. She didn't feel any more at ease. "Is she intelligent, this dragon?"

Regel looked thoughtful. "Cunning enough to stalk her prey—to strike only from a position of strength," he said. "The one time I fought her, I did not try to speak with her."

"You *fought* the dragon?" Semana raised her eyebrows. "I'd not thought you a dragonslayer as well as an oathbreaker."

"I am not." Regel frowned. "The battle was…one-sided." He checked his weapons, ensuring none had frozen into their scabbards. "We will skirt the dragon's territory as best we can."

Semana bowed to his judgment, but she wondered.

The morning dragged on into full day.

The going was rough. An unpleasant haze crept up and refused to burn off as the day waxed, making each breath a chore and cutting visibility to almost nothing. Regel had insisted they use Semana's relics as little as necessary, so as not to attract the dragon or any other sentry to their path. This necessitated at times hiking through snowdrifts up to their waists or climbing precariously over treacherous ravines. Ice broke underfoot and stones shifted with their weight, and if Semana hadn't had her flying boots, she'd have plunged into at least one frozen-over river.

Going leagues and leagues out of their way grated on Semana's nerves. As the hours grew long, she became weary, and that weariness became frustration. It all felt so pointless. The prospect of one, quick, bloody battle grew increasingly attractive.

Finally, the growing anger proved too much for her, and Semana spoke up as they paused to rest some three hours after highsun. They had found their way out of the forest to a low spot by a mostly frozen brook, where a gentle rise of snow led up the far bank to a smooth white field. The hill was high enough that Semana could not see over it. In that direction, she saw the tops of snow-tipped trees and then clouds roiling to the south. She might have found it beautiful, were she not so focused on rebuking Regel.

"Perhaps we should try to kill this dragon of yours," she said. "Its pelt would make a fine trophy, and the tales speak of dragons hoarding treasure. Surely the Deathless would appreciate us removing such a dangerous foe from their threshold. It would be a service."

Regel didn't answer right away, but waited until they had crossed over the little brook. There he shed his pack and pulled out his carving of the moment. "When I faced the dragon in her lair, I was not alone," he said, cutting off a sliver with his small knife. "Three Deathless had come with me, and we were not enough."

"This Rose you spoke of?" Semana asked. "Was she there?"

Regel shook his head. "The dragon's predations had strayed close to Necthana," he said. "We set out to slay the beast, against my better judgment. I wielded Frostburn, and we had several relics among us. We managed to dissuade it from attacking the city, but—" He shook his head. "I was the only one who escaped the dragon on that day."

"Deathless can die?" Semana smirked. "So much for the legend."

"They can, with difficulty," Regel said. "They surrender mortality for another kind of life in death. Eternity stretches before them, unless it is cut short."

"A great tragedy, then." Semana bit her lip. "The fae couldn't have been too happy about that."

"On the contrary," Regel said. "As a people, they consider death at the hands of a worthy opponent a blessing from their goddess."

"Ruin?" Semana asked.

"Death."

She thought back to what Gilt had said to Regel in the flamewell, about being honored to die upon his sword. They seemed mad indeed, but perhaps it was a madness she could use.

"And even if we could kill the dragon, we should not," Regel said. "It is part of the equilibrium of the region. Its territory guards the approach to Necthana, and it prevents the northern tribes of Children from amassing to march against Tar Vangr."

"So as glorious as our hunt would be, we shouldn't try," Semana said. "Your faith in us almost brings me to tears."

Regel shrugged. "I'd rather see you angry than dead."

Semana had a witticism all prepared for that, but Regel's body abruptly tensed and he held up a hand to stay her. The sounds of the forest—the faint chirp of snow birds and the rustle of small animals in the brush—had vanished, swallowed up in an immense quiet that became suddenly thunderous. Semana realized they were not alone, though she couldn't say how she knew that. Regel gestured with his carving for her to remain quiet, and reached for the pack he had just set down at the foot of that little rise.

Abruptly, Semana realized what had happened. She felt something—something cool and growing colder inside her. It reminded her of sensing Gilt in the flamewell, but whatever she felt now it was much, much bigger. Older. And far, far greater.

"Semana—" Regel started to say.

A tremor ran through the white hill at his feet. Snow fell away near the pack, parting to reveal a disk of liquid blue, unexpectedly dark against the white ground and gray sky. An eye.

"Go!" Regel was shouting, and she didn't need the encouragement.

They ran through the icy terrain, which exploded up around them in explosions of stone and murderous white shrapnel. The ground rocked underfoot as a massively long muscular form wrenched itself from the ground. Semana slipped, fortuitously ducking a wedge of stone that would have taken her head off, armor or no. Regel scrambled behind her, the pack with their supplies abandoned in his wake to vanish amongst the flying snow and dirt. He staggered and leaped with remarkable grace for a man his age, trying to keep his balance in a world tilting wildly back and forth.

He wouldn't make it, Semana realized. Not on his own. Damn and burn.

Semana turned on her heel and rushed back toward Regel. His eyes went wide as she ran back into danger, but he could not move fast enough to stop her. She slammed into him even as she sent magic into her boots and lifted off the ground. She scooped the Oathbreaker up and away from the earthquake. The cold air burned in her lungs, but at least the ground wouldn't crush them.

Arms wrapped around Regel, Semana rose up into the sky and looked down at the creature.

The dragon unfolding from the earth stretched unbelievably far, and in more than two directions. Great sheets of the snow drift rose and skittered free with practiced movements, revealing great canopies of wings of silver and crimson. From this angle, the dragon's rise seemed casual—like a cat stretching or a hound shaking off rain—but it wreaked perilous havoc indeed. The ground pulsed like a disturbed pool of water, the trees sliding off it like algae.

The creature roared like rolling thunder, and just the sound buffeted them like a high wind, and Semana had to grit her teeth and fight to remain stable. Regel shouted at her, but she couldn't hear him.

"What?" she asked.

The dragon unfurled its massive wings into the air, like a pair of leather capes that billowed around its comparatively small, wiry frame. Its wings stretched as wide as its prodigious length, from the crown of its horned head to the barbs at the end of its tail. It had a head like a wolf's skull, long and tapered toward the snout, silver-white in color with red slashes as its jaws spread wide.

The creature gathered its wings around itself, powerful limbs poised under its bulk, and hurled itself into the air. Cracks shot across the icy ground, radiating from the point of its launch. The air whirled up and around them with suddenly massive force. The dragon boiled up into the air after them, whirling around itself like a spinning dancer. It moved faster than Semana could have imagined of such a huge creature, with grace both beautiful and terrifying.

"Semana!" Regel shouted.

With a start, Semana realized the beast had almost caught them. She stared into its mouth with three rows of jagged teeth, each of them the size and hone of a falcat. She felt as much as saw magic crackling in the depths of its gullet, and dived out of instinct. They fell just below a rushing firestorm of lashing energy spat over them. White fire turned the very air into rimefrost, which shattered as the dragon flew through it. The dragon displaced the air with an explosion that knocked them spiraling down.

Stunned for an instant, Semana swam through the air and caught Regel just in time to pull them out from under the swooping creature. The dragon had reversed its momentum and its course with marvelous agility considering its prestigious bulk.

"Down!" Regel shouted to be heard over the rushing wind. "Down!"

Semana knew he was right. They could not hope to elude the dragon in the sky, much less fight it.

Trailing swirling plumes of smoke, they spiraled down into the edge of the remaining forest, where a series of ridges and boulders might provide at least a little bit of cover. Semana had crashed enough times to know to pull her limbs into a ball and relax her muscles before the impact. They smashed aside branches and hit the ground amid a raining storm of snow and grit.

Semana's armor flared with magic to cushion the impact somewhat, but she distinctly heard a wet crunch as Regel smashed into the ground beside her. They rolled end over end, embracing each other tightly, until finally they smashed into a boulder. The world went gray—

~

The world faded in around her, and Semana awoke to shadows playing across her face. She realized she must have been unconscious for just a few heartbeats. She felt nauseated and her head pounded as she struggled to focus. Details swam around her and the world took on a floating quality. It all seemed so far away, if it was real at all.

As she floated back to awareness, Semana stared up at the gray sky, perceived through a jagged net of ice-frosted leaves, and thought she could make out the faint outline of the sun. She felt almost as though she would rise out of her body above herself and see the world from a different vantage point. It all seemed so peaceful.

Then a great shadow swooped overhead, and it forcibly woke her back to herself.

The *dragon.*

Semana sucked in a sharp, deep breath, and the cold air seared her lungs. She tried to sit up, and her chest and abdomen loudly protested the movement. Her body felt like it was pulling itself apart, but at least she could move.

Fight through it, she told herself. *No fear.*

A roar sounded overhead, almost deafening her in its thunder. The dragon was not directly over them—she would have felt the wind of its passing—but it was searching. And it was close.

Regel lay beside her, unmoving, his face as white and sallow as old bone. She shifted out from under his arm, which flopped uselessly to the ground.

"Oathbreaker," she said, patting his cheek. "Regel!"

No response. Damn. At least mist rose from his lips, indicating that he still lived.

Semana fought her way to her feet, trying to focus through the shivering terror of the dragon's passing. She bent and tried to lift Regel, but he was nearly seven stone of dead weight: far more than she could carry or even drag. Doing so might do him more harm than good.

How useful Tithian would have proved just then, with his healing touch. He had always been the one to keep them on their feet, while her magicks cut others down. She could not turn it to aid. Unless…

She empowered her silver glove, and its magic bore Regel aloft like a babe in arms. Semana concentrated to keep the hold gentle. Usually, she only lifted folk in duels, where she cared little for the subject's safety or comfort. No doubt Regel would be sore for days, but at least it served.

Now she had to decide where to go next, and fast. Smoke rose from her glove, and a foul odor surrounded them. Even if dragons could not sense magic—and most of the tales claimed they could—surely this one would see or smell the smoke and come for them. Through the blood connection, she felt it and knew it could feel her. The sheer power of the dragon's blood, even far away, made her giddy and slow. She could picture it swooping down through the trees, which would present as much hindrance to its passage as grass might to a boot, and snatching them up in those lance-sized claws—

No. She couldn't think that way. She had to focus. Had to move.

The fall had left Semana disoriented, and she hardly knew the directions of the compass. The sun lurking behind the clouds offered no great help. She could pick a path, but would it lead her to safety or deeper into the beast's territory? Regardless, she couldn't stay here.

Something flitted through the shadows of the trees behind her, and she wheeled, green magic crackling around her mask in preparation for an attack. Her heart thundered in her chest.

Gilt stepped out of the shadows as though they had spawned him. How she hadn't sensed his unique blood, she could not say, but if she hadn't seen him with her own eyes, she'd have had no idea he stood there. Perhaps he'd learned to block her Blood Magic?

"Come," he said, holding out a hand. In the other, he held a naked sword of black stone, its point gleaming sharp. "I will guide you."

Semana didn't need a second invitation. She took Gilt's hand, shivering for a moment at the spark of power between them. He felt it too, and his face looked suddenly uneasy.

Then they were scrambling among the trees, seemingly on a random course, as thunder roared behind them. At some point, Gilt had grasped Regel and carried him like a bundle over his shoulder. Semana knew the buoyancy her glove had given the man helped, but the way Gilt's tightly corded muscles rippled under his cloak, she suspected he could have managed even without it.

They ran through a thicket of trees and hesitated at the edge of a cliff overlooking a valley that contained a maze of rough-hewn rock. Ancient water had carved a fractured web of narrow passages through the blackened stone, like tunnels bored through sand by insects. Semana could not say for certain at this distance, but they looked deep enough to traverse and narrow enough that the dragon could not follow them.

"What is that?" she asked Gilt.

"Our way." His starry eyes narrowed. "She approaches."

Semana didn't need to ask. She felt the blood singing in her veins.

The dragon dropped from the sky and landed on the slope just ahead of them, making the world shake under their feet. It could have slain them from above with its breath or smashed them underfoot, but instead it paused and stared directly at Semana. Its blue eyes swam with mist and darkness, drawing her in deep. Looking into the dragon's eyes, feeling its power breaking her body from the inside out, she thought she could see beyond the veil of the World of Ruin into—

Gilt's hand tightened on hers, breaking the hold of the dragon's hypnotic eyes.

Then the beast roared, its triangular mouth opening in three directions. Semana stared into a forest of fangs with not one but three tongues to match its three jaws. Magic crackled in the depths of its throat, blue and white and silver and burning. She remembered what it had done to the very air, and realized it was the same as her Frostfire. Was this the power of her Blood? If so, it was far greater than she could ever wield, and it built to a destructive crescendo that would consume them all.

Semana channeled all of her strength into the mask and sent a swirling helix of Plaguefire directly into its gullet.

The dragon jerked back with a shriek of pain and surprise. It vomited gouts of Frostfire tainted with green and black poison, which fell sizzling to the frosted stones. The dragon lost its footing and scrambling to hold onto the slope, roaring and crying out in a chorus of choked, guttural noises.

For a heartbeat, Semana thought she had killed it, and though her heart leapt in triumph, there was a tiny part of her that mourned.

Then the dragon smashed its thick tail into the edge of the ravine where they stood, shattering the ground under their feet. Gravity ripped Gilt's hand away, and Semana found herself falling, sliding, and bouncing down the slope toward the rocky maze. The dragon fell beside her, claws and wings thrashing at her madly, every strike gouging deep furrows in the ground beneath them. One talon clipped her, and it took all the power of Mask's cuirass to deflect the bony claw enough not to let it impale her like a boar on a spear. Boulders tumbled past, jarring against her with bruising force.

Semana screamed in answer to the dragon's roars, lashing out with whatever magicks she could muster: the invisible blade, her Plaguefire, and even her Frostfire. It swarmed out of her, raw and uncontrolled, burning and freezing the beast in equal turns. Power thrummed through her Blood, and she could taste the dragon with her whole body. Locked together in a death spiral, they became one, and Semana could not say where she ended and the dragon began.

Then the pain grew too great, and she vanished into numb darkness.

EIGHT

When Regel woke, he found himself half buried in snow and loose rock. He had only hazy memories of the flight through the forest, meeting Gilt, and the confrontation with the dragon on the slope before they all fell. His bones felt weak as though freshly reknit and his exposed skin itched raw where the landslide had torn it open. Even as he lay there, his magic worked to put his body back together. He wondered if he had survived the fall, or if his magic had brought him back from Ruin's threshold.

Fanning the embers of life, Davargorn had called it. The magic could not reach beyond the veil of mortality—only pluck a man or woman back from death's clutches. Regel would remember that.

He observed before he moved, casting his senses around his surroundings even before he opened his eyes. He'd fallen into a narrow crevasse of sorts, with walls that reached perhaps five paces above before curving into a ceiling that entombed the darkness beneath. The air was cool down here between the walls, like a grave not yet filled in. He opened his eyes, and beheld the cool black stone arching up overhead until the two sides nearly joined in craggy edges about two paces apart, like half-melted fingers on the verge of lacing together. Through the uneven rift he could see a sky the color of moldering bone.

Damn and burn. He knew where he was—where the Deathless had led them.

"Regel?"

The echoing voice sounded harsh and ragged, but it was definitely that of Semana rather than of Mask. He shimmied out from under the rubble, shaking off snow that had turned to slush, and levered himself up. Semana spoke again, this time slightly farther away. Limping on his damaged leg, Regel followed the sound down the tunnel. A shadow passed overhead, and he could hear the dragon's wings rending the air. He knew they could not go back, but the path forward might not offer much better.

He came upon them at a crossing of two paths in the maze, opening into a wider chamber with a small pool of brackish water at the center. Semana's pack had come open in the fall, and their supplies lay strewn around the chamber: bruised apples and shriveled potatoes seemed vibrant against the gray stone and snow. Steam rose around the open space in curling trails, like the breath of some unseen creature. From what Regel knew of this place, the impression was not entirely inaccurate. A ripple passed through the wall under his touch, every so often, and he knew they were not alone.

Regel paused a moment to observe his companions before approaching. Gilt sprawled on his back, unmoving, while Semana paced anxiously around him, full of nervous energy with no outlet. He might have thought it simple frustration at their situation, but she had pulled her mask off and he could see the look of concern on her face. Her bare face offered an unexpected intimacy. Periodically, she knelt beside the fallen man to touch at his face or chest, trying to rouse him to no avail. Every time, she stood back up, looking more agitated than before. It was rare to see Semana care for someone other than herself.

She tensed as she caught sight of Regel and they shared a moment of fraught recognition. He thought he even detected a touch of fear in her expression, which he'd not seen in her since Gardh, and before that in Tar Vangr when she struck down Ovelia. He did not like it.

"Help him," she said, pointing to Gilt.

Regel gave the sprawled man a sidelong look. "He passes well."

He began picking up the stray bits of gear and foodstuffs.

Semana stared at him, then knelt next to Gilt once more. "He's not breathing."

"He is Deathless," Regel said.

As if to confirm his assertion, Gilt abruptly drew in a breath, and his black eyes fluttered open.

Semana gasped, startled at his abrupt awakening, then immediately quashed any sign of relief. It would not fit with the persona of Mask, after all.

"You live," she said, her voice carefully flat.

"Not as you do, but yes." Gilt nodded. "My lady will not claim me until the time is right."

They gazed at one another for a long time, before Regel cleared his throat to draw their attention. "This place is not safe," he said. "We should go."

Semana shook herself and looked up to the narrow slash of sky visible through the broken stone above. In the distance, the dragon roar sounded like an approaching storm. "Will it follow us?"

"Not into the Cauldron," Gilt said. "But you struck the beast deeply. It will not forget you."

Semana clenched her hands into fists. "Good."

Regel bit back a sharp retort. He saw nothing good about the dragon marking Semana as its favored quarry, but now was not the time. "Let's move. The Cauldron holds other dangers."

That made Semana laugh long and loud, the sound broken and ragged. "Worse than a dragon?"

Regel glanced at Gilt, who was giving the princess a very serious look. “Madness lurks in this place, seeping into the frozen earth and rising back up when disturbed,” the fae said. “It takes form and defies death, just as we do. It is alive and it hungers.”

“Living magic,” Semana said in Mask’s ironic drawl. “Oh what a marvelous day.” She crossed her arms. “Anything else I should know? Such as where this magic came from?”

She looked first at Gilt, but when he said nothing, she turned to Regel instead.

“Legends say men dwelled here,” Regel said. “A fortress where another city took refuge beneath the earth from the coming of Ruin.”

Semana’s eyes widened slightly. “You mean the war that ended the World of Wonder,” she said. “People hid in this place, awaiting the Prophecy of Return?”

“That is the tale,” Regel said.

“The legend speaks true.” Gazing up at the broken spires of the long dead city, Gilt bent down and took up a handful of ash. “A great calamity befell the people of this land, and the poison seeped through.” The dark powder leaked between his fingers and glimmered in the air. “Become twisted savages, they clawed their way out before their time and became the madness that had unmade them.” He let the last of the dust diffuse into the air. “Now they haunt the land, seeking to visit their fate upon all.”

“The Children of Ruin,” Semana said. “That’s where they came from.”

Neither Regel nor Gilt spoke. They did not need to.

“No living spells thus far,” Regel said.

“Why so sure?” Semana asked.

“We would already be dead.” Regel glanced back the passage, which shivered as the dragon passed overhead. Even if they climbed out of the Cauldron, the dragon would be waiting for them. “We cannot go back. We must go through.”

Gilt nodded, and at length, Semana followed suit. “And you think we’ll make it?” she asked.

Regel looked at her in that cold way that indicated he didn’t want to lie to her.

“Very well.” Semana buckled the leather back over her face and head and breathed deep and ragged. “Let us go.”

Under the shadow of the wary, circling dragon, they descended through the maze of tunnels into the heart of that most cursed place in the lands of the north: the Ruined Cauldron. The burned out complex seemed like something out of an all-too-familiar nightmare, revealing to him the end of a world.

The deeper they went, the more signs of civilization they found—or what remained of one. Thick pipes of long corroded steel rose from the walls like veins, whatever they had carried a thousand years ago long since dried up. The weather-gutted remains of stone chambers pocked the twisting tunnels, their floors and walls cracked under the elements. The mummified remains of tables, tools, and the like dotted the place, all so fragile they turned to dust at a whiff of air. Regel couldn't fathom many of the devices: metallic cylinders with glass barriers at either end, tubes with pointed ends like the proboscises of mosquitoes, and numerous vats of cracked glass big enough to hold human bodies. Whatever purpose these devices might have served, Regel could not guess, but he suspected it could be nothing good.

They found no corpses. No skeletons, no shadows burned onto walls or floors, no desiccated bodies turned to stone with age. No tattered remnants of animals fallen through the cracks above into the maze of corroded stone and starved. Not even any plants, dried and shriveled into sculptures of dust.

The place was a tomb, and yet, he felt something alive around them. The darkness loomed like a lurking creature, waiting for them to look away before it pounced. Gilt had spoken of the magic lingering here, and Regel could feel it around them like an enemy gathering just out of sight around a corner. He kept one hand on the hilt of a falcat at all times, and he could see Gilt maintaining the same wariness.

For her part, Semana took in the odd environs with aplomb, seemingly unmoved by the sights that so unnerved him. She seemed even wonderstruck rather than disgusted, though perhaps that was his imagination. Not for the first time he wished he could perceive her expression through the mask.

They came at length to an open valley at the center of the Cauldron, where the tunnels converged at the edge of a deep well torn in the earth. Wisps of gray mist rose from the stone underfoot that was more than just disturbed dust. Some sort of structure the size of a castle must once have stood here, its crumbling stone foundations the only evidence of its long ago existence. The wind hissed around the edges of the yawning pit, giving rise to a moaning sound no living creature could emulate. It seemed as though the World of Ruin was whispering to them. Regel was not about to listen.

Leading the way, Gilt paused, assuming the stillness that marked the Deathless fae. With familiar grace, Regel followed suit, though even he could not hold himself so completely motionless.

Semana looked at the two of them askance. "What is it?"

"Can you not feel it?" Gilt asked.

Regel could. The feeling that something lurked just out of view, quiet at first, had built into a roar that could not be ignored, and now it came from everywhere around them. Their presence had awoken an old power in the Cauldron, and it had stalked them for some time, always keeping its distance, watching. Now, though, it had prepared for them and lay in wait. Somewhere.

Here.

He heard a cough from behind him, where Semana stood, and of a sudden darkness encircled Regel, cutting off his senses. His charge and their guide vanished. He groped through the scintillating motes of darkness but found nothing. He heard nothing but a faint buzz in his ears, blocking out the rest of the world as though he had left it behind. Everything was gone.

It happened inside Regel next. He suddenly felt tired, as though a parasite had drained him dry in the course of a moment, leaving him hollowed out. His body felt weak—his bones fragile, his stomach empty, his skin dry and cracking. He felt old. Withered.

He had disappointed so many people. Made so many mistakes.

Darkness rose up inside him and outside. Faces emerged in the mist—visages he vaguely recognized and rocked him to his core. Faces of those he loved and those he had only seen in dying. All the folk he had killed or watched die. Some of the living whose lives he had scarred.

He had failed. Failed to protect Lenalin or Orbrin. Failed to save Ovelia or Semana. He did not have the power or the strength or the will to do what needed to be done. Whatever he touched, it broke apart like dust on the wind.

The darkness suffocated him. He could accomplish nothing. Every time he tried to make a difference, it only made life worse for those he cared about.

He had no purpose any longer. The world had moved on without him.

All passes to Ruin.

When the mist lifted, Regel stood alone at the very edge of the abyss in the center of the valley. Mist deep in the pit wove circles and spirals in a beautiful and terrifying pattern. It was hypnotic. The tips of his boots extended a little over the emptiness, and he could feel it inviting him to fall.

He wanted nothing more.

A faint sound drew his attention—a fragment of a distant scream. It startled him and didn't last long enough, but it broke his focus on the swirling depths. Something had fooled his senses, he realized, and the scream broke through the haze.

Regel turned away, searching through the fog for a sign of—something. Companions. He dimly remembered that he had those. A dead man who lived and a girl. A young woman, he thought, but he'd last known her as a girl. She meant something important to him. She was…

Light flashed in the mists ahead of him, and a powerful exclamation of power cut through the ringing silence. He beheld a figure floating among the mists, swathed in black and rippling with silver magic. Her power burned the mist away in coiling swaths of gleaming flame.

Semana.

His sluggish mind came back to itself, and Regel could hardly breathe against the choking magic. Something had hold of him: a monstrosity that had stolen upon him gradually and pulled his life from him like an unseen leech. It had stolen upon him subtly at first, but now it screamed. Thousands of voices cried out in languages he did not understand, producing a cacophony of madness that set his teeth on edge. He saw faces once more in the mist, twisted into tortured angles and impossible distortions. Faces emerged from screaming mouths and bled apart, eyes and noses and mouths melting like ice in the sun.

Then the mist wrenched away from Regel, screaming and roaring as it flowed around and past him into the void. Regel staggered but caught himself on a jutting boulder as the magic boiled around him, fleeing Semana's rage into the pit.

They stood alone in the ruined valley, the wind roaring around them.

Only the two of them.

"Gilt," Semana said, anxiety edging her voice. "Where's Gilt?"

Regel shook his head. He looked down into the unfathomable darkness.

NINE

As of the sixtieth day out of Tar Vangr, they'd covered roughly two hundred leagues. Winter had come in full force, and every step northward delayed the spring. They'd made good time considering, and as the Cauldron fell further behind, Regel started to believe them truly out of the reach of the Ravalis.

"Watch your step," Regel said as he crept down from stone to slippery stone into the snow-choked ravine. "The footing is treacherous."

"Watch *yourself*, old man." The air wavered around Semana's boots, and she floated lightly over the stones. "Unless you want me to carry you." She scoffed. "Unlikely."

They'd come to the Narkggr Wound the previous eve, at which point Regel remembered the terrain grew very rough, even in summer. Reality did not disappoint his recollection: under snow, the canyon became a slippery maze with sharpened rock thrusting up and at dangerous angles. After the first thin ice bridge crunched and collapsed underfoot, he picked each step more carefully, thrusting his feet in securely before putting his weight down. The cold made his bad leg ache, and moving it was torture. Not that he could show weakness to Semana, of course—the princess watched him like a hungry wolf, ready to pounce at the slightest provocation.

The silence between them had lasted since the Cauldron, and they'd shared words only as circumstance demanded. A darkness hovered around Semana, and it was not just the disappearance of Gilt. The battle in the Cauldron had taken something from her, just as it had struck him deeply as well. He still saw those faces when he slept—familiar but alien both at once. He slept only as much as he needed and meditated when he could not, searching vainly for stillness within himself.

As he sat awake at night, he saw Semana doing the same. Was it worry for Gilt?

At least they were almost there. The Narkggr Wound marked the edge of Necthana lands. Once they passed it, they would have nothing else to fear—assuming the Deathless welcomed them.

Regel suspected Gilt had not perished in the Cauldron, but rather returned to shadowing them rather than accompanying them directly. He thought he'd seen signs of the fae's passage: a shadow that lingered too long or stretched too far, or a certain tree brushed clean of snow to mark their path. It could be another Deathless, but he did not know why another one would help them in that way.

Regel had not told Semana his suspicions, and he was not certain why. Instinct told him to keep that information to himself, at least for now. It was hardly the first secret he had kept from her.

What, then, was Gilt's purpose in following them? Had Gilt become so fixated upon Semana that he disobeyed the directives of his queen? Semana did have a way of inspiring such fanaticism.

That made Regel think of Ovelia. He wondered how she fared, and whether he'd made the right decision to leave her behind. She would certainly have aided their journey on numerous occasions, and he would have loved to have someone he could confide in. Semana didn't know Ovelia was alive, but he suspected she would learn the truth in time. How would she react when—

It was only as he fell that Regel realized he'd allowed his musings to steal his attention. His bad leg couldn't support his weight when his footing shifted, and it went out from under him, spilling him with a splintering splash into the partly frozen stream. Ice crunched and shattered around him, damp seeped through his clothes, and his flesh went numb from cold and shock. He fumbled to catch himself as he slid and tumbled among the rocks, but his fingers could not catch on anything solid. He bumped and slid and fell into a gully at the bottom of the ravine, splashing freezing mud all over himself. There he lay, wincing, half submerged in a soup of mud, snow, and tingling water that threatened to burn away his clothes and skin even as it sapped his body's heat.

He lay there, looking up at the sky. The clouds flowed overhead in a series of slowly shifting shapes, like the gowns and tunics of Vangryur dancers at a formal revel. The silver and gray reminded him of Lenalin's gowns. He'd spent many nights hiding up in the balcony or behind a set of spyholes, watching as she danced with partner after partner. How he had wanted to be any one of those men.

As he watched, the clouds darkened, and he caught sight of something metallic that glinted in their depths. It made his heart pick up its pace, and his frost-stung body went rigid.

Semana appeared at his side, looking down at him with wide eyes. She'd lifted her mask to her brow, and the light made her few locks of escaping hair gleam like liquid silver. Regel saw genuine concern in her hazel eyes, which he never would have expected.

"Pass well?" she asked. "Regel?"

The bright object in the sky blocked out the hazy sun for an instant, darkening the world.

Pain stabbing his leg, Regel sprang up and shoved Semana back under the overhang. He caught her wrist and clapped a hand over her mouth before she could protest. Then he nodded upward.

An ornithopter dipped out of the clouds, three rings scything around it and groaning against one another at the apex of their orbit. The canyon walls and the wind above had muffled the mage-engine's whine before, but this low it became a whirring, clanking monstrosity. Corroded chains hung from the ship, ringing off the turning rings as they passed beneath. Its horn uttered a wailing dirge, like that of a dying general sounding the retreat too late to save the day. The ornithopter cast beams of light arcing around the canyon, its crew clearly searching for something.

The skyship was small, sized for ten warriors or so, but at that altitude its rings put out enough wind to make Regel tremble on his feet. Snow swirled around them, biting into their exposed skin. Semana thrust his hand off her mouth so she could pull her mask back on. They stood, poorly concealed against the canyon wall, as the craft hovered not far overhead, blaring and blasting snow in all directions. The wind bit into his freezing back and the snow came alive against him, tearing at his clothes.

Regel felt Semana's glove growing warm against his hand and saw green flames start to course around her leather-bound face. Within the slits of her mask, her eyes turned bright red. Her breathing quickened, and he could feel the tension in her arms. The growing fury. Magic.

"Wait," he said, struggling to keep his voice steady.

Then—too slowly by half—the ornithopter rose back into the sky and disappeared amongst the gray clouds. Regel and Semana stood another hundred count, but the craft did not return. Finally, Semana shoved Regel off and strode out into the canyon where she could see.

"The Ravalis?" Semana asked. "I thought we'd left them behind."

"Perhaps." Regel had a darker suspicion, but he kept it to himself.

"They were right atop us," Semana said. "How did they not see us?"

Regel shook his head. "The way is watched," he said.

"Not that you could walk it anyway." Semana passed her hand over his sore leg, her fingers glowing lightly. Regel felt the blood tingle in his veins, making the muscles ache. The silver glove let slip a wisp of dissolute smoke as the magic simmered. "I don't think this has enough power to carry you all the way, and we'd choke on fumes long before we found out," she said. "We need another route."

"Outpost nearby," Regel said. "When last I passed through. Might..." He winced. "Might still be there." He pushed off the stone wall of the canyon and teetered to his feet, favoring his bad leg.

"Please. You're embarrassing me." She waved her left hand, and Regel felt her magic settle around him, lifting him. He felt lighter, and his leg hurt only a little when he put weight on it.

"Thank you," he said.

"You're welcome, *father.*" Semana smiled sourly. "So long as you don't mention it again." She slid the mask back over her face, and her voice turned into the broken rasp of the sorcerer-slayer she resembled. "I'd hate for folk to think me merciful."

As the wind roared around them, Regel peered between two stout oaks at the cluster of frost-choked huts below, alert to the tiniest detail. Smoke wafted thinly from covered stacks at the top of two of the buildings. Thick boards on the windows kept out the worst of the winter, but Regel could see light emanating faintly inside one of the hovels. A pair of yew trees grew on either side of the tiny settlement, looming over the center square like twin specters. Regel watched for an hour and saw no movement.

"Safe?" Semana asked.

"Perhaps." Regel took off his mask to wipe the lenses clean of the dirty snow. At least the snow did not burn this far from Tar Vangr's corruption. Most of his body had gone numb in the cold, and he found himself wishing Semana still possessed her fire gauntlet. They would find shelter from the snow and wind in those houses, and that made an approach not only worthy but necessary.

"How many, do you think?" Semana leaned languidly against the tree beside him, running her fingers obsessively over the wires of her silver mesh glove. Her impatience was palpable.

"Smallborn—perhaps a thinblood," he said. "Hunters. No knights. A score of folk. Perhaps."

"Is that all?" Semana stretched, popping the bones of her arms and shoulders. Her cheeks looked shallow, her grimace thin. "If they attack us, we can kill that many between us without effort."

"We should pass on," Regel said. "Recall Gardh."

The rebuke had come out of him before he'd thought, and he immediately regretted it. By her expression, though, Semana hardly seemed offended.

"I am thinking of practicalities," she said. "You were the one who made us leave Gardh in haste. If we hadn't escaped through the kitchen, we would have starved long ago." She looked at him sourly. "And then you lost half our supplies fleeing the dragon."

Regel bit his tongue. She was right, and no matter how sharp her words, he took some relief hearing them. He'd rationed the little food they'd managed to scrounge during their escape from the dragon, but they could not press on much further without more.

"Pigs." He inclined his chin toward a covered pen between two of the huts, its roof partly collapsed under an impressive snow drift. At this angle, he could not see inside the structure, so perhaps a farmer could have gone around behind where he could not see.

"No pigs," Semana said.

Regel noted a flicker of radiance in her bare right hand. "Blood magic."

"Yes." Semana raised her chin, attuning her senses to something he could not see. Red mist swirled around her hand and arm. "Dangerous but useful. They have no pigs down there. Blood I sense, but all of it men's blood."

"Alive or dead?" Regel asked.

"Hard to say." Semana shrugged. "Maybe if I were closer."

They'd spoken little regarding Semana's new powers, and that only in the aftermath of Gardh. In retrospect, Regel understood that it was blood magic she had used to defeat Vhaerynn at Tar Vangr, but burned if he could say how she had come by it. Since her display of prowess at Gardh, he'd grown increasingly uneasy, and he's questioned her once or twice. Semana had brushed off his concerns, but her troubled expression attested that even she had doubts. There he had let the matter drop: he knew little enough of magic, and he hardly told her all *his* secrets. This one, she could keep. For now.

"We have no other choice," Semana said. "Barter with the living or scavenge from the dead. We should get on with it."

"One last look."

Regel drew out the carving he had been working on since Tar Vangr and focused upon it. It had begun to take shape in the moments he'd had to cut, but he could not say for certain what it would become when he finished. Most of the time, he saw an image in the fragment of stone or wood before he started carving, but this time, certainty eluded him. Some manner of beast, he thought, but whether it would be a fox or a dragon he could not say. He let his mind quiet and his senses fly free, but the roaring wind garbled anything he could determine from the cluster of huts. He could hear absolutely nothing, and smell only the sharp tang of decay and something oily and sweet.

When Regel came back to himself, Semana was staring at him, her eyes faintly red with rising magic. Beneath, hunger had rendered them dry and bloodshot. Against his better judgment, Regel stepped first between the trees, shaking off the snow that had packed onto his coat, and Semana followed behind.

Fifty paces brought them across a clear stretch of snow to the tiny hamlet, the wind pummeling them with every step. The branches of the yew trees waved at him like fingers, but whether to entice or warn he could not say. Some niggling doubt whispered a warning at the back of Regel's mind, but he stifled it. He kept one hand on the hilt of his falcat, however. The pig pen was empty, as Semana had said, the gate left to clatter against the fence in the wind. It sounded like the clack of bones.

"Anything?" Regel conveyed the question more with a look than an audible word.

"No one alive in there," Semana shouted over the storm. "Lots of blood, but none of it warm."

She indicated one of the doors, which rattled in the wind. Smoke gathered around her silver glove and the door jerked taut. Finally she threw her arm back and wide, and the groaning door ripped itself open to hang haphazardly from one hinge. The storm whistled greedily into the newly opened space as Semana stepped inside, her mask glowing with power. Regel pressed himself against the wall near the door of a second building, drew his sword, and tested the latch. The door swung easily open to clatter against the opposite wall. When no cries or caster bolts emerged, he peered inside—and suddenly the chill reached his blood. Now he recognized the faint smell he'd detected: inside the chamber, the stench of rot grew overpowering. The humidity inside made sweat break out inside his mask.

"Regel," Semana shouted over the wind.

He set his jaw. He knew what she would say.

The chamber into which he peered was a charnel pit. Crude symbols traced in blood and feces smeared the walls, and pieces of corpses hung from the rafters, strung up with blood-slick twine or rubbery entrails. The blood had frozen black in long, ropey icicles from the grisly totems. Every bit of furniture lay in shards on the floor, many pieces thrust through disembodied torsos or pieces of limbs. He could count the number of dead only because someone had left a haphazard stack of eight heads in the center of the room, every expression contorted in terror and agony. Maggots squirmed in their mouths, noses, and empty eye sockets.

"Father?"

Regel turned to Semana, who stood on the threshold of the other hut, grasping both sides of the doorway with trembling arms. He could not see her face through the mask, but the choking sounds that emerged from her—audible even over the wind—made his heart crack. Her eyes were wild and enraged. She had seen the same thing in the other chamber, and it took the strength from her limbs. She tottered toward him, barely able to balance, and he caught her in an awkward embrace. This, he had not expected.

"What," she said, her voice weak. "What—?"

"Do not look," he said. "Children of Ruin did this."

That made Semana tense. She looked him in the eye, then pushed past him into the chamber. The thick stench made her cough, but she stood tall. "Barbarians I have met before, but this—"

"You've only seen Luether," Regel said. "The Children of the wilds don't even pretend at civilization." He adjusted his mask to block out the smell. "I had not thought to find them so far north."

"Why would they leave this?" Semana waved her silver glove, and several of the hanging pieces parted like curtains of beads. "Is this some manner of… message?"

"Art," Regel said. "The art of the mad—" He stopped. The sweet smell that he'd detected outside grew stronger, beneath the overwhelming stench of rot. He'd ignored it before, but now his instinct blared a warning at him. He shoved aside one of the corpses to reveal a cask of brittle wood, its top cracked open to the air.

"What is it?" Semana asked.

"Out!" Regel turned and tackled her out the door just as a flaming arrow whipped over their heads and slammed into the wall.

The gas caught, then the casks of alchemist's fire, and the hut exploded.

Semana shook her head and coughed violently, and the world came back. She must have lay senseless for less than a ten count, and her entire body shivered in pain. Her limbs felt like wet logs, barely responding when she tried to move them. She tasted bitterness in her mouth and spat out gobs of saliva-soaked snow. Chunks of smoldering wood and twisted metal studded the clearing at the center of the little hamlet, thrown madly away in the explosion. Behind her, the hut had become a burned out husk, smoke reaching toward the sky like the fingers of a grasping skeletal hand.

She sensed blood approaching her from all directions, this living and wild.

All around, dark figures wrapped in leather and fur strode out of the swirling snow, their hands bristling with jagged blades and studded cudgels. They'd left their faces bare to the elements, and Semana understood instantly why: every grotesque visage was a different nightmare. One man had chunks of glass thrust out through his lips like a second row of teeth, and one woman's face bore so many deforming scars she resembled a dismembered corpse more than a living creature. Another man seemed normal enough, but when he waggled his tongue at her, it flailed in two separate pieces like that of a serpent.

Children of Ruin.

Regel rolled out of the flames a few paces to her right, trailing sparks, and lunged into Snaketongue with a vengeance. The man barely got his three-bladed spear up in time to block Regel's first falcat, and the second blade hacked around his defense to slash his face open. The barbarian toppled, screaming in a burst of blood, and Regel whirled past him like a black and crimson hurricane toward the scarred woman. She blocked his strike, catching both blades on her club, and hurled him back with a grunt and a cackling laugh.

"Up," Semana told herself. "Up!"

The barbarian with the glass teeth stood over her, his serrated sword high for a deathblow. Regel was trying to get back to her, but the scarred woman cut him off. She lit the pitch smeared along her ugly cudgel, and the weapon burst into orange flame. Regel backed off with a hiss. Semana was on her own.

Good enough.

Semana's silver glove flashed hot and she lashed up at her would-be killer with all its force. As though struck by an invisible hammer, he hurtled off his feet and sailed over the remaining hut, screaming as he disappeared into the storm. She forced herself to one knee, then to her feet, where she stood shakily.

From above, Semana heard a roar she had at first taken to be the storm. The clanking ornithopter had swopped in over them, and was hovering aloft, casting down beams of light and blaring horns. Its three rings had frozen in a single encircling band of bright-burning magic, and bundled figures dropped down from the craft on hanging chains. They climbed down, hand over hand, and dropped into the snow. As soon as they were down, the rings engaged around the ornithopter again, whirring to keep it aloft with winds that sent snow swirling in all directions.

A dozen assailants stood around her—some from the ornithopter, some from out of the storm—every one of them lighting spears and swords with flame. Several took aim with their spears, but Semana waved her silver glove around herself, and the projectiles shattered off a shield of invisible force to fall useless into the snow. The show of magic set the barbarians back on their guard. They kept the circle around her, stepping slowly back with weapons raised protectively. They feared her. Good.

"Enough!" Semana called upon her Frostfire, and the flames wreathing the remaining weapons winked out. Some even dropped their suddenly rime-encrusted weapons. "I am the last daughter of winter. You are nothing to me. Nothing!"

Overhead, the ornithopter's clanking roar drawing her attention, and she saw dark shapes maneuvering an attached heavy caster into position. The ground soldiers had been a distraction, it seemed. The rings around the ornithopter locked out wide once more and the caster took aim. She redirected the force of her silver glove above, just in time to catch the first casterbolt. It struck like a falling boulder and shattered off Semana's shield with enough force to launch itself through the remaining building. She fell to one knee, shaken by the blow. That weapon was meant for destroying warmachines or crippling other skyships, not for dispatching one slight woman in leathers. The barbarians clustered around had started to chant and bang their weapons on the ground or stomp their feet.

The ornithopter's heavy caster turned over, lining up a second six-foot casterbolt.

It fired again, and this time Semana swatted the bolt away like an insect. Her silver glove burned hot on her hand, shrouded in foul-smelling smoke, but she could not relent. Regel was locked in a duel with three opponents now, the scarred woman among them. He was trying to get to her, but what could he do? Semana was alone. The chanting grew louder, the barbarians emboldened. It matched the pounding of her heart in her head.

The third casterbolt fired. She blocked that one as well, the air splintering as casterbolt stuck the magic shield. It broke through and sailed down, end over end, to crash into the snow a few paces from Semana. The silver glove was white-hot now, its magic all but expended. She could not block another blast. The chanting and pounding was deafening and Semana felt weak on her feet.

Undeterred, the men on the ornithopter aimed the fourth and final bolt.

"No," Semana said. "*No.*"

Green flames rose around her, and she raised her hands up, channeling the power from her mask between her outstretched fingers. It burned and stung and made her sick, but she gritted her teeth and roared in the face of the pain. The rest of the world went suddenly silent, and every eye stared at Semana.

She directed the Plaguefire forth in a torrent of arcing tendrils and sent it sizzling up at the ornithopter with a matching scream. The magic cut through the heavy caster, rotting away its barrel and projector to nothing in an instant, and withered its operators to moldering skeletons that crumbled away as it tore past. Semana brought her arms down with a guttural roar, and the roiling power swept across the body of the ornithopter. It bowed at the middle, issuing loud cries of distress.

The craft gave a shudder and wheeled wildly to the right, its rings once against spinning furiously to try to keep it aloft. Weakened by the magic, two of the concentric rings tore themselves apart with a shriek under the pressure. Tarnished gold fired in all directions, and shards stabbed into the ground around Semana. Bits of metal rang off the last of her invisible shielding magic.

Half a ring hit not three paces from her, bounced, and shot through the circle of barbarians, leaving two warriors shattered to bloody shreds in its wake.

Overhead, a chunk of the crippled vessel fell away, narrowly missed the last scything ring, and crashed into the earth with a clap of thunder. Trailing smoke, the ornithopter groaned and cried as it tried to limp away, its one ring spinning madly to generate enough force to keep it aloft. Finally, the drooping aft half of the ornithopter slammed into the furiously-spinning ring, which shattered against it with enough force to break them both to shards, while the forward section shot off and smashed its way through the remaining building in the little town, causing an explosion of foul fumes and alchemically-treated pitch that drove Semana to her knees and smashed the world into unbalanced, ringing chaos. Semana stared, blinking, at a shard of metal that had pierced the ground not the length of a hand from where she stood. It smoldered and rotted away before her eyes.

A pain in her gut drew her right hand, and her fingers came away bloody. A piece of the ornithopter was lodged there, black blood welling around it. Burned and damned.

When her hearing returned, Semana realized the barbarians were still pounding their weapons and chanting. There were more now, if that was possible: a score at least, of all different shapes and sizes, with faces that ranged from light to dark but all enraged. She could see the frost biting into their hands, and some of them bore bloody bits of fresh shrapnel lodged in their chests, limbs, or even faces. And yet they stared at her, seemingly inured to pain. Behind them, Regel's battle had ended, but Semana did not know how—she simply heard no more sounds of clashing blades.

Had her warder fallen? It hardly mattered. She would fall soon enough.

The chanting had changed as well: at first, it had seemed like a nonsensical cacophony of sounds rather than words, but now she heard something coherent in it. "*Dar-Karsk,*" they were saying, or something like it—a name? And "*terens,*" which sounded like the Old Speech. Master, perhaps?

"*Dar-Karsk Terens,*" they chanted. "*Dar-Karsk!*"

The ring parted to admit a tall man in a mottled gray cloak. She could smell the garment at a distance, so choked with rot and mold that it made her gag. In the depths of his hood, the man's reddish eyes burned like embers in the light of the burning structures. Semana glared up at him, teeth gritted against the pain and weakness spreading through her middle.

"I suppose you're Dar-Karsk," she said through the agony. "Should I be frightened?"

The man raised his hands, and the air started shimmering around them.

Magic.

Semana reached for more Plaguefire from her mask, but the bolt that had felled the ornithopter had drained it substantially, and her own strength was failing her. Instead, her hands began to sparkle with silvery, crystalline energies, and she blew out a relieved breath. The Frostfire could not be controlled, but at least it came now, when she had need of it.

She sent a bolt of Frostfire directly at the barbarian sorcerer. It slid through his chest without apparent harm and tore into the snowy ground behind him. Semana almost couldn't believe her eyes.

"That's—" she said. "That's a fine trick."

The barbarian sorcerer declaimed words of power—Semana had never seen anyone cast a spell that way before—and slammed his magic-blurred fist into the ground before him. The ground rippled toward her like a wave.

Blearily, Semana drew hard on the last dregs of magic in her silver glove, and a shield flickered in the air in front of her just as the ground erupted. Spears of earth burst forth and smashed into her shield with enough power to shatter the paltry magic and send her sailing back through the air. She slammed back into a wall laced with the gnarled roots of one of the yew trees. She both heard and felt her ribs crunch, and her body went instantly numb. She slid to a shuddering halt on the ground and sat against the wall, fighting for breath and her bearings. Above, the yew's branches had become burning cinders, and she saw a hunk of the ornithopter balanced precariously in the blackened foliage. How beautiful and horrible, both at once. This wouldn't be a bad place to bleed to death.

Fighting against the pain, Semana looked back into the clearing. A dozen barbarians stalked toward her, silent now—bearing witness. The sorcerer stood at their head, striding toward her slowly but steadily, completely unrushed. From somewhere, Regel was shouting her name, but Semana could not see him. She spat blood onto the snow. She scrambled to get up, and her legs still moved. That was good. She managed to get to her feet, with the help of the wall.

"Come on, then." Her words came out wet and she drooled bloody spittle. Her mask flared with choking power, recharging by draining what little of her own life remained, and the flames coursing around her hands turned green and ugly. "Come and die."

She hurled Plaguefire at the man in the mottled cloak, who raised a shield of stone out of the snowy earth to block. The power splintered his wall into dust and chunks of rock, knocking him to the ground with explosive force. The rest of the barbarians fell silent as corpses, staring at her in shock.

"Come and die at Mask's hand!"

Semana sent sickly threads of magic toward the rest of the barbarians, striking one in the chest as he raised his sword, another in the belly as he hesitated, and one in the back as he fled. She wrenched the life from them with her will, making their skin turn blotchy and their eyes bleed reddish pus. She felt them die in horror and agony, but she did not care. A sickly echo of their vitality flowed into her, filling her broken body with a profane kind of strength.

Semana staggered toward the sorcerer, who struggled to move on the snowy earth, and grasped the collar of his cloak. She wanted to see his face before she killed him, to look him in the eyes and know that he knew what befell. She raised her other fist, swirling with Plaguefire, over his face.

And hesitated.

He held his hands in clawed fists and while she could see magic about them, Semana held back. He was young—no more than five years older than she—and yet silver shot through his bright red hair. His skin had a deep russet undertone. And his eyes…huge and deep hazel now that his magic fell away.

They were *her* eyes.

She'd hesitated too long. One of the barbarians hurled a spear at her, and she struck it aside with the last magic of the silver glove. Another one rushed at her with a sword, but she slew him with Plaguefire before he had taken three steps. Then the man on the ground thrust his open fingers up at her and something struck her from behind and she jolted forward off him.

At first, she thought someone must have shoved her. She was still standing, but her feet did not touch the ground. Regel was shouting her name somewhere far away, his voice growing softer. Didn't he know she would win this fight for them? She was Mask, the greatest slayer in the World of Ruin. She would kill them all and prove her worth to her father, even if she died in the process.

Because *burn them all.*

She tried to step forward, but her legs wouldn't obey. She coughed, and blood flowed freely from her mouth. Her body seemed strangely disconnected. She felt so weak.

Then she looked down to inspect her wound and found blood-drenched yew roots growing from her chest, curling like grasping fingers. Five of them. They had run her through from behind.

The world blurred and slipped away.

BOOK THREE: CAPTIVES

Four years previous—Luether—Summer 978 Sorcerus Annis

Semana strained to hold herself parallel to the floor, all the muscles in her sides and stomach tight and sending jolts of angry protest rushing up to her brain.

"This is…tearing me apart," she said. "Like my muscles…coming undone…"

"Hold it," Tithian said as he knelt at her side. "Keep holding."

Silver *Fire*, it hurt. Her body gasped for breath and ribs ached. Her body weight drove her elbows into the ground, and every time she tried to bring her hands together, Tithian edged them apart with his toe. She'd long since lost the strength to glare up at him. She could do nothing but focus on holding the pose, willing her muscles to get stronger to endure the pain for longer.

"Do not fall because it hurts," TIthian said. "Only fall when your body fails."

"I'm…failing…now," Semana said.

"Then hold for longer," Tithian said. "Send your mind elsewhere. Ignore the pain. Do what is necessary."

Necessary.

She imagined Mask in her mind, floating above the deck of the *Heiress*, Plaguefire swirling around him. She imagined Ovelia Dracaris plunging her sword through the Winter King. She imagined the Frostburn, the most terrifying man she had ever known, weeping like a child at his failure.

She could do what was necessary.

Semana focused not on the effort but on anything else. The greasy Luether room, with its pitted walls and rough floorboards scratching at her leather armguards. The stink of unclean leather and old blood. The muffled moans from the next room. The sweat pooling on her forehead, dripping patterns on the floor under her face. The growing difficulty to draw breath. The pressure…

Finally the pain climbed past her iron will, and Semana collapsed to the floor. There was something pure and righteous about falling in such a way. She could rest assured that her mind triumphed over the pain, and it her body that had failed. She lay there, coughing raggedly.

Tithian cleared his throat. "Better," he said. "A three hundred count that time."

Semana glared up at him sourly. "Not good enough," she said. "You can hold a thousand count."

"Of course I can," he said. "I fight with steel every day."

She had to concede that point. Between Children of Ruin, warders, and rival hunters, Tithian had put his body to the test every day since the *Heiress*, and it was no wonder he'd built an impressive base of strength. Semana had glimpsed him more than once, returned from one task or another, stripping off his harness of leather and iron to unveil muscles that grew increasingly defined. As a boy, his club foot and mismatched eyes had made him gawky and odd, but as he became a man, he looked dangerous.

Their eyes had met on several occasions, but he quickly looked away rather than hold her gaze. It was...It was damned confusing.

As children, before Mask and the Bloodbreaker had destroyed that part of her life, Semana had looked upon Tithian as closer than the brother she barely remembered. She felt drawn to him and safe with him. He would never leave her or abandon her, and he'd proved that much in the last year. And now, once they had left childish things behind, she felt...different. He made her uneasy, and she could not say exactly why. Perhaps it was the hunger in his eyes, or perhaps the hunger inside herself.

Sometimes she thought about asking Tithian if he wanted to kiss her, but she could never quite decide whether that would be a good idea or a disaster.

In any case, she focused on the physical training, trying to distance her mind from the task at hand. Tithian may have had constant fighting to keep up his strength, but her favored tactic was magic, and that did nothing to enhance her muscles. Quite the opposite, in fact: after more than a year using magic on a daily basis, she'd started to recognize the feelings of wear and soreness that it promoted. It would take more getting used to, she thought, and building her body would only help with that. If only the combination didn't make her quite so tired.

"Good," Tithian said when she'd held the table position for another two hundred count—more than decent, for a second attempt so soon after the first. "Are you ready to go back in?"

Semana let out a deep sigh as she clutched her aching middle. "We should."

He gave her a hand up, and they stood together in the dingy room. Semana breathed hard, and Tithian stood waiting—ever patient, ever reliable. She thought, in that moment, that it wouldn't be so bad to kiss him. She had few enough other choices, after all. Her task took precedence, but perhaps...

"Tithian," she said, her voice soft.

"Master?"

He held out the black leather death mask for her to put back on, and took care to look away. Something about that deference or the presence of the thing cooled her ardor.

"Nothing of import."

She took the mask and buckled it back onto her head, making sure to get every wisp of her short-cropped hair. She became Mask again, as she did every day—layering darkness over the Winter Princess she could no longer be. For now.

"Forward," Mask said, her voice crackling. She hardly even had to try anymore.

Tithian stepped to the door and pushed it open into the inner room of their suite, and the man bound inside immediately started screaming against his gag.

The smell of blood and piss assailed Mask's nostrils. Bound for almost a day, the hapless prisoner hadn't had a chance to void himself anywhere but where he was sitting. The room looked and felt like a butcher's slaughter room, the walls painted with layer upon layer of old blood. Perhaps it had been such a place in years past, but here in the fallen city of Luether, it could well have been a home and the blood on the walls that of its former inhabitants.

He couldn't see them through the leather belt buckled around his head, but he could hear them and that was enough. Tithian's club foot gave him a very distinctive walk—step, slide, step, slide—and his cloak rattled softly against the sword at his belt as he moved. Semana knew this was by design, as he could move with near perfect silence when he wanted. What it was precisely in his cloak that made that sound, Mask did not know. He'd promised to make it a surprise. For her part, Mask heard her legs popping as she moved—a sound she needed no artifice to produce. The corrosive power of her Plaguefire had done that well enough all on its own. All in all, the effect was terrifying, which pleased Mask.

"Riesk of the Quick-Fingers." Mask's hollow voice danced off the walls. "You have the misfortune to possess knowledge I need. This process need not be more painful. Speak, and go free."

"Stay silent," Tithian said in his own voice like shredded gravel, "and suffer."

The voice surprised her, and she knew he'd meant it as such by the way he looked to her for approval. Mask ignored him in favor of the prisoner.

"Riesk of Summer Lives," she said. "I care nothing for your insurgency. Throw down the Ruin King or die in the attempt. It makes no difference to me. All I crave of you is information. Understood?"

Riesk nodded slowly. His body still trembled, but he was calmer now.

Mask pursed her lips inside the mask. She'd told Tithian torture wouldn't work. In her experience, it proved an ineffective means of acquiring information. But the lad was gifted, and he'd been so pleased when she acquiesced to his request. If it made Riesk more quiescent, all the better.

"Let him see," Mask said.

Tithian unbuckled the belt from around Riesk's head, and let it slip down to his neck. The man's eyes went wide as he stared at the two of them. Tithian he'd seen before. Indeed, from his muffled cries of pain over the last day, Mask suspected the two were good friends by now. Riesk had not seen the sorcerer herself, though, and the expression of mingled horror and terror on his face made all that training she'd down with Tithian very much worth it. She waved, and Tithian pulled free the gag that kept Riesk quiet. He panted and spat blood and spittle down his chin. His eyes remained on her.

"You know of me—I see that," she said in a broken whisper. "Do you remember when we met?"

His eyes narrowed at the oddity of the question, but Mask could think of no better way to ask. Any other way she phrased it, it would seem far stranger. And alas, she could tell by Riesk's confusion that he had never met the old Mask. But perhaps he knew someone who had. She tried a different course, angling for information from another direction.

"Your Master, the Fox of Luether," Mask said. "He or someone in his organization hired me for a task, one I completed as instructed. But I was betrayed. I would know the identity of the one who turned against me. I know it was not you. Give me a name, and your suffering is at an end."

Riesk's lips formed words. "That simple, is it."

She'd intended to seem reasonable—a respite after a day of pain and torment—but what she conveyed instead was a sense of security. Riesk didn't seem grateful for the chance to bargain, but rather overly reassured. Arrogant. This was going poorly.

Tithian picked upon Mask's growing anxiety and stepped close to Riesk, menacing him with a blade. "Talk," he said. "One name, and this all ends."

Riesk looked up at him. "Can't tell you what I don't know," he said. "The Fox doesn't hire slayers to do his business. You want a name, ask him."

"Give us his name then," Tithian said, "and we will."

"Tithian," Mask said, but it was too late.

The damage had been done. Riesk had made that last suggestion in jest, but now he closed up at the suggestion of betraying his master. "I'd sooner die," he said. "And that I'll tell you for free."

Tithian opened his mouth to retort but could summon no words. His face was turning red.

"Squire," Mask said. "Attend me."

They removed to the near window, where they could look down into the street of low-city Luether. In name only did it resemble the Tar Vangr cityscape Mask remembered from her childhood. Most of the buildings had become burned out husks, usable only for squatters or one of the many illicit revels that culminated in violence during summer nights. Sometimes one man or woman would die, sometimes a dozen—the rules varied as wildly and unpredictably as the whims of the Ruin King. Dusk had come an hour before, and Mask could see fires already lit for that midnight's festivities. This was a bad city—one they should leave as soon as they had the chance.

Tithian joined her at the window, looking frustrated. "He has nothing to tell us," he said.

"We have to know." Mask closed her fists hard on the windowsill, and lingering traces of Plaguefire softened the calcified wood into rotting mulch. She realized she was too loud, so she cut her voice to a whisper. "We traced the information to him and his organization. You said he was the best source we could find."

"The best I could capture," Tithian said. "A dead end. We need to try again."

"It's been a year and two seasons. I don't know how much longer we can do this."

Tithian touched her hand. "As long as we have to," he said.

Mask pulled away, and instantly she could tell she shouldn't have. Tithian's face darkened and his body language grew hostile. She hadn't meant to offend him. He'd just been trying to comfort her, but comfort was not something she wanted.

Then they saw a group of people flitting through the street, moving with too much organized purpose to be Children of Ruin looking for a fresh brawl or stragglers to waylay. To another observer, they might have escaped notice, but Mask had a keenness of vision that had served her well all her life. She knew they were moving together, and that they were coming here.

"You said no one followed you," Mask said, the words almost a curse. She pointed.

Anxiety broke through Tithian's calm. "I didn't see anyone."

"Of course you didn't." She nodded back over her shoulder. "Your people?"

Riesk spat at Semana. "Summer Lives," he said.

Tithian's body contorted into a combative posture, and he bunched up his muscles to pounce like a ravenous beast on Riesk. She stayed him with a hand on his arm and turned slowly.

Mask turned around, so she could see Riesk grinning bloodily at them. "Time to release me," he said. "Whoever you are, you aren't Mask. Lay down your arms, and I'll spare your lives."

He couldn't have seemed more at ease if he'd planned this. Maybe he had indeed planned to get captured and then rescued in some sort of scheme to slay them. Had she followed the right trail after all? Was Riesk himself involved in the plot to slay the Blood of Winter? Or was this simply the legacy of the great Mask, drawing enemies she neither knew nor could prepare to face? The princess and her pageboy might have been fledgling hunters themselves, but the old Mask's career stretched back decades as far as she knew. Never before had she considered the sheer audacity of trying to assume the sorcerer's life.

The visage was cracking. The mask slipping. She didn't know what to do.

"Master," Tithian was saying, and Semana realized he meant her. "*Master!* What do I do?"

Semana shook her head. She didn't know. She felt lost and confused. "Deal with him," she said.

Riesk chuckled. "Deal with me," he said. "Lad, you should let me go, before—"

His words cut off with a ragged, choking sound. Tithian had stabbed him in the throat, blood oozing around the small knife in his hand. For an instant, all three of them seemed equally surprised. Even Tithian did not seem to have expected such an outcome. He stared down at the blade in apparent disbelief. Then, slowly, his expression hardened as Riesk choked and gagged and tried to breathe.

"I'll let you go," Tithian said, his lips widening into a statue. "This is a mercy."

"Tith—" Semana said, but when he looked up at her, his eyes were filled with that same hunger as before, mingled with something that made her skin crawl. *Joy*.

"Know me before you die," he said, grinning in Riesk's face. "I am Davargorn, slayer and destroyer. I claimed your life, as I will that of all your blood. I am Davargorn, your bloodbreaker."

Mask held up a hand. "Wait—"

He plunged the knife into Riesk's throat and up into his brain. The man's eyes bugged and he sputtered nonsensical sounds as he stared into the mismatched eyes of his killer. His body wrenched taut and tried to escape but could not move.

Then Tithian—nay, *Davargorn* was his name now—wrenched the blade free in a torrent of blood, spit, and bile.

The princess fell back against the door and sank to the floor to keep from staggering. Deep inside her, Semana wanted to scream and vomit, but Mask had to keep her locked down. She covered her mouth with one gloved hand as though that might keep the sobs inside.

She should be harder than this. She could be. She *must* be.

"Trapped," she whispered. "I am trapped."

"Master?" Face covered in Riesk's blood, Davargorn gazed at her, his oversized white eye gleaming like the moon. He still held the dripping knife. "We must go."

Heavy footfalls on the stairs below told Mask he spoke true. She had no choice.

She climbed to her feet, beckoning him over, but when he pointed the knife at her, she recoiled.

"Leave it," she said. "There will be more steel."

Davargorn hesitated a moment, then dropped the knife clattering to the floor, spraying spots of blood across the long darkened boards.

They were out the window, embracing one another, when the door crashed open inside.

TEN

Present Day—The Winter Wilds—Spring 982 Sorcerus Annis

SHE AWOKE FIRST TO a sense of lightness—no sound or touch or sight to behold. Her body felt buoyant, drifting without foundation or connection to anything around her.

The world bled out and flattened around her, and everything about her seemed to peel away with it. She saw for the first time its fragility, as though reality were but a tattered pelt stretched over jutting bones. If she reached out and took hold of it, she could pull the skin away and discover what lay beneath.

And even as she thought this, visions bloomed throughout the darkness. She shook, terrified and alone. A name rose in her mind, but she had no mouth to call for help. She could not stand. She…

No. She was power. She was a weapon. She would not fear.

Strength rippled through her universe, cementing her place within it. She willed herself to be here. She belonged here.

Her perspective broadened until she was at one with the world, and not just her own. Other worlds she did not know spiraled out around her, each with their own rules and laws and magic. She saw a thousand flashes of other lives, which traveled through majestic places she had never seen and could scarely imagine. Some were dark and cold as death, while some shone bright enough to blind her by comparison. She saw dripping forests and soaring peaks, cities drifting atop gargantuan fronds of some pink plant, and towers built upon the inverted peaks of mountains.

Faster and faster the rainbow of worlds appeared, melting over one another in an unending torrent of visions. Sprawling urban landscapes flickering with thousands of lights became muddy battlefields filled with fire and smoking war machines, then shifted into tranquil garden oases populated by meditating figures in bright robes that in turn bled into the flames of a world affire.

What magic was this? She wanted it.

She needed it.

She tried to stretch out her arms to touch the other worlds, but she had no body—only a will that drifted through the kaleidoscopic hurricane of reality. Faster and faster they emerged, until she could not make out their distinctions. A barrage of light and dark and thousands of colors she had never seen before riddled her mind, and she could not stand it. She clawed desperately for somewhere to ground herself, wishing desperately she could shut her eyes. But at the same time, she longed to know this power. She would wield it herself, and pierce the veil between worlds.

The worlds spiraling around her bled into a single bright light, blinding and disorienting her. She felt dizzy and weak, and realized she was fading away. The light was burning her, but she felt no pain. The scope of the universe shrank around her and she shrank with it, slowing and dimming.

Soon, the light would swallow her, and…

Semana opened her eyes, her body numb and empty in the wake of the strange vision.

For a moment, staring up at a blank white ceiling, she thought she had not escaped the dream. It had merely shifted into the reality she knew now. She had a body, but one that had grown so very weak after her ordeal. She felt as if she were gradually bleeding back into physical existence. The world crept into her awareness slowly, and with it an awful sense of loss. This world was all she had now, when she had glimpsed so much more.

For now.

The white ceiling above was a bleached skin of some animal, she realized. A tent that flapped gently in a cold breeze. The room was simple: a cot piled in furs upon which she lay, a thick rug of fibrous rope, a chest for belongings, a brazier that shed dim, muddy light and heat. Semana saw also a number of papers strewn over a stump that doubled as a desk, upon which stood several crude, weak candles. The tent boasted very little in the way of furniture or heavy objects. Efficient and quickly moved.

Semana seemed to be alone. She touched her forehead, the movement making a ringing sound. Around her bare wrists clinked numerous thin metal bracelets—plain rings of corroded iron and tarnished silver, mostly, but here and there she found gold as well.

She remembered the Children of Ruin taking her. And her wounds. Mortal, she had thought.

Increasingly uneasy, Semana sat up and immediately curled around her midsection, which burned and itched as though someone had cut her open and thrust a smoldering coal inside. Unsurprising, considering the tree roots that had stabbed through her like spears studding a boar. She found a design painted on her breast and belly with some sort of crusty, red-brown substance that smelled terrible. It flaked off when she brushed it, leaving a sticky residue in its wake, and she inspected her stomach for the wound. But her skin was bare and smooth, with only five small red marks just below her ribcage, as well as a jagged scratch along her lower side. She felt around at her back, and found no wounds there, either.

Fully restored—and from mortal wounds. How long had she slept?

Her stomach curdled with ravenous hunger, and Semana saw a loaf of hard bread and wafers of dried meat set out on the table beside the cot. Meager rations, but they looked delicious. She stuffed the crust of bread into her mouth, hardly pausing to chew before she set to the meat as well. Venison, she thought. She had downed about half of it before she abruptly stopped, letting the crumbs of the food fall to the ground. She felt at her bare face with fingers that had begun to tremble. It was only then Semana came to the full realization what had been taken from her, and that her armor was nowhere to be seen.

Instead of fear, however, anger rose up inside her. Yet another humiliation to avenge.

The sounds of sharp converse came from the sealed flap of the tent, and Semana realized she would not remain alone for long. She swung her legs off the bed, and it took a few shaky steps to make her numb limbs cooperate. The flap opened, admitting the cold night breeze from outside.

When a hulking guard pushed into the tent, Semana stood tall and firm, arms crossed, heedless of her nakedness. "Not another step," she said. "Unless you want to die."

The ugly man had skin the color and consistency of hard cheese and wore boiled leather and wolf pelts over a body thick and strong as an old, gnarly tree. For a barbarian, he looked surprisingly intact if heavily scarred. Then he bared yellow teeth in a defiant grin, the skin of his cheeks and jawline stretching in multiple directions away from deep red furrows. In effect, his mouth looked like the base of a starfruit. Definitely one of the Children of Ruin.

He said something guttural and reached for one of the three stubby blades that hung like jagged icicles from his belt.

"I warned you."

Semana called upon her blood magic and reached out for the guard, but all that happened was a wave of nausea. The sudden revulsion had the strength to make Semana stagger back to one knee, but having her magic refuse her command startled her more. The poultices smeared across her body tingled, making her skin itch and burn. Perhaps they thwarted her magic somehow?

Whatever the explanation, the question would become moot in a moment. The guard stepped forward, dagger scraping free of its scabbard, and she glared up at him. His size dwarfed her, and his blades and armor gave him a clear advantage. Casting about for a weapon, she saw nothing that offered a chance to defeat him, and escape seemed dubious. Perhaps she could get one of his daggers, but what then? Regel had taught her the basics of swordplay, but her real talents lay with magic, not steel.

Then the guard abruptly stood up straight as though struck. His eyes widened, and he fell to one knee. He reversed his dagger and extended it to her, hilt first, then arched his head to bare his neck. He said something deep and even reverential that she did not understand.

"What?" Semana asked, but no reply was forthcoming.

A second barbarian stepped into the tent, saw Semana standing there and the other bowing to her, and assumed a grim expression made deeply unsettling by a lack of lips. Her mouth was just a red, gaping wound that revealed rows of jagged teeth. The woman looked vaguely familiar, and Semana recognized her as one of the Children of Ruin who had waylaid her in the tiny hamlet. This one stepped toward the one on the ground and raised a flanged mace over his head.

"Wait." Semana held up her hands to stop the barbarian. The woman paused and looked at her with a dubious expression. Five years as a slayer had taught her to read faces like pages in a book, but she could not easily discern this woman's intentions. "What—what is going on?"

The woman lowered her mace and pointed to Semana. "*Teren-sa*," she said, then pointed to the supine barbarian. "*Drek skaka*."

Semana saw silvery flames crackling around her fingers, and realized the Frostfire must have manifested around her at some point. That must have been what the first guard saw, just before he presented himself for death. If the markings had inhibited her blood magic somehow, at least the Frostfire could still manifest. Not, of course, that she could control it well enough to be a reliable weapon.

As she marveled at the silver flames, the barbarian woman nodded with a pleased expression on her face. Then she raised her mace suddenly and, before Semana could protest, she brought it down on the kneeling guard's head. The man made a breathy mewling sound, confused and not a little frightened. Semana watched, unable to move, as the woman smashed the mace into the man's head and neck, over and over. The first blow created a massive red welt, then the barbarian's neck gradually bent like warped wood. His hands clawed at the dirt and he made incoherent groaning sounds. On the third strike, his neck broke open and blood spattered his killer's face and hands, the ceiling of the tent, and Semana's own feet. By the sixth stroke, the barbarian resembled not so much a man as a sack of meat and bristling bone. The previously pristine interior of the tent became a mess of gore.

When she had finally finished, after the eighth strike, the barbarian looked up at Semana with a broad grin. Her lipless mouth made the smile truly hideous, as her dark skin bled right into the roots of her sharpened teeth, glued together with blood spatter. Split scars marked where her lips had been torn and burned away.

Perhaps she sought approval through that look? Semana blinked, then drew in a breath and blew it out slowly. She had killed men and seen more killed before her, but this…

She put her hands behind her back, so that her trembling fingers would not give her away. Then she nodded. "Yes," she said. "He offended me, and his death was well done, you vicious madwoman."

The woman looked at Semana with a fraction of understanding—more than the man had shown, at least—and nodded eagerly. "*Rus Teren-sa.*" She knelt and whispered words into the gore, then flicked blood from her mace, seemingly indifferent to the grotesque scene the murder left in the tent.

"I don't speak your tongue," Semana said as calmly as possible. "Do you speak mine?"

The woman shook her head, whether in answer or incomprehension, Semana couldn't say for sure. She pressed the mace to her chest. "*Kalik,*" she said proudly.

"Kalik. That's your name. Right." Semana put her hand over her own chest, but had to think a moment as to what name to give. "Mask," she said at length.

Kalik furrowed her brow and her expression grew stormy. She pointed the bloody mace at Semana. "Mask," she said. "*Teren-sa.*"

"That's your word for me. Well." Semana indicated herself again. "*Teren-sa?*"

Kalik nodded, seemingly mollified. She nodded deferentially to Semana and looked at her with expectation.

"Exceptional," Semana said. "Trapped here with only an idiot for company. That's what I'm calling you, Kalik: idiot."

"*Terens ka,*" Kalik said, pointing to her. Then, experimentally, pointing to herself: "Idiot."

Semana nodded. "That's right."

Kalik gave her a wide, horrid smile that almost made Semana vomit up the meat and bread.

The barbarian pointed toward the tent flap, which whipped open in a cold breeze. Semana felt the wind on her naked skin, and while the cold did not touch her, the breeze reminded her of her nakedness. Kalik gestured toward the night outside. "*Terens ka*," she repeated. "*Vas tastha*."

"You want me to go with you, idiot?" Semana pointed to herself, then the darkness.

Kalik nodded enthusiastically and gestured again.

"Where is my armor?" Semana hugged herself, hoping that would convey the need for clothes, but Kalik only shook her head and continued to stare at her.

Semana stepped toward the corpse on the floor and tentatively took the edge of his leather cuirass. She shook it lightly. "Armor?" She indicated her own body. "My armor?"

"*Carpas*." Kalik nodded in sudden understanding. She waved Semana back, then set to stripping her splintered companion of his leather harness and armament.

At first, Semana didn't understand, but when Kalik offered her the hapless guard's breastplate, it made sense. She accepted it with a sour smile of gratitude. "I suppose I can't walk about nude, can I, idiot?" She smiled brightly at Kalik. "This will have to do for now. I'll find my own armor, then I'll kill you and escape, well? Does that pass well with you, idiot?"

The barbarian smiled and nodded. She waited while Semana awkwardly donned the armor of the dead barbarian. It was heavier than it had appeared, and Semana realized quickly that metal plates ran through the leather, crudely stitched over but effective. When she had donned it, Kalik gestured toward the flap leading out of the tent.

"Yes, idiot," Semana said. "Let's away."

A cold wind swept through the brisk midnight air over the little valley of cookfires laid out before Semana and her guide. The tent stood on the fringe of a much larger encampment with scores of weathered tents, and in the bright moonlight off the snow she could make out some of the people: Children of Ruin, one and all. Numerous totems like crude battle standards of lashed bone, wood, and blood-stained leather stood forbidding sentry outside many of the tents, marking particular clans or famous warriors, perhaps. It resembled an army camp, full of men and women sharpening blades, sparring, and boasting. The smell of roasting meat mingled with sweat and the tang of shit to create an aroma of barely caged violence waiting to be set loose.

The stench reminded her a bit of Luether, but even worse. There, at least the barbarians had been the rare powerful, rather than everyone she saw.

Death in any of a thousand forms lurked in the camp, waiting for her to make a mistake or cross the wrong screaming savage.

Semana should have felt fear to see herself surrounded by so many foes, especially when she had neither her armor or relics, but instead she found herself in awe. As a child, she'd heard tales of the Children of Ruin as wandering, insane specters, women and men driven mad in the wild. They were little more than animals, the tales said—dumb brutes who existed only to gobble disobedient babes. In her years as Mask, she and Davargorn had avoided working for the Children, who could rarely be trusted to school their own actions, much less hold true to any agreement. In Luether, the paranoid Pervast the Ruin King barely held the animals in check through a combination of charisma and anonymity. Few if any had ever seen him, and thus few could threaten him, but all feared and respected him. Without a leader, the whole city would descend into chaos and destroy itself.

What she saw before her now, however, was no pack of wild dogs but an organized, directed, capable army that posed an unexpected danger for any force foolish enough to wander into its path. If Children of Ruin could organize on such a level, perhaps they posed a greater danger to Tar Vangr and even Luether than anyone realized. This army must have an organizing force to keep their natural inclinations in line. Like as not, the sorcerer she faced back near Narkggr was the leader here.

She would learn the truth in due time. First, to secure her place here among the Children of Ruin. Establish herself.

"Where is my ally?" she asked Kalik. "Sour old graybeard with cold eyes. Regel Winter."

The woman shrugged, apparently not comprehending.

"Frostburn," Semana said.

That name struck a chord in Kalik, and her expression grew grave. "*Den davar*," she said, her words almost reverent.

When she used the word "davar"—the word for "one who kills" in the Old Tongue—Semana caught her first glimpse of the roots of the language. She'd not studied the language of ancient Calatan in years, and her memory of it had rusted from disuse. "Den" was similar to "daen," she thought, which meant "cold," and "cold killer" seemed like an apt description for Regel.

"*Den davar.*" Semana nodded. "I must see him."

Kalik said something Semana didn't understand, but her body language told her well enough the request would come to nothing. She did not get the impression that Regel had perished, however—likely, he had become a prisoner of the Children as well.

"Very well, idiot," she said. "Take me to your commander. No doubt you've been instructed to do that already." She fought to come up with the word from Old Calatan. "*Terrin?* Master?"

"*Terens,*" Kalik said.

"Yes." Now Semana recognized the word for "ruler" despite the unusual pronunciation. "*Terens.* Take me there."

"*Teren-sa,*" said Kalik, and they were on their way.

That wasn't the first time the barbarian had called her that. What did it mean? That these folk thought her a potential master? Semana considered the implications, and did not mind them one whit.

They were no Deathless fae, but they were an army.

But whose?

As they skirted the edge of the camp, Semana still drew quite a few intrigued glances. Ruin had painted its Children's skin and hair all manner of hues and tones, but she'd never seen one who bore bright silver-blonde hair like Semana did, making her as surely an outsider here as in any civilized mage-city. That, and she had none of tattoos or scarification that marked the Children. She wondered what smooth skin and natural features meant among them—whether it was a good or bad thing. None of them attacked, at least. Indeed, most seemed to regard her with non-threatening interest or even deference.

When they wandered past two half-naked men wrestling in the snow—one pale, one dark—the pugilists paused in their combat to watch her. They were both missing half a face, such that together they made up one mottled visage. One took the opportunity to sweep the legs of his opponent and they ended up back on the ground, where their wrestling took on a sensual component that made the grapple no less intense. Soon enough, one of the men was crooning in pleasure as the other grunted.

Near the edge of the camp stood a crude stockade of lashed boughs set against a boulder, creating a space about large enough for half a dozen bodies. The Children had only a single prisoner, however: an old man who wore ragged hides and snow. His arms were lashed around the massive, splintery log upon which he lay. At first he seemed as foreign and off-putting as the barbarians of the camp, but on closer inspection, she recognized his icy eyes and grim face.

"Regel," she said.

His eyes flicked to her, but he did not otherwise move. Snow lined his beard, which had grown in thick and gray since she had seen him last. She wondered again how long she'd slumbered?

"I'll see you freed," Semana said. "Patience."

If Regel heard, he made no acknowledgment.

Kalik led her away from the camp up a winding path among boulders and tree boughs that hung heavy with snow. It occurred to her—as it often did in such situations—that leading her to a remote location would provide an excellent opportunity to murder her without any witnesses, but she could not guess how the barbarian camp might react. Based on all her interactions with Children of Ruin, public torment and executions inspired and entertained them, so she should be safe out of open view.

It also occurred to Semana to murder Kalik and make good her escape, but she saw three important obstacles to such a path. First, her armor and all her relics lay somewhere in the camp, she knew not where, and trying to get them back would no doubt require her Blood magic, which didn't seem to want to obey. Second, she lacked the supplies for a trek across the wilderness. And, for a third, she supposed she should free Regel as well. She needed a guide, and he'd proven useful thus far. And he *was* her father, or at least so he claimed.

"Are you still taking me to the *terens*?" Semana asked.

Kalik rounded on her and put two fingers to Semana's lips to silence her. It was brief, but Semana caught a flicker of fear in her eyes. But was she afraid of Semana, or of her master?

Urging silence once more, Kalik beckoned Semana onward.

About a hundred paces removed from the encampment, they came to a patch of boulders devoid of snow, where steam rose into the night. A hot spring, but nothing like the flamewell Regel had showed her during their journey. Semana felt warmth here but not the same overweening vibrancy of life granted through contact with the Narfire. Perhaps it was the proximity of the Children of Ruin, but she felt only anger and violence in this place.

Two slender figures—one male, one female—lounged on the stones near the mouth of the hot spring, shivering in their nakedness despite the radiant warmth. Kalik led Semana between them, and she took the opportunity to inspect both as she passed. In coloration and feature, they varied as did the sun and moon, but they bore the same dull expression and the same set of chains around their necks, wrists, and ankles. Their bodies showed not a little evidence of punishment—particularly the man. They averted their eyes, as though looking at Semana would invite further torture.

Slaves. The thought set Semana's teeth on edge. A disgusting import from the Lands of Summer, slavery did not occur naturally in the world as far as she knew. Thus, she had not expected to find the demeaning practice among the Children of the north. Strange.

At the heart of the spring, a naked man stood with his back to her, submerged halfway up his buttocks, arms extended so that two mostly naked slaves could rub his well-sculpted muscles with reddish rocks dripping with water. They made slick sounds against his skin, scraping it free of what looked like muddy clumps and leaving warm, ruddy trails in their wake. These slaves were male and female as well, and as different from each other as from the first two Semana had seen. This *terens* apparently had eclectic taste. Semana crossed her arms and waited.

Kalik said something low and guttural, and the man glanced over his shoulder. His thick, water-slick hair hung down his back, obscuring his face. "That will do, Kalik," he said.

"Yes, Dar-Karsk," she said in clear, if heavily accented Calatite. Semana stared at the woman, who smiled at her with her deformed mouth, then spoke: "Pass well, *idiot*."

As she turned to go, Semana looked back to the man in the spring, around whom the naked slaves draped a thick gray cloak that floated on the surface of the water like a grime. "She understood everything I said to her?"

"Yes." The barbarian sorcerer made brushing motions with his hands in the direction of his slaves, and they bowed and shrank back. Dar-Karsk stepped up and out of the water, and his cloak slithered up behind him. He had a thick, deep voice like stones being crushed to gravel. "I instructed her to watch over you but not to speak Calatite to you," he said, still not looking at her. "Kalik may lack a full face, but her tongue is quite talented."

"I'm sure." Silvery fire crackled around her fingers. Her Frostfire stirred, but she could not say why. Semana crossed her arms, tucking her fingers and the magic into her armpits. "Why am I alive?"

The sorcerer sniffed. "Direct," he said. "That is a thing worthy of esteem." He let the water fall from his cloak and adjusted his hood. He turned to her halfway so that she could see his face in profile, hidden in shadow under his hood. "I am Dar-Karsk, Rotpriest of the Children of the North Wind, and you are the great Mask, the flesh made weapon, the destroyer of dreams. Your name is well known to us—your true face, less so. It is an honor to meet you in battle and out."

"Not an answer." Semana raised her chin. "I'm waiting."

"As I've waited six days for you to awaken." He stepped toward a stack of gray-black clothes and claimed a pair of loose hose. "You live because you have power. You slew my warriors and earned your life. Do not squander it in a vain effort to antagonize me."

Six days asleep, at his mercy. Semana suppressed a shiver. She would not bow to his intimidation. "Don't deflect," she said. "Your magic all but slew me. How do I yet live?"

"So you do not know." He paused in pulling on his right leg, then drew it up. "Interesting."

"Know what?" Semana asked.

"That is a question for your companion," Dar-Karsk said. "The great Frostburn, in our camp. Imagine. A double honor."

"I saw Regel," Semana said. "He did not answer me either."

The rotpriest kept his silence as he laced his breeches.

"If you'll not answer my questions," Semana said, "I'll have to guess. Somehow I live, and you've healed my wound and blocked my magic. You could have killed me in my sleep, but you did not. If I yet live, it is because I hold some value to you. What is it you want of me?"

"Direct *and* perceptive—exactly as I had hoped." Dar-Karsk pulled the robe tight about himself and secured it with a length of hemp rope. "In truth, I *do* intend to make use of you, in a mutually beneficial way. You and your companion are both of value, and so you continue to breathe. For now."

"You have plenty of power." Semana gestured to his slaves, who knelt at the edges of the pool. They cringed at the attention. "And you hardly seem to lack for flesh. What can I offer you that you do not already have? Coin? I have none. Only my sharp tongue."

He smiled, an expression barely perceptible under his cowl. He was making an effort not to show her his face, she realized. "In due time," he said. "But first, perhaps you wish to refresh yourself?"

"With you just standing there?" Semana scoffed. "Not likely."

He laughed. The humanness of that sound surprised Semana, considering his rough voice. "Come. I see that you are wearing the armor of a dead man, and I can smell the blood and sacred herbs on you from here."

"Sacred herbs, is it?" The foul-smelling stuff itched on her skin when he mentioned it, and she resisted the urge to scratch. "I've worn worse."

"I had heard the great slayer Mask never removed his armor—*her* armor, I should say." Dar-Karsk waved his hand over the pool, and the water shivered in the wake of his hand. "You need prove nothing to me. I know when I have met an opponent to be respected and feared."

And so speaking, he turned his back fully once more.

It took all of Semana's iron-hard willpower not to spring forward and throttle him. His display of power—making the water move with his own, strange magic—stayed her hand.

"Well." She unbuckled the crude brigandine harness and it clattered to the ground with a crunch. The rotpriest stood a touch taller at the sound, then relaxed as she slipped under the bubbling surface.

The hot spring did not feel as wondrous as the flamewell, but Semana appreciated the water's warm caress all the same. It soothed her sore muscles, particularly her battered midsection. She scratched at her limbs, but the flaky designs drawn on her skin hardly seemed affected. Silently, the male slave extended his rock toward her, and she accepted it warily. It looked porous and felt soft and spongy. With the rock, her ministrations proved more effective in cleansing her skin.

"Pleasant, is it not?" True to his word, Dar-Karsk did not face her. "Ruin is a harsh world, and our small diversions make a significant difference."

"As you say." Semana tried her best to keep the relief out of her voice, so as not to give him any satisfaction. She scrubbed her chest with the rock, and the brownish sludge flaked off into the water without trouble. "At least I'll get this shit off. What is it?"

"Herbs, blood, and—well, you said it yourself."

Semana fought down her gorge. She scrubbed harder.

"Shall we speak more?" Dar-Karsk asked at length.

"Are you going to answer my questions?" Semana asked.

"Those that are mine to answer." The rotpriest spread out his robe and sat on a boulder overlooking the pool. "Not the miracle of your healing. That was not my doing."

"Whose, then?" Semana asked.

He remained infuriatingly silent.

"Speak, then, of this task you have for me," Semana said as she sponged her back. One of the slaves started toward her, no doubt to assist, but she glared at the woman until she retreated. "You kept me alive to a purpose. I would as soon accomplish it and be on my way."

"Would you indeed?" Now he turned to look at her, and she sank into the dark water up to her chin, arms crossed over her bare chest. "I suspect you'll not get much farther."

"Regel and I were doing well enough before you waylaid us," she said.

He shrugged. "The farther north you travel, the deeper you journey into the land of Worldfire. I cannot guarantee your safety from them as I can from my own people."

"Worldfire?" Semana asked.

"The magic of the Ruin Druids, who rule the Children as speakers for the gods," he said. "They control the earth and its elements. You live because my warriors are loyal to me, not them. If you met an actual Druid, you would not be speaking now. They are jealous masters and hate magic not their own."

"Magic such as yours." Semana focused her efforts on her left arm.

"Yes and no." Dar-Karsk's words turned bitter. "I am a man, and so I cannot be one of them. I have studied their ways for a decade, but I will never rise higher than the rank of adept."

"Powerful enough, for an adept," Semana said. "My power did not so much as touch you."

At that, he smiled slightly, but there was no mirth in it—only a vague uneasiness. "I have magic of my own. Not Worldfire, but its antithesis. *Anathema.*" He brought his hands together so that the respective fingers touched. "The druids did not know when they imparted their secrets, and I have killed all who learned the truth. Though not you, of course."

"I see." Semana finished with her right arm and held up the dripping sponge stone, considering. "And you need my help against them," she said. "To take your rightful place."

He turned to her, and the moonlight reflected off his yellowish teeth.

She paused, then rose out of the water, baring herself fully to Dar-Karsk's view. He watched her levelly, betraying no reaction, but he certainly seemed fascinated. Semana let the water run from her limbs and drip back into the pool. They stared at one another.

"Bring my armor," she said. "I will aid you, and then we will go along our own paths. Agreed?"

He nodded. "Agreed."

Dar-Karsk waved, and half a dozen barbarians appeared, melting out of the boulders where they had held bows and javelins at the ready. The sorcerer had never truly faced her alone. Wise.

Kalik appeared with a burlap sack over her shoulder. She discarded it at the edge of the pool, and Semana saw the familiar black leather within.

"I had my slaves use snow to clean it," Dar-Karsk said. "I hope I did not overstep."

"As if I have a choice." Semana had not expected an audience, but it mattered little.

"I must ask that you not use your relics in the camp," he said. "The Children are but simple people. They believe in *gods*. They might take strange magic…amiss."

"And what do *you* believe in, Dar-Karsk?" she asked.

"Myself." She saw a hint of a smile in the darkness of his cowl. "You."

Semana stepped to the sack and drew out her leathern breeches and cuirass. Gone were the wraps for her breasts, but she could endure the minor discomfort for now. She slipped the armor on, making sure to bend away from

Dar-Karsk as she did. He did not even try to disguise his interest: indeed, he rose and stepped quietly toward her, almost close enough to touch her. He reached out, but she turned to confront him, her armor donned but not yet fully buckled. She lifted up her leather mask and considered it.

"I want to tell you something, Dar-Karsk," Semana said. Frost spread along the ground from her bare feet, covering the hot spring's surface with a thin rime. The other barbarians fidgeted nervously.

"Indeed?" Then he stiffened, and his expression became one of confusion. His own body had become a stranger to him, its blood and bone and muscles firmly in the red-glowing hand of the pale-haired woman who stood before him.

Semana's eyes flared with crimson light. Her voice rasped. "You've made a mistake."

Semana pressed the mask to her face, and instantly a halo of green fire surrounded her. It lashed out with tendrils of sickly magic that struck at their barbarian escorts. Weapons clattered to the frozen ground as the magic wrenched the strength from the guards' limbs. Their legs turned gelatinous and they fell to their knees, gagging and choking. Kalik vomited over and over, her lipless mouth drawn wide like that of a skull.

"What passes?" Dar-Karsk kept his voice level, but Semana heard the threatening panic there. "Why can't I move?"

"Blood magic," Semana said in Mask's voice. "Since I washed that silver-burned *shit* off me, I've been able to summon it. I waited for just…the right… moment." Semana turned to Dar-Karsk and smiled through the mouth slit of the mask. "Now."

"Intriguing," Dar-Karsk said. "I underestimated your power. You are more glorious than I could have imagined."

"It's hardly glory, but thank you," Semana said. "I told you about the Plaguefire, now let me tell you about necromancy. Your blood is mine to command, your body mine to control." She raised her hand, and one of Dar-Karsk's hands reached up to his throat. "I could kill you with your own hands, but I won't. That would be too easy. Painless by comparison. You call yourself rotpriest, eh? Ironic."

And so speaking, she focused the Plaguefire around him into a gnashing green cloud that snapped and nipped at his flesh. Through it all, he stood still as a statue, unable to strike back.

Leaving him frozen there, Semana looked out over the encampment, which had begun to rouse itself to the day's activities. The first breeze of dawn stirred the wisps of hair that had escaped her mask. She felt powerful, and not just because of the magic. Perhaps a queen might feel this way surveying her subjects and her world. But of course these were enemies, and they would sooner die than serve her. A choice in which she would happily oblige them.

"I will kill you now," she said. "Then I will take my companion and leave this place. I will kill any of your burning barbarians who get in my way. Those who bow to me, I will use as they are useful. I want you to know this, before you die choking on your own guts."

The rotpriest shrugged his shoulders slightly—as much as the blood magic would allow. "I know trust is a rare, hard thing in these dark days," he said. "But I assure you, I would never bring you to harm. Quite the opposite. I am your only friend in the World of Ruin."

"Somehow I doubt that." Semana focused the Plaguefire around him, dwarfing him. "You tried to kill me. Or will you deny that it was your magic that struck me down?"

"I'll not deny it," he said. "I will never lie to you, Semana."

That made her hesitate. "How do you know that name?"

He smiled, which she could barely see in the depths of his cowl. "Hold out your hand."

Silvery flames crackled around her fingers, and Semana tried to will them away. "What?"

Wordlessly, he presented her with his bare hand, fingers splayed.

Semana wanted to laugh, but somehow the gesture had no mirth to it. Here the man stood, defenseless, his own magic barely simmering beneath the surface. She could kill him at her whim. She would do as he asked, then send power through his hand to kill him. And as he crumbled to his knees and then to the ground, she would smile down at his corpse and know who had the power.

She put up her hand and spread her fingers, around which silver Frostfire danced. The green flames of her mask mostly swallowed the power, but some spark remained. Fitting, she thought, and almost didn't see the silvery flames dancing around the rotpriest's hand as well.

Then their hands touched, palm to palm and finger to finger, and the silver flames surged together like two parts of a lock clicking together. The silver flames spread up her arm and around her body, and suddenly her sickly green Plaguefire turned to silver Frostfire, banishing the power of her mask entirely. They stood there, hands together, burning with the same power, for a long moment. Then the rotpriest spoke, and his words sounded different—softer and smooth, with the accent of a civilized man. Some of his diction stumbled as before from unfamiliarity, but gone was his gruff demeanor and harsh voice.

"Among the Children of Ruin, I am Dar-Karsk the Condemner, Priest of Ruin and harbinger of doom," the rotpriest said. "But among your people—our people—I went by a different name. One that I have not forgotten, just as I cannot forget you." With his free hand, he pulled back his hood.

Semana caught her breath. His hair had dried since the pool, brightening from its original muddy color to a deep, vibrant crimson like old blood. As she watched, the silver Frostfire bathed him in light, illumining his features in a way she had not seen before. His hazel eyes—identical to hers—caught the moonlight and glowed brightly with both mirth and violence. Before, he had seemed merely familiar—a long ago, forgotten memory, but now...Now she *knew* him.

"What?" Amused at her expression, he smiled with his set of long teeth. "Did you think yourself the only one capable of resurrection?"

Words hardly came. "Darak," she said. "It—it cannot be."

"It can, little sister—and it is," he said. "I am Darak Ravalis nó Denerre, once Crown Prince, and one day King of Tar Vangr."

He laid his other hand on her shoulder, and their joined flames rose around them in a halo of silver into the night sky, only to fall back around them in crackling trails of fire.

Darak smiled at her. "With your aid, that is."

ELEVEN

Legs crossed and hands folded in his lap, the old man sat atop the bluff overlooking the barbarian camp below. The brisk wind bit at his exposed skin and tore at the fringes of his weathered leathers. He could feel the cold, but he had learned long ago not to give it power over him. He had much greater worries than the chill upon his old bones. One of which was, even now, marching up the hill toward him. She would arrive in a thirty-count, so he breathed in deeply and let himself drift.

In his right hand, Regel held a half-finished carving upon which he allowed his mind to focus while his senses flew wide. He heard the guttural whispers and challenges in the camp as well as snippets of a thousand conversations, only some of which he understood. He smelled the sweat and rage of the warriors as they sparred or had furious sex in their tents. He could taste the vegetable soup thickened with rice and deer blood, mingled with herbs to bless the soldiers with strength and madness in equal turn.

This was an army marshaling for war, he knew, but what war? Ten days among the barbarians, observing their preparations and progress, and he had not yet learned to what purpose Darak intended to put them. It did not help that few spoke even a dozen words of Regel's tongue, and none seemed willing to share even the briefest of conversations with him. They came to him periodically for his special aid, but more usually his escorts took him to one of the white tents at the center of camp. Under close supervision, he'd not found an opportunity to ask any questions.

As if drawn to his thoughts, a familiar presence entered Regel's awareness, and he knew then that the time had come for the confrontation he dreaded.

It had taken four days since he'd first seen her awake at the camp. Four days for Semana to decide how to confront him. Four days to work through the feelings of betrayal and uncertainty. She knew he had lied to her, but if she knew the full extent of those lies…

Regel shook his head. This would hurt.

With his keen senses, Regel appraised Semana as she drew up the path. She seemed more substantial—stronger. The camp's regular supply of bland but rich food had done well for her body, replenishing the weight she'd lost on their trek and then some. She had taken to wearing the acolyte garb Darak had given her, a robe of thick wool dyed so deep red it appeared almost black. Even without his enhanced sense of smell, Regel could tell that the Children mixed blood into the sticky dye. It matched the deeper, older scent of blood and grisly murder she wore beneath the robe. During those many years wrapped tightly in Mask's armor, the legacy of violence had seeped into her skin, and Regel wondered if any amount of scrubbing could expunge its taint.

He wondered too if Semana even *wanted* to rid herself of it. At first, when she had revealed her true face in the bowels of the palace of Tar Vangr, he'd felt so certain she did. Mask's attack five years ago had marked her, but it had taken until the barbarian ambush for Regel to understand how. He had thought the trauma had made her a victim, but he had come to see something else beneath that black leather death's head mask. Something very different indeed.

Semana approached him now without a mask, though he could see the darkness all around her. Her face was cold and set, but anger made her grimace.

"Did you know?" she asked.

It would be that question, then. Regel closed his fingers around his carved focus, and his senses flooded back into his body. He heard again the howling wind in his ears and realized that while he'd let his senses wander, his body had started to go numb in the chill. He hugged himself for warmth.

"Did you know?" Semana asked again. "Did you know my brother lived?"

"I had suspicions," Regel said.

Semana grew tenser, closing in on herself. "Did you search for him?"

Regel shook his head. "Orbrin refused."

"Why did you think he yet lived?" Semana asked.

"Darak had a well of strength to him that few fully understood," Regel said. "Paeter thought it came from him, but I knew the truth. It is a trait you both share with your mother."

"So you say."

That did not appear to have soothed her even a little. Damn.

Semana looked out over the camp, joining Regel's silent vigil for a long moment. Below them, the soldiers seemed restless, arguing and bickering over trifles, challenging one another with chest-slapping shows of bravado. Without discipline or even the bonds of shared heritage that united many such forces, they stood constantly upon the edge of descending into anarchy.

Semana saw it as well. "What keeps them together?" she asked.

"Fear." Regel inclined his head toward Darak's gray tent, its edges trimmed with rot like his robe. "You've seen the Children defer to your brother—men much larger and stronger than he—as though he is an immortal creature, not just a man."

Semana dismissed that observation with a wave of her hand. "He has great power, you know," she said. "The magic of Ruin herself is his to wield."

Regel looked at her askance. "He calls forth the Narfire?"

Semana's expression became contemplative. "He calls upon the magic of the land itself. Every rock, every tree, the air itself. These are his weapons. And he wields the Frostfire in our blood."

Regel had known that, but Semana's casual revelation surprised him. "You should take care," he said. "Ears not ours still hear our words."

He nodded to the two barbarians in gray weather cloaks sitting upon the rocks just down the bluff, both of them large, gruff men who'd spoken not a word to Regel each day they followed him about the camp. They'd stirred when Semana approached, but had not stayed her. Whatever arrangement she had with Darak, apparently she had enough free run of the camp to avoid such entanglements. Not for the first time, Regel felt like the camp's only prisoner.

Semana shrugged. "Perhaps your warders speak our tongue, perhaps not," she said. "But if they fear my brother as you say they do, it matters little. You will not deflect me so easily."

"You have more questions." Regel nodded. "Ask, then."

"Only one." Semana spread her arms wide. "How do I yet live?"

That question he'd dreaded above all others.

When she saw he would not answer, Semana took a step closer, eyes rigid upon Regel. She held him with the fury of her gaze. "We should have died in the ambush. Darak's magic sent branches through my body," she said. "How do I yet live?"

He shook his head.

"You see, I think I already know." As she spoke, Semana loosened her robe around one arm and drew up her leather sleeve. "My brother keeps you here because I wish it, but also because you are useful. I remember Ovelia speaking of your healing hands—ironic, for a slayer, no?" She bared her arm to the cold air. "You saved me somehow. But why keep it a secret?"

Regel rose and held out his hands to placate her. "Semana—"

"Very well." Semana drew from beneath her robe a knife with a sharp curve, the crude sort of implement the Children of Ruin carried with them at all times. Without hesitation, she pressed the blade against the skin of her arm and drew a bright line that welled with blood. All the while, she stared right at him without wincing or evincing the slightest pain. He saw only a fearsome, terrible will in her eyes.

Regel tensed but did not move. "Do not," he said. "As your father, I—"

"As my father?" Semana's voice wavered slightly, perhaps from the pain or perhaps something else. "You have claimed that right, but you have not earned it." She flicked her blood from the knife into the driven snow. "If you'll not find your courage on your own, then I shall aid you."

Then she reversed the blade over her chest, as though to plunge it into her own heart.

"Wait." Regel raised one hand.

Semana stayed the blade, allowing him to step toward her. He laid his fingers on her arm, over the wound, and closed his eyes. He let his mind and body sink away, much as he did when he used his sensory focus. This communion was far deeper, though, making his body tremble and waver as though it would cease to exist, and hers along with it. Semana shrank back, but he closed his fingers around her arm and held firm. Regel Winter, the man once called Frostburn, Oathbreaker, Lord of Tears, and the Shadow of the Winter King, vanished, leaving only the light.

The connection came quickly, as it had that bitter night at the ghost village. He reached inside Semana, and for a time they seemed of one flesh, one mind, and one spirit. He felt the hurt in her arm, and at a touch of his spirit, he bathed it in healing flame. The magic seared her flesh like a hot poker that touched for an instant and then was gone, leaving a tingling scar. Awe rippled between them, and Regel realized he was feeling Semana's thoughts. He had never before used the magic on someone fully aware, and the strange echo of her spirit and his made him dizzy. Her heart thundered in the space between them, and his beat faster to match.

He felt her pain and wonder because he had *become* her, in a very real sense.

Then it ended, and she flinched away from him. The communion broken, his senses rushed back into the mortal world, which seemed bleak and muted by comparison.

"What—?" Semana shook her head. "I knew it. You have magic of your own."

Regel looked away. "Barely," he said.

"That is why Darak is keeping you here," she said. "You heal his warriors, he spares you and feeds you. Yes?"

Regel nodded gravely. "I prefer bandages and poultices," he said. "But yes."

"How long?" Semana's eyes veritably glowed with excitement in the muted dawn light. "How long have you had this power?"

Regel shrugged. "Not long," he said. "I am a child with a stick, not a warrior with a sword."

"I could help you," Semana said. "I've seen magic like this before. Tithian wields something like it, though his is much…colder." She shivered, then looked back at him with a hopeful expression. "I could help you learn to use it."

"As Darak is helping you." Regel ventured a guess. "*Using* you."

"Hardly," Semana said. "I can handle my brother well enough."

"He is not the callow boy you remember," Regel said. "He cannot be trusted. Every word he says to you is an attack. Make no mistake."

"What do you know of it?"

"I have heard him promise to aid you in taking back Tar Vangr."

Semana's ardor diminished somewhat. They kept their sessions secret from the rest of the camp, but Regel had sneaked away from his escorts on more than one occasion to watch. Darak wielded Frostfire with a confidence that rivaled the power King Orbrin had demonstrated so many years ago, and under his tutelage, Semana might prove more powerful still.

"He will use you," Regel said.

"He will try," Semana said. "Darak is my mother's child, but so am I. How do you think I survived all those years? Or controlled Tithian so fully?"

"So that is it," Regel said. "You would use Darak as he would use you."

"He is teaching me." This time, Semana did glance at the barbarians keeping watch. The men seemed oblivious. "His tutelage is one of many ways in which he is useful. He and his army."

"His army," Regel said. "Not yours."

Semana's mouth crooked into a slight smile. "Not yet."

They stood unspeaking for a time, each weighing the other from two paces apart. The wind filled the silence, not with words but meaning so potent neither could ignore it. Semana had another question, one darker and harsher than the others, and Regel willed her not to ask it. He saw the end of their parternship behind those words: the death of whatever tenuous trust they had built over their journey together. He wanted to stop her—to take her in his arms and reassure her—but they had both made decisions, and he would face the consequences.

"So," she said. "You said you discovered this magic not long ago."

"Semana—"

"No more lies." She held up a hand to silence his protest. "Did you have this power on Ruin's Night?" she asked. "Is that how you survived Tithian's assault? I had assumed he healed you, but perhaps you healed yourself. Tell me."

"He healed me," Regel said.

"But it woke your own magic," Semana said. "And if you lie to me again—"

"I will not." He shook his head. "But—"

"Did you heal the Bloodbreaker?"

Silence fell once more between them. Semana's gaze bit into Regel and tore at his flesh, leaving him raw and bleeding. The terrible secret between them had finally emerged, and it unmade him.

"You did," Semana said at last. "You tell me not to trust Darak, but you have been lying to me all this time. She is alive, and you let me think she is dead."

Regel stepped forward and took her hands in his. "I am your father," he said. "I would never let you come to harm."

"No." Semana grasped his forearms so hard Regel thought they might break. "You may have put your seed in my mother in a moment of her weakness, but that does not make you my father. Far from it."

Her silver glove flaring with magic, she shoved Regel backward with a strength he had not expected, and he hit the snow-covered dirt hard enough to bruise. His bad leg screamed with pain.

"You are no father to me," Semana said. "I have had men in my life worthy of that name. Syr Sargaunt, the old captain of my guard, was there to protect me and to teach me how to be strong. King Orbrin was there to wipe my tears and whisper soothing words. Even Paeter, wastrel and bully and narcissist that he was, was more a father to me than some shadow lurking in the dark. None of them sought to control me, and none of them lied to me as you have." She raised her chin. "I would rather have such men for a father—one a warrior, one a king, and one a prince—than a creature such as you."

"Semana," Regel said. "Please—"

"No," she said. "You may be my father in flesh, but not in spirit."

With that she stalked off and left him struggling to rise, his strength all but vanished.

From down the hill, Regel heard his escorts chuckling at his misfortune. They traded words in their guttural tongue and slapped their crude swords against their shields. Resolved not to call out to them for aid, he gritted his teeth and tried to push his bad leg into place. He still felt the sting of Davargorn's casterbolt deep in the bone, and it grew almost unbearable in the cold. The wind hissed around him.

He realized at length that his escorts had ceased their converse, and indeed, they had vanished when he looked up. It took him a moment, but then he saw their crumpled bodies amongst the rocks that lined the path. He opened his fingers around the carving to enhance his senses, but immediately he discovered the needlessness of the gesture. A shadow in the shape of a man loomed over him, wind billowing his cloak out against the gray sky. The man's jet-black eyes stared down at him, and the expression on his dark face was pitiless.

Regel understood.

TWELVE

Semana stormed up the hill toward Darak's command tent, curses on her lips.

In previous days, she'd taken care walking through the camp to attract no undue attention and offer no gesture a barbarian might take for a challenge. Today, however, she had no patience for caution. She wanted to rage and destroy. Any Children of Ruin who got in her way would end their days coughing up their lungs into the half-frozen dirt, and she wouldn't even break stride. Semana almost wished someone would challenge her, just so that she could make an example of the poor fool.

How dare that man deceive her. He had lied to her for so long: allowed her to think Ovelia dead when he himself had wrested her from Ruin's grasp. If he could lie to her about something so important, why should she believe another burning word he spewed?

Regel yet lived because Darak found him useful, yes, but also because she had told her brother not to slay him. Now she had half a mind to command Darak to kill the old man, whatever his uses. Or perhaps invite him to watch while she did it.

One thing held her hand: his magic, like Tithian's but…pure. Untainted.

Her erstwhile squire had proven capable of great things with his power. For one, he'd caused her hand to grow a new finger to replace the one she'd cut off. The fresh digit tingled now that she thought of it, reminding her how odd it felt. Partially numb and never quite right. Tithian had never been a handsome lad, but his magic had misshapen her body over the years until he looked almost as bizarre as a Child of Ruin. He healed by thrusting pieces of a body back together. Just so, his magic aided others only imperfectly. Hence, she had assumed Tithian had healed Regel, as the man had a pronounced limp where his injury had laid him low. There seemed to be no such weakness in Regel's healing magic, however. Semana's own mortal injury had left only faint scars, and her insides felt perfectly well, if sore. And just now, when Regel had sealed the wound in her arm, she'd felt warmer—closer—than ever with Tithian.

Where had the power come from? The Oathbreaker was not of any great Blood: gutter born and bred, with nothing to his name but the good fortune of tricking the Blood Denerre into accepting him. He was a useful instrument, but a common one. Why would the Narfire bestow such power upon such a man, born nameless and alone? Perhaps his birth had been a trick of Ruin, to laugh at those who would call themselves noble.

One boon, however, of springing from Regel's blood meant that Semana might inherit this magic herself. It hardly seemed a fair trade for the disappointment of calling the man her father, but so often she had longed for such magic of her own. She wondered at the blood they both drew upon, and from whence this power had come. She needed to think more on this, and perhaps consult a sage for answers. When next she was in Tar Vangr…

So many thoughts whirled inside Semana's head that she hardly noticed Darak's tent was dark despite the rising sun. She pushed right in without hesitation, then pulled up short, confused.

"Darak?"

Semana knew immediately she was not alone in the gloomy interior of the tent, and that her brother was not here. The hot, close air scratched at her exposed skin. She summoned the power in her shielding breastplate, tasting the metallic odor on the air as the magic bloomed and cast a dim blue illumination around the room. Her eyes adjusted slowly to the dark, and not for the first time she wished she could see as Tithian did. The faint light let Semana see Darak's wide bed and scant furnishings, including the makeshift throne he'd used his magic to make grow from a stump. She saw no one.

"Show yourself," Semana said. "Or are you afraid?"

A woman stepped out from behind the throne into the thin light. She wore a dress made of little more than tattered blue and gray sashes that would have been scandalous at a noble revel for how they revealed more than hid the curves of her powerful frame. Over one arm draped a gray robe like the ones Darak favored, as though she had just doffed it upon arrival. The mark of a rotpriest. Semana could see little of her face other than her luminous green eyes, which burned with growing rage.

"I am not afraid," she said, her words heavily accented. She dropped the robe to the ground and took up a gnarled staff leaning against the bed beside her. This she tapped thrice on the floor with ceremonious precision. "Who are you, child, to challenge the Mistress of the Burning Rain?"

"Ha," Semana said. "Am I meant to be impressed by that name?"

The attack came suddenly, but Semana had anticipated it. The air around her grew heavy, glittering with moisture trapped in fog. Semana caught her breath even as the stuff began to burn at her skin and lungs. A flash of power from the silver glove, and Semana sent the foul air billowing away from her in all directions, including toward her attacker. The rotpriest swept her robed arm across, sending the acidic cloud to dissipate away from her. It beaded on the throne, sending up faint whiffs of steam.

"Is that all?" Semana held out her silver glove toward the woman. "I will show you—"

Then, abruptly, the magic of the glove drained away. The relic had been fully charged a heartbeat before, and suddenly it had no power left. The dim blue light that protected her faded as her breastplate ran out of power as well. The thick leather felt heavier than before and Semana fell to one knee, shocked. She grasped her mask, hanging from her belt, but even it seemed to have no magic left. What sorcery—?

The rotpriest stood over her, darkness swirling over her head like miniature stormclouds. The malevolent stars of her eyes pronounced doom upon this interloper who had dared challenge her, whoever she was. The woman's gnarled staff crackled with thunder inside the tent.

"Afferath!" Darak appeared behind Semana, close enough to reach out and touch her shoulder. He held a staff of his own, this one a smooth shaft of ash enwrapped in a red vine. Bright light burned from its tip, not unlike the radiance of the sun. "Stand down."

They faced each other, the two rotpriests, each burning with magic. Then the woman lowered her staff. "Your whore attacked me," she said. "I suggest you see to her."

Spurred by the insult, Semana shook off her hesitation and glared up at her. "I am no whore, and not his, either," she said. "And unless your mind is feeble, woman, recall that *you* attacked *me*."

A force shoved her from behind, and she found herself on her face on the canvas floor of the tent. Darak had kicked her in the back, she realized, and even now held her down with a foot between her shoulder blades. She tried to look back at him, but he drove her face deeper into the dirt. Instead, he stared at the woman, his chest big, his eyes promising violence.

"This one is under my boot and does not concern you," he said to her. "You will stand down."

The woman scoffed. "I *will*, will I?"

Semana fought to breathe under Darak's weight. Her hands twitched into claws.

At length, her magic dissipated, and the room's natural light returned. Now Semana could see her opponent—this Afferath—more clearly. From the shape of her cheeks and chin to the angle of her eyes and bold nose, Semana had never seen anyone quite like her in all her travels. The woman seemed Semana's opposite in many ways: muscular and robust compared to Semana's slender frame, dark and cold of complexion where Semana had fair hair and warm toned skin. Beautiful, and yet, there was something about the form of her face and bearing that made Semana uneasy.

Afferath wore a curious circlet upon her head: a ring of gold set with numerous sapphires carved like tears or raindrops. It was one of the few pieces of jewelry Semana had seen amongst the rugged Children of Ruin, and that made it stand out vividly.

"On your feet, slave," Darak said.

Semana glared up at him but he had eyes only for Afferath. They faced each other like proud bears competing over territory in a game of intimidation and bravado. Considering that Afferath had nearly killed Semana over gentle mockery, the challenge took on a deadly undercurrent.

Finally, Afferath relaxed first. She drew from around her neck a thong upon which hung a branch with silver leaves. Mistletoe, if Semana was not mistaken. Over this she whispered a prayer in the guttural language of the Children, then she handed the prize to Darak, who took it with a bow. Another ritual Semana did not understand.

"You've not broken this one, I see."Afferath laughed. "I thought you more of a man, Dar-Karsk."

"Need I show you?" Darak stepped around her and sat on his stump throne. "You did not complain so loudly the last time."

"You did not try hard enough, then." Afferath stood over Semana, looking down at her critically and without esteem. "Ware this slave. She has some degree of power. Enough to turn aside a simple attack." She looked dangerously at Darak. "Surely you've not been training her? The ancient laws—"

"Ruin forbids a man to train a woman, I know." Darak inspected his nails. "So you taught me."

Afferath drew up tall, offended at his easy dismissal of her concerns. "It is anathema."

"So many things are." Darak seemed unconcerned. "Speaking of which, have you had any sway over the circle? Regarding my proposal?"

If Afferath heard the question, she made no sign. Instead, she prodded Semana with her staff, and it was all she could do not to lash out. The druid had drained away the powers of her relics, but Semana could feel the woman's blood calling to her, veritably begging to be seized. Could Semana catch and bind Afferath before the counterstroke? She did not think so. Blood magic took longer than other magic, and her instincts told her not to risk it.

"I could always use another apprentice," Afferath said. "Tell me, is she versed in the arts of the night? She is pleasing enough to behold."

"She is mine, Afferath. I'll not part with her." Darak laid a soothing hand on Afferath's arm and offered her a handsome smile. "And you know I am yours, *master*."

"As you say." The druid sniffed with derision and looked down at Semana. "Please him well, slave, and lathe him deeply, but do not wear him out. He must have strength for the coming moot."

Then Afferath took her leave, the rotted –hem of her robe whispering along Semana's back.

Semana waited a ten-count before she climbed to one knee and looked up at Darak where he sat on his throne. "What the burning Nar was *that*?" she asked.

Darak looked at the mistletoe, then tossed it to land with a rustle in the dirt. "That was one of the Druids I spoke of. Afferath of the Burning Rain: lover, master, and means to an end." Darak leaned his chin on his hand. "I would not call her an ally, but she's least among my enemies. She has her uses."

"Not what I meant." Semana sat up as gracefully as she could, though her back continued to ache with the indignity of lying beneath Darak's boot. "What you did to me. I am not your slave, brother."

"Appearances." He shrugged. "It is fortunate you did not claim to be my sister. The price of wielding Worldfire is solitude. I might have lovers or slaves, but friends or blood? As a rotpriest, I would have been honor-bound to slay you. Afferath might have killed you herself on principle. Or for pleasure."

"My thanks, I suppose," Semana said. "Though if you humiliate me like that again, I will not be so patient." She folded her arms and glared at him. "Do not forget that I still have power."

His hazel eyes considered her dubiously. "She drained your relics, did she not?" he asked. "A potent Worldfire trick—a small expenditure of will but difficult to master. She took the magic of your arms and pulled it into herself. All power serves our mother, and so we can take it when we wish."

"And yet, you have never done that to me," Semana said. "Even when I attacked you that first day, at the bath. Why not?"

"Mayhap I trust you, dear sister," Darak said. "But wait, you were threatening me, and that deserves address." He rose and crossed to a table set with several chipped jugs of various sizes, where he selected a hollowed out horn into which he poured an amber liquid. "Pour you something?"

Semana shook her head.

"I shall drink your portion, then." Darak poured extra mead into his own horn. "I think you know that the Frostfire cannot harm me. So I think you must have meant that other magic that you wield."

"Blood magic." Semana raised her chin. She understood something important in that moment. "That is what you wish of me, is it not? The aid of my Blood magic at this moot, whatever that is?"

Darak smiled with obvious, almost paternal pride. "Twice each year, once in the spring and once in the autumn, when day and night pass in equal balance, the Druids of Ruin gather at a great moot upon Iseldra's Folly."

He gestured out the open tent flap, where Semana saw, in the distance, a great mountain covered to its midsection in stunted trees and badlands, then shorn into blackened ruin above. It looked as though some great catastrophe had struck most of the top roughly from a mountain, leaving a broken, craggy badland where its peak should stand. Smoke rose lazily from it, and the sky above darkened. Dimly, she remembered some sort of story about the landmark, but it seemed to matter little now.

Darak went on. "There they conduct certain rituals to their many gods of the land and sea and sky. Chants, invocations, celebrations of the seasons, and other such frippery. Such things hold little interest for me, as they would any thinking man, but the Children imbue them with deadly import. You and I will make no deprecating noises or express anything less than the utmost faith in these rituals. Indeed, both of us shall take part, and make the blood sacrifices that are required of us."

"You presume much, brother," Semana said. "I'll not give a drop of my blood to these savages."

For a heartbeat, anger flashed across Darak's face—his cheeks reddened as though he'd taken offense—but he reined in his emotions. "As a simple slave girl, your blood means little to them," he said. "It is mine—the blood of a Druid—that will awaken the old powers of Ruin and give their rituals power in their eyes. I do not need you for that, but rather the second part of the day."

"And that is?" Semana crossed her arms.

"The challenge," Darak said. "A battle for the right to stand in the circle. The Children believe only the strong deserve survival, and only the strongest deserve reverence." He drained his horn of mead and cast it aside to bounce across the hard-packed earth. "For years I have been denied my place among them, but by destroying one of my rivals, I will win favor and earn the mantle of druid."

"I thought no man could be a druid," Semana said. "Your Afferath called it *anathema*."

"Weakness is the greater crime against Ruin," he said. "The druids rule through fear. They have never encountered a man who could challenge, much less defeat one of them. As a wielder of Worldfire and Frostfire, I am unprecedented. I will be the first male druid of the circle in a hundred years."

"If you have such power, then why do you need me?" Semana said. "Surely you can defeat them on your own. And if not, then you are not strong enough to stand among them, are you?"

Again she caught that flash of anger, which she did not like—not even a little bit. "I cannot use Frostfire against them openly," Darak said. "I warned you the Children were a superstitious lot. The first druids I met ten years ago…they did not take well to my power. I have learned to hide it."

"What about those near the pool who watched our Frostfire join?" Semana asked. "I've not seen any of them since. That is not a coincidence, I think."

Darak shrugged. "They were valuable servants," he said. "But you are more valuable."

"Perhaps—" He spoke so casually about murdering his own people that Semana felt parched. "Perhaps I'll have that drink after all."

She crossed to the table with the mead and spirits—no wine among the Children—and her hand trembled against one of the bone jars. A drinking horn sat upon the table for her. In truth, she wanted nothing more than the soothing, bitter tea she'd consumed all those years as Mask. At first, she'd drunk it only for appearances, but she'd come to enjoy the taste. It was hers and hers alone, and in that moment, she felt like a small leaf trapped in a strong current, desperately in need of some control over her world.

Darak's hand lay over hers, so subtly it startled her. Semana looked down at his gentle touch, then up into his eyes. They were so like hers it felt like looking into a silvered glass. He caught her arms like a rabbit in a snare, and as much as she did not like to feel trapped, she could not easily pull away.

Then she saw what looked like a black scab on the back of his wrist, and before her eyes it grew down the back of his hand. Revulsion gave her the wherewithal to pull free of his grasp.

"What is that?" Semana screwed up her face in disgust. "Growing on your hand?"

"Apologies." Self-consciously, he scratched the muck off his hand and it disintegrated into specks of smoke in the air. "Have you noticed, when I use my power, or when Afferath struck you down, it produced no desecration? No foul smells? No smoke or taint in the nearby air?"

"No." Semana had cared more about staying alive, but she need not say as much. Then her eyes widened. "Are you saying this Worldfire of yours does not—?"

"Make the world rot?" Darak shook his head ruefully. "Worldfire offers too much power for a mortal body to channel safely, and so it damages us." He showed her the skin where the lesion had been, which was faintly gray. "The more we use the magic, the more we…rot, as it were. Hence the name. My slaves lathe me every day to cleanse me of the marks, but they will always return." He slid his sleeve back over his wrist. "Ruin is a harsh mistress, but her rewards are great."

"That's—that's horrible." Her own magic could make her tired or sore, but imagining one of her relics causing such disfiguring harm to her body turned Semana's stomach. "I did not know."

Darak sucked in a breath, and for a moment she thought he might rebuke her. Instead, he blew it out slowly. "Spare me your pity," he said. "I'd have thought becoming Ruin's greatest slayer would put you past such things as sentiment and intimidation. Did I misjudge you?"

"It was not pity." Semana drew up straighter. "But if it was, I would offer it, whether you accepted it or no."

Darak glared at her, frustrated but intrigued. "Pass well," he said at length. "You will help me at the moot. If I am strong enough to defeat one of the druids on my own, all passes well. If you aid me, we will ensure that none who bear witness live to tell. Understand?"

Semana returned his gaze levelly, smiled, then turned back to the table. "Perhaps," she said.

"*Perhaps*. Ah." Darak smiled ruefully. "The voice is yours, but the words those of the Frostburn. He warned you against me, I expect."

"And if he did?" She poured mead into the horn. "If he is convinced you intend to betray us?"

Darak smiled widely. "Our greatfather's slayer is wise, but has he not lied to you before?"

Semana thought of Regel's healing magic, which he'd kept secret for so long, and about Ovelia's survival. Had she known the Bloodbreaker yet lived, Semana would never have left Tar Vangr, and none of this would have come to pass. In a way, perhaps Regel had been right to keep the truth from her.

"Necessary lies," she said. "I do not thank him, but in his place, I might have done the same."

"And before that?" Darak asked. "He's told you, for instance, how he knew how our father beat our mother but that he refused to intercede? The actions of a man who loves, but is too much a coward to act upon it?" He raised his chin. "He is as much to blame for her death as Paeter."

That struck Semana like a slap. "We were only children. How would you know—?"

"He told me," Darak said. "The day he abandoned me in the wilderness, alone. Regel was the one who took me out to my exile, or did he never tell you that? How he tried to kill me?"

Semana's mind roiled, and she almost dropped her mead horn. She hadn't considered…Then she caught herself. She'd not seen her brother in many years, and she had no particular reason to trust his wild accusations. Next she saw Regel, she would confront him, and he would not lie to her. Until then, she would treat his words as what she suspected they were: an attempt to manipulate her.

"Why do you seek to carve a rift between us?" she asked. "What do you stand to gain?"

She saw a hint of frustration, which only reassured her. He would have to try a different tack.

"No rift," Darak said. "Perhaps the Frostburn has only your welfare at heart, but in this matter, he is mistaken. I mean you no harm, not when you can offer me so much." He laid his hand on her shoulder and turned his reassuring smile on her. "When we can offer *each other* much."

The gesture might have had more impact had Semana not seen Darak do the same to Afferath only a hundred-count before. And she would certainly not fall victim to his charm as easily as some savage. Lightly, she shrugged his hand off. "Stop pressuring me, brother. I will think on it."

"Think on it." Darak bit his lip to restrain himself. "I had forgotten how Calatite women could dither. Men of the wilds are more decisive."

"And barbaric." Semana raised the horn to her nose and inhaled. The aroma was pungent and thick, like the spirits of the mage-cities but with rough notes of earth and rain. "I will think on it."

She could tell her defiance had angered him. Darak took after his father, and the Ravalis were infamous even among the fiery summerblood for their volcanic temperament. However affable their audience might seem, beneath roiled a fierce struggle. One that she would win. Her obstinancy would provoke him—draw him into a misstep.

"Ware that you do not spend too long *thinking* on it," Darak said. "I can offer you—"

"What?" Semana took a sip of her mead, which burned down her throat. "Have you even considered what to offer me? To secure my loyalty? To justify this trust you have placed in me?"

He looked at her, confused for a moment.

"I thought not." Semana grimaced. "You told me all your plans—your hopes and aspirations. You told me about the heresy you plan to commit, to become the first man to stand in the circle of druids. And somehow, you thought I would help you. Why, because we are Blood?"

"That is not enough?" Darak asked.

She gave him a dubious look. "I have never found it so."

Darak drummed his fingers impatiently on the arm of his throne. "What do you want, then?"

Semana stepped toward where he sat on the throne and waved. At first, he did not understand, then his expression grew cold and dangerous. He rose, glaring at her like a spited child, and stepped aside. She settled onto the throne and gazed out the wind-snapping flap and over the tent.

"This," she said. "I want a throne, but not of your little army. I want what is mine by right of my birth and blood." She turned her cold eyes on him. "I want Tar Vangr."

Darak's easy confidence faltered. "You ask me to promise something that I cannot easily deliver. You know as well as I that no horde of barbarians has ever so much as penetrated the outer gate of the City of Steel. Even if—" His eyes narrowed, and Semana fancied she could hear his mind working.

"Too long among the barbarians has slowed your wits, brother," Semana said. "I wouldn't ask you to send this paltry rabble against the walls of Tar Vangr. All I would win would be a mass grave of dead lunatics. No." She gestured to the silver mistletoe branch Afferath had left, which still lay on the floor. "Your teacher showed me something much more valuable you can offer. Power. The circle of druids. With Worldfire, I could throw down the city at a whim."

Darak thought about it a moment, then nodded. "Very well, sister," he said. "You've my vow, if such you'll accept. Help me win a standing in the circle, and I shall bend whatever magicks are mine to command to your cause. Together, we shall win back your city."

"My city," Semana said. "Not yours?"

He hesitated.

The flap of the tent burst in and a breathless sentry stumbled in, eyes wild. He stammered in the language of the Children, and Darak replied in kind. As the man headed off, shouting wildly, Darak's expression soured into something positively hateful.

"What did he say?" Semana asked.

"The Oathbreaker," Darak said between clenched teeth. "He has escaped."

Semana felt a brief thrill, which made her smile. That wasn't the right expression for the moment, though, because Darak's scowl only deepened when he saw her apparent pleasure. He reached toward her—only about halfway, before he caught himself and withdrew his hand. But Semana noticed, and Darak saw that she had.

"He'll come for you," he said. "Stay here."

Then he was gone, leaving Semana standing there in a whirl of thoughts and conflicted feelings. Her fury yet burned at Regel, but it seemed to have simmered to something more manageable that let her think. Of all the figures of her past, she had the least loathing for him, aside from the secrets he'd kept from her. The deception infuriated her, yes, but it did not mean she wanted him to suffer.

Surely Darak was right, and Regel would make an attempt to rescue her. And knowing him, he would succeed. But was that what she wanted?

At least one thing was certain: she was *not* staying put.

THIRTEEN

SNOW CRUNCHED UNDER LEATHER boots with a sound like grinding glass as the seekers approached, breath steaming low in the winter air and cold steel gleaming.

Behind a petrified log, Regel crouched low amongst the frost-laden brambles and willed his heart to slow and his breath to deepen. Two of them he saw, and one he did not: a man and a woman of powerful build cloaked in boiled leather and furs. The man fairly bristled with daggers of various makes and shapes, a number of them thrust through loops of scarified skin on his powerful arms and legs. The woman carried herself in a strange, loping gait, thanks to limbs too long for her compact body and jointed in two places each, rather than one. She looked mundane until she unfolded one long arm from under her robe, revealing a wicked axe that seemed to float in the vicinity of her body as though held by someone else entirely. Just looking at her made Regel feel uneasy, so he closed his eyes and let his senses expand, negating the need to watch.

He intended to remain hidden as they passed. Preferably they would not find him at all, and then he could continue on his way. But if he had to kill them, he would take down the unseen third first, then pick off the others when they came to investigate their companion's absence.

A fight would not be to his advantage, based on positioning and his defenses. He had no armor of any kind, and he wielded only a crude sword from one of his slain warders and a pair of stout knives. Old and battered past the point of reliability, the sword held most of its weight toward the tip of the blade, discouraging Regel's own style, which relied more on finesse and precision than strength. The too-short daggers would make clumsy hand-to-hand weapons and even poorer if thrown. He wondered how the Children of Ruin made do with such inferior arms, which led him to a shuddering fantasy about what a horde of barbarians could accomplish when properly supplied with fine steel and armor.

Destroy what remained of sanity and humanity in the world, no doubt.

After they passed, he waited a ten count, then a twenty count, with no sign of the third seeker. He knew someone was there: someone light of step, favoring oiled leather, and carrying a bow—

The creak of a bowstring alerted him with less than a heartbeat to spare, and Regel tensed to launch himself aside just as an arrow sunk into the log by his face. He caught sight of a lithe figure slinking behind a thick trunk for cover before he could throw a blade. He had no chance to silence her before she loosed a ululating cry that resounded through the icy forest, drawing hunters.

Regel bit his lip, not wasting breath on a curse. He tensed for a leap over the log even as the archer reappeared—just enough to loose another arrow, but neither close nor revealed enough for an effective throw. He jumped with the aid of both arms, wincing as his leg protested, and pain bloomed in his right hand. Regel cleared the log, but his arm jerked painfully taut against it as he stumbled over the other side. The arrow had gone through his palm, pinning his hand in place. Damn and burn.

Awkwardly, Regel drew the jagged sword into his left hand just as the two forward scouts burst from the trees ahead of them. Grinning madly with a mouth full of mangled teeth, the man pulled two daggers from his bare arms and drew them back to throw, even as the woman uttered a guttural warcry and charged, hooked axes spinning in her skeletal hands.

The first dagger, Regel managed to cut from the air, but the clumsy sword couldn't catch the second, which sank into his belly like a hammer. He hardly had a chance to feel the sucking pain before the woman was on him. He warded her off with the sword, but perhaps he should have let her in close. Her long arms gave her an impressive reach, and it was all he could do to dodge aside from one axe chop and catch the other up high with his sword. The attacks were weak from lack of leverage, but he couldn't counter them. At least the dagger man held off on throwing another blade as he waited for an opening.

The woman hissed at Regel and struck again, her axes rushing in from both sides, and he managed to duck one and block the other. The axe hit hard enough to knock him down and to the side, his stuck hand wrenching his arm painfully around the log. She cut at him fast and hard, like a threshing spider with its prey. He worked his blade fast up and down to deflect her attacks, but it left his arm exposed. All the strength in his body ebbed and drained out around the burning knife in his gut.

"*Davar-daen!*" The woman's face lit up in triumph and she aimed her next strike at his arm.

Regel winced, kicked hard off the ground and propelled himself over the log, using momentum to break the arrow's shaft and rip his hand free in the same motion. He could feel the shaft grind against his bones and and blood fountain forth, but he was loose. He pulled his arm back just in time, and the axe sank into the log. He landed on the log and brought the iron sword down into her wrist with all his strength, then elbowed her in the jaw with the same arm. The woman staggered free, screaming in pain as blood streamed from the stump of her arm, and her disembodied hand twitched on the haft of her axe.

He went for a killing thrust with the clumsy sword, but a thrown dagger cut across Regel's face and his left eye exploded with pain as though from a punch. He fell dizzily aside, vainly keeping the sword up in a show of defense. The world spun, and he touched at his face with his bloody, damaged hand: whole and intact, though he could only see haze through his left eye. The dagger had struck handle-first, hard enough to ring his skull.

Distantly, he heard the lopsided woman screaming in rage at the dagger wielder, which made no sense to his addled mind. What she should have done was attack while he staggered hardly able to defend himself. As the world came back into focus, Regel started to make sense of it. The axe woman had marked him as her quarry, and it was a point of honor that she would be the one to kill him. Wonderful.

As they argued, Regel clutched the hilt of the dagger in his belly. It had bit in close to his side, missing his innards. The blood coming out was clean and red. Good. A pierced kidney would have killed him much earlier, or at least crippled him going into this fight.

The woman roared in challenge, holding her remaining axe out wide as well as the bony spur of her bleeding stump. If the maiming caused her any pain, she seemed to have found a way to ignore it. Regel wished he had that power. One thing that had proved clear about his healing magic: it did not work quickly. The wound was starting to hurt less, but would it make the necessary difference?

They faced each other, Regel and the axe wielder, each cradling a damaged right arm to their chests. His sword dripped with blood and gobbets of flesh that had caught in the pitted blade. Her mouth had spread so wide in her roars of pain and rage that her lips started to split. She spat blood and spittle and muttered something in her cruel tongue. Regel had never had an affinity for languages, but the point seemed clear. He bent low in an aggressive stance, scanning her movements for the right angle of attack.

She made the first move, barreling in with a wild cat's hissing roar. She smashed her axe so hard into his intervening sword that the blood-smeared steel sheered off at the force. The axe raked across Regel's arm, carving a jagged flap of flesh to rise into the air. Blood seeped around the wound and splashed in the wake of the axe where her strike had left a deep divot just above his elbow.

Regel's left arm screamed at him in rage but he tried to ignore it. He forced himself to smash the broken hilt of the sword up and into the woman's face, which drove her back half a step. Unbalanced, he tackled her and they tumbled together into the snow, blood tracing their path.

Those long limbs had a dramatic flexibility to them, particularly with the two joints, and Regel found himself trying vainly to pin the barbarian. She wrapped her legs around him and handily slipped free of his holds, turning them around to her own advantage. If not for the significant disadvantage of only having one hand, she would have beat him by now. Ovelia knew far more about this sort of duel than he, and not for the first time, he regretted not trying harder to learn from her. An odd memory of one particular day of fierce lovemaking came to him as he wrestled for his life, and he pushed it aside.

The barbarian ended up atop him, straddling his midsection, her one good hand incapacitating his right arm. He tried to reach one of the stout knives at his belt, but her distended leg was in the way. She drew back her stump, gleaming with shards of yellow bone through a coat of blood and mud, and stabbed at him with the broken wreck of her wrist. The bone tore across Regel's cheek as he jerked his head aside, and he felt hot, fresh blood flow from the cuts. She drew back for another strike.

Bleeding, in agony, his vision shrouded in sweat and the haze of pain, Regel had nothing left. In a fit of madness, he seized her ruined wrist in his half-numb left hand and jabbed the bony spurs at the end into her face. The two joints made it comparatively easy, actually, which was maddening. He felt as much as heard one of her eyes pop like an overripe peach. The woman screamed and reared back, lightening the pressure on him for just a heartbeat.

It was enough. Regel seized one of the knives in his good hand and jabbed it into her stomach. He pumped his arm over and over, stabbing the blade into her chest and stomach half a dozen times before she let out the first sound of pain. She punched him again, this time slamming her torn arm into his forehead. Blood fell into his eyes, but he kept stabbing. He hardly knew if he still held the dagger or whether he'd lost it in one of the strikes. It hardly mattered.

She hit him again, but softer this time. She had significantly less strength to expend. His already damaged eye swelled shut from the beating, and Regel could dimly see through the other. He kept stabbing and the barbarian's whole body shook, flailing desperately as it approached collapse. She tried to punch him again, but this time her arm only ended up in the blood-softened snow. She didn't push herself back up, even as he kept stabbing her, his arm moving slower and weaker.

Finally they lay together, Regel struggling for breath, and the barbarian shuddering in her death throes atop him. She felt as heavy as the dirt piled on a grave, but he managed to slither out from under her weight. He coughed and tried to climb to a sitting position, wiping at his face with filthy hands.

The glint of steel in the dying rays of the winter sun reminded him of his situation, and he looked up to see the dagger wielder standing over him, a blade in either hand. Regel knew he didn't have the strength to dodge or deflect either throw. He blinked the blood from his eye and panted, desperate to think. He expanded his senses and the world seemed to slow…

Gilt stepped out of the barbarian's shadow and smashed him to the ground like a fearsome wind. Even before the barbarian hit the ground, Gilt seized the daggers floating in the air where he had dropped them, then fell upon him. With unerring deftness, one dagger went into his kidney and the other into his heart. Gilt caught and cradled the dying man, who looked up into the fae's dark face with wild terror. For one slow heartbeat, Gilt looked deep into the dagger man's eyes, seeing the depths of his soul and the terrible deeds he kept locked away there. The fear drained away, replaced with something like peace.

Then with a twist, Gilt snapped the man's head around and let his lifeless body flop to the ground.

Regel coughed and climbed to one knee, wincing as he touched the wound in his side. "Waited enough?" he asked.

The fae shrugged. From under his cloak, he pulled out a short bow adorned with feathers, along with a quiver of arrows of familiar green fletching. Regel compared the shaft he'd broken out of his hand to these arrows, and sure enough, it was the same. Back past the log, he thought he saw the archer's boot protruding out from around the covering trunk. Gilt had been there, and Regel probably owed the Deathess his life. Again.

He got to his feet and bent over the dead dagger-wielder. These blades at least were of quality, with the distinct disadvantage that he'd have to pull them out of the man's flesh in order to claim them, because that's how he had carried them. This particular Child of Ruin had no use for sheathes, it seemed. Regel started with the two the barbarian had been holding: the first a straight and narrow Vangryur blade, the second a wide-bladed crescent, perhaps from the Free Isles.

He claimed four more knives of different shapes and sizes, drawing them gently from the barbarian's body. He'd been a ruthless killer in life, yes, but even in death he was still a man.

Gilt watched silently, his cloak wafting slightly in the breeze, his dark eyes weighing.

No sword, and Regel had never been much for axes. Another pitched battle wouldn't pass well for him anyway—not until he healed and found a better armament. It would have to be stealth.

Gilt started walking away, but Regel did not follow. He saw an opportunity, and he started limping back toward the camp. He did not bother to call back for Gilt. No need.

Every step ached. His crippled leg hurt particularly as he walked, every step sending fresh lances of pain down through his knee and up into his hip. He could only see out of one eye—he hoped the other would see again when the swelling went down—and his face itched and burned as though cut by a thousand tiny shards of glass. His right hand was a mass of blood and pain, and his left arm was mostly red and black from the long, rough cut in his bicep. His midsection felt like one huge sucking wound.

Semana. He had to help Semana.

Gilt appeared out from behind a boulder nearer the camp, waiting as Regel made his slow way. The fae's eyes held no judgment, but his stance indicated curiosity.

"I'm not leaving without her," Regel said. "Want to stop me? You'll have to—"

He stumbled and would have fallen, but he caught and steadied himself on the boulder.

The Deathless touched Regel's cheek tenderly. There was power in his body, and the energy between them felt suddenly electric and alive. He nodded in the opposite direction: the path to Necthana.

"No," Regel said. "I've made my choice."

"And she has made hers." Gilt's voice rolled like thunder. "You should respect it."

Regel gazed out over the trees to the towers of smoke rising from the barbarian encampment. At this distance, he could hear the warhorns of men and women preparing for a march. If he did not go to Semana now, she would not be here when he returned. But even if he could sneak through the camp, and even if he could confront her alone, would she turn from her path and go with him? After the lies he had told her and the truths she had spoken to him?

"We have to try," he said. "Whatever it takes."

Semana moved quickly from Darak's tent and down among the ranks of the barbarians. The whole camp was up and on its feet, tearing down tents and packing up weapons, saddling shaggy winter horses and filling wagons. They made ready for a march, she realized, and not to seek out Regel.

If she meant to slip away, this was her opportunity: during the confusion, she could vanish, and by the time Darak realized she had gone, she would have found Regel and they would go far from here.

A shadow interposed itself in her path, and she found herself looking up at possibly the largest man she had ever seen. Semana was not short, but her head only came up to his belly, and he looked more than twice as wide as she stood. He was a solid mass of muscle and bone covered over in boiled leather and dark furs. His face looked half formed from clay, and Semana realized only after a moment that it had been badly burned—probably purposefully. He wore silver mistletoe on a thong around his neck, which Semana took to mean he was Afferath's man. He looked down at her with unfeigned interest.

"Stand aside," she said in the high speech, hoping it would translate to the barbarian tongue. In any case, Mask's gravelly voice seemed well suited to the words of the Children.

"No, Starmane," he said in passable Calatite.

Starmane. That was a name she had not heard before. It also meant she hadn't done as well hiding her distinctive silver-blonde hair. "I belong to Dar-Karsk," she said. "I am his acolyte. To strike me is to invite…" She struggled for the word. "Conflict."

"Mountain's Rage fears no boy that rots," he said. "Mountain's Rage takes what he wants. If Dar-Karsk has claim on her, let him fight for her."

Instinctively, Semana reached for the power in her silver glove, but she found nothing there. It hadn't yet regained its charge after Afferath drained it. She dared not risk Frostfire openly. The blood magic beckoned, but she had only just begun to taste the barbarian's blood when he laid one massive hand around her upper arm and laid the other on her chest, his fingers thick and hard as steel rods. She flinched but could not get away.

"Ample and strong," he said. "Good. Endures pain."

If this was what passed among the Children of Ruin as flirting, she wanted no part of it. In part, it was her difficulty with the language, but mostly it was simply who she was. She instinctively pulled away, and Mountain's Rage's lewd smile turned to stormy, offended anger. Rage rose in her as well, sublimating into cold, calculating violence.

Their little confrontation had drawn onlookers from all sides: distorted faces and cruel smiles. Confronted with this giant of a man, at the center of a horde of barbarians, Semana felt the air crushing in on her from all sides, making it difficult to breathe. *No.* She would tolerate the pressure, but she would not let it make her small. If she kept delaying him, it would give her blood magic time to work.

"Step back, fool," she said, not bothering to speak the words of the barbarians. She could taste the brute's blood. His strength beat against her. Could she overcome him before he could strike her down? "Step back, or I will slay you where you stand."

Her words meant nothing to Mountain's Rage, but he understood her tone. He smiled, but there was nothing gentle in it. "Strong," he said. "Good. Mountain's Rage will enjoy breaking—" His words trailed away, and his face contorted in the expression of a man suddenly ill at ease. "Break—breaking—"

Later, Semana would recall that she'd heard the voice first, but in truth, the man did not speak. He seized the attention of all through force of presence alone. The darkness bled from him and made the gathered barbarians tremble with a sudden chill none could credit. For her part, Semana knew immediately what had come to pass, and it filled her with dread and excitement both.

"Away."

Gilt's voice was mild, but it rippled through the crowd of barbarians like a stone dropped in a pond. And they obeyed, even if none could explain why. Perhaps they saw him for what he was: a true heir of Ruin, while they were but pretenders. The barbarians shuffled away, and Semana found herself face to face with the specter of darkness she'd thought lost to them. It struck her as odd that she'd cared so deeply about his disappearance.

"Semana," came a far weaker voice. The darkness around Gilt lifted, revealing Regel standing in his shadow. The man looked terrible—exhausted, wounded, and barely up on his feet. He looked at Semana with eyes that were beyond desperate. He reached weakly toward her. "We have to go."

Semana took a step back, just out of his reach. "You look awful, *father*."

The contempt she put into that last word should have ended it, but Regel's expression only grew confused. "We don't have time," he said. "We need to leave—"

Semana stood firm, arms crossed. "Why yes, I pass perfectly well," she said. "And Gilt is alive. Yet another lie you allowed me to believe, Regel." The omission was not a surprise, but it infuriated her all the same. "I assume he rescued you, and now you would rescue me, is that it?"

Regel stared at her, uncertain. How sad, to watch the man who knew everything grow confused.

"And you," Semana looked to Gilt. "You've been following me all this time, waiting for the right moment to—what? Whisk me away? Here, in the heart of the enemy's camp? You are bold, Deathless."

"Yes," he said.

He spoke seemingly without guile, which annoyed her as much as she appreciated it. Everyone in her world had either lied to her or tried to murder her: Ovelia, Regel, Darak, Afferath, these barbarians, everyone. Not since Tithian had she had a companion she could trust, and she was glad he lived. Still, his appearance now was…inconvenient. And that he'd brought Regel did not speak well for him.

"Semana." Regel looked around at the barbarians, who had started to break free of their stupor, eyeing them with increasing curiosity rather than awe. "We need to—"

Semana held up a hand to silence him and continued to address Gilt.

"I see that you've appointed yourself my warder—what I don't see is the why." Semana glared up into Gilt's face. "Are you captivated by my dubious charms, or do you seek to defend the scion of your precious Frostburn? Because we're not on the best of terms." She glanced toward Darak's tent. "I'm sure he's told you his suspicions of my brother. Do you share them? Or perhaps you are jealous?"

"Yes," Gilt said without hesitation.

His abrupt answer surprised her, then irritated her. He never seemed to answer a direct question. "Which?" she asked.

"*Semana.*" Regel talked right over Gilt. "We must go now, while the pass to Necthana is clear." Again he extended his hand. "Come."

The mention of the Deathless City made Semana pause. She needed an army to overthrow the Ravalis, and she'd thought Darak the solution. Again, however, she thought of a horde of Deathless as strong and beautiful as Gilt. If she refused to go, did she trade a keen sword for a dull knife?

Around them, the camp stirred, broken of its lethargy and had begun to grow restless. Semana saw Mountain's Rage dispatch a messenger, no doubt bound for Afferath. Whatever she chose, she had to move quickly.

Gilt gazed at her levelly, cutting like a blade to the truth behind her words. "She will not come," he said for Regel's benefit.

"No," Semana said. "I am not finished here."

Tragedy etched Regel's face. "Semana, you don't know what you're doing."

"The problem, Oathbreaker," Semana said, her voice breaking into Mask's rasping drawl, "is that you think that."

Regel fell back a step as though she had slugged him in the gut. He seemed to age at least a dozen years, his featured growing weathered and frail. And just at that moment, Semana was pleased to see it.

Regel disappeared back into Gilt's shadow, steadying himself on the Deathless's arm. Gilt merely looked at Semana, his face placid. Then he nodded, perhaps in understanding or in resignation. "The way to Necthana will remain open until the day eclipses the night upon the equinox."

"That is the same day as the Circle's great moot," Semana said.

Gilt gestured toward the white-capped mountains a dozen leagues to the north. "I tell you this so that you will know when retreat is no longer a choice."

"I never retreat."

Now the crowd around them had grown, and she could see someone forcing a path through the barbarians from the direction of Darak's tent.

Gilt eyed her levelly, then nodded. "You are intriguing, Semana Denerre nô Ravalis."

For a first, Semana did not know what to say. "Thank you?" she tried, but when she looked, he had vanished like mist on the breeze, taking Regel with him.

Damn and burn. Maybe she should have gone after all.

Darak appeared through the ranks of the barbarians. He must have seen the last words passed between Gilt and Semana, because in the depths of his cowl, his face betrayed a storm of emotions: uncertainty, a little fear, and above all, relief. He looked pleased.

She nodded to Darak, and as though that had broken some spell, he came toward her and took her hands in his. "He was going to take you," her brother said under his breath. "But you stayed."

Semana nodded. "Yes," she said. "I won't leave you. Not again."

Darak seemed pleased at that response. Then his expression deepened to something dark and serious. "Before, you asked me if I loved Tar Vangr," he said. "The answer is no. I left that life behind me long ago. " He shook his head. "Take your city of cold, unfeeling stone, and be welcome to it. I prefer the winds and fires of Ruin."

"Then we shall bring those upon our enemies." Semana offered him her hand. "Together."

"We shall destroy them all." Eyes smoldering, Darak bowed low and kissed the back of her hand. "Together."

Semana's heart leaped. This was what she had wanted. It was not how she had imagined it, perhaps, but for the first time, Semana felt hope enter her heart. The desperate dream she'd nurtured had a chance of coming true.

A cold voice brought her back to reality. "A truth revealed, a mystery uncovered."

Afferath stood across from Semana, flanked by Mountain's Rage and a hulking barbarian woman she had not seen before. They had been watching the whole time. The druid's cold gaze fell upon Semana with new admiration and curiosity. "This acolyte has more secrets than you told, Dar-Karsk."

Suddenly, Semana became very aware of how many eyes fell upon them, and she started thinking of what that all must have looked like. Darak had come to her unescorted, and he looked small and vulnerable compared to Afferath and her companions. Semana, however, knew well that a Ravalis became most dangerous when cornered. Belatedly, the watching barbarians bowed their heads in deference, as though they'd only slowly recognized his presence.

Darak spread his arms and raised his voice to address the collected barbarians. The wind caught his words and swept them throughout the camp. Worldfire, she thought.

"Blood of my blood, blades drawn with mine," he said, his manner one of heightened excitement. "Today, one of the little Gods of Ruin has shown favor upon us and our cause."

God? What god? That sounded ridiculous until Semana realized he meant Gilt. To the backward Children of Ruin, surely a Deathless fae must seem like a god. Oh, her clever brother. No wonder he had talked his way into their highest esteem.

Darak joined Semana at the center of the camp but strode right past her. He waved his hand over the ground where Gilt had stood. "The very ground echoes with his touch, churning and seething with unfulfilled desire," he said. "His blessing is as yet unclaimed, but it will be." He pointed to Semana, his eyes wide, his voice growing ecstatic. "This woman. She is his chosen one. Surely if she stands beside us, he will come again, and our strength will grow."

To Semana, these invocations sounded like gibberish, but the gathered barbarians declaimed shouts of triumph and fervor. They stirred to frenzy all around her. No longer did she sense rivalries and loathing, but rather a communal sense of lust and rage. They desired blood and death and pain. Darak called Gilt a god, and they believed him, one and all.

No, Semana realized—perhaps not *all.* Afferath stood apart, arms down at her sides, hands clenching to fists and opening once more into claws. Rage grew in her, but rather than cast it up into the heavens as an offering to the goddess Ruin, Afferath directed it toward Semana. The druid could not know the truth, but she could certainly suspect it. And that, Semana knew, was dangerous. A challenge.

Darak seemed to realize it as well. "Afferath, Mistress of the Burning Rain." He extended one hand to the druid. "You stand in witness of Ruin's miracle. Will you deny it?"

All eyes turned to Afferath. She hesitated, then wrenched her damning gaze from Semana. The barbarians were watching her now, keen on her reply. She raised her chin to Darak. "I confirm it." She spread her arms wide. "Go forth. Rut. Kill. Consume. Give glory to Ruin!"

At her pronouncement, the barbarians roared in a tumult so loud it made Semana's head ache. A nearby one punched her neighbor in the face with a fist full of nails, making blood fly. The man tackled her in return, and their lips locked in a fearsome kiss that became a gnashing flurry of teeth and tongues. As she watched, they tore at one another's clothing and thrust into one another right there in the clearing. A man crammed his member into a kneeling woman's mouth and she gnawed on it with sharpened teeth even as she tugged at his massive balls. Two women shoved fingers, then whole fists into each other while a third took turns thrusting her tongue into their mouths.

All around Semana, more barbarians coupled or grouped: men with women, men with men, women with women, and many whose sex Semana could not begin to guess. They flailed with fists and feet, subduing would be partners and pulling others in harder. All around her, the Children of Ruin boiled over into an orgy of violence and pain that she could scarce believe, let alone understand.

"Girl."

Semana turned to find Afferath behind her. The druid clasped her about the face and kissed her full on the lips. The sensation was wet and hard and Afferath tasted of smoke and rain. Afferath's jaw ground against her own through the layers of flesh, and the druid's tongue shot out and scraped at her firmly shut teeth. Then bright pain bloomed in her lip as Afferath bit her. Semana recoiled, but she could not break free of the druid's much stronger grasp.

"Do not forget yourself, child," Afferath said.

Finally, Afferath noted Semana's struggle and pulled away, her face beyond angry. She raised one hand languidly and struck Semana a sudden blow to the face with the heel of her palm. The strike put Semana on the ground as surely as a hit from a hammer. The world blurred, and she found herself looking up at Afferath. The druid needed no words—her angry glare carried it all. That, and the clouds swirling around her, crackling with lightning. Her magic had turned her fists into living stone.

"Stay down," Afferath said. "If you would live, do not defy me again."

Perhaps it was her mother's will in her, or her father's stubbornness, but Semana got up.

Blood drooled from her mouth onto the frozen earth, and her face resonated with pain in exploding waves. Anger rose, but instead of heat, Semana felt only cold inside. She looked down at her shaking hand, pillowed under her chin, and saw silvery flames crackling around her fingers. She remembered Darak's warning, but right then it hardly mattered. She would have her vengeance.

Then her brother stepped between them, the winds swirling around his limbs. He had eyes only for Afferath, and she for him. They confronted one another, both burning with Worldfire. She raged with the power of the storm and the strength of mountains, while Darak's power was more subtle. Semana could feel the silvery Frostfire burning inside him, lurking just beneath the surface. Some sort of understanding passed between them, a conflict without words or actions—only will.

Finally, Afferath lowered her fists, and the clouds parted around her. She nodded to him, and he bowed. Slowly, he drew open his robe, then let it fall to a puddle around him, leaving him standing naked in the circle of the writhing army. Black mold snaked across his back and dotted his arms and legs, but his scarred body seemed mostly pure. Afferath nodded once more, smiled slightly, then strode toward him. She took his cock in her hand and stroked it with her thumb, making Darak shudder. He glanced at Semana and offered her a small smile.

More than a little nauseated, Semana had seen quite enough. She stumbled away, and none of the occupied barbarians stopped her. She wondered if she shouldn't have left with Gilt and Regel after all.

But no. Her brother had promised her they would destroy her enemies.

She would hold him to that promise.

BOOK FOUR: SEEKERS

Five years previous—Tar Vangr Bay—Spring 977 Sorcerus Annis

THE HEAT OF BOILING magic below the surface turned the dark ice to slush, which flew in waves as the rattling ornithopter skimmed the surface of the bay, its silver rings vibrating with a low whine that set his teeth on edge. The salt water stung his nose and seared his skin, and his legs had long since cramped in the small space for passengers.

Regel Winter could bear it, though. He had to know for sure.

The third day after Ruin's Night found him vainly scouring the wreckage of *The Heiress* yet again, looking for any sign of Princess Semana or the crew. It had been easy enough to slip among the volunteer searchers and rescue teams dispatched to the wreckage. All the credential the directors of the recovery effort had required was that Regel had his own ornithopter and was willing to help. They didn't care about his name or ulterior motives—they were too shocked about the downing of the skyship and the apparent death of their beloved princess.

The last days had seen the city go from confused horror to deep and lasting sorrow. First *The Heiress* broke up over the bay in a series of spectacular explosions, going down with all hands. Then word emerged that the Winter King Orbrin Denerre was dead, murdered at the hands of his most trusted warder, Ovelia Dracaris. They were already calling her the Bloodbreaker for her infamy. And, of course, on the same night the Crown Prince Paeter Ravalis had fallen to Regel's own blade, which caused less shock and anger, but did little to stave off feelings of insecurity. Chaos ruled at the palace, and Regel knew it was only a matter of time before the Ravalis moved to punish whatever scapegoats they could offer up as blood sacrifice for the debacle.

At least his name had not entered into it. Most of Tar Vangr thought Frostburn, the Shadow of the Winter King, was but a myth. Demetrus Ravalis knew better, of course, and if they had the treacherous Ovelia in custody, surely she would not hesitate to name him. His old hideaways were useless—the places he'd taken Ovelia, the private darknesses they'd shared… That, he could not think about. If he did, he would start screaming and perhaps never stop.

The madness of it all clawed at the edges of Regel's mind, threatening to unmoor him from the world entirely. He could cling to sanity only out of a vainglorious fantasy that Semana might have survived despite the crushing weight of reality.

Ornithopter crews scoured the site of the crash, desperate for survivors. It was difficult, heartbreaking, dangerous work. The ice-choked water could chill to the bone at the slightest touch, and seemingly secure footing on a floating bulkhead might give way unexpectedly and swallow a would-be rescuer whole. Worst of all, the skyship's mage-engine hadn't fully discharged, and it filled much of the bay with roving, wild magic. Power scythed like spears of lightning or turned air to acid, choking and burning the lungs out of any hapless seeker who had the misfortune to step into a tainted area.

Despite the hazards, some had hoped that survivors might be recovered from the wreckage that first day. Crews had worked dawn to dusk in search of anyone trapped in the sinking morass, but all the bodies they pulled from the cold waters were mutilated and frozen black. That first night, after the mage-engine finally exhausted itself, the creatures of the Dusk Sea went about their work, leaving dull red patches of blood and disembodied body parts floating in open areas free of debris. Few held out any hope that anyone or anything would have survived longer than that.

Regel Winter was one of those few.

Theirs was one of three ornithopters out on the water that day, tracing over reaches of the bay they had crossed numerous times before. They sent down divining rods and hooks in search of more bodies, salvageable devices, weapons—anything that might offer some clue as to what had transpired. For all their efforts, they had found a corpse around midday, or at least part of one: the torso of a well-built man, one arm neatly lopped off and the rest of his limbs mostly eaten away along with his head. Regel had started to discount the find as irrelevant, but he recognized a tattoo on the left shoulder depicting the wings of a mechanical dragon.

"Syr Sargaunt," he said, his stomach sinking. "Damn and burn."

"Knew him?" Serris looked over at him uncertainly, holding the controls steady as they hovered a pace or so above the dark waters.

Regel nodded. "Princess Semana's elite bodyguard," he said. "He would not have left her side. If he is dead..." He shook his head.

"Sorry." A bit of blood oozed out to stain the bandage on Serris's cheek where Paeter had slashed her face open just three days before. "Take him with us?" she asked. "Proper burial rites?"

Regel shook his head. They didn't have the time for such things. Being out on the water was already drawing suspicion. At this point, they must resemble illicit salvagers: carrion birds trying to claim what they could after everything was picked over. All it would take was one Ravalis patrol, and that would mark the end of it.

He detached the body from the hook and let it slide back into the water, whispering a farewell. Despite their differences, Sargaunt had been a good man, and Regel knew he had given his life to save the Princess. Alas, it appeared that it had all passed in vain.

"Keep going," Regel said. "Turn north toward the city."

Wordlessly, Serris flicked a lever, and the rings began to turn around the ornithopter once more, propelling it onward in their ongoing search. For never having flown an ornithopter before, Serris had proved remarkably adept, if a little shaky. Confidence would come with time.

Regel sighed and extended his senses, seeing without seeing, searching. But the sea was cold and dead, just like his world.

He could not say exactly how much time passed between the discovery of Sargaunt and when Serris cleared her throat. Three days they'd known one another, and she already knew well when to speak up and when to leave him be. The woman had proved more than just a worthy squire: she'd offered him a shoulder to lean upon and a willing ear, when he felt like talking. He'd chosen well with her.

"Master," Serris said in his ear. "Master, we should go. Nothing for us here."

She was right, of course, but he hardly heard her. His eye caught on something, and his heart sank to behold it. "Take us down," he said.

"But the engine's charge—" She started to protest, but he cut her off with a sorrowful look.

"Please," he said. "I need to see."

They sank toward the dark waters, and Serris set the rings to supporting the ornithopter as it hovered. Below them, part of one of the great gold rings that had propelled *The Heiress* protruded out of the water, bent and partly split apart through the force of the impact. Ancient runes scribed along the gold flickered with the last vestiges of mostly spent magic, weathered and dimmed through the lapping waves. He'd seen this part of the wreckage on previous days, noting its position at least five paces higher, though now it had sunk to a tiny hump over the water.

It was not the tarnished gold ring that caught and held his attention, but something attached to it and streaming raggedly in the wind: a scarf of crimson silk. The ornithopter hovered in close enough for Regel to touch the frayed fringe of the scarf, and he recognized it instantly as the very one he had given to Ovelia to give to Semana. He'd found it among his things—a last keepsake from her mother—and though he had never allowed himself to have a relationship with the girl, he had wanted her to have it. It meant something, even that indirect message of affection. That…

"Master?"

Tears streamed down Regel's face, even though he'd not noticed at first that he wept.

"Get us back to the dock," he said. "This place is nothing but a graveyard."

Sure enough, the Ravalis were out in force on Tar Vangr dock. Regel saw four or five dustknights milling about, inspecting boats docked and ornithopters simmering with energy. One of them waved their ornithopter down, indicating an open landing spot amongst a sea of crates.

Serris touched Regel's arm. "I'll talk to them," she said. "Know how to handle men like that."

Regel nodded and made no move to rise as she lifted the cockpit and climbed out. As she headed toward the dusters, she walked with a casual grace that neither accentuated her sensuality nor denied it. Serris was a woman in command of herself and this situation, whether the warders knew it or not. And seeing the duster's easy reaction, he understood entirely why Serris had approached them in that way.

He looked back over the bay. The world seemed so small and stale. Empty.

"Hold there," said a man on the dock.

He recognized that voice, from somewhere in the dim recesses of his memory. There was so much in the way—so much despair and self-hatred and recrimination—that it blocked his thinking. Only the tone pulled his attention from his vigil, and he looked back around to where Serris stood amongst four men arranged around her like like a kill squad. Three of them were faceless Ravalis warriors in humming power armor, while the fourth stood tall and arrogant in his gold-inlaid plate armor and azure half-cloak.

This man, Regel recognized. Davrik Rolan, lesser heir of a thinblood loyal to the Ravalis, and until recently, one of Paeter's boon companions. He had been there on Ruin's Night, when Regel cut down the Crown-Prince and escaped into the gloom, and that meant he might recognize Serris. From his confrontational, in-control body language—arms crossed, shoulders back, chin slightly raised—it seemed he did. He looked down at her with the smug confidence of a predator that has sighted its prey.

"Where did you get that, fair one?"

He reached out and touched at the bandage wrapped over Serris's face, but she recoiled before he could touch her. This elicited a series of whistles and gentle mockery, as the three dusters shifted from acknowledging her strength to uniting against her. How like the Summerblood to turn against a woman at the slightest provocation. Regel suspected he would never understand the source of their contempt for the feminine. In his own experience, the fiercest, most dangerous foes he had ever faced had been women.

"You can't be making much coin trawling for scraps like this, sweetling." Davrik gave her a lewd smile. "Perhaps you should come with us. I could make it well worth your time."

"Flattering," Serris said, her voice dry as dusty bones. "But no." She'd taken a subtle dueling stance and Regel saw her hand reaching around toward her lower back. "Better step back, little man, if you value your pride. Shame to put you down in front of your little boys."

That made Regel sigh. When Serris said she knew how to deal with these men, he hadn't thought she meant provoking them into a fight. He climbed out of the ornithopter, his tired limbs finding new vitality in the face of this emerging threat.

Her bold words seemed to have impressed the dusters, who turned their jeers and smiles to Davrik. Apparently, they didn't much care for the minor heir of Rolan. Perhaps Serris had played this right after all. Regel could tell, however, that her bravado was just that: an act. She trembled slightly, confronted with these four armed and armored men. He'd only drawn her up from slavery three days before. Serris would need more time before she could use her powers with real confidence.

His precious masculinity challenged, Davrik couldn't well back down from Serris's implied threat. His face grew stormy and he reached for her. "See here, you gutterborn slag—"

"Hold."

They looked up as he approached, their faces growing somewhat wary. Always on the small and wiry side of strength, Regel's physicality had never truly intimidated his foes, and that had always served him well. He faced the four of them, one hand on the edge of his cloak, the other hidden. His interference changed the dynamic considerably, and all the ease Serris had inspired turned to steely caution. The dusters stood on edge, hands near to weapons.

Davrik goggled at Regel, then an easy smile spread across his flushed face. "What say you, graybeard?" he asked, trying to draw Regel into his circle of allies. "Is she not a fetching thing, this one?" He teased his fingers along a lock of Serris's blonde hair, and she jerked away as though stung. "Do you think she has the same curls between her legs, too?"

"Stand away from her," Regel said. "I won't say it again."

Casters came up in the hands of two of the dusters, while the third reached for the hilt of a sword. Davrik's smile became a sneer. "This is not your business," he said. "I suggest you move along."

Casually, Regel swept his cloak open to reveal Frostburn drawn and hungry in his other hand. The blue mage-glass blade made the air around it crackle with the chill. It hungered for their blood. Craved their warmth. He'd not fed it in three days, and Frostburn held a bottomless depth of need.

The dusters' eyes widened. They'd heard the stories, and they knew that blade. The casters pointed in his direction trembled. The one with a mere sword shook, the point wobbling toward the ground as though the blade had grown too heavy for him.

By contrast, Davrik merely furrowed his brow and reacted with confusion rather than fear. He did not recognize Frostburn or understand its significance. How like a thinblooded lordling, to ignore the tales of mere smallfolk to his own peril. And how ironic, that the last time that sword had tasted blood, it had done so in the same brothel he'd frequented that night.

"What dust magic is this?" He gestured idly to Regel. "Take him as well. No one threatens the Blood of Rolan—" He noticed the wave of fear that had transfixed his companions and grimaced. "What troubles you, cowards? Cast upon him. Kill him if you must...What? What passes?"

They had started to back away as a group, weapons shaking as they covered Regel. One—the duster with the sword—broke and ran full out, his armor clanking as he went.

"What?" Davrik asked. "I don't—" He looked to Serris, who was beaming back at Regel, and snatched at her arm. "You! Don't think I don't know you, little whore! You're coming with—"

Serris pulled the dagger Regel had given her out of the sheath at the base of her spine and jabbed it into Davrik's bent wrist between the plates of his armguard and the edge of his gauntlet. He screeched in sudden pain, released her, and staggered free. Serris looked at the blade with wonder, hardly believing what she had just struck him so effortlessly, then followed Davrik, menacing him with the point.

The heir of Rolan ran away, cursing his seeping wound and hurling invectives back towrd them.

When they had all fled, Regel sheathed Frostburn and let his cloak fall back around himself. He'd come so close to using the blade once more, after he had sworn never again to draw it.

That would have been yet another failure to add to his weight.

"Should've handled that better," Serris said. "Next time, I will."

Regel nodded. He had no doubt.

"They'll report this." Serris wiped the dagger off on the hem of her own cloak. "We should go."

Regel stared down at his hand, still cold from Frostburn.

"Ornithopter still has some charge left," Serris said. "We could take it and go wherever you want. We could—" Her eyes widened as she beheld Regel, his face stricken with a deep, preoccupying despair. Her eyes softened. "Master."

The tears had frozen on Regel's face, and he started weeping anew.

Uncertainly, Serris touched fingers to Regel's face. "It was not your fault," she said. "You do not have to do this." She laid her hands along his cheeks as they stood there on the pier.

"No," he said, catching her wrists in his hands. "Thank you, but no. These tears—I *should* weep. I cannot forget, and nor should any of us."

"So we won't." Serris touched the last tear on his face, then put her smoke-stained finger below her eye. It left a black smudge shaped like a teardrop, and he suspected she'd left the same mark on his face. "Not ever."

Then she leaned in and kissed him on the lips.

It was a gentle thing, that kiss, but not chaste and certainly not innocent. Serris may have been fresh to the ways of battle and intimidation, but she knew how to kiss and caress. More, the warmth in her recognized the cold in him, and Regel wanted nothing more than to embrace her and forget about his failings and his darkness.

They drew apart and looked at one another, Serris's expression conveying an offer.

Regel laid his hands on Serris's shoulders and looked into her face. She seemed so young and vibrant—so full of power and purpose—and he felt so old and empty. And she was kind: a trait rarely preserved among those who had grown up in such harsh circumstances as she had.

"You don't have to do this," Regel said. "My tragedy is not yours. I thank you, but—"

"Want to." She took his face in her hands and pressed her nose to his. "You object?"

In all his years, Regel Winter had known many women, but he had only loved one—Princess Lenalin—and she was long dead. Ovelia he had slept with many times, but both of them had pretended she was Lenalin. It had simply not occurred to him there might exist others who might desire him.

"I loved one woman," Regel said. "I'm not sure I can love another."

"Think this love, old man? This is solace. Take it or no. Don't fool yourself." She smiled wryly. "Don't know if you're worthy of me, come to think of it."

He gazed at her, this young woman he'd chanced upon in the commission of his final duty, and wondered how he'd ever thought their meeting random. Her hand on his chest felt warm and comforting, and that was what he needed.

"I'm not…" He shook his head. "I'm not ready. Not yet."

He would have understood had she grown angered or annoyed, but instead she merely nodded and touched his hand. "Right," Serris said. "Tell me when you are." She rose. "I'll power up the ornithopter. Take your time."

As she walked away, Regel looked out over the bay, where the last pieces of The Heiress sank slowly beneath the surface. He had to accept that Semana was well and truly gone—that she had died never knowing the truth—and it cut him to the core. All those he loved, gone. His world, ended. But perhaps…

Perhaps something yet remained. Some measure of justice—or at least vengeance.

Serris had reminded him that he had something yet to give, and much yet to do.

He nodded to himself in the failing sunlight, as the cold winds of dusk rose to swirl the powdered snow around him.

Regel Winter was not done yet.

FOURTEEN

Narkggr Wound, The Winter Wilds—Present Day, 982 Sorcerus Annis

Five days past the barbarian camp, Regel and Gilt found themselves at the borders of Necthana, land of the Deathless fae. Like a great scar risen on the World of Ruin's flesh, the hulking Narkggr Wound grew nearly impassable as the snows deepened, but they'd managed even despite Regel's crippled leg and his slowly healing wounds. He'd not allowed himself to complain, even when his aches grew far worse in the cold. In truth, his mind remained far behind.

At the height of the mountain pass above Narkggr, Regel found himself gazing back toward the valley of the barbarian camp. At this distance, he couldn't have picked out discrete forms or even tents, but he expected to see something. Instead, he made out only a blighted black stain on the valley floor, as though the very presence of the barbarians had burned the land of life.

Gilt moved on a few steps before he realized Regel had stopped, then waited for him silently. They had no words to exchange. The fae seemed to understand he needed a moment.

Regel had spent the first day in a blind despair, eating, drinking, and saying nothing. The first hour or so after their escape had been their one chance to take her, and she had turned them away. Again he had failed her. He could not stop failing her.

Brute pragmatism kept Regel from rushing back to free Semana despite what she had said. Even if he managed to reach her, even if he could transcend his wounds and overcome the numbers arrayed against him, he could never have managed to escape with her. They would have died together, and then he would have failed her another way.

Gilt had spoken of the matter only once, to claim that Semana had made the choice of her own will and he should respect that choice, and Regel had spent days trying to refute that assertion. She was confused. She was bewitched. She didn't have the slightest idea the danger she was in. She had rejected him not because she didn't want his help, but because she didn't trust him and didn't know what to think.

So much effort did Regel spend convincing himself of these facts that he began talking to himself. Arguing with himself. When Gilt regarded him in obvious concern, Regel rebuked the Deathless angrily or ignored him entirely.

It was only as the fourth day dawned, finding him cold and bone-weary, that Regel started to wonder if the Deathless had spoken true. All the lies Regel had told Semana and all the secrets between them had bubbled up, and there was no way to put that flame back in the ground. She needed time to forgive him, and he needed aid to rescue her. Aid that he hoped to acquire from Necthana, if the Deathless could be roused from their slumber.

He had to try.

"You are right," Regel said to Gilt. "I see that now."

Gilt had the respect to reply with silence.

They journeyed for a time among the stones of Narkggr's heights, streaked with sparking colors like flints etched through the stone. By reflex, Regel started to explain the dust and its purpose, but of course Semana was not here to listen, and Gilt knew the nature of these mountains better than he. Thus, Regel stilled his words and took care not to step too close to any of the swirls of color.

The appearance of the dust veins meant they had almost reached their destination.

"Here," Gilt said, indicating the summit that lay before them.

Regel nodded. He had anticipated this, and now he found himself trembling.

Ahead, over the pass, there seemed to be nothing. Narkggr marked the edge of the world of men, and beyond lay only a forest of eternal snow pierced with stone so cold it turned flesh to ice. Nothing could live past this point, and in a way, nothing did. It made for a fitting place for the Necropolis of Necthana, where no mortal could enter—at least, not of their own power. Only those who had forsaken the path of the living could walk that of the dead, though they could guide a mortal through.

He remembered the last time he had walked this path—four years ago, when he had thought all was lost to him. He'd gone to Necthana and thought never to return, but something pulled him back. Duty. Business left undone. He had that once more, and thus he would not find himself trapped in the Necropolis anew. He would be able to leave, but not before he had what he needed.

Gilt looked at him wordlessly, an unspoken question in his jet-black eyes.

Regel swallowed any doubts. He unbuckled his borrowed swordbelt and let his weapons fall to the ground. He might need them, but he could not take them. "I stand ready."

Gilt's power swelled, dark wisps of magic coiling around them like frayed ribbons. Regel could feel it like a cold mist that suffused his soul rather than his flesh. He shivered, having forgotten exactly how this felt. His spirit came unmoored within his body, then tore free with a jolt that felt like falling. Had he not known what to expect, Regel would have screamed in sudden terror, but as it was, he bit his tongue and suppressed the fear.

On the shadowy wings of Gilt's power, they passed just under the surface of Ruin, slipping out of sync with the stone and air around them, which darkened and blurred to his senses. The world was still the world, but its life bled away, leaving a hollow landscape like a dull reflection of the realm they had just left. The edges of things fractured and fell out of focus. Regel felt himself sinking down through the stone under his feet and had to will himself to remain aloft. His own body lost cohesion, and as he looked at his hands, he saw his fingers turning bone white and bleeding into one another.

The *ren shala*, the Deathless called it—the shadow path.

This was how the Deathless moved unseen, seeming to flit from place to place with impossible speed, appearing and vanishing just as quickly from the air. His feet passed through the rock as though it were water, and he traced one hand through the mountain wall, causing it to ripple like a disturbed pool. Solid stone and earth proved a permeable barrier to the *ren shala*, though it could not pierce living things or travel through iron or steel. Nor could such metals follow a traveler into the shadow path, which was one of many reasons Deathless trained without weapons and never carried arms crafted of metal.

They could have walked the *ren shala* from the outset and thus reached Necthana in half the time, but Regel was only mortal and the less time he spent between worlds, the better. Also, doing so would loudly announce their presence to any Deathless standing sentry. Then the Deathless would know of their approach long before their arrival and make ready a welcome, or else prepare an ambush that would see them dead before they reached their goal. Regel honestly could not say which they should expect. Not every fae would welcome his return: he'd left more than one enemy when he'd abandoned Necthana not long ago that he might return to Tar Vangr for one last chance at life. To return now…

Regel found himself questioning this course. Without Semana to protect, what was there to be gained in the Deathless City? She would have grounded Regel—given him a reason to return to the world in time. Without her, would it be a haven or a snare?

He looked up, having never seen the sky while walking the *ren shala*, and what he saw gave him pause. It seemed cloudy as before, albeit a deeper and colder gray, but now he saw streamers of black like coiling lightning. He thought, for one terrible moment, that he saw the bindings that held the world together. And if he focused upon them, he thought he could see something more—something beyond....

"Frostburn?" Gilt was a sliver of darkness in the vague shape of a man. The Deathless's face blurred in the distortion of the magic, and it gave Regel an object upon which to focus. Too long spent thinking or wandering the shadow path, and one might never leave it.

"Yes." Regel made himself stare at the carving in his hands, as when he extended his senses. His shadow body drew back together where it had started to unravel. "Lead me."

"Stay close," Gilt said. "There are darker things along the path, and they hunger."

Clasping hands, the two of them stepped forward and down through the mountain, as though into standing water that parted to swallow them whole. They sank into the earth, Regel's senses deadening as stone enshrouded them. He'd taken a deep breath, but mostly for his own reassurance: along the shadow path, he did not need to breathe, and there was no air to breathe even if he needed it.

As they delved deeper, Regel wondered if he had erred in trusting Gilt. He hardly knew this fae or his motives, and while he did not think Gilt meant to slay him, he couldn't say for sure. It would be easy along the shadow path. If the Deathless released his hand, the mortal Regel would wander aimlessly in the *ren shala* until the magic ran out, he went mad, or a horror walking the same path found him.

He felt a rush of warmth as something vaguely alive caught around his middle, then broke with a slight pressure. They fell onward, but now Regel knew they were not alone.

A warm presence stood out in the cold world of darkness, floating somewhere off behind them. Several, he thought. One of them detached from the space in which it lingered, whispering through the space between worlds like a spider creeping along its web. Whatever monsters stalked the *ren shala*, he did not wish to know. Perhaps they would pass it by.

He closed his eyes and hoped he had chosen rightly.

Time passed differently in this world, but it still felt like an eternity before Gilt drew him up into an open space. Regel had felt the choking pressure of stone all around his body for so long that the newfound freedom made his mind fly apart in all different directions. He staggered free of Gilt's hand and fell wretching out of the shadow path and back into the mundane world. He found himself in a dark cavern of some kind, with purple-blue illumination bouncing off the walls from a distant source. Below and ahead of them, at the end of a winding catwalk that stretched a long spear's cast, Regel beheld a dusky glass wall that marked the bounds of the city.

Necthana, City of the Deathless. They'd made it.

As he doubled over at the base of a mottled stalagmite, Regel's stomach heaved up the meager breakfast he'd managed earlier that day, and the bile made his throat burn all the way down.

"Gilt." Regel choked on the name.

He had only to look up at the Deathless—to see his eyes glittering in the ambient light—to know they were not alone.

Four Deathless appeared out of the semi-darkness, stepping out of the gloom itself as though they'd always been there. The first was a bare-chested man with rippling muscles and a strong jaw, holding a shaft of wood about the length of his leg. The second was a woman, dressed similarly but for the linen bands that wrapped her hands, wrists, and forearms up to the elbows. She had no weapon but for her fingers curled into claws. The third and fourth Deathless had an androgynous look to them, as was common among the fae. Their black cloaks rippled at the movement of powerful limbs beneath, and one of them held a short bow crafted of gray wood.

The four were obviously different from one another, but they shared three important qualities in common. The first was an otherworldly quality and beauty about their bodies: they seemed like creatures that belonged to another age and another world, ethereal and irresistible in their power. Secondly, each of them bore designs inked upon their faces in white and black ink that shimmered in the faint light. Lastly, they bore vividly black eyes like those of Gilt, which seemed far darker than the blackest midnight.

The four stood waiting, poised on the threshold of an attack.

Before, Regel had wondered if they would find welcome or an ambush. This felt like the latter.

Gilt put out his hands toward them, wrists locked together. "Peace," he said. "We—"

"Silence," said the woman, her voice barely above a serpent's hiss. "You bring a man. Why?"

Regel drew himself up tall despite his weariness and lingering injury. "I am the Frostburn, anointed wielder of the cold flame of Necthana," he said. "I will speak with the Deathless Rose."

The words caught the fae by surprise, and the man with the staff in particular seemed startled. His eyes first widened in surprise, then narrowed in challenge. "The great Frostburn." His deep voice echoed off the walls and filled the cavern like a war drum. "An honor, if you speak true. I am Dawn."

"I do." Regel stretched his muscles as unobtrusively as possible. He knew what would come next.

"I am Blood," said the woman, pointing her clawed hands at him. "You will prove your worth."

"I am Dew," said the one with the bow. "You will prove yourself or die."

"I am Silver," said the last Deathless. "If you die, you will feed Necthana."

"Well." Regel raised his hands to match Blood, who seemed to lead. "Let us begin."

Deathless schooled their features as a matter of course, but he could tell from the fae's unfolding body language—muscles easing, shoulders turning toward him, legs opening slightly—that she was pleased. Compact and powerful of build, Blood had a dark complexion and an imperious look, like someone accustomed to command. Regel wondered who and what she had been in life.

"I think you grow old and weak, Frostburn," said Blood. "You will not so much as touch me."

"Words are not blows," Regel said.

She leaped through the shadows to slam into him with a leaping knee. She hit like a battering ram, sending him staggering back, his whole middle shaking with the impact. Blood flowed along the stone with him, landing two punches to his face, and launched a second kick for his groin. He managed to twist his hips so that the hardest part of her shin slammed into his thigh instead. His leg went numb immediately and his balance fell wildly apart. He stumbled to one knee, inadvertently ducking the spinning kick that followed her assault. Blindly, he launched himself forward, slamming one shoulder into her midsection to drive her back. She vanished before he could tackle her, though, leaving him kneeling on the cavern floor.

He wondered why she had taken the name Blood. Had she turned her back on her own Blood, perhaps, or sworn never to shed blood from a foe? That seemed too much to hope for.

Darkness flitted away from Regel and resolved into Blood, dancing free and regaining her balance. A red mark spread on her midsection from his hit, but it hardly seemed to pain her. She inspected the mark with a look of obvious distaste. He'd proven himself against her, anyway. If he'd had to fight her to the death, things might have ended very differently.

"Not so weak, it seems," she said. "Dawn."

“I am honored to fight the Frostburn.” In one hand, Dawn raised his staff horizontally and drew his other fist back. Regel could tell he was one of the newly Deathless, elevated through a ritualized operation. That would make him both inexperienced and impusive. Dangerous.

“Hrn.” Regel wiped his mouth. No blood on his fingers.

He chanced a look at his companion. Gilt faced Dew and Silver, the three of them locked in a balanced triangle. Even without moving, Regel knew they held each other at bay in a battle of will. Gilt had not yet provoked the other Deathless, but if he moved to aid Regel, they would intervene as well. He was on his own.

Dawn came in slower, staff spinning around his body like an ornithopter ring. Regel took two wary steps back, settling into a defensive stance that left him light on his feet.

The staff snapped out like a striking snake, and Regel lunged aside as it thrust past his ear, then ducked to let it slash over his head. Dawn struck fast and hard. A tiny clip on the shoulder knocked Regel staggering, a thrust to the belly winded him, and he narrowly evaded a deathblow that would have caved in his forehead.

He caught a strike coming for his right side, but Dawn stepped around him, reversed the staff, stepped past, and smashed Regel across the opposite cheek. He spun and toppled to the floor, arms breaking his fall, barely keeping his face from striking the stone. Regel spat blood onto the stone.

Dawn stepped back, spinning the staff twice to let blood and spittle flick away into the dark, and Blood grimaced in his direction. “You do him no mercy,” she said. “Finish the old man, or I will.”

“There is no honor in slaying a wounded man,” Dawn said. “The legendary Frostburn will die on his feet, as has been foretold.”

Regel seized the opportunity to push himself up to one knee, and from there shakily to his feet. “Come then,” he said, adopting a combative stance once more. “Let’s finish this.”

Dawn rushed at him, staff whirling, but this time, Regel was prepared. He ducked the first attack and stepped wide, then bobbed under the backswing. He came up inside the Deathless’s guard and closed his hands around the staff, one inside Dawn’s grasp and the other outside. Try as he might, Dawn could not twist the staff free of Regel’s grip, and they wrestled back and forth in the center of the chamber for control of the weapon.

“Well fought, Frostburn,” Dawn said. “But you are only a man.”

Regel replied by slamming his forehead into Dawn’s hooked nose. Cartilege crunched and the fae staggered back, trailing blood. Regel wrenched the staff from Dawn's weakening hands and slammed its end into the side of the man's head. Or would have, if Dawn hadn't raised up an arm with lightning speed to block it as surely as a shield set against a spear.

Darkness flowed around the Deathless, and he stared out at Regel with eyes like pools of ink.

Moving with impossible speed, Dawn seized the staff, ripped it free, and struck Regel heavily in the side of the head with it. The sheer force of the blow sent Regel staggering back, but he kept his wits about him enough to get his hands up to protect his head from further blows.

And they came. The Deathless launched a withering assault, striking as hard as the strongest barbarian but also with the speed of a duelist probing for weakness. He pulled shadow to strengthen himself, and Regel could see it devouring him from the inside out. Black flames hissed from his lips and fell like burning teardrops from his eyes.

"Enough," Blood said. Even she could see how the battle unfolded and had lost her taste for it.

Dawn kept attacking, and Regel kept defending himself. His arms and legs had gone almost numb from the beating, and blood flew with every whip-crack of the staff. But he stayed standing. His mind was far away, on the daughter he'd left behind. Compared to that pain, this, he could endure.

"I said, *enough*." Blood grasped Dawn's arm, restraining the staff from striking anew. She glared into the other fae's red, heaving face from scarely a hand's breadth away. "You disgrace yourself to strike with anger. You left passion behind, or did you forget your death?"

The words had a palpable effect on Dawn, who recoiled as though she had slapped him. The anger faded and tranquility returned. "Yes, Master," he said. "My life is dead, but I remain."

Blood put one hand on his cheek, running her fingers along his bleeding brow. The gesture was almost a tender one, which surprised Regel. It seemed the Deathless had not left all passion behind.

He sensed the creature before it arrived: a tingling that started at the base of his skull and spread outward from there. Perhaps he'd caught something of it on him: some connection that led the creature to him and allowed him to sense it. He reacted without thinking, throwing himself forward at the two fae. He slammed into Blood and knocked her sprawling, even as the massive creature roared out of the darkness just behind him. He felt its massive bulk displace the air as it fell abruptly out of the shadow path, just long enough to pounce on Dawn, who went down screaming as its jaws locked around him.

Regel hit the ground, tackling Blood under him, then looked around at the creature, which resembled something out of his worst nightmares. Mottled black and gray, it had a dozen hooked legs longer than a man was tall and a shaggy furred body like that of a wolf spider. The top half of its form, however, more resembled some sort of horrific, half-opened flower bud. As Regel watched, it unfolded seven different jaws to draw Dawn's shuddering body halfway into itself. Hooks the size of a human hand adorned the edges of its mouths and spines covered its body above the muscular trunk. It smelled of musty death and uttered a groan like that of a man who has eaten too much and will certainly vomit.

"*Ren Sakat!*" Blood shoved Regel off her and leaped up and into the darkness as she rushed at the monstrous thing. She had no weapons, but she threw herself at it with wild abandon, kicking and punching its spiked hide heedless of the damage she would inflict on herself.

An arrow slammed into the creature from Dew's bow, and Silver screamed and attacked it with twin falcata. The tiny shaft seemed to harm it only a little, but Silver's swords hacked into one of its barbed legs. The creature issued a sound like a thousand discordant screams as a second cut tore through one muscular limb in a burst of greenish blood. The injured leg erupted like a sack full of viscous liquid suddenly pierced, smearing the Deathless and prompting fresh shrieks of pain. Regel could hear and smell it searing the fae's flesh. Blood caught some of the spray as well, but she only hissed.

"Frostburn!" she cried. "To arms!"

Regel nodded through the haze of pain and horror. He grasped Dawn's staff, fallen not too far away, and swung it with all his strength at one of the thing's intact legs next to the damaged one. It struck with a satisfying *crack*. The creature scrabbled to maintain its balance, failed, and smashed to the ground with a shuddering impact. Scalding ichor splashed on Regel, but he got his cloak up in time to block most of the spray. The stuff bit at him even so, and he tore the garment clumsily off. By the time he discarded the cloak to the ground, the acid had eaten through half of the fabric, smelling of rotting flesh and ash.

Putting the creature down had opened it to the attacks of the others. Dew put several more arrows into its more vulnerable, seven-sided mouth. Silver managed to stab and cut while moving, striking quickly and retreating into the shadow path before it could counter with splashes of burning blood. Gilt had joined in the assault as well, dancing alongside Silver like a twin specter, a long obsidian sword flashing as it cut ribbons of flesh from the monstrous thing. Just as it reeled, moaning and shrieking, Blood appeared from the air and slammed into it with both feet.

The creature should have fallen, wounded and maimed, but instead it wavered, growing instinct, and faded back into the shadow path from whence it had emerged. It left with a deafening roar that Regel could not stop hearing.

Blood screamed in rage, pulling shadows around herself as though to pursue, but another, commanding voice stayed her. “Hold.”

Instantly, the gathered fae stopped what they were doing and dropped to one knee.

The Deathless Rose, queen of Necthana and master of the darkness after death, stood amongst them, tall and regal in swirling black and white robes that seemed to defy gravity. They rose from her angular frame in dramatic rising frills, like the wings of a dragon stretching for its morning flight. As Regel remembered, her smooth scalp showed no sign of hair, which combined with her bold features to make her beyond striking. The paint marks on her face, unlike those on the other fae, were of vivid red, like fresh blood. She held up one long-nailed hand to stay the other fae from their task.

“Do not follow,” Rose said. “The shadow stalker has the advantage in its own world.” She looked down at Dawn’s corpse, which lacked a head, arms, and top half of its torso. “Do not mourn our brother fae. He died long ago, and destiny has collected that which remained. Honor him instead.”

The gathered fae deferred to her command, nodding their heads respectfully. They looked introspective and at peace—even Silver, whose skin showed indications of no small amount of burning. Blood, however, had eyes only for Regel. She stepped toward him, rage burning on her face.

“Why did you save me?” Blood asked when she came close.

“What?” Regel could hardly hear through the ringing in his ears.

She shoved him hard, and he staggered against the wall. She pointed to Dawn’s corpse, which had withered down to the bones. “Why save me, and not Dawn? He was young. His death passed not a year ago.” She pointed to her chest. “Because of how I look? Is it your instinct to protect a woman?”

“No, I—” Regel started.

Blood smashed a left hook into the side of his head, shattering his words. As he groaned in pain, she caught him by the throat and held him hard against the wall.

“Whatever I was before, I am not weak, nor am I a woman,” Blood said, her lips scraping against his ear. “I am Deathless. Remember that.”

She gave him one last shove, making his bones shiver, then stalked off. The darkness swallowed her before she’d gone more than half a dozen steps. Silver and Dew followed suit, glancing in his direction before walking away through the shadows. Soon, Regel stood alone in the chamber with Rose and Gilt.

"I did not intend offense," Regel said.

The Queen of Necthana turned toward him, the complex marks on her face lighting up with a particular pattern. He'd grown adept at reading her thoughts from the colors, but over the years away he'd fallen out of the habit. Regardless, when she smiled slightly at him, he felt dizzy with her approval.

"Do not fear," she said. "Blood is young. She has never truly forsaken her life or its passions. Perhaps the final death of her lover will aid her in this."

Regel drew in a deep breath and blew it out in a sigh. He remembered the way Blood had touched Dawn's face. "I did not know," he said.

"You could not have known." Rose looked as serene as ever. "They became Deathless together, each succumbing to a different flaw. You do Blood a service by removing the source of hers."

Regel suspected Blood would not see it that way. He would mind his step in Necthana henceforth.

Belatedly, Regel remembered Gilt was there, watching patiently. The fae had suffered only a minor wound in the assault on the shadow stalker: his left wrist oozed dark blood that seemed more black than red. The Deathless looked unconcerned but instead fixed his gaze upon the cavern ceiling, away from Necthana and his Queen. He kept silent, but that faraway look and his posture might as well have screamed his thoughts.

"You're going back," Regel said at length.

Gilt nodded slightly.

"Why?" Regel asked. "You said we should respect her decision."

"I do respect it," Gilt said. "And I respect her. I will protect her when she needs me."

Regel nodded. "She won't like that."

The fae shrugged.

Then the shadows wrapped around him, and he was gone.

Regel stood alone with the Queen of Necthana. She who had sheltered him as a child, who had trained him as a boy, who had made him a man. She who had armed him with a mighty relic of her people and given him his first name. She looked exactly the same as she ever had—thirty years had not put a single wrinkle upon her face or taken any of the light of her faintest smile. She was a woman who could love or kill with equal warning, utterly in control of herself and her world. So far beyond the concerns of human life that Regel's fears and regrets seemed suddenly trivial under her obsidian gaze.

Was it any wonder he had fled here after Orbrin's death, when the world seemed too far lost to Ruin to have any meaning?

But he had not stayed in Necthana. This was not his world—not then, and not now. That, he told himself to remember. If he did not, he would lose himself and become as the fae: silent, all but devoid of passions, unconcerned with the mortal ways of Ruin above. *Deathless.*

"Well do we meet," Rose said.

Regel nodded. "Not for long," he said. "I need your aid. My—"

"Hush." She touched long fingertips to his lips to silence him. "We will speak of these things later. First, you will rest and regain your strength." She scrutinized him. "You have grown old."

"You have not changed," he said. "Not a single day."

Silver Fire, but she was beautiful. Not in the fashion of mundane women, though her russet skin and vivid eyes would be the envy of Tar Vangr. She was more. *Greater.* Regel knew from personal experience Rose had not been a woman in life, but she seemed pleased to be called "she" now. She was Deathless: such concerns no longer applied to her. She captivated Regel regardless, however he tried to maintain his concentration around her.

"You are weary," she said. "You need rest."

Again he nodded. He could do nothing else but agree.

"Good." She wrapped her arms around him, and he lost himself in her cold embrace. The shadows rose around them, and he felt again that sensation of falling.

Then Rose pressed her lips to his, and the world vanished around them.

FIFTEEN

The Winter Wilds

The mountains towered above them, their shadows casting a long chill across the gathered host encamped below it. The Children of Ruin spread through the small valley, over a thousand fur-wrapped forms milling about the business of a war camp. More arrived by the day, as they drew closer to Iseldra's Folly in the north. The power rising in the vale all but sizzled in the snow and the heat of the clear day.

"We shall destroy them all," her brother had said. "Together."

Even now, fifteen days later, standing on the threshold of Darak's tent and looking down at the barbarian camp, Semana could not stop thinking about those words.

For years, since the night Mask attacked her skyship and Ovelia slew her greatfather and all of it went to ruin, she had scarcely allowed herself to dream that it might be possible. Her Blood spilled and gone. Her protectors destroyed. Alone, but for Tithian. The last heir to Tar Vangr with her hopeless quest.

And yet, there Darak dozed in his own bed in the depths of the tent, whole and powerful and influential. And most importantly, he was on her side. He offered her all she wanted—all she had ever dreamed. To reclaim Tar Vangr. To punish those who had destroyed her family. To restore her birthright and become the queen she'd been born to be.

Victory seemed so close Semana could almost taste it on her tongue.

So why the unease that lingered at the back of her mind, telling her to be wary?

A small group of figures detached itself from the larger camp and stalked up the hill toward the tent. Semana easily recognized Afferath at a distance, having seen entirely too much of her in the previous days. The druid never went anywhere without her four burly escorts: bodyguards, servants, lovers, all of it. One was the hulking Mountain's Rage, who never failed to ogle Semana whenever the opportunity arose. Two of the others looked similar enough to be brothers: muscles sculpted in the same way, skin mottled and scarred and tattooed in opposite patterns, like mirrors of one another. Semana had come to think of them as "Right" and "Left," based on which hand they favored when fighting and where they tended to stand flanking Afferath. The fourth was a cold-eyed woman whose name Semana had heard once: Breaker of Frost and Ice. Semana couldn't say exactly why she bore that name, but she suspected the barbed morningstar the woman perpetually carried would do a fine job of breaking whatever she swung it at.

Semana looked at the ground as Afferath approached, offering the least obeisance she could without also giving offense. "Hail, Mistress of the Burning Rain," she said in the language of the Children. She became more adept with the dialect by the day.

"Yes." Afferath looked away, profoundly indifferent. After their first encounter, her passing interest seemed to have faded, and now she barely acknowledged Semana as a living creature. "Has your master risen? He and I have matters."

Matters. Semana worked hard to hide her distaste. "He slumbers still, my lady," she said. "Shall I wake him to receive you?"

"Respect." Afferath glanced at her dubiously. "How refreshing."

Afferath's bodyguards shared a chuckle and glared at Semana. She tried to ignore them. Something about her brother's former master made it impossible for Semana to rest easy around her. And it wasn't just her hold over Darak's power and his body. She didn't know their secret truth—how could she?—but she seemed ever on the verge of discovering it. If she'd thought for a single moment that she could kill Afferath and get away with it, she would have.

"Do not awaken your master, girl," Afferath said. "I will do so, and he shall be quite pleased to receive me—and what I have to offer."

"I'm sure." Darak stepped to the threshold and stood right behind Semana, a little too close for comfort, and put his hands on her shoulders. "What can I do for you this day, Afferath? Some business before the moot, is it? Or perhaps a service I might pay you."

"Both." She flicked the strings loose around her throat and shoulders so that her tattered dress slipped down her brown body. She glared at Semana as at a mangy dog in her way.

Semana not appreciate how Darak had positioned her between them, both physically and as an obstacle. She wanted no part of their sensual intrigues. "And me, master?" she asked. "Shall I go?"

"He hardly cares, slave girl." Afferath stepped out of the skirts puddled at her feet. She ran her hands through her hair to pull out any snarls. "Make yourself useful for once."

Semana looked to Darak for support, but he had looked away, his attention fixed on Afferath's bronze body. Not a surprise. She stepped out, glad to be quit of that place for the moment. Afferath's escorts, each of them marked with the silver mistletoe of their mistress, eyed her speculatively. Semana kept her eyes downcast and contented herself with imagining choking them with her magic. Especially Mountain's Rage. His face, she would gladly watch contrort and turn purple.

Trying not to hear the vigorous moans that soon emerged from the tent—or think about her brother's role in them—Semana headed down the hill toward the camp. Her heart lightened each step she took from the tent.

The valley had come alive with excitement for the coming moot. Everyone seemed to be up and about, shouting challenges, bickering, or picking arguments. She saw a scrap between two men who boasted so many shards and hoops of metal in their ears and faces that she could hardly imagine rivalry over who looked more like a monster was not the source of their conflict. A group of women watched them with marked interest, but they quickly fell to fighting amongst themselves. The camp had become like a tavern packed full to bursting with brawlers, braggarts, and comrades celebrating a coming revel. People, not the monsters she had always learned to fear.

Semana's bare leg scraped against a log, and she winced as much at the pain as her carelessness. It felt odd to walk in the skirts and tunic of an acolyte, rather than Mask's armor. Darak had judged it too dangerous and advised she hide the armor as best she could. As yet, he knew nothing of where she kept the armor, and that was a secret she gladly kept for now. She had started to feel Darak's disdain weighing on her. Ostensibly he treated her poorly in public to maintain their cover as master and slave, but increasingly she could not shake her impression that he enjoyed it a little overmuch. When Afferath insulted and belittled her, Semana could feel Darak's tacit approval of his sister being shown her place.

He meant to help her, but only on his own terms. He was in control, and it had begun to irk Semana more than a little. She did not like being controlled.

She'd rebelled in small ways. The armor she'd hidden away in her belt, but she continued to wear the glove of interlocking silver rings for her left hand, as it resembled jewelry of some sort more than armor. If he even knew of the invisible hand magic that the glove produced, he'd said nothing to correct her. Semana knew well enough not to use it openly amongst the barbarians, and particularly the druids.

Darak had judged the development of her magic to be worth his time and effort. He had spent the last days teaching her about Frostfire and how to wield it. The power manipulated the heat in objects or in the air, turning ice to water and then to mist or the reverse almost instantly. Also, Darak had confirmed her suspicion that the Frostfire protected her from extremes of cold or heat. Her brother shared the same invulnerability to the harsh cold of the north that had preserved her over the long trek with Regel. According to Darak, the power suffused ever fiber of her being, manifesting naturally to lower incoming flames or raise the temperature of her flesh in contact with the cold. This also explained why the power could not affect other wielders: Semana could never touch him with her Frostfire, nor Darak her.

All of that she might have learned herself, but she kept up with his lessons for a second, secret purpose: they gave her an additional chance to observe the Worldfire churning inside Darak. It was stronger than his Frostfire, weaker than most of her relics, but it had a flavor and power all its own that she found intoxicating. Semana knew she could learn to wield it as she had Vhaerynn's blood magic in the palace of Tar Vangr, given time and opportunity. Darak had realized that the propensity for wielding the Worldfire lay within her, and he had deigned to teach her the basics of drawing power to strengthen her body and speed her healing process. She had to take care, as Darak would likely not react well to learning that she could summon flame, guide the winds, and shape the earth just as he could. He might lose his mind entirely if he learned she could wield the magic better than he did.

How would that serve his need to dominate her?

It had often struck her as strange that the few other sorcerers she met struggled to learn the basics of their magic, sometimes for years on end. True magic was rare in the World of Ruin, and using even simple magical relics seemed difficult for most people. Jealous of their secrets, those few who could wield any magic of any kind locked themselves in high towers or concealed their art through flash, artifice, and distraction. What a tragedy for them that Semana, to whom magic was an open book, could learn and duplicate their magicks only by witnessing their use for just a few moments. It would not have surprised her, for instance, if Vhaerynn had considered himself the only practitioner of blood magic in the world until Ruin's Night, and indeed, he would have guessed rightly. Semana had never imagined wielding the power herself until she had needed it, and then it had come to her call as though born to her touch. She had ever reason to believe the magic of the druids would come to her just the same.

And with the Worldfire at her call, Semana foresaw a day when she would rule as Afferath did. One day. Soon.

Would it affect her as it did Darak? She wondered what it would feel like to rot from within and without as she used magic. The relics had sapped her vitality—particularly the Plaguefire in her mask—but the Worldfire seemed to draw its power from the wielder's body, draining life to sculpt the worldHow long would it take before she no longer had to fake a limp or assume a scratchy voice, because they would simply become natural?

When would the armor of Mask become no longer a disguise, but truth?

Semana thought of Regel and what he meant to the Children of Ruin. Finding his escorts dead, their throats slit and neither having even managed to draw a weapon, the barbarians had immediately assumed the infamous Frostburn had done the deed. Semana had heard the whispers. To the rest of the camp, Regel's mysterious disappearance had come not as a shock but as something to be lauded. Always among the barbarians' favorite villains, legends of the deadly Frostburn's exploits and supposed powers had filled the army that night. He was practically a Deathless fae himself. Some tales connected Gilt's visitation to the matter, insisting that the Deathless had spirited away his ally, whilst others claimed they even now did great battle among the clouds. The way they spoke of him, Regel sounded more like one of the gods of Ruin than a mortal man.

The barbarians were less certain what to think of the young woman who had appeared at his side.

As she made her way through the camp, Semana became aware of the barbarians eyeing her curiously. Regel had absorbed their attention when he was here, but now that he was gone, their questioning gazes had turned in her direction instead. Her acolyte robe—and thus Darak's implied protection—kept them at bay, but each day more and more faces turned to her as she passed, casting speculative glances in her direction. Many of those watching her wore silver mistletoe around their necks or on their patchwork hauberks. Their glares were a particular challenge.

Afferath's barbarians had joined them at the previous encampment, cohabitating with those loyal to Darak with only a few clashes. Tradition made the forthcoming moot a peaceful gathering of the Children of Ruin: those who would draw steel against one another became as brothers and sisters as they approached the sacred mountain. Their inborn inclination to rivalry remained, however: it simply sought a new outlet. Being small and vulnerable made Semana a natural target, and Afferath's contempt only exacerbated the issue. Unerringly, the foreign barbarians stopped whatever they were doing and stared at her as she walked past, producing an effect both eerie and intimidating.

When had she started thinking of Darak's barbarians as her people?

Tempting as it was to pull her cowl lower and pick up her pace, Semana knew it would only perpetuate the passive harassment. She had to make an example. Her. Not Regel. Not Gilt. *Her.*

Semana searched through the ranks of the barbarians and settled on an appropriate mark: a man, red of hair and fairly good looking, wiry of build and none-too-scarred. A bit of southern heritage explained the red hair, but his skin was very pale beneath caked on layers of paint and grime. He'd seen twenty winters or so, she estimated. She was not always the best at judging attractiveness, but this one looked smooth and well-formed, marking him as a good enough warrior to guard his face. He wore a sword, boiled leather, and a series of necklaces, earrings, and bones that adorned his face and neck. Semana had spent enough time among the Children of Ruin to know the plethora of trophies from previous campaigns. He was not the most impressive barbarian she could have challenged, but she could see his strength and importance within the camp. Good.

He saw her approaching as he sat with three other barbarians, playing some sort of game involving polished stones and small blades. Their eyes met from twenty paces or so, and he watched her approach with wary interest. It made her a touch uncomfortable, which turned into simmering anger. Good. She could use that.

"You," she said as she came upon the barbarian and his companions at their game.

One of the four—a rectangular man, solidly built with a face that was half burn scar—got up and crossed his arms to bar her path. A woman with hair that stood up in a dozen spikes glared at Semana like an intruder, while the third barbarian smiled mockingly at her with a mouth of fangs. Each of them had a small handful of colored stones, each crudely painted in different shades of a color: blue, green, and yellow respectively.

Then the leader said something guttural to his big beast of a companion and waved. The man stepped aside with a warning glare at Semana.

Their red-haired leader tossed one of the stones in his hand down into a circle drawn in the midst of their little group, upsetting two other colored stones and ringing off a razor the size of an arrowhead. With a grimace, he bent down to collect both stones, then picked up the blade. He worked it around in his fingers, examining the edge.

"What do you want, acolyte?" he asked at length, in the language of the Children.

Distracted by the game, Semana took a moment to realize he had addressed her. She wet her lips, pleased that she'd spent so much time on her accent. "I challenge you," she said.

The bold words made the woman with the animal fangs titter like a hyena, and the other two barbraians looked at one another dubiously. The red-haired man looked away.

"And why should I accept this challenge?" he asked.

"Because it is a challenge," Semana said. "And I see you are not a coward."

This time, the reaction to Semana's statement was silence. The other three barbarians looked at her dangerously, and the one with the wild hair reached casually toward an axe that leaned against the stump upon which she sat. The big man loosed a low growl Semana thought at first was the sound of stones rolling down the mountain.

Their leader, however, did not openly react. Instead, he drew the blade along the skin of his wrist, biting only shallowly, then let it and the blood fall back into the circle of stones and blades.

"*Vas*," the man said. "He is Bellows In The Deep." He indicated the big man, who grunted. "These are Fierce Wind and Rending Gash." He nodded to the two women in turn. Then he looked directly at Semana, his eyes burning with hunger and amusement. "I am Crown of Fire."

"A strong name," Semana said. "I am Mask."

Crown of Fire considered the name for a moment, rolling it over on his tongue like wine. Then he nodded. "I accept your challenge," he said. "But how shall we fight? You have no weapon."

"This game, perhaps," Semana said. "Surely there is a winner and a loser."

Crown of Fire nodded. He said something to Fierce Wind, who snapped back a retort, but eventually scooted over to make space for Semana. She held out her green stones to Semana, but when the princess went to take them, the woman let the stones fall just out of reach to the half-frozen earth instead. Semana picked them back up, trying hard to ignore Rending Gash's laugh and the scathing look Fierce Wind gave her behind her back.

"You have played the bloodstones before?" asked Crown of Fire.

Semana shook her head. "Teach me."

The barbarian smiled slightly, which was not a bad look for him. He hurled the small knife he was fiddling with back into the pit, where it stuck quivering in the center.

"This seems like an unfair challenge," he said.

"Teach me."

His smile widened. "This is the pit," he said, gesturing to the mess of stones and blades arrayed between them. It looked a bit like a spider's web of garish colors and mud-specked steel. "These, the stones." He rattled his own handful of red stones, then gestured to the multiple colors represented in the pit. "Toss a stone into the pit. Claim the stones it touches as it falls. Do not collect your own stones. When your color is gone, you toss no more. The victor holds the most stones when only one color remains."

"And the blades?" Semana could guess the answer.

He grinned and showed her where he had cut his wrist. "If you strike a blade, claim it and open the flesh of the hand that threw the stone. Draw blood, and continue. Do not, and lose. Understand?"

Semana nodded, her mind racing through the possibilities and potential strategies. She noted that many of the blades lay across or near large clusters of stones. Going for those stones would be risky indeed, and the more she cut herself, the worse her aim would be. Lovely.

Crown of Fire gave her a bemused look. "You may choose another challenge," he said, then grinned lustfully. "A rut match, perhaps. I would enjoy your body, and you, mine."

"Pass." Semana rattled her handful of stones painted a variety of shades of green. "I cast green?"

"Fierce Wind's color," he said. "Alas for you, Wind has left her stones in a terrible way. She is a terrible player."

The barbarian woman spat some curse Semana did not know. She filed that away for future use.

"Shall I throw first or you?" Semana asked.

The barbarians murmured to one another approvingly. Crown of Fire raised an open palm in a gesture of welcome.

Semana threw her first stone. It flew much harder and farther than she expected, skipping off two stones—one blue, one red—before coming to rest against a small knife. Crown of Fire chuckled. Not an auspicious first throw.

Smoothly, without breaking eye contact with Crown of Fire, Semana reached into the pit and picked up the two stones, leaving her green stone where it lay. After a heartbeat, she also raised the knife: a blade about the length and width of her thumb, one edge sticky with half-dried blood, the other spattered with mud and frost. She put it against her skin and made sure every barbarian was watching.

The knife bit into her roughly—hungrily—with none of the sweet kiss of a well maintained and sharpened blade, such as Tithian might have carried. If anything, it hurt *more* than she expected, for she had to dig in and tear her flesh open, rather than cut smoothly. At least she could ignore the cold. Finally, blood welled and the barbarians murmured their approval. Pain radiated up Semana's arm, but she tried to shut it out. She looked over at Crown of Fire, who smiled.

"Your skin is so smooth," he said. "First cut?"

"I've been cut before."

Semana started to set the knife on the ground beside her, but a hand caught her wrist. Fierce Wind glared up at her and shook her head furiously. She said something that sounded like a protest.

"The knives return to the pit," Crown of Fire said. "Throw it where you will."

That, Semana had not expected. She'd seen him cut himself, then throw the knife back into the pit, but she hadn't realized the latter action was part of the game. She took the knife, considered, then tossed it far from any stones. At least she wouldn't be cutting herself with that one again. Crown of Fire's companions, however, grunted and chuckled. Apparently, that had been a bad move.

Crown of Fire threw a stone of his own. It skipped off the green stone Semana had just tossed down, along a knife, and came to rest against three more stones: two blue and one yellow. He claimed four stones, then took up the knife. He traced a thin line near the other, then sunk the knife with dizzying precision into the pit right next to a pair of his own red stones, creating a natural and painful shield beside them. Semana saw that another knife stood on the other side of the stones, making it all but impossible to strike those two stones without also collecting two knives and thus two cuts.

Now she started to see the strategy, and it did not bode well.

They took turns tossing stones and knives into the pit, along with Bellows in the Deep and Rending Gash. They eliminated both fairly quickly, as the game had tended that way in the first place before Semana joined. Crown of Fire took out Bellows in the Deep with a brilliant throw that skipped off both of his last two stones, while Semana managed to strike the last of Rending Gash's yellow stones, which lay next to each other. Fierce Wind might have gone out first anyway, but Semana kept her stones far enough apart to make it difficult to eliminate more than one of her stones at a time. She also collected cuts on her arms, which began to pulse with the pain. She alternated throws between hands, using her left on easy throws and saving her right hand for more difficult ones. She envied Tithian his dexterity with left and right both: it would have come in handy in this game.

As they played out the game over the course of perhaps half an hour, they collected more and more onlookers. At first, they came from nearby fires, but then from farther away. When Semana looked up, she saw about twenty Children of Ruin watching them closely, with more arriving by the moment. They were placing bets on the outcome of the game: how quickly Crown of Fire would win and by how many stones, or how many stones he would strike with his next throw. Only a couple voices spoke in favor of her victory, and that inspired Semana more than she had expected.

As the game progressed, Semana came to two important realizations. For a first, this game required less strategy than nerve and grit, which fit with barbarian culture quite well. The onlookers applauded throws that took big risks, and chanted encouragement and challenge when a knife was claimed. And of course, it was a valid strategy to collect knives—and thus scars—to use to protect one's own stones. And for a second, she realized that as she cut herself more and more, and the stones became increasingly slippery between her fingers, she could imagine no way in which she could defeat the far tougher and more skillful Crown of Fire.

Not if she played fair, anyway.

Over the years of being Mask, Semana had practiced the art of using her magic subtly. The silver glove produced smoke and burned the air when she called upon it to produce great effects. But when she used it to cause only minor alterations—such as guiding a small stone—it distorted the air only slightly, and any stench it shed could be more than swallowed up in the reek of so many unwashed bodies crowded around them. Over time, she practiced using the glove in conjunction with her throws, guiding the stones she tossed to better and better effect. She would have won with one or two guided tosses and never risked striking any blades, but Crown of Fire would grow suspicious if she went from novice to master in a single game.

Instead, she grew better and better slowly and plausibly, ensuring he would not knock her out of the game, and steadily built her supply of painted stones. She waited for an opportunity, when Crown of Fire would present her with a chance to eliminate his red stones from the game entirely. With only two players, that became very difficult, as new stones kept falling into the pit, and as long as Semana kept her throws separated from one another, Crown of Fire couldn't claim more than one stone at a time. Meanwhile, she tried not to let the pain in her arms drive her to distraction.

Finally, when there were only a few stones remaining, a commotion up the slope split Crown of Fire's attention. Calling on the power of her glove, Semana sent a stone down, bounced it off one of his stones, and sent it skittering along the base of the pit, missing two intervening knives, and edged against the stone he had just thrown. That put his count down to one red stone remaining in the pit, while she had three green ones, all protected by a series of knives she'd placed at dear cost. Rending Gash loosed a whoop of triumph, drawing Crown of Fire's attention back to the pit. He stared in disbelief at his two stones, so far apart, rocking in the wake of Semana's throw.

"Not possible," he said under his breath.

"I saw it," said Rending Gash, her voice gleeful. "You're about to lose, Fire."

He glowered, then looked to Semana. Gone was his flirtatious façade, replaced with growing anger that she—a young woman, an outsider, a novice to the game, any of the like—had almost defeated him. Comprehension dawned on him slowly, and Semana sensed a touch of fear in the look he gave her. He had grown somewhat pale from blood loss. Fully a hundred barbarians had gathered, and Crown of Fire stood to lose face in front of all of them.

Loud voices intruded on their confrontation. The barbarians surrounding them parted ranks, and Darak swept through, his rotpriest robe damp at the edges where the hem trailed the half-frozen ground. He took one look at Semana's bloody wrists and hands and scowled at Crown of Fire.

"What means this?" Darak asked.

The red-haired man's perfect confidence with Semana faltered when he confronted a rotpriest, and he positively shook when Afferath appeared behind him. "Dar-Karsk," he said, stumbling up to his feet. "I can explain—"

"A fine game of bloodstones." Afferath smiled at Semana's blood-slick hands. "I say play on."

"No," Darak said, angry eyes fixed on his sister. "I'll not have my slave damaged for a foolish game." He'd almost said sister, Semana realized. Darak raised a hand shimmering with magic toward Crown of Fire, who was ostensibly under his command. "You there. Yield and submit to my will—"

Semana rose. "The challenge is not done," she said, interrupting his threat.

They all looked to her expectantly, none more than Darak, whose expression contained a mixture of anger and concern. He did not like her countermanding him. Semana had not set out to challenge his authority directly, but if it passed that way, she would be content.

"I am not afraid," she said. "I will continue playing, as Mistress Afferath commands."

The druid indulged Semana with a tight smile that conveyed approval for once, then nodded. The gathered barbarians applauded and whooped with delight. More bets fell upon the last throws of the game. Semana would have to take especial care, now that everyone was watching.

"It's not over yet." Crown of Fire ran a stone between his fingers, blood trailing down his thumb from the half-dozen cuts on his forearm. He gave Semana one last defiant look, then loosed.

It was a brilliant throw. It caught one green stone, bounced off two knives, and rolled toward her last two stones. Indeed, it would have struck both, had it not slowed just enough that it only touched one. Crown of Fire stared in disbelief, waiting for the stone to continue, but it tipped back and fell beside Semana's second to last green stone and the knife it was leaning against. He had gone from certain victory to cutting himself three times.

The barbarians around them had gone mostly silent, but Semana could hear some quiet murmurs as some changed their bets in light of what had come to pass.

Such skill and effort. Semana almost felt bad about cheating. Almost.

She focused her silver glove on the stone she meant to throw, rather than his red stone that she had slowed and stopped before it ended the game. It was not a difficult throw, particularly with her magic guiding the stone, and she picked up both of his stones, skipping over the intervening knife just for flair. Gaining two stones put her one over his count as well. Crown of Fire stared at her, taken aback.

"A good game," she said.

Crown of Fire nodded. "Yes." He turned away, curling his fingers against the pain in his hands..

Sounds of laud and congratulations swept through the assembled barbarians, and Semana understood that her victory had ment more than a single challenge to one man. From the sounds of things, she had chosen wisely in challenging Crown of Fire, who stood high in the esteem of the camp. And now they looked upon her with—if not the same level of admiration, at least the same sort of sentiment. She could build upon that. Even Afferath seemed to regard her with less open hatred than usual. Perhaps her willingness to inflict so much pain on herself had won even the druid's grudging respect.

Not everyone was pleased, however. Darak flashed Semana an angry grimace, as if to assure her this would be addressed. She smiled at him in turn. He had the power for now, but she had learned how to build power of her own. He needed her, just as she needed him, but she would stop him exploiting her as he had for entirely too long.

Soon, brother, she thought. *Soon.*

SIXTEEN

Necthana, the Deathless City

TIME EBBED AND FLOWED in unpredictable currents among the Deathless, for they were a people for whom the passage of years meant little. Regel lay in the wide bed in Rose's royal chambers, gazing up at the ceiling and wondering if he was becoming a part of it himself.

Necthana resembled a scintillating hive of bees rather than a mundane city. Instead of the towers and apartments that housed the residents of other mage-cities, Necthana filled the cavern with stairs and floors and domiciles crafted of dusky mage-glass. Purple radiance burned at core points in the city, diffusing through the glass to illumine most of its workings. Most folk could see one another much of the time, making privacy a foreign concept. Regel had almost forgotten this, until he rose naked from his bed and found himself face to face with two young Deathless—themselves also nude—through the glass wall of his chamber. They stared at him for a time, their expression unreadable, then returned to whatever wrestling or lovemaking they had indulged in before his rising. Among the fae, he found it difficult to tell the difference—all things seemed both amorous and deadly serious.

For all its transparency, Necthana had always struck Regel as close and cramped. The Deathless had no open spaces, but only countless spiraling corridors and staircases leading to sleeping rooms or meditation chambers. Everything neat and efficient and peaceful.

"Trapped."

He realized only belatedly that he had spoken. His voice sounded odd to his ears after so much time. How much time? He could not say.

Underground, he had neither sun nor seasons to watch, but only welcoming darkness and the constant hum of the power that thrummed through their mage-glass complex. He wondered how long he had slept each day, and whether measurements like days or fortnights meant anything anymore. He felt detached from his body and from his life. He had come here to a purpose, but it seemed to fade further with every breath.

Each day in Necthana passed much the same. He woke to a meal of mushrooms, nuts, and fresh water. When he had finished, a fae was there to guide him around part of the city, as one might walk a dog or other pet. Some guides were men, some women, some neither. He saw the same sights, wondrous as they were, and experienced the same aches in his body, particularly his crippled leg. After a time, his guide would lead him back to Rose's chambers, and each time, his guide would offer to pleasure him. Sometimes he would take the fae up on it, sometimes not—it never made a difference to what came to pass next. At first he thought a new fae escorted him every day, but after a time he wondered whether he had seen some of them before, and then he wondered if they were only a handful of unique individuals.

Rose would join him, bearing another platter of food, and they would speak of many things and nothing, each conversation fading into the mists of unstructured time and faulty memory. Sometimes they would lie together, sometimes not. Sometimes they would have sex, sometimes not. And each day, he woke to a new meal of mushrooms, nuts, and fresh water.

This morn—if indeed it was morn—the plate sat beside the bed, awaiting him. The baked mushrooms smelled of succulent fruit syrup broiled in dark places. The nuts were the same every morn: one sort that was curved and off-white in color, another gray-shelled with mottled pink and brown meat inside, not too difficult to crack but requiring some small effort. He had not counted, but he suspected the proportion of the two kinds of nuts was the same each time. The water had no taste and was always exactly at the same temperature as the chamber itself.

The routine provided him just enough variety that he hadn't lost his mind but he felt himself drifting. It was the same as it had been both of the previous times he had come to Necthana. Once, he had even sought the numbing monotony—to allow him to escape and forget.

The only thing that changed was him. His gray-threaded beard lengthened. The lines deepened around his eyes. His body had recovered as well, his magic repairing the wounds he had suffered in fleeing the Children of Ruin. The wounds closed up shortly into his stay, the marks themselves vanished within days, and then he could not even use the ache to remind him of passing time. And when the pain was gone entirely, how would he remember that he yet lived? Or would he be Deathless then?

"Semana," he said, and fire rose up inside him.

Yes.

Semana was the image around which he sculpted his life and maintained his sanity.

His guide of the day—a fae he judged to have been a man in life—stood waiting at the door, as still and quiet as a statue.

"Rose commanded you to come to me," Regel said. "She gave you strict instructions."

The fae said nothing but merely regarded Regel as he rose and stretched. Dark eyes flicked over Regel's naked body, then back to the floor.

"Inform your Queen that I shall wait for her here," Regel said.

The fae looked up at his face as though seeing him for the first time. "That is not Rose's way," he said. "You will wait?"

"As long as she takes."

The fae nodded and disappeared through the door, leaving Regel alone. He slid on a pair of loose hose, drew the string tight at his waist, and moved to the closest thing Rose's chamber had to a window: a wall the bordered the core of Necthana. He watched Deathless come and go, up dizzying staircases and through long corridors bordered on all sides by other dwelling chambers. Looking down into the center of the strange metropolis of glowing glass, one might imagine a colony of ants or perhaps the workings of a mechanism rather than the movements of living creatures.There were no secrets in Necthana: no intrigues or lies. This was not his place.

"I am not accustomed to being summoned."

Rose stood before him, tall and dark and statuesque in her proportions. She had always been bigger and stronger than he, from the moment they met thirty years ago, when he was just barely a man, to now, halfway between his fortieth and fiftieth winters. Time had ravaged him but it had not touched her: she remained as perfect and beautiful as ever, timeless and terrible in her majesty. This was her world in a way it would never be his, no matter how hard it wanted to keep him.

Regel took a moment to consider whether Rose's words held anger, but as always, he could not tell. Over centuries of existence, the Deathless developed a sort of stoic inscrutability that far outstripped any mortal he had ever encountered. In her role as the Ravalis spymaster, Ovelia would have wept with envy at Rose's skill. Regel realized it had been some time since he'd thought of Ovelia, and that gave him the extra touch of drive it took to push through Rose's strength of presence.

"How long have I been here?" he asked. "As the world above measures time."

"Not so long." Rose shed her mantle and draped it over the bed linens, revealing her muscular arms, dark and glistening with sweat. "Twenty days."

Regel's heart lurched, but he managed to keep his composure. It could have been years. He trailed his fingers along a darkwood dresser. "Am I a prisoner in this place?"

Annoyance flashed across Rose's face, and it was a testament to their closeness that she allowed him to see even that much of her true feelings. "I would not keep you against your will. You know this."

"Yes." Regel looked out into the greater city once more. He drummed his hand on the mage-glass. "And I thank you for allowing me to heal from my wounds."

"You healed within three days," Rose said. "Your magic saw to that."

Regel paused, his hand hovering over the translucent wall. He saw Rose dimly in the glass, and yet her black eyes lost none of their luster for the reflection.

"You knew," he said. "How long?"

"Always." She joined him at the window and splayed her long fingers around his against the glass. "When you came before us as a child, I knew you and your power."

"And you did not tell me."

"Some secrets cannot be told." Rose stepped in close against him, pressing him gently against the glass. Her breath was cool on his ear. "They must be learned."

He understood that only too well. "Semana Denerre lives," he said.

This time, he saw genuine surprise on her face. That, she had not known. If she had—if she'd known during his period of mourning that his daughter yet lived and she'd not told him the truth—he doubted he could have forgiven her. Just now, her expression seemed both sad and angry, the way he had felt for years.

"Semana Denerre lives," Regel said. "And I need your help to aid her."

Tension rippled through Rose as she pressed against him, and he could feel her distancing herself before her physical body moved. She drew away, leaving him slightly dizzy in her wake.

"Walk with me," she said.

Rose led him through the pulsing glass corridors of Necthana, navigating the maze of glass with the confidence of centuries of familiarity. He followed along behind, envying her remarkable smoothness and efficiency. He had trained among the Deathless and practiced the arts of movement, but Rose made him look like an awkward child.

Before, when he'd gone on these walks through the city, he'd attracted no great notice. The fae couldn't be bothered to note a mortal walking through their midst—a mere shadow to their power. But when he followed in the steps of Rose, Queen of Necthana, every fae paused to look upon them. They sensed her without seeing or hearing, as if they could *feel* her presence. Regel caught glimpses of that awareness himself—in the depths of the meditation the Deathless had taught him for expanding his senses—but it seemed to come so naturally to them, as though they had to try consciously to ignore the minutiae of the world rather than notice it.

They headed down to the core of Necthana, the closest thing the fae had to a square. The chamber was wide and open, with space enough for perhaps five hundred bodies gathered around a central point. Regel had once seen a conclave of Deathless assembled in this place to hear Rose speak, but he did not know if the city housed so many now. He doubted there were so many fae in existence, in fact.

At the heart of the square rose a delicate cylindrical column of mage-glass that split into multiple branches as it reached high above their heads. Inside this glass, surging like blood through an artery, sprang the Narfire: the very lifeblood of the world under their feet. Rivers and tributaries of the Narfire sprang up in various parts of the world, and Regel had never seen a city thrive without its blessing. The Narfire of Necthana was different, however: instead of its pure silver-white hue, the flames darkened as they flowed into the Deathless City, turning gray blue like the core of a flame that has reduced its fuel to mere embers. The Narfire rose through the mage-glass and became purple as it diffused through the city, growing lighter and lighter as it moved further. Regel had never seen the Fire behave in such a way.

"The secret magic of the Deathless," Rose said, as though she could hear his very thoughts. "How often have I told you a secret of my people?"

"Many times," he said. "But every time, there is more to tell."

She nodded. "I will tell you another," she said. "When the World of Wonder had died, but before the Prophecy of Return reached fulfillment, Necthana was a mage-city like any other—drawing upon what little of the Narfire we could reach, calling upon our ancestors for guidance in the darkness below the burning world above."

"I know the Deathless were men and women once." Regel frowned, confused. "But what has this tale to do with my request?"

If it were possible, Rose might have looked sad. "We had no supplies," she said. "In our haste to ready ourselves for the long dark, we did not properly prepare with all the things our city would require. Food. Water. Necessities. We knew after the first ten years that we could not support all our people until the Prophecy would be fulfilled. Not without…sacrifice."

That one word—*sacrifice*—hung on the air.

Rose laid one long-fingered hand against the glass column as though taking comfort in its warmth and support. Regel wanted to ask what she had meant, but he suspected he already knew, and just imagining it birthed a persistent chill deep inside him. He had seen the darkness of Necthana and knew the depths to which the Deathless might sink. He imagined the worst, and it did not surprise him.

"Our people were dying," Rose said. "We could not look to the surface for aid. To venture above would doom our scouts and all of us. A radical solution was proposed, and our sorcerers devoted all their time and resources to it. In our desperation, we sought the darkest magics. We embraced death, those of us who had survived found a path forward. Not into life—but into something more."

She spread her fingers over the glass, and the Narfire within clustered and flowed around her hand, drawn to it despite the barrier. She looked into the flames, searching for secrets only she could see.

"You speak as if you were there."

Rose looked to Regel then, and he realized something about her for the first time. She was old—that, he had known when they first met—but he had never felt the weight of her ancient majesty as he did now. With the familiarity of experience, she spoke of events that had passed over a thousand years ago. He had always assumed her wisdom sprang from the shared knowledge of all the Deathless who had come before, but now Regel had to confront the concept of an entity whose awareness stretched back farther than he could imagine and whose mind might never fade. He understood, in that moment, a fraction of what being Deathless truly meant, and it left him off-balance.

She drifted back up the stairs toward her chamber, and Regel followed in her wake. She moved with purpose, as though some business drew her attention. He wondered what she sensed that he did not.

"I was among the first to transition, so long ago," Rose said as they walked. "Our world is one of privation, but also of survival. We take the names of the things we swore never to behold again, to remind ourselves of sacrifice." She looked distantly sad as they climbed the stairs. "The magic that preserved Necthana rid us of trivial needs such as food or drink, nor did we produce more of our own kind to require expanding the space allotted us. And so, we never answered the Prophecy of Return, but instead remained in our holdfast as Ruin destroyed your world above. Mortals cannot even reach our city. We endure through the ages because we do not interfere."

Regel nodded, transfixed by her words. It was only through force of effort that he remembered what had brought them to this moment. Semana's face burned in his memory.

When they arrived back at Rose's rooms, he stopped in the threshold and waited. The sweet scent of flowers lingered inside the chamber, though of course there were none to be seen. She had left them behind a thousand years ago when she took that name.

"So you will not help me," he said. "Neither you, nor any Deathless."

"It is not our way," she said. "We take no part in the struggles of your kind."

"My kind." Regel crossed to her, fists at his sides. "Are we not of the same kind? Do you not bleed as we do?" He clasped her hand tight in his. "Do you not love as we do?"

Rose looked at him not like an old lover, but like a mother unto her child: fond but ultimately disappointed. "Stay," she said. "Surely you know by now the World of Ruin has nothing to offer you."

He drew away when she reached for his cheek. "Not only do you refuse to aid me," he said. "But you offer me that which I have already refused?"

To her credit, Rose did not follow him, but merely crossed her arms over her chest. "It becomes less an offer by the day," she said.

That took Regel aback. "What do you mean?"

Any trace of compassion had fled Rose's timeless face, and her black eyes stared down at him without pity. "There are many among the Deathless who believe you, a mortal, know too much about our city and its people," she said. "Some would see you dead. Others would have you remain. Few indeed would allow you to depart from our lands in safety."

Regel felt suddenly uneasy about his daily walks along the avenues of Necthana, where anyone and everyone could watch him. The fae eyes that had traced his path no longer seemed curious or companionable, but jealous. Conspiratorial. "You are their queen, are you not? Your will is law."

"The fae determine their course by vote," Rose said. "My voice carries weight, but it is not absolute. You have several strong voices arrayed against you."

What a terrible way to govern, Regel thought. "Who speaks against me? Perhaps I should plead my case to them."

At first, Rose returned his request with only a wary look, then shrugged slightly. "The Deathless Blood demands your death," she said. "In Blood's mind, you are to blame for the death of Dawn."

Regel nodded. He had expected as much. "There are others?"

"Many," Rose said. "Deathless Amber, Rain, and Mist are the three most powerful voices, but they do not know you personally." She paused. "Your greatest foe is the Deathless Summit."

"Summit. Of course." Regel narrowed his eyes. "Then I will go and face him. Prove again that I am worthy to remain—and worthy of aid."

Rose's mouth turned down slightly, and Regel felt her disappointment like a wave of sorrow. "You misunderstand," she said. "These voices have already spoken, and the vote already cast. I came to you only to convey the decision."

Regel felt a chill, and he looked away so his reaction would not show on his face. "I will go to Summit anyway," he said.

The Queen drew away toward the door. "You will do as you must," she said. "As will I."

Then she was gone, leaving him alone in the glass chamber. The city closed around him, warm and dark and inescapable.

SEVENTEEN

The Winter Wilds

As the sun dipped toward the distant horizon to their left, they reined up at the crest of a rise and beheld Iseldra's Folly, the mountain they had spent the last fortnight approaching. The last sunlight reflected off the driven snow, casting up a banner of blinding light that receded as the shadow lengthened across the valley. The majesty of that natural edifice, towering above the snow-covered plains, cast a wide shadow that encompassed the vast army of people camped like a sprawling town below.

At first, Semana thought the encampment some kind of dark forest that fringed the base of the mountain, so numerous were the tents. At this distance, it seemed to vibrate with movement, and smoke drifted up from thousands of cookfires to adorn the sacred mountain with a greasy haze that bent the light of the setting sun. When she realized those were all people, Semana felt more than a twince of unease to behold such a massive host. She'd thought Darak and Afferath's thousands large, but they were nothing compared to this vast nation of Children of Ruin. She'd not thought so many barbarians could exist, much less come together. They dwarfed the population of Tar Vangr, she realized.

"Impressive, are they not?" Darak asked at her elbow, sitting astride his horse and entirely too close for her comfort. "If only some voice could unite them, imagine what they could do."

Semana nodded. She edged her own horse away, and the beast grunted in a way that was anything but subtle. Afferath, watching from a knot of her honor guard half a dozen paces to their left, watched them both with a critical eye, the sun gleaming off her burnished face.

The druid had claimed she cared nothing for the relationship between Darak and his "slave," but Semana saw those gazes and suspected otherwise. When Darak had claimed shaggy horses from one of his barbarian lackeys for Semana and himself to ride, Afferath had given him a long, dubious look. Fortunately, five years constantly assessing her outward presentation as Mask had taught Semana well how to be cautious while observed. She had spent their time on the road acting every bit the demure acolyte for anyone watching, and considering how many barbarians served Afferath, Semana assumed someone was always watching.

Semana had also kept her eyes open, and so learned much in her time among the Children. On their road, they'd collected quite a few more Children on their way: tribes of barbarians that emerged from snow-dripping copses or snow-choked caves, each with a rotpriest or lesser druid to lead them. Chieftains and spirituals leaders both, these vassals commanded their own tribes, but in turn answered to the Circle of Great Druids. As a member of the Circle, Afferath exercised control over all the barbarians that followed them, both in her immediate retinue of fanatical followers and any other tribe that joined up. She could overrule any rotpriest of any rank, including Darak, and even questioning her was a crime punishable by significant pain or even death. To her was given the force and responsibility of judgment.

Just that morning, Semana had watched one barbarian—driven past good sense through a combination of drink and ardor—demand that the barbarian woman Fierce Wind be given over to him, simply because he wanted her. Darak had declined to rule against it and might have let him have his prize, but Afferath had chanced to wander past at just that moment, and she offered him some cutting words about whether he could win a mate without one being assigned to him. He'd made the mistake of swinging his massive war club at her, and Afferath had summoned the wind and broken every bone in his body with a gesture. He collapsed to the ground as a limp husk.

The druid dispensed death casually, as though life hardly mattered.

The brutality of it shocked Semana. Afferath hadn't murdered the man to any efficient purpose. She could have stopped him any number of ways, particularly with the power she wielded, and too few had seen the confrontation in the early hours to make it an effective demonstration. She'd done it because she could, and the joy on her face indicated she might have taken some satisfaction from the deed. Semana had ducked away before Afferath could turn that grin upon her.

"Semana." Darak's voice was soft in her ear, drawing her back into the moment. "You look ill. Do you pass well?"

She nodded. "How much longer?"

He turned to look down into the valley, squinting against the glare. "Two hours or so," he said. "We'll get there before full dark. It looks like most of the nation has gathered already. We'll have to camp on the outskirts."

"Nation?" Semana asked.

Darak grinned. "How many Children of Ruin did you think there were?" he asked. "Because we are many more times that many."

That, she could believe.

Darak clicked his tongue to urge his horse down the slope, signaling their own horde to follow him. Semana watched him casually swaying in the saddle and wondered at the transformation in her brother. She had last known him as a lanky, brooding boy, fond of books and tea, who still had a soft spot for his sister and her antics. Now, he had become a cold and confident man, prone to anger and thirsty to prove his strength against any challenge. In solitude, when none could see, he could speak openly with her, but around others—particularly Afferath—he became distant and condescending. When they shared his tent by night, Semana saw Darak as she knew him, but in public, she barely recognized him.

"Hail, rot priestess," said a man standing beside her horse.

Semana glanced down, then looked away before a smile would betray her. "Crown of Fire," she said. "What is it, warrior?"

The barbarian grinned up at her through slightly yellow teeth and ran his hand through his crimson hair. Despite the chill, he never seemed to wear a shirt or tunic of any kind, which Semana found unpleasantly distracting, particularly when she meant to keep her wits about her. Around him, she had need of them all the time.

"We camp tonight below the sacred mountain," he said, holding up his scarred arm. "Perhaps you wish to play another game?"

Semana scrutinized the marks on his arm—old scars and new, including the cuts he'd dealt himself in their previous challenge, which had left little more than red welts. He seemed to heal quickly. Her own wrists ached in sympathy. "Perhaps," she said.

His smile widened. He had interpreted her gentle deflection as flirtation. "Perhaps a different sort of game."

Semana glanced at Crown of Fire sidelong. Ever since their game of bloodstones, Semana had gathered increasing attention from the barbarians of Darak's tribe, and none more than Crown of Fire. Due to Darak's claim on his supposed acolyte, Crown had never pushed particularly hard, limiting his propositions to guarded suggestion and innuendo, but Semana knew what he wanted. His interest served her purposes. She would turn his infatuation into adoration and thus to abject loyalty, and he would bring his companions and his own admirers. While Darak busied himself rutting his druid, she would make his barbarians loyal to her. One by one, she would win them over.

The thought of actually lying with him made her vaguely ill, but she would keep him dancing.

Semana realized Crown of Fire was waiting for some sort of answer. She opened her mouth to give it, but at that moment, a shadow passed over them, too fast and too deep for a drifting cloud. Semana glanced up, and saw a flash of silvery wings against the darkening sky. Stark terror clenched around her stomach like a fist and her breathing quickened, and that came just at the sight of the beast. When it opened its many-fanged mouth and loosed a powerful roar that resounded through the valley like a thunder clap, Semana's whole body went numb with panic.

"Dragon!" someone cried behind her, and screams of fear rose through the barbarians' ranks.

"A true daughter of Ruin!" Afferath's voice rose over the din. "She blesses us!"

Semana looked to the barbarians arrayed in the valley, then up at the dragon descending toward them, its mouth wide with hunger. Its goal was anything but blessing.

Beneath her, the horse spooked at the dragon's awe-inspiring presence, and skittered down the steep ridge into the valley. Caught entirely by surprise, Semana tensed on the reins and tried to pull the beast to a stop, but the horse was past caring. It ran, uncontrolled and wild, bucking when she tried to control it. She swore at the brute in the tongues of Calatan and the Children, but nothing seemed to stick.

Around her, scores of howling barbarians streamed down the slope, whooping and yowling prayers to their Ruin goddess. One of them slammed into the horse and spun to the ground, but the force knocked the beast skittering off-balance. It shrieked and tossed its head, and the next thing Semana knew, she was slamming into the ground amidst the rushing tide. There she lay, stunned, as Darak's horde rushed toward the fray despite his wind-elevated commands to hold ranks.

Far ahead, down in the valley, the dragon descended upon the outskirts of the encamped barbarians and loosed a blast of Frostfire that turned a score of them to desiccated ice sculptures. Spears and arrows scythed up at the beast but glanced harmlessly off its scales to rain back down and fell barbarians by the score. With a cry of irritation rather than pain, the creature beat its wings and launched itself upward, the wind of its passing shattering the victims of its breath into reddish-white chunks of frozen flesh. As it rose, barbarians scattered like rodents from the path of a pouncing lion.

The world snapped back into focus as one barbarian almost kicked Semana in the face. Booted feet splashed through the slush around her, stomping perilously close to her face. A breath later, someone tripped over her, knocking the wind out of her lungs with one hobnailed boot. She lay coughing and half-drenched, her acolyte robes mangled with muddy slush. She coughed into her hand, which came away bloody. Semana scowled. Her body felt weak and battered, and she was pretty certain something had broken in her chest.

Maybe it was the Frostburn in her. Maybe it was her mother.

She got back up.

The valley had fallen into chaos. The dragon circled in the air, wheeling about for another pass. The encamped barbarians had rallied some sort of defense, but Semana knew the dragon's strength would more than match it. She sensed magic brewing at the heart of the camp—perhaps one of the Druids, or perhaps several—but it would not come fast enough to make the difference.

If this army—potentially *her* army—were to survive, she had to act.

Semana dropped a hand to the tarnished buckle of her belt. The black leather strap looked like it belonged with a very different sort of attire, and indeed it did. Semana summoned the magic within, bidding it open to her mind, and the relic answered. Heatless flame spread across her body, unraveling her acolyte robes like feathers blistering away. In heartbeats, instead of the mud-ruined robes, she wore her ensorcelled black leather, from scuffed boots to blood-stinking cuirass to riveted mask. The suit fit her like a second skin, and power suffused her body as her many relics hummed awake.

The mud bubbled around Semana's boots, and she launched herself into the air with the force of a loosed arrow. The hurtling air scratched at her mask and made her eyes water, but she smiled all the same.

She was Mask once more.

How could she have pretended not to be for so long?

The dragon swooped down, wings vibrating with the force of the air beneath them, silver fire crackling around its multiple jaws. Even in the depths of its focus upon its prey, however, the beast's head perked and its eyes turned toward Mask as she flew toward it, power burning around the silver glove on her left hand. The sorcerer thrust her hand forward like a charging knight, and the manifested power smashed into the dragon like a shattering lance.

The beast loosed a startled shriek and tumbled in the opposite direction, smashing down onto the edge of the camp and tumbling through like a rolling boulder. Barbarians scattered in all directions away from the furrow of its crash landing, and Mask watched more than one body fly bonelessly into the air, like mud flung up in the wake of a spinning wheel.

The manic hew and cry among the gathered barbarians died away, and all stared in shock at the source of the strike. A sea of faces looked up at the sorcerer floating above, crackling with power.

Mask realized she should say something—issue some inspiring speech or declaration. But just at the moment, all she felt was terror and elation. Her heart hammered out of her chest and her lungs couldn't seem to get enough air. Her hands were shaking, and she thanked the Fire for the darkness and black leather that hid the signs of her fear. And she wouldn't trade it for anything.

The dragon rolled back over onto its belly and gathered itself like a hunting cat ready to pounce. It looked directly at her, its head like an arrowhead pointing straight at her heart. Silvery flames dripped from between its teeth, and it hissed in challenge. It completely forgot about the barbarians it had come to attack, sweeping them aside like flecks of dust with its massive wings. The dragon only had eyes for her.

Mask summoned plaguefire, which burned in a corona around her head. Her silver glove hummed with the amount of power she forced it to create. If she only had a moment—

She didn't.

The dragon cast itself at her, jaw gaping open and frostfire surging forth in a scorching geyser. Mask barely threw herself aside of the flames, and one of its claws clipped her hard enough to evoke all the shielding power of her armor and shatter it in a single blow. She tumbled crazily through the air as it hurtled past, buffeted like a tiny bird caught in a windstorm. Something smashed into her with bone-jarring force, knocking her back up into the night sky.

Her wits jumbled and fell over each other as she tried to think. She realized dizzily that it was one of the dragon's tails that had chanced to hit her and juggle her back into the air. The three tails streaked after the beast, stabilizing and guiding its flight not unlike the way she used her silver glove. What an odd thing to think, when she was fighting to stay alive.

In the depths of her confusion, Mask thought of the first time she'd tried to fly, five years ago in Tar Vangr. Saw again Tithian's concerned face as he watched her botch the landing so badly. Not for the first time, she regretted their parting.

A cry rose from the barbarians below, and Mask saw the dragon curling in the air to strike anew. She fought to rein in her terror and focus. She could do this. She *must.*

The boots surged with power and she caught herself in the air, bobbled a bit, and floated autonomously perhaps a long spear's cast from the ground. The fog swirled around her, cutting her vision to a very limited range. A roar echoed around her, announcing the dragon's approach, but she could not see it amongst the clouds. Whether it could find her or no hardly mattered. It had only to fill the fog with Frostfire and—

The world exploded around her in silver flames. Mask shrieked and curled into a ball, desperate to shield herself from the roaring destruction.

The moment stretched. She could feel the intensity of the power boiling around her, crackling over and under and through her. It shattered against her like waves crashing on rocks, sending silvery spray in all directions. The power recognized her. It knew her. It answered her. It consumed her and begged to be consumed.

At length, Mask realized she was not dead.

Far from it, in fact. She had never felt as powerful as she did just at that moment, bathed in the silver dragon's breath and breathing in the Frostfire like oxygen. It tasted clean and perfect, like pure rain free of Ruin's bile. Even as a child, raised among the powerful and privileged, she'd never tasted anything so pristine. The power bathed her and purified her until her body veritably *thrummed* with energy.

Mask rose, carried aloft on the wings of the magic in her boots. She escaped the haze of silver fire, which hung below her like a cloud of death. The dragon surged past, its scales glittering in the glow of its own fire. The creature was beautiful in its gleaming majesty, an engine of power and destruction that none could oppose.

None but her.

Mask summoned Plaguefire and hurled it at the dragon, cutting a line of green and black corruption down its marvelous scales. The creature shuddered, loosing a baying cry of pain that made Mask shudder. It tried to fly away, but she pursued, maintaining the arcing chain of green and black magic that connected them. It pulled her and she flew along with it, using her boots to keep herself stable. The dragon dragged her through the sky like some sort of parasite attached to its thick body.

The dragon's breath had charged her full of energy, and she directed the power inside into the mask. Somehow, the relic drew power from the surrounding world as usual but also from her own body, making more powerful than ever before.

They sailed into the sky together, Mask's plaguefire lashing at it over and over like a threshing machine. Each strike burned a hole in its armor, rotting the silver and white scales before her eyes. She left dozens of scoring marks along the dragon's hide, cracking and tearing and damaging it. The dragon rolled and flailed its claws at her, seeking to pry her away like the unwelcome pest she was. Unfortunately for the beast, however, Mask was much too small and nimble to be cast away so easily. The Plaguefire kept stinging as the dragon flew on, and a piteous moan sounded from its mighty throat.

At first, Mask was delighted, but her ardor began to fade. She had wanted only to harm the mighty beast, but the higher they flew and the more damage she inflicted upon the dragon, the heavier her heart weighed on her. This began to feel not like a battle but more like vandalism. With the ugliest of her magic, she repeatedly blighted the most beautiful thing she had ever seen without pity or hesitation.

There had to be another way.

The dragon slowed abruptly, extending its great wings out to block the wind and seize all sound before it. Unhindered, Mask shot ahead, drawing level with the beast's glittering eye. In that pendulous orb, she saw bestial pain and fear, but also an intense sorrow that was anything but animal. It no longer wanted to fight: it only wanted to fly far and fast. It wanted to escape.

The dragon's desire mirrored what she felt in her heart.

Mask let go.

The Plaguefire burned out, and the crackling cords of magic connecting her to the dragon dissolved like mist. Just before it pulled away, the dragon glanced back and she thought she saw joy on its face. If she hadn't known it for a wild beast, she'd have thought that glow in its eye born of respect. Perhaps even affection.

Then it beat its wings hard and shot into the gray clouds above. Buffeted on the wind of its passing, Mask fell away back toward the ground far below. For a number of slow, calm heartbeats, she floated in the empty sky, the world dull and slow. She reached out her arms and legs, feeling the embrace of the rushing air for a moment, then pulled up and propelled herself on her boots.

From this distance, the World of Ruin below looked surprisingly peaceful. Through low-hanging clouds, the massed army spread like a black blanket at the foot of Iseldra's Folly, the summit of which she could make out about level with herself. In the spreading dusk, she could see dim red and green lights glowing within. It looked as if a great blow had shattered the mountain top, leaving ragged stone spears that reached into the sky like grasping fingers. In the mountain's palm, steam and smoke licked upward from what looked like a forest of some kind. But that made no sense. Surely trees and other living things couldn't thrive among rubble and broken stone.

Mask glanced down at the army and considered. Darak had exhorted her to keep a low cloak to avoid questions that might reveal her secrets, and swooping back among them openly would do quite the opposite. She owed her brother nothing—least of all her obedience—but in this case, she had to admit he had a point. Afferath distrusted her intensely, and even if she did not seize the opportunity to slay her outright for using anathema relics, she was one of the High Druids. If she persuaded others of the Circle to turn against her, it might present a significant obstacle to her greater goal.

The falling night and her black leathers gave her an opportunity, and she flew away from the barbarians massing in the middle of the valley, searching for a likely place to set down unnoticed. They did not seem to be actively engaged, but the tension on the air threatened to choke her. Barbarians snarled at one another, beat their chests, and brandished their weapons menacingly. One wrong word or move, and it could fall to blows, sacred mountain or no.

A familiar voice rang out, and Mask wondered why it surprised her.

"Ruin sends her dark angel to protect us!" The winds carried Darak's voice wide as he stood high in his stirrups. He threw his arms wide as though invoking the power of Ruin herself. "We are blessed, my brothers and sisters! This will be a moot unlike any other!"

Of course Darak knew the truth, and of course he would do this. Her brother never missed an opportunity to take advantage of every situation, even if—*particularly* if—it meant seizing the glory from his sister. She suspected this was the skill that had kept him alive and powerful for so many years.

Darak went on, and his sermon gave Mask a chance to land behind a wagon, out of immediate sight of any who might be waiting. All had seen the sorcerer in black leather, and so that armor would draw more attention than it deflected. The wagon was full of supplies—rough blankets, foodstuffs that smelled salty enough to choke on, and all manner of rope and the necessities to build Afferath's glamorous tent. No one would miss one blanket, which Mask filched with the aid of her silver glove. It shifted and fell off the back of the wagon right into her waiting hands. She looked back around.

"Just as Ruin has blessed this moot, so has she blessed Afferath, Mistress of the Burning Rain!" Darak said. "For the angel did not appear until she took the field!"

Mask had to fight not to chuckle at that. A hundred paces away, Afferath sat astride her own horse, fuming and doing her best not to show it. The barbarians around her were not so easily taken in either, and looked disapprovingly at their mistress when they thought they could get away with it. She had reacted to the dragon's presence by calling it a blessing from Ruin, but that had not worked out well for anyone involved. Now Darak's speech, despite pushing some of the credit toward her, represented a clear challenge to her authority. Mask hoped Darak knew how to wield the weapon he had just drawn.

Something moved in the darkness behind Mask, and she whirled, unseen hand immediately thrusting forward and up. She caught a man and slammed him against the wagon, where he hung gasping and choking. His crimson hair gave him away immediately: Crown of Fire.

"Ruin…angel," he said. "Praise…to you…"

Mask tilted her chin. "Silence," she said in a ragged voice.

Crown of Fire obeyed immediately, his eyes wide with religious fervor.

She knew she should kill him. But if she did that, his loyalty would evaporate and she'd have to find a new contact among the barbarians. No. Better to make him hers, and she thought she knew how.

She let Crown of Fire slide to the ground. To his credit, he staggered only once, then quickly righted himself. He sank to his knees and presented his throat. Splotchy bruises had started to appear on his dark skin, but he hardly seemed to feel them.

"Get up." Mask tossed the blanket in his face.

Crown of Fire rose, his face furrowed in confusion. Then his eyes widened as Mask activated the belt. Her leathers, glove, and mask melted away, vanishing into the relic's magic, and Semana stood before Crown of Fire, her hair mussed and her body naked but for the belt clasped tightly just above her hips. The barbarian stared at her in awe, wonder, and not a little desire.

"Well?" She turned her back and extended her arms.

After a heartbeat's hesitation, Crown of Fire stepped forward and draped the blanket reverently around her shoulders. Semana could feel his warm breath on her neck and smell his anxious sweat, and his hard body brushed against hers for just a moment. Neither arousing nor entirely unpleasant. She turned to him, and his eyes were very bright in the last rays of the setting sun.

"Am I your master?" she asked. "Before all others?"

He nodded immediately, his bright red tongue flicking out to wet his lips.

The barbarian reached for her, but Semana drew back before he could touch her hand.

"Acolyte." Darak stood at the edge of the wagon, where he had come looking for her. Behind him, the barbarians in the valley had erupted in sounds of joy and revelry, rather than battle.

"Master."

She avoided looking Darak in the face, as that would be a challenge. Instead, she turned her gaze on Crown of Fire, then moved her head dismissively. He headed away, sparing only a single glance for Darak. Was that jealousy on his face? Perhaps.

When they were alone, Semana adjusted the blanket around herself and finally met Darak's eye. "How did you find me?" she asked.

"The same way I found you at the ambush site," Darak said.

"You can smell my Frostfire." Semana knew it was true, because she could detect his power that way: simmering, faint, but definitely there. After what the dragon had breathed into her, she suspected she reeked of the power for miles if anyone knew to recognize the smell.

Darak nodded. He stepped closer, and Semana felt the sudden urge to back away. She suppressed it and stood her ground instead. "You're wroth with me. For disobeying you."

"Wroth? Hardly." Darak smiled widely. "Our journey has been nothing but victory. First one of the Deathless Fae of legend graces us with his presence, and then the dark angel of Ruin flies for us. Do you have any idea how much those folk down there love you right now? How much *I* love you?"

He beamed with pleasure. Manic joy made his dark complexion ruddy, and he looked much younger than his twenty or so winters. She had never seen him so ecstatically happy, even when the barbarians had answered his speech with their orgiastic revelry. She was about to remark on it—rib him with some sly witticism—when he reached in, seized her face, and kissed her full on the lips. It was not a gentle brotherly kiss, but something harder—hungrier.

In her surprise, her whole body seized up, confused and unable to react.

Darak broke the kiss and drew away slightly, keeping their faces close together. He ran his thumb over her lips. "I knew I chose rightly with you."

He smiled brilliantly, caressed her cheek, then walked away.

Semana just stared, fighting as hard as she could to stop her legs trembling.

EIGHTEEN

Necthana

As a city, Necthana stood as one sinuous whole, without streets or avenues to demarcate houses or separate domiciles. Staircases climbed up between wings of chambers, a little like close alleyways that offered no opportunity to hide one's doings. The Deathless passed their time in close proximity, their deeds open to all to see, just as they had for over a thousand years. Rose's chambers at the heart of Necthana allowed all of the Deathless to see her rooms at all times.

The chambers of the Deathless Summit, however, varied from this tradition. Poised on the northernmost edge of Necthana and reserved for one fae and his entourage, it sought and achieved a kind of autonomy that would seem foreign to the Deathless. Most of the walls were covered over with dark tapestries inside, affording a level of privacy unheard of in this city. Several corridors leading to these chambers stood blocked off with stone and repurposed mage-glass, leaving only one primary entrance that stood under the constant watch of two fae who meditated out in the courtyard. So fully did they blend into the pedestals upon which they sat they might have been statues rather than people.

It reminded Regel of a holdfast, or at least the closest one could create in Necthana.

He presented himself at the entry gates, and the watchers stirred. Their bodies had not moved, but Regel could feel their wills awakening. They scrutinized him silently but pointedly.

"I call upon the Deathless Summit," he said. "Will you bar my entrance?"

The warders gazed at one another, communicating silently. They turned back to their meditations.

Softly, Regel blew out a breath of relief. It was the closest to an affirmative he would receive. He adjusted the leather packet slung across his back so that it did not cramp his shoulders.

He ascended the steps, glancing around the unusual chambers. He'd never set foot inside Summit's halls, of course—not on any of his previous visits. Tapestries depicted a series of fantastic landscapes: towering mountains of crimson and gold, sweeping valleys that sparkled as though with real daylight, and forest scenes of swirling color and majestic beasts. Regel, in all his travels, had never encountered such wonder. This sort of beauty seemed impossible in the World of Ruin.

Could these tapestries date from the World of Wonder? The artifacts within Necthana shared the timeless quality of the Deathless: ancient but not old, never fading or growing dusty. Those images could be thousands of years old and he would not know it.

"Come, oh mortal man," said a voice that echoed off the walls of glass. "Be not afraid."

Regel gritted his teeth.

He crossed through the hall of tapestries and into what looked like a study crammed with shelves of books, scrolls, and pedastals crowned with sculptures and trinkets. The relics drew his eye: a necklace of dull multi-colored beads, a rod about the length of his hand etched with flames, a sword broken in three places, and a chipped vase inset with colorful designs from another world. The artifacts looked as old and exotic as the tapestries, and Regel guessed they hailed from far, far away in the World of Ruin. The knowledge stored in this single room might have rivaled that of the greatest sages of Tar Vangr.

Then he saw it. Affixed to the wall behind the large darkwood desk, emitting blue-white tendrils along the mage-glass like creeping vines, was a sword crafted of blue mage-glass. He could feel the sword's cold power calling to him even at this distance.

Frostburn.

"Beautiful." The voice, deep and penetrating, sounded like thunder rolling off a mountain. "And deadly. But you knew that already."

The fae unfolded from the darkness where he sat at the desk. The purple light of Necthana's walls reflected off the silvery skin of his hand as he turned a page in the book splayed on his desk. He was the palest of the Deathless that Regel had ever seen, his delicate features and complexion suggesting a winterborn heritage. He had strong, well-hewn features and a modest dark beard with touches of gray. The many furrows on his face spoke of a long life spent in the harsher parts of the world, facing the ravages of weather but never losing the magnetism that made his visage compelling.

"Summit," Regel said.

"Rose's pet." Not looking up, the fae gestured to a goblet filled halfway with thick black wine. "That is for you. A truly ancient vintage. One of my favorites."

Regel left the wine sitting on the desk. "The Deathless Rose tells me that yours is the loudest voice that speaks against me," he said. "How can I allay your concerns."

Summit carried on with his reading as though Regel had not spoken.

This Deathless, Regel knew from old. They had met near thirty years ago, when he had first come to Necthana. Summit had opposed him from the first, advocating for his immediate execution or his expulsion from Necthana at the very least. Only facing the fae in combat had granted Regel the chance to prove himself, but it had not led to anything like friendship between them. Quite the opposite.

"Do you hate me so much?" Regel asked.

"Hate you?"

Finally, Summit looked up at him, and his regard lasted a long moment. Then he closed his book and stood, drawing up to his full height, which put him rather taller than Regel. Imposing.

"Did you ever hear the tale of my naming?" the fae asked.

"No." Regel wasted the wine: bitter but powerful. Much like Summit himself.

"I suppose you would never have heard it," Summit said. "You were ever Rose's pet, and I doubt my name or origin ever crossed the pillow between your faces."

Regel shrugged.

"I was the first outsider to become a Deathless." Summit stepped back around the desk and sifted through papers and leather bound books. "I was an explorer, you see, in those first optimistic centuries of the Calatite Empire. I discovered Necthana in the autumn of 336 SA by your calendar. I remember the date only because I kept a journal of my life, and that was the final entry. Ah."

He held up a book for Regel to see. The leather was ancient and branded with a script he did not recognize. He could readily believe the book dated from six and a half centuries ago.

"Mountains were my passion." Summit indicated the wide map hung on the wall behind his desk. "I scaled ranges in the blasted realm of the setting sun, in the unapproachable east, and in the lands of eternal summer in the south. But the best among all of these—where my dreams bloomed and my fancies led me—were the peaks of the northern ranges." He swept his hand over the north of the map. "They had no names, in those days. I was the first to reach the…" He paused, hesitating to say his own name. "*Top* of many mountains. And so many such peaks bore the names I gave them, at least for a time."

Regel noted Summit's hand drifting to the northeast edge of the map. "And you discovered Necthana," he said.

Summit's lip curled and he looked genuinely amused. "You know I did not," he said. "The Deathless discovered *me*, in fact. One had been watching me for some time—a constant, silent companion on some of my more treacherous climbs. I think you know the Deathless Gilt."

Regel nodded. "He is a scout," he said.

"Among other things," Summit said. "There have ever existed among the Deathless those who wish to explore. To press for a wider world. Who cannot be contented with a realm that does not change. It is a disease to them, curiosity: a vestige of the old way that will not expire. Gilt came upon me in my extremity and aided me when my need was great. I would have died, were it not for Gilt's curiosity. It drew us together, along with my own drive to learn. To understand. To find..." He trailed off, uncertain of the right word.

Again, Regel nodded, but this time he saw a deeper truth. Now he knew why Gilt had followed them, and why the Deathless had gone back for Semana. Discovery drew him, and the princess represented something the World of Ruin had not known in centuries, if ever. He knew the word.

Hope.

Summit had lost himself in thought for a moment as well, caught in a memory from six hundred years earlier. "We became exploring companions and lovers and, in time, Gilt brought me to Necthana," he said. "I received a...poor welcome. Many sought my destruction immediately, and were it not for Gilt and for Rose, they would have had it."

"She protected you?" Regel asked. "Rose did?"

"As Rose protected you," Summit said. "The Deathless Rose ruled the Deathless even then, and with such a position came a great voice. Rose spoke for me, and thus I endured, even surrounded by my enemies. In time, with training and with proving, I became Deathless, and when the ritual asked me to forswear that which I most loved, it was the peak of my passion—the eternal goal of my adventures."

"The summit." Regel nodded. "Why are you telling me this?"

"For the same reason anyone speaks to anyone else," Summit said. "To be understood."

Regel furrowed his brow. "But I do not understand," he said. "Your tale is not unlike my own. Thirty years ago, I sought the fabled City of the Dead, and Rose drew me into Necthana. You sought my expulsion or destruction. I learned the ways of the Deathless, and you stood over me, advocating at all times for my failure. Why would you work against me, as others worked against you?"

This made Summit smile slightly. "I do not hate you. I envy you." He gestured to Frostburn on the wall, which had begun to drip long trails of icy condensation along the glass and floor. "You walk among us as a living man, gaining access to our deepest secrets and our greatest magic. You never had to compromise what you were—you did not have to die to earn your place among us. I thought I could change Necthana, but I only became its slave. You, however." He closed his black eyes and breathed out wistfully. "You are free. And for that, I envy you."

He came around the desk until he stood within easy reach, handsome and intoxicating. This close, his body smelled of rich cloves and fresh kefa. The power within Summit stirred, and Regel could feel it warm against his skin. The fae reached across and laid his hand across Regel's own on the table, his skin unexpectedly cool in contrast to the power in his body. Summit leaned close to whisper in Regel's ear, as though they were old friends rather than enemies.

"You have such strength in you, and Necthana needs your strength. I will speak for you." Summit's words were sweet in his ear. He took Regel's hand and guided it to his own cheek, its skin rough and weathered from exposure centuries before. "You may thank me."

"Thank you?"

Summit leaned in and kissed Regel gently, his lips cold and bittersweet. Regel could not have pulled away, even had he wanted to. His body drew into the kiss, pulled toward the power inside Summit as surely as a scrap of metal to a lodestone. Regel's heart raced as though it would burst out of his chest. Desire and need drowned his anxiety and he lost himself in the Deathless's embrace. Time stretched and his mind spread with it. The fae's hand slipped down the front of Regel's breeches.

"You belong here," the Deathless said. "With us."

Just at the moment, Regel could hardly argue.

Summit pulled him around and pressed him against the desk, the both of them falling atop it together. The fae climbed onto him smoothly, never losing the connection between their lips, and Regel pulled them close together. Garments came undone and skin pressed against skin.

"But I know you will not stay," Summit said. "What is to be done?"

Regel kissed him back, hard and needful.

Frostburn gleamed on the wall, redoubling its magical output. The trails of frost crept toward them as though hungry for their heat, just as the Deathless body atop Regel craved his warmth. Summit's touch reached into Regel and stirred the magic inside him. Power leaked out of his heart, diffusing into the rest of his body like blood dripping into water. Summit drew it from him, absorbing it as though—

Feeding.

"Wait," Regel said between kisses. "Stop—"

He tried to get his hands under Summit—to lever him away—but the Deathless was too strong. Fear beat hot inside him, replacing any desire he had known. And with it, anger. Regel smashed the heel of one hand into Summit's head, but the blow was not strong enough to knock him away. The Deathless loosed a murmur of annoyance then kissed him anew—harder and more assertively this time.

"Give me your power," Summit said. "Give in, and this will all end."

Regel felt weak, as though the Deathless had already drained most of his strength. Out of the edge of his vision, he saw one of Frostburn's trails of ice creeping across the desk toward them. He had no choice. He strained to reach across. His fingers scratched on the wood, just barely touching the ice…

A rush of cold flooded through him, as though every ounce of heat had vanished from his body. Atop him, Summit stiffened in surprise and tore away, gasping and choking at the effort. He caught himself on one knee on the floor, his robe hanging open and his black eyes glittering up at Regel.

"What have you done?" Summit fell to a coughing fit, unable to restrain himself. "You cannot defy me. You need me."

Regel barely heard. That tiny touch of Frostburn's power had overwhelmed him, and he needed more. He scrambled off the table, his body clumsy, and staggered across the study.

"Where will you go?" Summit asked. "You cannot escape Necthana. You cannot walk the shadow path unguided."

"Perhaps not." As he passed, Regel pointed at the piece in Summit's collection that had given him hope. Not Frostburn, not any of the inspiring art, but the broken pieces of an ancient steel sword: metal in a city where none could pass. "But that means there are other ways in and out. I will find one. With this."

He laid his fingers against the blue glass blade on the wall. He touched its sparkling silver hilt.

Summit's eyes widened. "You cannot have that. It is the deathright of my people. You cannot—"

"No." Regel stood at the wall, reaching up. "You erred thirty years ago, and you still err today. You think this a weapon, but *I* am the weapon."

He closed his fingers around its hilt, and the blade took him. Passion and heat drained from him, and in their place he knew only the hungering void. Too long had he passed without the sword, and he could not resist its pull. He wrenched it off the wall and swept it around, the blade cutting the air itself.

The long curved blade of blue mage-glass cascaded from Regel's hand, the air shimmering and freezing around its edge. Its very proximity hurt, sucking the will out of all things living, dead, and Deathless. Necthana's hatred flowed through the blade, as though a single shard of Ruin had broken off and formed a weapon that a mortal man might wield.

"I *am* the Frostburn," Regel said.

The doors burst open and half a dozen Deathless streamed in, staves and truncheons at the ready.

In the depths of Frostburn's cold fury, a tiny part of Regel smiled.

BOOK FIVE: MASKS

Two Years Previous—Luether—Summer 980 Sorcerus Annis

THE HIGH WINDOW OF the tower exploded out into the late day sun, sending a sun-sparkling shower of glass, stone, and dust raining down over high-city Luether below. A mostly naked man tumbled in the midst of the cutting storm, blood streaming from his mouth and nose, his torn dressing gown streaming up around him like broken wings in the hot air. He fell for half a heatbeat, the rushing wind stealing his screams, and abruptly lurched to a halt, dangling in midair and suspended by nothing visible.

A figure wrapped in black floated out through the hole the magic had ripped in the side of the tower, smoking boiling up around the burning energies that held it aloft. Mask looked down at the man caught in her magic, who coiled and fought like a fish suspended on a hook. Long wisps of golden hair flopped wildly in all directions, exposing thick bald spots on his head. He could not move in any direction, but his thrashing succeeded only in flipping him over so he could stare with wide eyes at the fall. His hands scrabbled furiously at the air for supports they would not find.

Borne on the power of her boots, Mask floated around the man and lifted him vertical with a casual wave of her left hand. The air wavered around the silver glove, its power hot and steady. She pulled herself parallel to him as he dangled in the air, legs kicking under him as though trying desperately to swim. His limp blade danced pathetically along with their motion. The sorcerer had to suppress a gag.

"Where?" she asked, her voice crackling.

The man's expression hardened a bit when he saw her, but only a bit. Lord Muldrand of Blood Tomp was a proud man, and when he faced an enemy, he chose bravado over sense. When first she had come to him in his chambers, he'd seemed too stupid to be afraid. Dangling a hundreds of paces over certain death weakened his resolve, however.

"What do you mean?" He had to shout over the wind. "I don't know what you mean!"

"Where." Mask reached toward him with her right hand and traced one sizzling hot talon of her war gauntlet through the air just above his chest and rotund belly. His body tensed and tried to pull away from the deadly magic, caving itself in toward his spine. "Where is the Ravalis Shroud?"

Muldrand feigned a look of surprise. "I don't know him," he said. "Who—?"

Mask sighed. She waved her left hand as though swatting a fly, and sent Muldrand sailing back into the tower through a window on a lower story. His bulky body shattered the thin wood shutter with a hollow crack, and she heard one of his arms crunch grotesquely against the stone of the sill, followed by Muldrand cursing and weeping in pain. A flicker of concern rose up inside her, but she smashed it back down with cold anger and indifference. Next time, she'd have to aim a little better.

Blood Tomp was one of the few remaining Bloods of power in Luether that persisted after the rise of Pervast the Ruin King. A rich and powerful house, Tomp had a history of outspoken opposition to foreign influences and the "tyranny" of any ruling body that pushed for alliance or even tolerance for "enemies" of Luether, such as the Winter King and his attempts to forge a pact before the fall of Luether nearly twenty years ago. Ironically, Muldrand and his Blood had immediately kneeled to the barbarians upon their conquest of the mage-city, and today spent their time desperately trying to remain useful to Pervast whilst decrying the Summer Lives insurgency and its "foreign" customs and backers, all without any evidence connecting their efforts to Tar Vangr. His was one of the faces of the Ruin King, allowing the edicts of the Children of Ruin to come through a voice more recognizable and sympathetic to the people. He leveraged his charisma through regular speeches to crowds of Luether's dregs, whether at public executions or the Children's less well attended but frequent gatherings on the street. Blood Tomp decried the traitors of Summer Lives, blamed folk from other lands for the problems in theirs, and preached slavish devotion to the Ruin King by offering the illusion of riches and fame to be earned thusly.

It made sense, Tudran's scheme to survive and even thrive under the rule of the Children, and it made Mask ill just to think on it.

True, the sorcerer had no great love for the Fox of Luether and less for the cause of "redeeming" a lost city like Luether, but she had even less compunction about bringing grief to a toad like Muldrand. He represented the worst of Luethaar: kowtowing to a monster like Pervast and selling out his own people whilst presenting himself as a patriot. He was nothing but a sweaty opportunist, stuffing his fat belly and deep pockets with the suffering of those who thought him friend, and playing whichever side would line his coffers. He was a miserable, bigoted, two-faced worm of a man.

And he was the pivotal next step in her ongoing quest to find those who wanted her dead.

Muldrand's groans and curses of pain took on a new caliber when he started screaming in panic, and the sound of crashing furniture emerged from the tower window. That would be her squire now.

Mask sighed. Time to get on with this.

She floated inside the room, where Muldrand had huddled in a corner to escape the destruction. A table crashed into a wall, cracking into several pieces, and Mask's squire hefted a chair to hurl in its wake. The finely crafted wood groaned and split, upholstery nails popping loose to plink like tiny daggers against the stone. It was hard to tell through the articulated bones on his death mask, but she suspected he was smiling. Tithian seemed to enjoy destruction of all kinds.

Davargorn. Mask had to correct herself. He'd begun to favor the name the other Mask had given him that terrible night back in Tar Vangr. As he explained it, to him, Tithian was just as dead as Semana was to her. He would not use that name again—at least, not until their quest was done.

Muldrand looked as horrified at the destruction of his furniture as Davargorn's obvious capacity for violence. His tone suggested he'd mostly recovered his composure, and fear had become anger.

"Do you have any idea how much coin I paid for that?" the Lord of Tomp asked. "That table was imported at great cost—at great cost, I tell you—from the Free Isles. The wood salvaged from three different pirate ships, all sunk in the Battle of Faradis—"

"Really." Muscles rippled along Davargorn's bare arms as he wrenched one of the legs off the chair, which came free with a disconsolate moan of wood warping. He patted the haft in his other hand. "I'll have to thank those pirates for giving me such a fine cudgel for beating you."

Mask rolled her eyes and suppressed a sigh. Davargorn meant well, but he had yet to achieve proper skill with intimidation. When it came to inflicting pain, he showed an unnerving aptitude, but his delivery of threats left much to be desired. The implied violence only seemed to confuse Muldrand. The man seemed too stupid to be afraid. Perhaps she should dangle him outside the tower again.

"Is coin what you want?" Muldrand asked. "If that's what this is, we can make a deal. I'm a very rich man. I'm richer than you know. That's one of the best things about me."

"I'm sure," Mask said, drawing their attention.

Davargorn glanced up at her with a little bit of annoyance: he didn't like it when she seized his moment, but he was too much her slave to complain. For his part, Muldrand looked uneasy and scooted a little further into the corner.

"What's this all about?" Muldrand asked. "What passes? I'm a smart man. Very smart. You can talk to me. We can work something out."

He was stalling. Mask heard footsteps and angry voices outside the chamber. They'd taken care of his personal warders, of course—left them beaten and unconscious in the halls above—but blasting out the upstairs wall and throwing Muldrand out into the open air had drawn some additional attention.

"Time grows short." Davargorn smashed his improvised club against the wall with a sharp crack of wood on stone. The end splintered, sharpening to a forest of jagged points. He menaced Muldrand with the tearing club, which succeded in frightening the man where words had failed.

Mask took hold of his arm, restraining the club. Davargorn looked at her, mismatched eyes livid through the bones of his mask. She shook her head slightly, and they struggled silently for a heartbeat. The anger inside Davargorn practically screamed at her, clawing and thrashing to get out. But she was in control, not him. Always her.

Finally, his eyes parted from hers, and he lowered the club.

Fists and boots pounded on the door, and warders shouted for Lord Muldrand.

Mask looked to the fat lordling on the floor, not bothering to hide her contempt. "We will meet again, Lord Tomp," she said.

Muldrand took some heart from the voices of his warriors and smiled smugly up at them. "I look forward to it," he said. "And when you do, we'll have a nice talk, we will. You, me, and my—"

The words shattered in a wet grunt as Davargorn swatted the ragged club across Muldrand's face. Blood and spittle flew in its wake, and Muldrand's head smashed back against the wall. At first, he could only stare at them, stunned and confused by what had transpired. Then three red gouges started welling on his previously handsome visage, and Muldrand rubbed at his ruined face. He fell to his knees, screaming horrified, choked, gargling screams, incoherent and filled with wordless nightmares.

Mask wrenched Davargorn away from the blubbering man and all but hurled him out the window ahead of her. The door shattered open just as they fell out over the city, and a casterbolt whizzed through the air above them. Davargorn put his arms around her compact body and Mask activated her boots only when they had fallen a spear cast toward the ground. They swooped away through the sizzling heat of the Luether summer while castermen loosed vainly after them, blowing bricks and crumbling stonework off the surrounding towers.

They flew out over high-city Luether, the sun uncomfortably hot through the black leather of her armor. At first, flying together with the boots had proved an awkward experience—two bodies clinging together for their lives as the world passed crazily beneath them—but now they had become very accustomed to it. Sometimes, Mask even gave Davargorn the boots to wear himself.

They headed for the edge of the high-city mage-glass so they could descend to low-city unmolested. In Tar Vangr, there might have been sentries posted to shoot down illicit fliers, but not here among the Children of Ruin. They were all too busy reveling in cruelty and blood.

Mask had long ago learned not to bother speaking while they flew, and Davargorn didn't look like he had much to say either. His eyes were far away—his jaw set in a thin, angry line. He burrowed against her, holding her tight, and she could feel his anger like a radiating lamp inside him, making him burn to the touch. He knew he had done wrong, and was even now considering how to defend himself.

They would definitely discuss this. Of that, she could be certain.

They set down on the roof of Illustra's, a mostly defunct brothel they kept as one of their safehouses in Luether. The various tasks Mask and her apprentice undertook for coin—mostly intimidating street toughs or roughing up a perceived rival—permitted them a certain influx of coin, which they used to keep waystations and boltholes in various buildings throughout the city. Since Summer Lives had raided their first hideaway two years ago, they'd avoided any permanent housing. It made them too vulnerable—too easily discovered.

Of course, their anonymity hardly mattered if they couldn't work together toward a common goal.

When they descended the rickety scaffolding into their rented room, Davargorn went immediately into his regular routine upon their return: checking the various snares and wires he'd set up to mark their absence. None of these measures would prevent intruders, but if any were disturbed, he would know someone had been there.

"What the Fire was that?" Mask demanded.

"What was what?" her squire asked, his voice drawn out in indifference.

"What you did," Mask said, her voice gravel-choked and coldly angry, "was reckless and could have unraveled our whole task. If you'd killed Tomp, how would we have followed him to his meeting place? Where would we be, if I hadn't stopped you?"

"Tomp is a fool," he said. "The Shroud would never meet with his like. I saw that clear."

"A fool yes, but *whose* fool?" Mask asked. "The Shroud would not meet with him directly, but his *liaison* is the one we want. I've told you time and again—I am the mind, you the body."

Davargorn grunted in acknowledgement but made no other comment.

"We've never been so close to the Ravalis Shroud," Mask said. "Don't you see that? If we find him, we find who sent killers after us. "

"After *you*, you mean," Davargorn said under his voice.

Mask slitted her eyes. "I thought we were in this together."

Davargorn shrugged and moved on to a hollow spot on the wall. He pulled aside a board low on the wall and checked the level of dust in the crawlspace.

It took quite some time for Davargorn to go about his business, and all the while Mask stood there, fuming with rage. She wanted to scream at him for what he had done. She had to rebuke him, at least, lest he take it as passive encouragement to defy her. But just at the moment, she couldn't even get him to look at her.

"Davargorn," she said. "*Tithian*."

He preoccupied himself inspecting a doorjam, across which he'd strung a hair. Perhaps the hair was hard to see, and that was why it took him so long, but Mask suspected a greater motive at play.

She reached up and unbuckled her mask. The sound drew Davargorn's attention, and he looked up with wide eyes as she removed the foul thing and let it fall to the floor. She became Semana again, but this time it took longer and felt harder to make that transition.

Davargorn hurried toward the mask, picked it up, and shoved it in her direction. "Put this back on, for the Fire's sake," he said. "I'm not finished checking the room. Anyone could be watching."

Semana raised her chin imperiously. "Look at me."

Tithian tensed but looked pointedly away.

"Look at *me*." Semana seized his masked face in her hands and turned it toward her own. "My face. This is still me. But I'm losing myself. Every day that passes, every lead we follow that leads to nothing, more of me goes away and I become that *thing*." She pointed at the mask she'd thrown on the floor. "Do you think that's what I want? To become a monster?"

"Isn't it?" he asked.

Semana was stunned. "What?"

Tithian looked at her levelly and at length. As children, he'd never have looked at her that way. He was always her subordinate, and even now, he considered himself her squire, she his master. But at the same time, the way he looked at her now—seriously and without guile—was alike unto the look of an equal. Semana wasn't sure she was quite ready for him to look at her that way, and she broke first.

She turned and refused to meet his eye. "I don't know what you mean," she said.

"I think you do." Tithian put his hands on Semana's upper arms, making her tense up.

"This is the overwhelming purpose and goal of my life—to reclaim what was taken from me," Semana said. "Do you think I would let you or anyone disrupt that?"

"And do *you* think we can go back to what we were?" Tithian asked. "Four winters have passed. This is our life now. These, our faces." He held up her mask near his own. "Can you tell me, Semana, in total truth, that you do not accept these things? That no part of you *wants* this?"

Semana hesitated. "I—"

That, she could not do. She could speak the words, but she could not swear to them.

"Is that what *you* want?" she asked. "This life of pain and blood?"

He did not answer at first, and the moment stretched between them.

"Perhaps," Tithian said. "At least when I wear this mask, you don't see—"

He paused, and Semana caught the significance of his near slip. She sighed inwardly. So it was still his face that bothered him. Of course.

"You don't see the boy I was," Tithian said. "I'm your equal. Your companion. Your friend in a way I never could be. When we wear these masks, we are the same." He raised his hand to gesture out the window toward the setting sun. "We're free. You must see that."

"You see freedom." Semana touched the mask in his hand. "I see a prison."

His mismatched eyes turned to her, soft through the bones of his mask. "Semana—"

A discreet tap sounded on the door, and both of them tensed. The façade of Davargorn built right back up over Tithian, and he turned toward the door, a blade palmed into his hand. Behind him, Semana bent and slipped the mask over her face and head. When she had buckled it in place, she inhaled the familiar stink of blood that never seemed to go away and sighed. Gone was Semana Denerre nô Ravalis, last heir of Winter, and in her place stood a weapon that existed for only one purpose.

Death.

"Come," Mask said, her voice shredded and broken once more.

The door opened to reveal Eltes, one of Illustra's boys, who stood sweating and uncertain on the threshold of their room. He had good looks: delicate but well built, his every muscle chiseled the best his diet would allow and further augmented with oil and perfume. Illustra had made a game of sending her most attractive prostitutes to Mask and Davargorn's room, perhaps in an attempt to allure them and perhaps gain some advantage over her dangerous guests. If it weren't harmless, Mask would have had Davargorn put an end to it that winter, when she had sent two boys and two girls to them, her youngest and most vibrant flowers, certain that they would at least prick some interest. Little did Illustra know that, young as they were, these lads and lasses had been older than the assassins themselves.

Eltes had been to the room before, and left empty-handed every time, except for a healty offering of fear gifted of Davargorn and his hunter's glare. This day, in his trembling hand, Eltes held a yellowed envelope with one word printed upon it in rough ink: MASK.

"Come, boy," Mask said. "Is that another task I spy in your hand?"

Eltes nodded dumbly, not meeting Mask's crimson eyes. He wisely kept his gaze on Davargorn, who skulked around him at the edges of the room, watching like a hunting wolf that has spied its prey.

"Give it here," Mask said.

Eltes stepped forward but stumbled on trembling legs. His fear was a palpable thing she could almost taste, and she had to admit it made her feel better. She could forget all her doubts and focus instead on the task at hand.

Mask raised her left hand, and the invisible hand of her magic took the letter from Eltes's grasp and brought it floating toward her. She waved dismissively at the lad. "You may go."

Eltes stumbled and scurried out of the room as fast as his muscular legs would take him. Davargorn watched him go with some interest, then closed the door behind him and looked to Mask.

"Who is it?" he asked. "Who are we to kill this time?"

"Muldrand Tomp," Mask said. "It seems we'll both get what we want."

Davargorn smiled, but it was not a reassuring smile.

NINETEEN

Present Day—Iseldra's Folly, the Winter Wilds—Hopedawn 982

The horses' hooves pawed at the rimefrost that coated the skittering stones of the path up Iseldra's Folly. Today was Hopedawn, the height of spring where day and night perfectly matched one another in length. Starting on the morrow, the days would lengthen while the nights shrank until Midsummer and Bright Solstice, the longest day of the year, at which point they would begin to shrink toward Doomdusk and eventually Dark Solstice. Leaving camp before dawn, Semana, Darak, and twelve warriors had ridden half a day from the camp to the foot of Iseldra's Folly.

The great mountain rose above their heads, sparkling with a rainbow of colors, broken asunder three hundred paces up to form…what? Even flying the previous day, she'd been unable to see beyond the edges of the mountain, and as they climbed she wondered what they might find. She'd caught a glimpse of trees, and they had haunted her dreams that night. She could feel the swelling magic in this mountain, radiating from the summit. Red and green smoke rose from among the broken stone pillars, and faint voices drifted on the wind.

The valley below Iseldra's Folly had become a veritable city in its own right, with hundreds of barbarians bedecks in paints and raiment of a dozen different tribes. Semana wondered as to their names and ways, but when she asked her brother to name them, he changed the subject. If he meant to join the ruling circle, would it not behoove him to learn about his would-be subjects?

She picked out their varying markings and the similarity of their piercings and bodily modification, and guessed she saw representatives of a dozen different tribes. Some spoke softly in their barbaric tongue to one another, but inevitably they fell silent and looked once again to the display above. Some of them stood, some of them kneeled, but all of them watched the towering mountain.

Semana couldn't quite fathom this sort of mass reverence. It was like something out of a bard's tale of Old Calatan, when imaginary gods still held power over the hearts of mortals.

"So many," Semana said as they rode through the silent masses. "They are part of the moot?"

"They are the honor guard for the twelve druids of the circle," he said. "By tradition, each member brings to the sacred moot on Iseldra's folly brings twelve bands of twelve warriors. Many come besides: quartermasters, cooks, cobblers, slaves, and followers of all kinds, not to mention acolytes and lesser rotpriests like us. All told, thousands gather here, awaiting the outcome of the moot. It is a religious experience for them: a pilgrimage to Iseldra's Folly that they take every few years."

"Why here?" Semana asked.

"Legends." Darak glanced up at the ragged summit. "You'll see soon enough." He looked around, scrutinizing the barbarians with a derisive sneer. He reined his horse a little closer to hers. "Do not meet their eyes. These barbarians grow anxious as the moot transpires, and will be looking for an excuse."

"I am not afraid." Semana looked around at the armed men and women, who eyed them back with speculation at best, outright ire at worst. "Let them think what they will."

"Do as I say." Darak closed his hand hard around her wrist. "You are my slave, I your master."

Semana thought of what he had done to her the night before, and it filled her with uncertainty and anger. Silvery flames crackled around her fingertips as her Frostfire begged to be unleashed, even though the rational part of her mind knew it would not harm Darak. Then she remembered the hundreds of barbarian warriors around her and let her feelings cool to quiescence. For now.

Darak left his own honor guard—only a dozen swords, which befitted a lesser rotpriest—below the treeline, and he and Semana dismounted to make the perilous climb on foot. For the first thousand paces or so, they had the thick, gray trees to cover them on all sides, but then they broke free of the trees and came to a field of jagged rock, mostly gray but crusted over with various colors: reds, blues, greens, and even vivid purples. Every small stone seemed to be of a different color, and Semana wouldn't have guessed most of these hues could appear in nature.

The tricky path ahead crept up the mountain, crossing back on itself numerous times, and looked none too wide. They stopped for Darak to steady himself on his knees, breathing hard. Semana thought with satisfaction back to all the physical training Davargorn had put her through. Under her brother's boot, she had to take these small victories where she found them.

"What are these?" Semana levitated one of the stones toward her hand: a bright orange-red one.

Darak's eyes widened, and he drew on the Worldfire to sweep the stone away to skitter down the mountain side. At least, that's what it would have done, except that it exploded into a ball of flame the same color as the stone. Semana felt the heat on her face, even if there was no pain.

"The magic of the great cataclysm, trapped within the earth, vomited up," he said. "Dangerously unstable in its unrefined form."

"Dust magic," Semana said. "The flames wouldn't have harmed us, you know."

"Yes, but we'd have to explain why our clothes burned but our flesh did not," Darak said, panting. "Be a little... more careful."

Semana bit off a rebuke. Now wasn't the time or place to challenge his authority—at least not yet. She would wait for the opportune moment.

Wind clawed at the strands of Semana's hair that managed to escape her hood, and she felt entirely too light and vulnerable, and not just because all of this dust magic could explode at any moment. Beneath her rotpriest robe, she wore fresh woolens acquired in the wake of the previous night's events, and the exertion had dampened them with sweat. She did not feel the cold—not with the Frostfire surging through her—but she suspected another woman might be shivering in her place.

Darak coughed a few times and sniffered in the cold air. "Ready to proceed?"

"Yes?" Semana looked at him dubiously. She hadn't even wanted to stop for a rest.

"Well, hurry," he said, as though he hadn't been the one to make them pause. Her brother made a face as though he'd touched something sour with his tongue and gestured up at the rising sun. "Our path awaits. We should go, if we're to make the climb by the sun's zenith."

Semana nodded. Were she alone, she might have used her boots to fly all the way to the top of Iseldra's Folly and have done, but some barbarian would certainly see that. The forms had to be respected, she supposed. The last thing she needed that day would be one of the druids blasting her from the sky with a melting storm cloud or bolt of lightning. And if her magic touched off the raw dust magic that dusted the slope... Perhaps that was part of why the druids insisted on holding their moot at Iseldra's Folly, as the dust magic provided a natural defensive measure, or could ensure mutual destruction if anyone's Worldfire got out of hand. A delicate and dangerous place to break custom.

No, she would be patient. Choose her moment with care.

A hundred paces up, Semana looked down upon the small forms of the assembled honor guard at the foot of the Folly. Unsettlingly, the path offered the assembled barbarians a perfect, unencumbered view of the pair of them as they climbed. Were it not tantamount to sacrilege, the barbarians of various tribes could easily feather them with a barrage of arrows. And after they tumbled off the narrow path to their deaths, the howling wind would sweep neatly away any sign they had attempted the climb at all. It reassured Semana that she had her boots to catch her if she fell, but her sacrilege might cast a shadow on Darak's day of ascension, and wouldn't that prove a shame. She made a bitter face.

"Slave," Darak said from behind her. He extended his hand for aid. "Attend me."

Semana bit her tongue to keep back a retort and paused on the trail until Darak caught up with her. Beneath his rotcloak, he smelled pungently from the exertion of climbing up the mountain, and he had several of those brown-black growths festering on his skin. He'd commanded his slaves to lathe him vigorously that morn in preparation. At least he'd not pressed Semana to join them but only grinned at her in smug satisfaction. He had spent too much time enjoying himself in the last days, and it irritated her to see him continue doing so.

"We're alone," she said as she helped him climb up. "Do you have to call me that?"

"Yes," Darak said. "We draw close to the others of Ruin's circle, and their powers of scrutiny would surprise you. Do what I command, lest I punish you."

By his devilish grin, she couldn't tell if he was jesting or not. "You're in a mood."

Darak glanced up the slope toward the summit. "You've no idea how long I've awaited this day," he said. "So many years learning, training, hiding. All for this moment. And you." He put his hand on her arm. "Ruin made your path cross with mine. Neither of us will regret this, sister. I promise."

The unexpected and unwelcome intimacy made Semana shiver, but she tried not to show it.

For all the wilds had changed her brother, he was still Darak. Dimly, she remembered huddling together with him listening to their parents argue—always violently, rarely to any purpose. Darak's hands trembled as he covered her ears and his voice shook as he told her not to cry. That, she realized, was her earliest memory, and she clung to it fiercely now.

"I have imagined all the paths today might travel," Darak said. "And though there is risk, I see no way in which we will fail. I have planned for every contingency."

The ground shifted under Semana's feet suddenly—a stone skittering out where she meant to put her weight down—but Darak shot out a hand and grabbed her arm. They stood very close for a moment, ensuring Semana's balance had returned, and finally she pulled away.

"I will follow your lead," Semana said. "But do not think I've forgotten your promise to me."

Darak stared at her for a long moment, then nodded. "The moot first," he said. "We must focus upon the challenges of the day. Once I am a High Druid, you will have all the aid you require."

Semana nodded. She found herself thinking of Regel and what might have been, had she gone with him. At least she knew how to handle the Oathbreaker. Her brother was proving less pliable.

They reached the summit of Iseldra's Folly, a rocky expanse at the height of the broken mountain where high parapets of stone swept up to stop passage through all but a few, mist-choked narrow passages. Semana turned back and gazed in wonder at the wide, snow-covered world around her. She'd noted the precipitous drop-off from the winding trail, where a false step might lead to a bone-shattering slide down a hundred paces to the next loop of the trail.

Only at the top did she understand the full scope of the climb. Through a soft haze of gray cloud, the world spread out before her in a sea of white snow and gray-green trees, rolling up and down in sharp mountains like tiny blades stabbing up for an unwary giant's foot. On the southwest horizon, she could just see the greasy shadow that rose into the air above Tar Vangr. The grand panorama reminded her of looking out over the spiraling World of Ruin from the bridge of a skyship. She felt like a child again, basking in the fraying majesty of a darkening world.

"Beautiful and terrible, is it not? Such is the majesty of Ruin our mother." Darak swept his hand across to indicate the mountain-studded valley that lay before them. At his touch, the mist around them rippled and parted to offer a clearer view. Clarity lessened their vantage, though, making it almost… mundane. "Such awesome power, and yet this is the world she is to have sculpted? Pathetic."

"The way you speak of Ruin," Semana said. "As though she is a goddess and yet not."

"To the barbarians, she is one of many, but supreme over them all," Darak said. "It is a silly thing, their faith. They believe in a god for every high mountain or deep river, a god for every type of weapon and every battle. Yes." He saw her disbelieving look. "They believe gods spring into being when blood is shed—that the pain and screaming of men and women dying are the birth pangs of such a being. Ridiculous." He scowled in utter contempt.

"All these years among them, and you do not respect their faith?" Semana asked.

"What is there to respect?" Darak waved his hands over the teeming horde far below. "The ramblings of weak-minded, insane rovers, terrified of Ruin's utter lack of meaning. They invented gods to give them some sense of purpose—some reassurance that what something other than emptiness awaits them at the end of a fatal spear. They are like children, and not just because they call Ruin their mother. Their idiocy should be accorded no more respect than that of babes."

Semana should have agreed, but she found herself in doubt. Her blood had never cared much for the divine, and neither had her city. Tar Vangr had paid ceased to pay heed to the winter god years before her birth. And yet, she found cause to wonder. Also, she found his attitude ironic, considering how differential he insisted on being. His dismissive contempt seemed like a weakness, not a strength.

"What of this day's rituals?" she asked. "Surely the Circle is worthy of your esteem."

Darak gave her a sober look. "Only a fool does not respect power, and the High Druids have a great deal of it," he said. "They shroud themselves in the glamor of the divine. The Circle conducts its rituals only in those places where Ruin's majesty cannot be denied, and those uninitiated into the order of rotcloaks are not allowed to witness their rituals. But rest assured, the power of Worldfire has nothing to do with any god or goddess. I made no pact with any great power or swore any oath—well." He grinned. "None that I intend to honor. And few of the Circle of Twelve do so either."

A sound arose from beyond the stony barriers—something halfway between singing and howling.

"The call." Darak stiffened, and a shadow passed over his face. "We have tarried long. Come."

He took Semana's hand and pulled her none-too-gently toward the nearest passage leading into the summit caldera. The impulse arose to shake him off and chastise him for his roughness, but instead Semana followed along without protest through the narrow pass. She could bear the indignity.

Naturally hewn rocks jutted out at them, some matched so well to the opposite wall they might once have been connected until some great force tore them asunder. In places, it grew wide enough for two to walk abreast, while at times Semana had to slip sideways between the walls or even crawl under a low overhang. The sun behind the thick clouds hardly penetrated the tunnel from above, and the lack of light combined with the lingering mist to make it almost impossible to see. Fortunately, Darak held her hand and guided her along, warning her about particularly difficult spots as they made their way through. When it grew too dark to see, Darak cupped the air in his hand and it crackled into burning life between his blistered fingers. He carried this torch in one hand and held her wrist in the other.

As they walked, he spoke softly of the coming moot.

"After a series of ceremonies to honor the goddess of Ruin," Darak said, "the Circle will deliberate on whatever matters they consider important to the Children in the coming year. We are not expected to listen to those. I have on several occasions, and trust me, they are a waste of time."

"You've—" Semana grunted as she climbed over a withered fallen log that had come wedged into the passage in some past time. "You've been to a moot before? I thought men were forbidden."

"Forbidden as members of the Circle, yes, but not as seconds," Darak said. "It is common for the druids of the Circle to make the strongest and most handsome would-be apprentices fight for the right to share their beds. Whoever succeeds in defeating the others and pleasing her best wins the dubious honor of accompanying her to this moot."

Semana heard the dourness in his tone. "You speak from experience, do you?"

Darak sighed. "When Afferath said she needed a new apprentice, she did not speak in jest," he said. "Until last year, I was her favored apprentice. Safe to train, because I was a man and could not possibly supplant her in the Circle, potent with Worldfire, strong but smooth and soft from my childhood in Tar Vangr. A fine prize, and I pleased her well."

"Ugh," Semana said. "And just when I thought I couldn't despise the woman more."

"You sound jealous, sister," Darak said, his tone teasing.

"Hardly." Semana spat, both to clear the oily smoke from her mouth and in derision. "I couldn't imagine a single moment spent in that woman's bed. I don't know how you managed it."

He looked at her sidelong.

"What?" she asked.

He let it pass and went on. "An acolyte seeking entry to the Circle must select one of the High Druids to challenge," he said. "The challenged druid must defend her position in a ritual combat that lasts until dusk. The incumbent retains her seat in the event of a draw, or if she slays the challenger. If victorious, the acolyte who issued the challenge can only ascend to that druid's place, no matter which druids of the Circle are slain."

"In battles of their own, you mean?" Semana asked.

"Or against the acolyte," Darak said. "Druids who have been named in the ritual challenge are obligated to fight their attackers, but druids who've not been named may choose to participate in such a battle or not, depending on their own alliances within and without the Circle. Unchallenged druids sometimes use it as a chance to support their allies in the Circle or sabotage or murder their rivals. It is a political struggle wrapped in the robe of religious ritual." He scowled. "You can imagine my distaste."

She didn't have to: the contempt was written vividly on every line of his face. "It sounds complex," Semana said. "Hardly what I'd expect from barbarians."

Darak smiled at the corner of his mouth. "There is a simpler course we could take," he said. "Sometimes, an acolyte challenges the entire Circle, in which case by tradition any of the High Druids may be slain, and the battle ends when the first one falls. Then that is the seat the acolyte takes."

"But all the druids of the Circle would be obligated to attack an acolyte who issues such a challenge, yes? Who would be mad enough to attempt such a thing?"

"Indeed," Darak said. "It is better to have allies than all enemies, don't you agree?"

Semana nodded. "Afferath is your ally," she said. "You expect her to join you to fight whichever druid stands against you. Yes?"

"That is my expectation," Darak said. "She thinks she can control me, and if I become a High Druid, then she will have two voices in the Circle. And it gives her a chance to slay one or more of her rivals. A fine opportunity for her."

"Unless you try and fail," Semana said. "Then she will have made an enemy."

"Most of the Circle counts the rest of the Circle their enemies—once the ritual is over, they will go back to their squabbling stalemate and nothing will ever change." Darak shrugged. "Afferath has allies as well, and has assured me I can count on their support in my challenge. That is, if I earn their respect in the initial ritual of declaration. I am, after all, a man."

"I don't follow." Semana pursed her lips.

"Men can challenge the Circle of Twelve, but none has ever succeeded," Darak said. "By tradition, all unchallenged druids unite to slay any male acolyte first. To preserve their dominance. Afferath is confident, but traditions are strong things. Hard to break."

"So we are walking to our deaths," Semana said.

"Dearest and only sister." Darak flashed his winning smile over his shoulder. "Would I have brought you all this way if I did not have a plan?"

"Tell me, then." Semana glared. "Which druid will you challenge?"

Darak shrugged. "I must see the druids and their would-be challengers first."

"You've no plan?" Semana asked.

"I have planned as much as I can, without seeing the state of things today," Darak said. "The leader of the Circle of Twelve is called Erethar, and she I *know* I cannot defeat, with or without your aid. There are others I know I could not defeat. It depends also on which druid is yet unchallenged, and whether that druid has a second who will complement them and how."

"A second?" Semana was starting to put it together.

"The law of the moot allows each druid to have a second, as well as each acolyte who seeks to challenge them for membership. I was Afferath's second last year, and now you are mine."

Semana nodded. She had expected something of the sort.

"Not every Circle druid keeps a second or even trains acolytes at all," Darak said. "For instance, I have never seen a second stand beside Naor the Raging Flame. The woman is so arrogant and so dangerous, that's probably for the best."

"So we challenge her?" Semana asked.

"No." Darak looked at her sharply. "Having no second makes her seem vulnerable, but that woman is a raging firestorm of power. She needs no allies or support. We'll stay as far from her as possible. It would be best if she turns her ire a different way, which might happen if there are other acolytes there to challenge the Circle."

Semana watched as Darak ducked under a withered root branch that stretched claw-like fingers out to grasp at their faces. She caught it in her right hand, then cut it off at the root with a little burst of her glove's invisible blade. Then she tossed it behind them. Darak sniffed at the tainted air and looked at her accusingly, but she just smiled at him until he shrugged and pressed on. If she could not wear her armor, at least she could wear the glove.

"Other challengers," she said. "Others like *us*, you mean?"

Darak nodded. "There will be other upstarts who seek a place in the Circle themselves—in fact, I hope there will be, to occupy the others of the Circle. When acolytes challenge the Circle for membership, it is common for the allied druids to unite and slay interlopers quickly. Fortunately, the moots only transpire on the equinoxes, and so there are plenty of would-be ascendants every time."

"What if they challenge the same druid you challenge?" Semana asked. "Will you not have to deal with them as well?"

"Leave that worry to me, sister."

They continued on in silence for a time. Eventually the passage broadened and grew warmer, and Semana doffed her hood and shook out her hair. Darak smiled. "Let's rest a breath," he said.

"I thought we were making haste," Semana said.

"It's not much longer now," he said. "We chose well in our path. Some of these passages twist and turn for hours, and some do not even reach the summit. If we miss some of the ritual, I'll not mourn."

"Do you have any wisdom for the battle to come?" she asked.

"Most acolytes and challengers waste their stamina channeling Worldfire early in the battle," she said. "Use what you've learned from me for defense and strength, not for attack. I've a different plan for that." He eyed Semana, specifically her flowing, rotpriest robe and her lack of a backpack, and his face darkened. "Tell me you brought your armor."

She nodded. "Always."

His eyes widened slightly when Semana unlaced her cloak to fall around her.

"The magic consumes whatever I'm wearing," she said. "Have a care."

Darak shrugged and averted his eyes, though he did not turn his back.

Semana shed the rest of her rough-spun woolens and laid her fingers on the clasp of her belt, which pulsed with a bit of magic. In a heartbeat, Mask's dark leather assembled itself out of the air and wrapped around her limbs. "Satisfied?" she asked.

"Very." The corner of his mouth crooked up. "And you can put it back just as easily?"

With a second touch, the belt reversed the process, leaving Semana nude once more. She dressed quickly, and this time Darak openly watched her. It made Semana uneasy, and the feeling did not pass until she stood once again in her woolens. She thought of him kissing her in his jubilation—unpleasant but understandable, considering his great moment. The way he looked at her now…It unsettled her.

So too did her limitless patience. Why was she making excuses for his behavior?

"Store your glove in there as well," Darak said when she had finished. "We can't take chances that one of the High Druids might recognize it for what it is."

Semana wanted to argue, but he had the right of it. She touched the belt, and the silver glove startled to unravel, its links coming apart around her hand and vanishing into the air.

"The other druids must see you in that cloak, as you were wearing when you met Afferath," Darak said. "Your Worldfire is weak, but your other relics are strong. Everyone saw Mask yestereve, but no one will suspect the Angel of Ruin is a frail girl. When the ritual combat begins, you will not be known to our enemies, and so your magic will surprise them. A powerful druid can use the Worldfire to drain your relics, but it takes a moment. You might kill our target before she can react."

"So your plan is to ascend through trickery," Semana said. "Rather than strength or skill."

"As you say." Darak projected an air of affability, but she could sense danger beneath his words. "Do you object, sister?"

"Not at all," she said. "Strength is but one measure of power—cunning another."

Darak considered her for a time, then rose and extended her his hand. "We've almost arrived."

The summit of Iseldra's Folly was not as Semana had expected. To look upon it from a distance, the mountain resembled a blasted volcano, in which a massive eruption had ripped the top off and sent its remains streaming out over the countryside. And indeed, such might have come to pass in this place, at some long ago time. But if so, it did not account for the sheer vibrancy found within the volcano's crater.

Once they emerged from the misty passage into the interior, they stepped into a steaming jungle thick with vegetation on all sides. Sweat instantly broke out on Semana's forehead and neck, and the robe felt thick and cumbersome on her itchy body. Trees short and tall stood around them, their sandy-barked trunks thick and their branches strong, dripping oily dew from wide, blade-shaped leaves overhead. Sharp-thorned brush choked the sides of the narrow path, bristling with crimson thorns and nursing in their midst what looked like tight-wrapped bundles of gristle studded with green daggers where it grew from the vine. The plants seemed to grow directly from the rocks with no intervening soil to nourish them. Chanting resonated above and around them, too muddled for Semana to pick out words. Darak seemed encouraged rather than concerned, and he pushed them forward at a regular if gingerly pace.

As they headed down the densely overgrown path, Darak spoke, and his voice took on a mystic tone. "Centuries ago, the first Grand Druid Iselda of Verdant Stone defended herself against the combined strength of five other Worldfire wielders in a bid to determine who would reign supreme over the Children of Ruin," Darak said. "She thought, with her great power, that she could defeat all who dared challenge her. She was not wrong, but in her hubris she failed to consider the damage such a battle might wreak upon the landscape. The titanic magic brought to bear tore open this mountain, letting the Narfire bubble up to the surface, consuming all who stood near, including Iseldra even in her victory. In her wake, this mountain bears her name, and stands as a reminder to all to consider carefully the ground of a duel. A fine tale, and all too appropriate that the druids hold their moot here."

"The Circle has a sense of irony, then," Semana said. "To continue fighting in a place where such a battle slew all who fought in it."

"Or perhaps it is lost upon them," Darak said, his voice dry. "Some say that Iselda's magic still lingers in the land, true to her own name." He ran his hand along an oily leaf, then flicked his fingers clean into the brush. "Perhaps it's even true. How else do you explain vegetation growing from stone?"

"How indeed."

Semana knew better, however. She recalled the Flamewell where Regel had told her about the life-giving power of the Narfire. If Iseldra had truly broken open the earth to the Narfire below, of course the mountain would become a cradle for living things. Another gap in Darak's knowledge.

They broke from the jungle into an open space at the center of the crater, and Semana fell instantly onto her guard. The dominant feature of the clearing was a natural stone dais, around and upon which stood the mossy remains of some sort of structure crumbled to pieces centuries gone. Only a few of the support stones of its foundation remained: great slabs of heat-blackened rock like the bones of an ancient beast long ago fallen into death. Torches burned wetly around the clearing, their smoke curling upward toward the open sky. Numerous totems of wood, twine, bone, and leather stood in the holy circle to mark its boundaries, not unlike at the barbarian camp. These, however, were uniformly old, and must have stood there for years, largely untouched by the elements in the protected crater atop Iselda's Folly.

It was the people, though, who gave Semana pause: fifty or so, mostly women of various shapes and sizes, engaged in some manner of religious ritual. From Darak's description, she had expected a close cabal of sinister witches out of a tale, glaring at one another with malice or perhaps cackling over evil schemes. The High Druids were the queens of Ruin, chief among the barbarians, and so she found herself mildly disappointed that they seemed so earthly—*mortal.*

The women up on the dais wore sheer white robes through which the dark silhouettes of their bodies writhed in an increasingly frenzied dance. Those below wore rotpriest robes, and some favored the roughspun garments and cobbled armor of the Children of Ruin. Other than Darak, none of the men wore robes. All or most seemed to be chanting the same rhythmic sounds that had drawn them here, and Semana could still pick out no words. The proceedings bore a certain flowing beauty that Semana found intoxicating, and she wanted nothing more than to stand, watch, and marvel.

"Are those the Circle?" Semana indicated the dancing women. "I expected something more…"

"Grand?" Darak reached out and raised her chin to make her look beyond the dancers on the dais. Semana flinched away from his unexpected touch, but then she saw and marveled.

The Druids were in the *trees*.

She saw only three of them at first. She picked out a dark-skinned, lithe woman dressed in hunting leathers who balanced precariously on a surprisingly slender limb. So perfectly did the woman match the foliage around her, Semana would never have seen her had she not moved slightly in a dance of her own. A bow leaned against the trunk near her: a splendid weapon wrapped in thorny vines and flowers. Semana saw a second High Druid: a stout woman with gray skin and hair who brooded amongst a blackened, burned out trunk high in one of the trees. Flame dripped from her idle hands as though she had just emerged from a bath of fire. Finally, Semana saw a pale woman in a golden robe who sat serenely, legs folded and eyes elevated above the morass, as though watching something in the distance. In fact, this last druid was looking directly at Semana, and the scrutiny made her distinctly uncomfortable.

"No turning back." Darak indicated the woman in gold watching them. "Mayel saw us before we even came down from the ridge. She speaks of her 'other eyes' that see much. Come."

The ritual trailed off as they approached. The rhythmic chanting of the acolytes on the dais diminished as one by one their eyes turned to the interlopers. They attracted the attention of the High Druids in the trees as well, who stirred themselves or made faces at the distraction. Darak guided Semana up the dais, between the parting ranks of dancers, and they stood still at the top of the stairs.

"What is this?" The woman who leaked fire stood up in the midst of her hollowed out throne. Her voice boomed over the assembly with wrath and fury, like a brewing explosion. "What is this creature that comes before us, so late in our ritual, and daring to wear our sacred vestments?"

"A man, I believe." Afferath lounged in one of the trees, resplendent in a robe dyed bright blue that covered even less of her body than the one she'd worn upon her arrival to Darak's camp. She flashed a look of dark bemusement. "Surely you've seen one before, Naor of the Raging Flame?"

The gray-skinned druid glared at her with unmistakable menace. "You still your tongue, rain goddess," she said, raising one flaming hand. "Lest I burn it from between your lips."

The world rippled between them, as if the very air itself shook where it hung over the assemblage. All fell silent and turned to a woman who rose from her throne of laced branches in the largest tree, directly across the dais from Semana and Darak. She resembled a tower of basalt, powerfully built with skin black as the night. To call her young would have been untrue, but neither did she seem old. Hers was a timeless face that defied even the hard years of the World of Ruin. She silenced her fellow druids with a sweeping look, then fixed her gaze upon Darak. Standing at his side, she felt the weight of that stare strike him like a blow from her silver glove, and he flinched as though punched. Then, as though strengthened by his sister's presence, he straightened and raised his chin.

"Erethar the Unmoving," Darak said. "I am Dar-Karsk of the Windswept Ravine, once squire to Afferath, Mistress of the Rain, now a druid in my own right and power." He raised his hands, and flames sprang from his right palm and mist swirled around his left wrist. "I demand the right of challenge."

Silently, the Grand Druid glanced at the druid in gold—the one Darak had named Mayel the Even-Handed—who spoke for her. Her voice contained no obvious emotion except perhaps a bored sense of indifference, and she didn't even look at them as she spoke.

"Unwise," Mayel said. "No man has ever stood in the Circle. Dar-Karsk asks for death."

"Him and that little stripling beside him," said another, this one a much-scarred woman built like a bull. She squatted disconsolately in her arboreal perch and glared down at them, fingering a massive, many-times notched battle axe. "If you care so little for your slave, boy, give her to me instead." She grinned at Semana with a mouth full of bloody teeth. "Carr the Axe will treat her well."

Semana did not know if the woman meant herself or her weapon. Both, perhaps. She had never responded well to threats. "I am not his slave," she said without thinking. "I—"

Her cheek burst into hot pain, and she had fallen to one knee before she realized Darak had slapped her. He glared down with wide eyes and shook his head in warning. Then he looked back at the druids, who greeted the sight with mixed reactions. Some chuckled or laughed aloud, while other murmured to themselves or their neighbors. It sounded like wind flowing through aspen leaves. Naor of the Raging Flame stared at them, fire rising around her. Afferath was laughing, which made Semana hate her even more. Only Erethar seemed untouched, gazing at them levelly. The Grand Druid raised her hand and the voices cut off instantly, letting silence rush back to fill the clearing.

"I speak for myself, and only myself," Darak said. "I hereby issue my challenge."

Erethar considered him, then raised her arms to indicate the rest of the Circle. As soon as she did so, the other druids began to shout invectives and curse them both, then argue with one another. Naor roared words in a tongue neither Calatite nor that of the barbarians, while Carr made a lewd gesture. Mayel seemed unaffected, watching quietly, while Afferath threw insults back at her opposition.

"Let the boy come," said the archer Druid Semana had seen before. The shadows danced around her, making her difficult to see, and she held three arrows in her left hand. "The Night Wolf fears no challenger. Let him try."

"You want him for your bed, Fellis," Carr said. "I'll make a pact with you: you take the boy, I take the girl. I might even leave him alive and whole for you."

"I'll have them both, ugly one." The ornate bow was suddenly in the archer's hand, an arrow on the string. "If you step into my path, I will put an arrow through your precious axe."

Other druids shouted their own arguments, and Semana felt the weight of their rage upon her. The others gathered in the clearing looked at her angrily as well: acolytes who would ascend to the Circle, their muscular seconds who fingered their blades, celebrants furious at the disruption of the ritual—in that moment, everyone hated Darak, and Semana by extension. Her own anger, however, burned at her brother. She had half a mind to summon the magic of her boots and leave him to his fate, but surely one of the druids would stop her before she could escape. Perhaps she would try anyway.

Erethar raised her hand once more, and once more the clearing plunged into silence. She looked to Mayel, who nodded and spread her arms.

"You are a man, but the Circle shall allow your challenge," Mayel said. "Know that all others who have come have chosen which of the Twelve they would challenge, and all have been challenged. You must declare a challenge against the entire Circle or renounce your claim."

That was it, then. Darak's claim would have to wait until the next year. Surely her brother wouldn't be mad enough to—

"Accepted." Darak gave Semana a slight smile and turned to Erethar. "I challenge you *all*."

"What?" Shock gripped Semana's body, freezing her limbs in place. "What have you done?"

After a long heartbeat, Erethar nodded.

"Granted," Mayel said. "Let the challenge begin."

Semana sucked in breath to protest, even as the world erupted in flame.

TWENTY

Necthana

Regel staggered down the hall, twisting and turning to keep his face to each enemy. Frostburn traced dripping trails of icy magic through the air, like streamers left in the wake of fireworks, and it kept his attackers more or less at bay.

He'd cut down two of the six Deathless, but that left four following him now, hissing like snakes in his wake. Their black eyes gleamed at him, promising death for what he had done. In the near darkness, illumined only with the pulses of Necthana's lifeblood through the mage-glass walls, they resembled nothing so much as shadows given shape and something like life. They moved with speed and grace unmatched by the muscles of mortal men, their weapons whistling through the cold air to produce a threatening dirge. The hum was almost hypnotic, lulling Regel to restfulness—relaxing his muscles and soothing his rage. No mortal man should have been able to escape or fight them.

It might even have worked, were it not for Frostburn's insatiable hunger.

The sword enhanced his senses, not unlike focusing on a carving all the time, and as fast as his attackers could move, they seemed agonizingly slow to him now. Where just one had overmatched him upon his arrival, now he could hold his own against many. And they feared the touch of that blade with a passion he'd only seen on the faces of dying men and women. Frostburn represented the sum total of Necthana's magic, boiled down into a single point of cold, sucking death, and now he wielded it freely.

The Deathless Horizon—a man with jet-black skin and eyes—lunged at him, one obsidian dagger high, one blade low. Regel flowed back, ducking under the high strike and bringing Frostburn around to shatter the lower blade. Horizon cut in with the broken hilt anyway, scoring a tiny scratch along Regel's shoulder that he saw but didn't feel. The Deathless might as well have scratched a glacier. Regel slammed one knee into the fae's stomach and smashed the pommel of Frostburn hard into the back of his neck, putting him on the floor.

Three left.

Regel had to fight hard not to stab Frostburn through Horizon as he fell senseless. Over five years the blade had starved since its last victim, and Regel had not fed it well in the years before that. Its overwhelming hunger burned inside him like a raging forest fire, impossible to slake or stop.

Another fae rushed in, and Regel compressed low to duck a slashing staff. He and the fae leaped at once—Regel backward, his opponent after him—and exchanged one, two, three strikes in the air, then landed in smooth balance. Regel put one hand behind the dull edge of Frostburn to parry the fae's staff, which struck hard enough to push him back two steps. He raised his sword to point at the fae's face, and the staff snapped up to match.

"Blood," he said.

"Frostburn," the fae said.

He'd underestimated Blood before, but not again. Not with Frostburn consuming his emotions and uncertainties. It left only a cold sort of focus that permitted no ego or delusion. He knew exactly what his body could accomplish and what the fae's could. He knew how this duel would end even before it properly began. And from the uncertainty that crossed Blood's face, he suspected he was not the only one.

Summit staggered into view behind his attackers, ebony black blood leaking down his forehead. "You cannot escape, Frostburn." His voice echoed off the walls. "All of Necthana falls upon you."

The threats fell on Regel's ears and washed over him like water carrying nothing. He knew the danger of his current path, and yet he did not flinch. He kept watching Blood, waiting—

The staff shot forward like a loosed arrow, and he leaned around it to close the distance. Blood turned, flowing to Regel's left, but he had anticipated the move. Frostburn shot through the air where the fae would arrive. The blade cut into Deathless flesh, and black blood spattered the wall and floor. Blood staggered back, clutching one wounded arm and baring bright white teeth that glowed in the chamber.

The wound was not enough for Frostburn. The cold blood of the Deathless could not sate the blade's hunger. It craved the warmth and life of mortals. This was its purpose: to reap the world of the living. It could carve a path handily through any obstacles in its path, such as the Deathless, but every tiny touch of chilly blood only made it hunger all the more.

The Deathless closed around Blood and Regel seized the opportunity to back away toward the entrance to the hall. Summit's warders outside had snapped to attention, holding their own obsidian-tipped spears and blades ready. One look at Frostburn as Regel brandished it, however, and they stood back to permit his passing.

One last salute to the warders and Regel made his way off into the maze of Necthana.

Time stretched as he made his way through the City of the Dead, but Frostburn's focus allow him to remain ona single path. This power—this state of letting the sword conquer him…Rose had always warned him against it, and he knew well enough on his own to avoid it. But now he had no choice. He bled from half a dozen wounds, but the raw hunger drove him on. If he tried to fight back against Frostburn's ravenous need, he thought he would sink to the floor on the spot.

He left a bloody handprint on the wall and continued up the steps, trying to control his breath.

Healing magic rose up in Regel, but Frostburn consumed it hungrily. Indeed, Regel thought this the reason his magic had never manifested before: whenever it had come close, the sword had feasted on it. He could pause, set down the sword, and try to heal himself, but who could say how much time would pass as he did so. Instead he pressed on, hearing the echoes of pursuit and seeing flashes of movement reflected in the glass around him.

There was another exit from the Deathless City, he knew—one that did not involve the shadow path. He could escape without fae assistance.

In all his time in Necthana, Regel had never found such a way out, but he had not explored it all. He'd never been able to reconnoiter the halls in the northwestern corner, not too far from where Summit had carved out his own little corner of the complex. Considering Summit's adamant opposition to Regel's presence, venturing too close to his demesne had never seemed wise. He recognized now that Rose's insistence that he never approach that corner of Necthana had kept him from it.

Once, his feelings had barred his path, but now, with Frostburn absorbing those feelings into itself, he had no more hindrance. He could not bring himself to feel angry at the betrayal, either.

As he wielded it, Frostburn turned Regel into a cold lake covered in ice upon which snow had begun to fall. His wounds felt like small fish floating just above the bottom of the lake, and his experiences in Necthana were the muddy base. Certain things rose to the surface—the threat of a fae lunging for him, the echoing shouts of Summit calling for his blood—but they did not break through the ice. In the world, he was unmoved and unmovable, existing for one purpose: to find warmer prey.

The corridor leading to the unexplored section of the city stank of age. The whole city did, with Frostburn enhancing his senses to a dizzying degree, but this corridor in particular reeked with the dusty hollowness of disuse. Elsewhere, he could detect the faint traces of footprints and the lingering smell of breath, but not in this corridor. No one had passed through this hall in some time: years, decades, perhaps centuries. It came to a dead-end after twenty paces or so, where the purple lights of the Narfire coursed around the end of the tunnel in a smooth, scintillating wave.

That couldn't be right. It had to be here.

He dragged Frostburn along the glass wall, its wickedly sharp edge gouging a fine furrow all along the mage-glass, testing for weaknesses. He could feel the tiny vibrations through the sword as it met ridges and imperfections in the mage-glass. He could see the tiny flakes of glass crisping off the wall as the sword drew along, mingling with frost and condensation from its magic. So intently did Regel watch the tiny permutations of the path that he hardly noticed the pattern he had etched into the corridor: a spiderweb of scratches and scoring. One area in particular he slashed over and over again: the glass here felt different. Weaker. There had to be a way out. There had to—

"Frostburn." Summit's voice echoed down the hall. "This is your last chance. Stand down."

Thirteen Deathless had gathered to block his retreat, pinning him against the end of the corridor. They stalked forward slowly in twos and threes, obsidian weapons at the ready. They moved with caution, wary of the blue sword. They had no need to rush him but could take their time. He had nowhere to go.

His senses had betrayed him. He'd known for certain that Summit had some way into Necthana other than the shadow path—some way that permitted him to bring metal. He *knew* it.

Regel pounded the pommel of Frostburn against the mage-glass. Once. Twice. Again and again. He struck so hard most of the Deathless winced in spite of themselves. Regel could feel his arms straining to the point of giving way, but he kept hammering.

"Stop," Summit said. "You don't know what you're doing."

Cracks spread outward from the points of impact and across the wall. They intersected the cuts he'd made in the glass and blossomed further. Smoke leaked from the cracks and dripped down the damaged mage-glass, evaporating into mist before they touched the floor. The Narfire hungered for release just as the power of the Frostburn did. He saw it then: that it was the supreme arrogance of man, living or dead, to think such a primordial power could be contained. Controlled. *Harnessed.*

Cloaked in screaming shadow, one of the Deathless flew down the corridor at incredible speed and slammed into Regel, knocking him away from the wall. He brought his sword around and thrust it through the fae, feeling its cold power hunger for blood—

Then they were walking the shadow path, spiraling up through mage-glass and stone and thick rock, in a world of darkness and flitting images that evaded his senses. Regel held tightly to the Deathless, as to lose his grasp here was to wander eternally lost through the world beneath the world. There were others in the darkness—lurkers or other fae, he could not say for certain—and he felt them rush through them as through a crowded courtyard. Silent screams of challenge and hunger followed them, and Frostburn cried out inside his head, craving their unnatural flesh for its feast.

Up and up and up they flew, clasped tightly together, until finally they burst from the ground into the world above. Regel fell free of the Deathless's grasp just as the shadow world collapsed around them, and he found himself dazed as he knelt in the snow. A blizzard swirled around them, stinging his exposed skin and blurring his senses. Above, the sky was blindingly bright even despite the storm, and he had to shield his eyes against the light.

He covered his face, coughing for air, and looked through the snow to lights dancing atop a distant mountain. Iseldra's Folly, he thought. What could be passing there? An eruption?

Frostburn sang in his mind, sending painful cold arcing up his arm, and he remembered he was not alone. The Deathless who had brought him to the surface stirred, then climbed to one knee not three paces distant. He lunged, sword up, but the fae knocked aside his swing with a swipe of one powerful arm, then moved out of his path as smoothly as the greatest dancer. He staggered through the snow, fighting hard to keep his footing, and whirled on his attacker.

"Rose," he said.

In the depths of Frostburn's need, the name meant almost nothing to him.

The Queen of the Deathless stood before him, one dark hand pointed in his direction, the other staunching the flow of black blood from her side where he had stabbed her in their initial struggle. Sweat beaded upon her smooth brown scalp, turning to ice as it formed, and her breath steamed out quickly and ragged. Her black eyes held nothing but tranquility, however, and she soon straightened from her fighting stance into something dignified and inexpressibly elegant.

Darkness swirled around them in various spots, announcing the arrival of more Deathless. Five—ten—twenty and more. Fae emerged from the *ren shala* around them, grasping weapons or hurling silent judgment with their eyes and accusatory fingers. With Frostburn, Regel knew he could take six or eight of them, perhaps even ten, but not dozens. They kept appearing, until over a hundred Deathless gazes fixed upon him as he stood facing the Queen of Necthana.

Rose looked around to the gathered fae, then raised her hands. "Begone," she said. "I shall dispatch this thief alone."

The Deathless hesitated, whispering amongst themselves, but one by one they vanished. Summit remained until the last, regarding Rose with angry judgment before he too slipped into the darkness.

Finally, they stood alone, Regel and the Deathless Rose, facing each other on a field of snow.

He raised Frostburn in challenge, and she stepped back into a balanced fighting stance.

TWENTY-ONE

Iseldra's Folly, the Winter Wilds

FIRE EXPLODED ALL AROUND Semana, raging against a swirling vortex of winds so powerful they could shatter bone. As the flames spun away, she watched the clearing through the wall become a dancing kaleidoscope of colors and flashes of light and movement. The roar of the furious storm quashed any other sound, and she felt as though it would pull her apart.

Darak stepped through the winds to her side, dark veins rising across his cheeks. "Move!" he shouted, which she read on his lips more than heard him say. "Go!"

Her brother's face woke Semana from her hesitation. She reached out to the earth beneath her and felt its power strengthen her limbs. Her flesh grew firm as rock. Darak swept one hand up, parting the winds to give them a path out, and Semana ran. No sooner had they made the treeline than a powerful explosion tore apart Darak's tornado behind them and knocked them tumbling to the forest loam.

Semana lay stunned for a moment, staring up at the winter sky through the foliage. Two separate streaks of colors crossed through the haze—first a zig-zagging black form like a great bird, then a jet that was crimson like blood and fire. She thought it beautiful at first, but then the flames struck the black object, which exploded in the air. It tumbled down, burning like a falling star, and sizzling black blood rained down on Semana as she lay blinking. It tickled her skin and made her feel…befoulded. Filthy.

She was accustomed to the feeling.

Wordlessly, Semana pushed herself to one knee. Battle had erupted in the clearing, a vicious, violent melee that belied the orderly ritual that had preceeded it. The white-robed acolytes shed all pretense of civility and even humanity, their faces livid with rage and swirling power. One woman opened wide her arms, which became thrashing vines riddled with thorns like razorwire around an abandoned fortress. She lashed out to batter and rake her opponents, felling three before she cried out and slumped face-first onto the dais, a hooked axe buried between her shoulder blades. The High Druid Carr danced down from the tree and reclaimed the weapon, which she sank into the twitching acolyte's skull.

Another explosion drew Semana's attention. A series of combatants burst into cinders around Naor the Raging Flame, who walked past as casually as one might stroll through a garden. Around her roared a localized storm: a pyroclastic cloud of fire, ash, and darkness that tore apart all in its path.

"And that," Darak said quietly at her side, "is why we do not challenge Naor."

Her brother had climbed to his feet and stood at her side, shaking only a little. Semana could feel the power of Ruin surging in him, lending strength to his limbs. Most of the acolytes she had seen used Worldfire to produce impressive bursts of flame, blows of lightning, or other means of assault. This expression of the magic might impress an onlooker and could possibly slay a foe with a lucky strike, but it also left the practitioner vulnerable. Only a few—the High Druids, Darak, and herself—thought first to fortify themselves, using the strength of the mountains to boost their vitality and the rushing wind to speed their movements. He had warned her to do this, and she understood now. Had she attacked straight away, Semana would no doubt have died in that clearing.

"Magnificent, isn't it?" her brother asked. "Such bloodshed and death and for what? A monument to their own foolishness. Not one of these is worthy—not like me."

Darak watched the battle with smug satisfaction, but Semana's attention went elsewhere. She could not say what she had heard, but she acted on it all the same. She turned to the trees at their back, her silver glove burning with summoned energy. Wind rushed through the undergrowth and she bent her knees slightly, ready to spring in either direction.

"Well done, child." Afferath eased out from hiding, her skin blending almost perfectly with the dusky bark of the trees. "I see Ruin has begun to speak to you in the wind."

"No." Semana relaxed her glove's burn so the druid wouldn't notice. "But I heard you anyway."

Afferath narrowed her eyes and scowled in transparent distaste. Her daring blue gown seemed to be built for battle, with tight leather wraps securing her muscular body for more vigorous movement. Afferath leaned casually on her thundering staff, but Semana could see that she gripped it hard enough to make her knuckles pale. Nerves, perhaps? Even fear?

"Do you have it?" Afferath asked.

Wordlessly, Darak drew from beneath his rotpriest cloak the mistletoe token she had given him back in his camp. It was somewhat rumpled from his travels and the exertion of their flight into the woods, but Afferath acknowledged the item with a satisfied nod.

"We are allies, then." It was only as Afferath came closer that Semana realized her skin emulated not only the color but also the consistency of the trees around her. She'd scarcely imagined such use of Worldfire. "My own second has, sadly, perished in the battle. I always liked you better."

"You honor me." Darak gave her a slight bow. "I shall look forward to serving under you again."

"Ugh." Semana held up a hand to silence them. That same inexplicable sensation came to her—a warning of something about to happen. "Hold—"

It leaped through the trees, a pouncing storm of teeth and claws. The panther was easily the size of a grown man and must have outweighed Semana by half. It slammed into Darak, and he sprawled under its huge paws. The powerful legs kicked, tearing open the rotcloak and the leather jerkin beneath. Darak screamed in surprise and pain.

Wordlessly, Semana watched the creature savage her brother. She should have felt shock or perhaps fear, but instead all she found within was a dull fascination. Upon Afferath's face, Semana saw a grotesque kind of satisfaction—even *joy*, as though seeing Darak in pain brought her actual pleasure.

That, more than Darak's plight, stirred Semana to action. She drew on the power in the ground beneath her—felt the heat of the volcano surge through her feet, up her legs into her body, then down through her arms. She loosed the power as a fan of hot wind that washed over the panther like a crashing wave. The creature screeched a half-human cry and the force knocked it rolling away to smash into a tree. There it jerked spasmodically, screeching as smoke rose from its now pock-marked fur.

Teeth clenched, Semana fought not to gag at the stench.

The panther rolled to its feet and glared up at Semana with surprisingly human eyes. It crouched low, drooling blood and greenish bile into the undergrowth. The yowl that fell from its muzzle was pitiable, though whether the sound took its birth out of pain or a desire for mercy, Semana did not know. She saw fear in the panther's eyes, and it looked ready to bolt.

Then Afferath brought her staff down upon the beast like a pounding boot. The stout wood drove the panther to the forest floor and tore right though its torso. Blood splattered in all directions and the beast's eyes and tongue bugged out of its face. Then a pulse of magic flowed through the staff and the panther exploded in both directions, torn raggedly in half. Its hindquarters smacked back against a tree, while its head and shoulders bounced toward Semana, trailing gore in woozy circles across the small clearing. The hunk of panther landed at her feet and sprayed blood across her shins.

The High Druid withdrew her humming staff from the ruin of the creature's body and tapped it on the ground. "Just an acolyte," she said. "A wise foe would not have attacked the three of us here."

Semana couldn't stop staring at the hunk of druid at her feet. As she watched, it first seemed like a panther, then it became the naked upper torso of a dark-skinned woman—a girl really, Semana's own age or younger. Blood welled up in her mouth and her thin arms slapped limply at the ground. The torn ends of bloody entrails wormed out of her torso like frayed ropes. Why hadn't she died yet?

"Girl," Afferath said. "*Slave.*"

The acolyte gagged through lungs blown apart, gave a wet wheeze, and shuddered into death. Semana looked up, suddenly alert once more. Afferath had spoken to her.

"See to your master." She pointed her staff at Darak, who lay unmoving on the forest floor.

Warily—so as not to lose sight of Afferath and her deadly staff—Semana crossed around on the far side of Darak and knelt beside him. With relief, she saw that he was breathing, but she hesitated to touch him all the same. Mindful of the torn acolyte whose blood stuck to her feet, she shuddered to think of what horrible wound she might find beneath her brother's cloak, and if he woke…

A hand grasped her wrist in an iron grip. Darak's eyes opened wide and stared into hers, and his sweaty face shook slightly. Semana withdrew, and he sat up, seemingly untouched.

"How?" she asked. "Your wound—"

"Away from me, vermin." Darak slapped her hand away. He wound his hand back as though to strike her, but Semana scrambled back before he could launch the blow. He climbed shakily to his feet.

Afferath grinned, revealing the blood in her pointed teeth. "To the Broken Tower then."

"I follow you." Darak grasped Semana's hand. "Come."

His touch filled her with unease.

They hurried through the wood away from the cacophony of battle. The fringes of the caldera saw less of the fighting, and they gave Semana an opportunity to breathe.

Afferath led the way, moving with surprising grace and speed for such a massive woman. On closer inspection, Semana realized Afferath's skin no longer seemed rough and wooden, and her limbs stretched painfully until they resembled those of a great cat more than those of a human. Keeping pace with her made Semana breathe hard, and not just because of the elevation.

As he half-walked, half-jogged, Darak evinced only a slight limp from what should have been a crippling injury. Using the Worldfire for protection had proved not just wise but essential, Semana thought. Still, she noted bright specks of fresh blood appearing in his wake.

"You're hurt," Semana said when they fell behind Afferath's hearing. At least she thought so—for all she knew, the woman had augmented her ears the same as her legs. "You should let me see that."

"No," Darak said. "If I show a hint of weakness, Afferath will slay me herself—or worse, leave me behind." He glanced over his shoulder, eyes slitted warily.

Semana had seen no sign of pursuit, but if the druid turned panther had taught her nothing, it was to expect surprises from Worldfire. Such a powerful magic, if it could reshape one's body entirely. She had seen druids take wing or run like the wind, take on the limbs of animals or become monsters. Beside that magic, Frostfire and even the necromancy of Blood Magic seemed almost trivial.

"You and she seem to have a plan," Semana said. "Care to explain?"

Darak looked as smug as he could despite his obvious discomfort. "At the edge of the vale atop the mountanin stands a holdfast," he said. "It is difficult to reach unless one knows exactly how to get there. We'll arrive first, and lay an ambush for the first High Druid to approach."

"What if it's Naor?" Semana asked.

"It won't be," he said. "If Afferath has done her work, it will be Mayel or Carr. Either of those, you and I can slay easily enough. Particularly once you don your armor."

"*If* you can trust Afferath."

"She hasn't killed us yet." Darak shrugged. "Don't trust her. Trust *me*."

Semana frowned but nodded. "You say that as though I have a choice."

Their path led them to the edge of the volcanic crater, and a slope of shifting rock rose before them up to a natural hunk of stone overlooking the misty valley. To call it a tower was generous—Semana thought it reached perhaps twice the height of a man from the top of the slope, but it was the highest point she'd yet seen atop Iseldra's Folly. It seemed as good a meeting place as any.

At the treeline, Semana paused, balancing herself against a withered oak. A few gnarled trees jutted from the mountainside just ahead, but thereafter they would be climbing through the open. Afferath bounded up the slope, leaping without effort from boulder to boulder, and had soon disappeared into the haze near the base of the tower.

By contrast, just behind Semana, Darak faltered on the increasingly uneven footing and grunted.

"You strengthened yourself, but not enough." Semana put her hands on his shoulders. "Afferath has gone on ahead. Let me look at your wound." He started to protest, but she pulled him closer to her. "Don't argue. I need you at your best when the druids attack."

"What can you do?" Darak pouted in a way that was both familiar and irritating. "Unless you've a relic I haven't seen yet…"

"Just show me," Semana said.

Darak gave her an odd look, but he did as she instructed, hitching up his jerkin and pulling down the hem of his breeches at least three fingers. Beneath the leather, his flesh had a rough texture like that of oak, torn open with several deep gouges that oozed brackish blood. The wound smelled foul enough to make Semana gag, but she clenched firm against the reflex. She had to focus.

She'd seen Regel heal folk before, even felt the power herself. And if she was his daughter, then surely the magic lurked within her as well. She laid her hands alongside Darak's wound, making him squirm slightly, and slid her eyes closed. They breathed together, there in the misty valley at the top of the world, as screams rang out in the distance. The sounds of battle grew louder—closer.

Nothing. No healing. No power.

"What are you doing?" Darak asked at length.

Suddenly self-conscious, Semana let go of Darak. He knew nothing of her true heritage or the power she sought, and she did not want to arouse suspicions.

"Infected," she said, hiding her disappointment behind an expression of disgust. "I'm not sure how, though. It's still bleeding, and there hasn't been time for it to fester."

"That's merely the Worldfire," he said. "I told you it takes a heavy toll."

He indicated her hands, which had started to go sallow. A skin discoloration appeared over her left wrist. It had not had time to become one of the rotpriest lesions as yet, but it looked like a grub on her flesh. Feeling ill, she brushed vigorously and it flaked away to leave raw, pink flesh beneath.

"You're one of us now, sister," Darak said. "How does it feel?"

Semana shivered and stifled the rising sick in her chest.

A loud baying sound from the direction of the battle caught her attention: a horn that made a sound like the howl of a deep-throated wolf recently gorged and looking for more.

"The first melee is over," Darak said. "The High Druids will begin their search."

"For the last of the challengers?"

"What care they for cowards?" He shook his head. "They go forth in search of the others of the Circle. The moot cannot resume until twelve sit around the dais, and any High Druid who has perished must be marked as such."

"Afferath," Semana said. "They'll come to find her, and then we'll spring our trap."

Darak nodded. "Exactly."

As though the words summoned her, Afferath bounded down the slope and landed gracefully atop the boulder they crouched behind. "Come," she said. "The sun moves."

Darak pushed past Semana to start climbing the jagged stones.

The way up proved even more difficult than Semana had expected. The stones provided poor footing and often shifted out from under them. More than once, she started to slip, but Darak steadied her by the arm. Together, they made slow progress up the slope.

"When do I don my armor?" Semana asked. "You can tell me that about your so-named plan."

"Soon enough," Darak said. "For now, wait—"

His words cut off as something struck him from behind, driving Darak into the rocky slope. Semana caught his arm to keep him from falling, and the sudden weight made her muscles stretch painfully. An arrow bloomed out of his left shoulder, its fletching silver and black.

"Fellis," Darak said. "They're upon us."

Semana drew Worldfire around her and sent forth a wave of rushing wind that deflected the next two arrows that came rushing in their direction. She lacked the control Darak had demonstrated in the clearing, but her strength easily matched it. Through the wind, she saw a dark shape slink out of the trees and take shelter behind a boulder.

Afferath appeared, crouching low on feline legs, and looked Semana in the face. Her eyes had become slits like those of a cat and when she hissed when she spoke. "Go now," she said, putting her arm around Darak. "Give yourself for your master. I will carry him."

"I'll not leave him with *you*." Semana summoned up more power, making her body tremble with strain to hold it in. She raised a hand crackling with lightning to stay Afferath. "You do not touch him."

"It…passes well." Darak seemed only a little winded from the arrow, which would have killed an unwarded man. "Go, slave. Now is your moment."

Semana nodded grudgingly, not entirely convinced, but she understood.

This was part of Darak's plan. As Afferath bundled Darak up, she turned to the approaching archer druid and sent her will into her belt. It pulsed with magic that rose up and swirled around her in a dizzying storm of black and gray. In one heartbeat, the rotcloak flaked off and burned to ash, leaving her bare against the cold, and in the next, Mask's black leathers encased her in reassuring death.

She hadn't worn them properly in some time, but they felt tight, sleek, and reassuringly familiar. The silver ring glove raveled itself around her hand, the magic replacing its delicate links in crystalline precision. The stout black boots fit snug around her feet and calves, heavy and buoyant both at once. Last of all came the mask, which adhered to Semana's face as tightly as a second layer of skin. Her relics' power flowed through her, and she rose up off the slope under the power of her flying boots.

Something hard slammed Semana's head violently to the left, and she saw a black-and-silver fletched arrow spinning away from her amongst the stones. It hadn't bit through her protective magic.

First, *Fellis.*

Semana spotted the archer perched atop the boulder by the treeline and flew toward her. The High Druid paused a heartbeat, startled at the sudden appearance of the so-called Angel of Ruin they had all seen, then drew back her bowstring. An arrow smashed into Semana's shoulder but she barely felt it through the armor's ensorcelled protections.

Instead, her power flared and Plaguefire spread around her in a dazzling corona, not unlike Naor's cloud of flame back in the clearing. Fellis the Night Wolf stared at her with widening eyes as Semana flew toward her, green and black flames consuming the sizzling arrows as fast as the druid could loose them. The archer leaped to safety just as Semana smashed into the boulder, cleaving it in two with the magic of her silver glove. Fellis drew and loosed even as she fell, turning a somersault to land on her feet. She ran, launching arrows as she picked her way over the stones. The shafts rotted and fell apart as they flew toward their target, leaving only a rain of corroded arrow heads and withered feathers.

Semana rose up higher in the air and cast about angrily for her quarry. What she saw was a roiling ball of flame, one that shattered the nearby trees and stones.

Naor the Raging Flame had come.

"Child," the druid said, her voice like rolling thunder. "Such power you wield. You will surrender it to us. You will kneel to the Circle or die where you stand. Choose."

"I choose a third path." Silver flames swirled around Semana and she floated up from the ruined stone. Mask's ragged voice rose unbidden from her throat. "*Right through you.*"

So speaking, she shot toward Naor like one of Fellis's burning arrows, and struck the druid's cloud of flame like a hammer smashing into an anvil. Semana punched right through the burning field, the flames licking at her armor's glowing blue shield, and tackled Naor. The woman proved just as light as Semana had expected, and they went down in a tumbling heap, rolling over each other through the snow and rock. The flames flickered and died, their mistress's concentration broken.

Semana emerged on top and drew back her silver-gloved fist but Naor hit first, driving both fists up into her chest. Even with the armor's shield, it felt like being struck by a battering ram, and Semana found herself lifted up and away. She hit the ground and floated up immediately, narrowly rising above a jet of flame that emerged from Naor's mouth as though the woman were a dragon herself. Semana hurled a bolt of Plaguefire, which struck the high druid full in the chest and made her whole body convulse in sudden agony. She fell to her knees, vomiting flames and bile onto the ground.

Before Semana could ready a fatal strike, two arrows sizzled through her lingering aura of Plaguefire to bury themselves in her leathers. Fellis danced across, sending arrows her way with the speed of five archers. Indeed, for a heartbeat it seemed four shadowy versions of her followed her across the uneven ground, dancing nimbly in concert like acrobats at a revel. She could not tell which was the real druid, if any was. Semana swatted at the first Fellis with the power of the silver glove, but she'd chosen poorly and the invisible blade cut through mere shadow that broke apart into the night air. She took an arrow to the left shoulder for her trouble, which stung but did not penetrate deep enough to wound.

She needed a new strategy, and she realized what to do. Fellis's blood was moving too fast to seize, but Semana could use it to tell where she stood. She extended her senses and sensed life beating in only one of the shadowy silhouettes. That one she clenched hard upon: not enough to control, but enough to make Fellis suddenly stumble, grasping herself as though struck in the gut. Her last arrow went wide, and she staggered toward cover. Too late. Semana lined up a bolt of plaguefire to cut her down.

The sudden urge to turn struck her, and Semana followed it. A massive, single-bearded axe came spinning out of the darkness toward her face, its edge keen enough to cut the ashes rising around her. Magic roaring through her, Semana reached up her left hand with the silver glove and caught the axe by the blade. Her armor's shield screeched with the effort, but between that, the force of her silver glove, and the strength of Worldfire in her arm, Semana managed to stop the blade not three fingers from her face.

Across the way, Carr the Axe—the third High Druid to arrive—had been looking at her in triumph, but her expression fell first to confusion, then disbelief.

Blood trickled down Semana's wrist, but she barely felt the shallow cut. Without a care, she tossed the axe ringing onto the stones.

Three of the High Druids had come at her at once, and she was winning. The terrifying Naor was puking up her insides at Semana's feet, all but incapacitated. Fellis could do little more than distract her, and now Semana almost had control of her body. Carr had saved her for now, but she'd done so by disarming herself. They stared at the Angel of Ruin and hesitated.

Semana could do this.

"Come," she said to them. "Is this the most you can offer? You, the harbingers of Ruin?"

A great tremor swept through the valley, and Semana might have fallen had her boots not caught her up in the air by a thumb's breadth. Carr and Fellis both froze where they stood, then fell to one knee. Naor wiped her filthy face and bowed deeply.

Through the swirling smoke, Erethar the Unmoving appeared. She stood like a boulder that had always marked that spot and was only now remarked. Her midnight skin and impossible stillness made her seem like something more than human—an extension of the World of Ruin itself. Her gaze fell upon Semana, and her expression was grave.

Semana reached out to her relics, and found their magic draining away. She had lost her chance at surprise, and Erethar would not fall prey to her tricks. No matter—she had other powers. In particular, the blood in the High Druid's veins coursed gently—her heartbeat so slow and steady—that Semana could not help but feel it. The woman might have seen through one of her secrets, but this would surprise her. If she had time to strengthen her grasp.

"I know you." Erethar spoke softly, but the wind carried her words to Semana's ears. Her voice was deep and soft as distant thunder. "I have tasted your magic before."

"Do you?" Semana asked. "I am Mask. The greatest slayer Ruin has ever known."

"You are not," Erethar said. "And yet, so you are. You are but a child."

"I am a weapon." Semana could taste Erethar's blood now. "The weapon of your doom."

"Perhaps, if you so choose," Erethar said. "But I sense another destiny for you, if you take it. You who are heiress of Winter, child of Ruin, and queen of Blood."

That, Semana had not expected. "What destiny?" she asked.

A scream rang out, and Semana gazed over her shoulder. Up in the broken tower, she could see Darak and Afferath struggling. A blade flashed between them. *Treachery.* She should never have left her brother alone.

Erethar raised her arm as though flexing her muscle, and a tremor rippled through the ground, right under Semana's floating toes. The princess sucked in a breath through the mask. "Is that—?"

Then spears of stone burst from the ground, studding a line that rushed toward her. Semana kicked off the ground with the diminishing power in her boots, but even so one of the tendrils jabbed into her chest. Semana heard as much as felt something break inside her, and the force sent her tumbling back and up. Her insides exploding with pain, she flew toward the tower, willing her boots to carry her that far.

"You run from your path," Erethar said behind her, her voice disappointed. "So be it."

She raised her hand and curled her fingers, as though coaxing a butterfly away from a flower.

Abruptly, the magic went out of Semana's boots and she found herself falling, rather than flying. She struck the tower hard, all the breath rushing out of her body in a torrent, and flailed as she tumbled to its base. There she lay, gasping for breath, for what seemed like an eternity. She willed herself up, but her body would not respond. Was this what death felt like?

Finally, Semana's senses came back to her and she awoke to a world of pain. She tried to push herself up, but her left leg exploded with burning agony. Something pale protruded from her flesh: a shard of rock or bone? Warm blood flooded down her leg, soaking her skin inside her leathers.

"Darak," Semana said, her voice choked. She tried to move, but she felt so weak.

Helplessly, she looked blearily up the few paces to the top of the stony tower, where her brother struggled with Afferath. The druid bled from half a dozen wounds, but her hands grasped at Darak as though with a life of their own. They caught his throat and squeezed hard enough to make him stretch taut. She was the larger and stronger of the two, but he had the blade. His right arm kept pumping, jabbing the blade over and over into her middle. Finally, the grip weakened, and Afferath released Darak entirely. She fell back a step, her chest and belly a mess of torn fabric and blood. Semana watched as she touched Darak's face, leaving three streaks of blood from his brow to his chin. His expression was almost tender.

Then he kicked her in the stomach, and Afferath toppled back out of the tower. She hit the stone with a crack, face to face with Semana. The druid's head twisted sideways from the rest of her crumpling body, and her dying expression was shocked. Her corpse bounced and tumbled bonelessly down the slope, leaving a trail of blood in her wake.

Darak stood atop the Broken Tower and raised Afferath's blood-stained necklace in his hand. "I am Dar-Karsk no longer," he said. "I am Darak Ravalis nó Denerre, of the Circle of Ruin!"

The other High Druids—Naor and Fellis, Carr the Axe and Mayel the Even-Handed, three more Semana did not know—raised their necklaces in recognition. Some did so immediately, others with hesitation. High Druids were appearing out of the mist all around the slope, until eleven stood before them. Erethar appeared in their midst, watching these portentious events, and all eyes turned to her. Finally, she drew off her own necklace of diamond and onyx stones and raised it high.

A shudder of victory passed through Darak, and he smiled brilliantly. He became the conquering hero, covered in the blood of a friend turned foe.

And just like a hero in a story, he needed no one else.

"Darak?" Semana asked. "Brother?"

One by one, the druids disappeared into the mist, returned to the moot. Darak climbed down from the tower and walked right past Semana without pause. He did not seem even to see her.

She felt so weak. Dizzy. Blood soaked her legs and pooled beneath her among the stones.

The world stretched and pulled apart.

TWENTY-TWO

The Frozen End of the World

THE STORM EASED, AND they faced each other over the driven snow. Man and fae. Living and dead.

They fought at first with silence. Regel felt Rose's powerful will crushing him like a mantle. It felt like a cloud of heavy fog he could not see but could feel. It weighed upon him, making his movements sluggish and labored. The world shrank around them as each focused upon the other to the exclusion of all. She wore an obsidian sword but had not drawn it. Indeed, she placed a hand upon the hilt but seemed to be hoping she would not have to.

"I stand to you unarmed," she said. "Will you do me the same honor?"

That gave him the advantage, Regel thought in some dim part of his mind. She had hope.

He, by contrast, had only purpose.

Slowly, he shook his head, then raised Frostburn to point at her heart.

"So be it." The Queen of the Deathless raised her hands, fingers curled gently into claws. Her body relaxed, but that did not reassure Regel. He knew it only made her more dangerous.

The battle played out in their minds: move and reaction, strike and counter, feint and secret thrust. Like master tacticians, they watched the duel unfold, thinking through what the other would do in response to every stratagem. They knew each other too well to either to deceive or be deceived. After Regel had trained under, fought beside, and loved Rose for so many years, he felt as though he stood against himself. She was part of him, but it was a part that rested beyond the chilly barrier of Frostburn.

"This," Regel said. "This was your plan, wasn't it?"

Rose regarded him with the impassivity of a statue. Blood continued to drip from her wounds unchecked, and it flecked the snow at her feet.

Frostburn's focus allowed him to think clearly—to analyze Rose's tactics and strategy—and it all started to make a terrible sort of sense.

"You encourage me to face Summit, knowing he kept Frostburn," Regel said. "You wait until I reclaim it and seek a way out of the city. You arrive to solve this problem, and your voice grows greater over that of Summit. Perhaps

I might even kill him, and that removes yet another obstacle to your power."

Rose inclined her head. "You are not wrong."

Neither could say who moved first. Perhaps they moved as one. They were of two minds and bodies, but one and the same spirit.

They came together in a flurry, blue blade scything over and around Rose as she dipped and weaved through his guard. Regel cut across at her knees, but she leaped and planted both feet in his chest, driving him staggering back. He caught himself with one hand in the freezing snow and kept Frostburn pointed up at her. Between the chill of the sword and his surroundings, Regel could barely feel his body any longer. He dismissed his concerns as those of the flesh and thus unimportant.

"Politics. Even among the dead," Regel said. "Not so different from mortal men as you pretend."

She shrugged.

They clashed once more. She approached rapidly and smoothly, then launched herself through the air at him, her knee lancing forward like a spear. Instead of setting Frostburn to spit her, he rolled low and cut upward. Rose turned in the air and the blue blade sliced ribbons from her cloak but missed her flesh. She turned a flip and landed in the snow opposite him, the cold hardly seeming to touch her bare feet.

Regel came in with a series of scything blows from Frostburn, but Rose flowed around each one as though executing the steps of a complex dance that she made look simple. Back and forth she moved, hands tracing patterns through the air in time with her evasion. He finished his combination with a piercing thrust that would have sliced right through her, but she leaped into the air and danced onto the sword itself. There she balanced on one foot for a heartbeat, seemingly light as mist, her frayed cloak dancing around her like a living thing. Regel looked up and their eyes met. She seemed…sad.

Then Rose dealt Regel a rising kick to the jaw and launched herself backward off the sword.

Regel staggered and righted himself after a few heartbeats to find Rose standing in the snow, waiting patiently. She winced slightly and favored her wounded side, but it hardly diminishing the strength of her stare. Regel knew that if he had not struck her in their initial clash, she would have defeated him long before now.

"But I did not cooperate," Regel said. "I took the sword but I didn't kill Summit. Hardly even injured him. You got what you wanted—to show yourself sweeping in to clean up his failure, but I yet live. So now you will kill me, as the last obstacle. Yes?"

"If that is your destiny," Rose said. "We both know you will not stay in Necthana, and I cannot let you leave."

Regel attacked first this time, cutting in at her injured side. Rose moved slightly slower, and he caught the edge of her cloak as she leaped away, slicing another ribbon to float through the air. He felt the blade bite into something harder—flesh—and Rose loosed a soft exhalation of pain. When she landed, she staggered slightly on her left leg and reversed her fighting stance to position it further away from him.

"You made a mistake," Regel said. "You should have drawn your sword first. Then I might not have wounded you."

To this, Rose had no response. She merely slid her weapon from under her cloak, setting the obsidian blade to sparkling as the snow fell around it. There was a warmth to the black stone, and the snowflakes melted as they touched its length.

At least Regel had made her draw her sword.

Regel grittered his teeth. "For the last time, I ask for your aid. Nay." He drew the sword up high and pointed it at her. "I *demand* it."

They both knew he made the request in vain.

They fought again, tracing skirling patterns in the snow like wolves fighting for dominance in the pack: equal parts deadly battle as play. They tracked deep pits in the snow and tracing shallow trails that whirled in wild patterns along its surface. Their swords sparked and screeched off one another, tracing circles around each other like the rings of an ornithopter. Rose remained careful never to parry his cuts edge to edge, as Frostburn would shatter her blade as surely as it had disarmed Blood in the same way. The mage-glass blade burning with the Narfire could not be matched.

They drew apart, each landing in balance on a boulder in the snow. Rose kept slipping slightly on the rock and correcting, like a Luehaar device whose gears have fallen out of alignment but keeps running all the same. Regel faired little better: he breathed heavily, his whole body trembling. He could barely feel his feet anymore, and his fingers had frozen to the handle of Frostburn.

"Regel." Rose's voice sounded thin and anguished.

She pointed to the sword in his hand, and he looked with agonizing slowness. A thick rime of ice had built up around the hilt, his hand, and up his forearm almost to his elbow. Regel could not have said which unnerved him more: to see the sword claiming him, or to realize it didn't surprise him in the least.

"It is not too late," Rose said. "Return with me. You do not have to wield that sword."

Regel shook his head. He didn't have that choice. Semana needed him. Tar Vangr needed him. He could not turn his back on them.

"If you go now, that is the end," Rose said. "You will never return to this place, and you will never be Deathless. You will die, by violence or by age, and you will have struggled all your life for nothing."

"I struggle for those I love," he said. "It is enough."

"You love only yourself," Rose said.

He roared and hacked at her, his rage rising up in a cold flow of fury. Frostburn darted in and out, side to side, seeking an opening in Rose's defenses. She parried his blows, mage-glass sparking off obsidian and sending shards of black stone into the dust like tears of midnight. His arms pumped faster and faster, right and left and above, but she deflected each and every attack. He struck high, hammering down upon her raised sword until he felt sure her blade would snap in two. His hands felt numb from cold and from the force of the blows. Frostburn wanted to strike—*yearned* to kill.

They broke apart again, both of them panting for breath in the swirling snow. Even the Deathless grew weary in time, and Regel knew Frostburn could sustain him longer than any foe could continue fighting. As they fought on, only time stood between him and victory, and the Deathless knew it.

"Are you still Regel, and not the Frostburn?" Rose asked.

"I am both," he said. "I can be both."

"You can be the Frostburn—this is obvious," she said as they stalked around each other. "But to be the man Regel, you must love the things and people Regel does. Do you?"

"They are all lost to me," Regel said. "All but Semana. She is all that matters."

"And yet you do not trust her," Rose said. "She has made her choice, and you refuse to accept it. You will not allow her to be free. You seek to control her—to make her decision yours."

"She doesn't know what she does," Regel said. "She cannot. If she did, she would never make that choice. The Children of Ruin? Her traitor brother? She needs to be protected. She needs—"

"She needs you to trust her." Rose stared at him a long moment, her black eyes grown wet, and not from the floating snow. "If you loved her, you would trust her. You would *respect* her."

Now it was his turn to hesitate, and it almost cost him everything. He barely looked up in time to see her rushing toward him, and it struck him to his core. She seemed, in that moment, not a woman of flesh and blood, but a billowing swarm of black winged creatures—bats, he thought, or ravens. The beauty and majesty of her rush transfixed him, and only belatedly did his body start launching backward in an attempt to dodge. The world seemed to slow around them, as Rose's power washed over Regel and Frostburn inched upward until—

The blade of blue glass smashed through Rose's obsidian sword—turning the point from Regel so that only the flat of the sword struck his belly—and sank deep into her chest. The impact jarred the weapon out of his grip, and ice broke away from around his wrist and hand. His head slammed back against the stone and they both fell. They toppled together backward off the boulder into the snow, bounced once, and came to a rest. The snow cratered out around them, crushed by their weight and melted by their heat, such as it was. Frostburn fell into the snow a few finger-lengths from his outstretched hand.

Regel lay staring up at the gray sky, where the clouds were just starting to part. Color trailed through the sky, like beautiful ribbons of thread from a weaver's loom. They danced and curled around the high, wispy white clouds that hung above the parting storm clouds, suggesting a realm far different from this, high above. It gave him cause to wonder what else lay in the world that he'd not yet seen.

Far from the pollution of the mage-cities, deep in the wilds, Regel could see a kind of beauty in the World of Ruin. In the depths of Frostburn's chill, he wondered if he would even have noticed.

The voice that stirred him from his world of fancy was weak—hurt—but determined.

"What I told you…it was not a lie, but it was not true."

It was only then that Regel remembered himself and what had transpired. He shook himself and climbed to one knee, looking around for Rose.

She lay beside him, her tattered cloak spread out on the snow like the broken wings of a bird that crashed to earth. Gone was her elegance, turned to an awkward jumble of boneless limbs that seemed too long for her body. Black blood seeped out a dozen wounds, staining the blood a deep midnight blue around her. Her dark eyes worked to focus, and her lids blinked many times as he watched. Her chest rose and fell fitfully, and blood seeped up to stain her tattered silks.

Free of the cold of Frostburn, Regel's heart leaped to see Rose so gravely hurt. He put his hands over the wound and called to the spark of healing within himself. He felt nothing but cold. Frozen fingers and toes, numb limbs and a shivering core, but also deeper. Inside, there was almost nothing: just a warm ember that he had to grope to find in the dark. Finding it reminded him of when Tithian Davargorn had healed him in Tar Vangr—fanning the flames back into life. In its lust to feed, had Frostburn come close to killing him?

When he touched the spark, life started to flow through his body and into Rose. He closed his eyes, seeking that communion he felt when he healed a living soul. But there was nothing. Rose might as well not exist. There was no ember to fan, that it might flame once more. Whatever lay inside her was cold and dead.

Panic washed over him, and he thought for certain Rose had died as he tried to summon the magic in himself. He opened his eyes and saw her regarding him sadly.

"No," Rose said. 'That—that magic is of life, and I am Deathless. It cannot help me."

"What—what can I do?" Regel asked.

"Even the Deathless can die." Rose licked her chapped lips. "Listen to my tale," she said. "I shall—try to finish it."

Regel nodded. "You—" The words caught in his throat and he had to swallow hard before he could continue. "There is more you did not say?"

Rose nodded. "The magic…that slew Necthana…came not from us, but from above."

"Why are you telling me this?" Regel asked.

The fae continued as though he'd not spoken. "A small crack—a tiny imperfection in our stronghold," she said. "The darkness seeped inside. Not enough to kill, but enough to weaken us. To steal that which made us human. Taint our minds and turn us against ourselves. In the madness that followed, we slew freely and willfully."

She winced, as though at some fresh, unseen pain, then sighed.

"It was only later—too long later—that the survivors realized what had been done," she said. "The darkness killed us, but it did not destroy us. We endured, and we had become the darkness we sought to hide from."

"Children," Regel said. "You are Children of Ruin."

"Yes." Rose smiled, and black blood leaked out the corner of her mouth. "And no."

"What does that mean?" Regel's vision blurred through welling tears. "What are you telling me?"

Rose lifted a trembling hand to his face and used her black thumb to wipe the tears away from his cheeks. "The darkness can be endured," she said. "Hope remains, no matter what we become, or how deep the abyss yawns. Find the light within yourself. The wonder. Show it to the world. Make it—" She coughed blood onto his face. "Make it a better world."

The bright light of magic stirring inside him flared to life, reaching out to her in compassion and love. Without the sword to eat away at it, Regel realized, it had grown hot and strong. Frostburn, simmering near his hand, pulsed violently with blue light. It called to him and coaxed him. Demanded of him. It would swallow him again and guide his course until he fed it blood and warmth and life.

"Make your choice, Squire," Rose said. "Frostburn hungers for my blood—for the last warmth inside me. *Our* warmth. You are one and the same, you and the blade. In this, slake your steel in me as you did your body." She pressed herself up, putting the point of the sword against her heart. "Leave your World of Ruin behind and finally know peace. Or." Her eyes slid shut. "Take the sword and use it."

Frostburn was in his hand. He did not remember picking it up.

It hungered. It needed. It *yearned.*

The moment stretched, caught in the endless haze of Necthana, even though he had escaped its confines. Time ceased to exist between them and his racing heart beat endlessly into the dark.

"No," Regel said.

Power surged in him, burning through Frostburn's icy walls, and he pushed it into Rose as she lay dying. The dark void where her soul should reside swallowed it hungrily, like fresh water poured into a long dry well. The Deathless's body tensed under his touch, and she shivered.

"No," Rose said. "What are you doing?"

Regel didn't care.

If she had no soul, that was all right. He had his own to offer. He tore pieces of himself free and shoved them into Rose. He felt her blood and her body, so like his own, but no longer what it had been at her birth. At first, he thought she had been a man, but of course, that was not the case. She was always a woman, because that was what she was.

He dived deeper. He felt her—became her—saw the world through her black eyes. He experienced the World of Wonder—the colors, the lights, the sounds, all of them flashes of memory from a child too young to absorb them—and it left him dumb and blind. He knew love: passionate and compassionate, all of it powerful and heart-breaking. He experienced her fear and her anger and all her life in memories he could not see or feel but nevertheless knew intimately.

"Regel," she said in his ear. "You need to let go."

Then she shoved him out of her, and they were two people once more.

He was once again a boy of fifteen winters, staring up at the most beautiful woman he had ever seen. At the same time, he had seen nineteen winters, and they lay in each other's arms for the first time. At the same time, at the height of his twentieth winter, she gave him Frostburn and he stood, triumphant and powerful, the pinnacle of a mortal warrior. At the same time, he came back to her, a broken man of forty winters who had lost all that he once loved, and she conforted him. She was a part of his world, and though she meant to hold herself apart from it, neither could turn from the other.

Frostburn clattered to the ground, the frosted mage-glass singing against the frozen tundra.

Regel was kneeling beside her—against her—his arms around her. She was whole once more, her wounds closed and her hurts eased. Their heat had melted the snow around them down to a white, uniform stone he had never seen before. It stretched out in all directions—seamless and pure like the snow that had covered it—protecting the deep buried city of Necthana.

Rose's eyes opened and she blinked up at him. "How?" she asked. "I am death. You are life."

Regel said nothing, only held her tighter.

At first, Rose lay taut and tense, but ultimately she relaxed into his embrace. He was her child, her squire, her lover, and her friend. They were, the two of them, people in the world, drawn together in one perfect moment of understanding and sympathy. But both of them knew it could not last.

He drew away, their fingers interlaced until the last.

"What you told me of Semana," Regel said. "You spoke true, even if I did not listen."

Rose nodded. "She is your daughter," she said. "But she is her own woman. She will bring light to this world. Do not smother that light, lest she lose her way in darkness."

Regel nodded. For the first time, he saw that he was wrong. He had always been wrong. With Lenalin, with Ovelia, and now with Semana. Perhaps… perhaps it was not too late to reconcile with his daughter. To find some measure of hope in a darkening world.

"I must go," he said. "And I will not return."

"You will do what you must do," Rose said. "As will I."

She lifted Frostburn, her dark hand clasped hard around the blade such that black blood seeped around her fingers. At first, Regel thought for a horrible moment that she might stab him with it, but instead she began to wrap it in a long scrap of leather form her torn cloak. Ultimately, she reversed the sword and extended it to him, hilt first.

"You will need this," she said. "Whether you will it or no."

This time, Regel did not argue. He took the blade—his fingers chilled even through the leather protecting them. His eyes never left hers as he rose to his feet, and finally he turned away.

He heard the darkness swallow Rose, drawing her back into the depths of Necthana, but he did not look back.

TWENTY-THREE

Iseldra's Folly

As before, she floated in the spiraling storm of worlds, but this time she knew herself.

She was Semana Denerre nô Ravalis.

She was Mask.

She was Semana and Mask, either and both.

She was both the Blood Queen and her mask.

She was falling or perhaps rising, but either way she flew with increasing speed through a universe that spiraled out around her in scintillating colors.

She saw scores of windows into other worlds—hundreds—thousands. She glimpsed every fantastic world she had ever dreamed and so many more she could not.

The more she tried to see, the faster she moved, allowing her to catch only the tiniest glimpses of vibrant, impossible beauty she could hardly imagine.

"What is this?" she asked. "What are you showing me?"

Her words echoed through the darkness, bouncing against the windows into the worlds. She felt weak, and her body lost strength as she floated. Somehow she understood that the longer she remained in this nexus among the worlds, the weaker she would become, until she unraveled entirely and ceased to be.

She had to seize control—to pull herself out before it was too late.

Desperate to restrain her fall, she reached out to touch one of the windows, through which she saw a bright, sun-blistered world of sand and yellow sky, and she an intense rush of dry heat swept across her. Her mouth and throat parched in an instant, and she coughed at the desiccated air filling her lungs.

For a heartbeat, she was in that world, sailing through that pure, golden air, overwhelmed by the sweeping barrenness of the spectacle. Half-buried mountains of red-gold stone stood out among the dunes, and she felt the heat of the blazing sun in the distance. Far below her, making a snail's progress along the sandy terrain, she saw a caravan of black wagons covered over with colorful blankets to shield them from the glare. The animals drawing the wagon resembled the horses of her world in some particulars but not others. They bore humps of flesh on their back, as few as one and as many as three, and they had six legs where the horses of the World of Ruin had only four. She saw people riding the wagons, too, who pointed up at her and exclaimed words she could barely hear, let alone understand.

She wondered what they would be like, these people of another world.

Then the world blurred around her, and she found herself once again in that space between worlds, where she could see limitless possibilities extending all around her. The worlds spun in all directions—up, down, and to all sides, always fleeing her grasp. She was doing something she should not—existing somewhere she should not. Reality itself opposed her, drawing away from her touch like a skittish bird that has never known a cage.

But she was a cage. She was the master, not the prisoner. The ruler.

She was the Blood Queen.

Power flowed through her, and she reached out to the fabric of reality swirling in the void. The magic pulsed in her head and her heart, much like when she sensed the blood of living things around her. It slipped in and out of her grasp, elusive and ephemeral, but it was there. She didn't yet have the power to control it, but she would. That magic had to exist somewhere in this place. It hid somewhere among the thousands of worlds that spooled out around her like threads spinning out into the darkness.

And if she could not discover it, she would create it.

For now, she clung to the world that came most readily to her call: a bleak window filled with smoke and blood and sorrow. She put both hands around the edges of the window, feeling its cold power burn through her. It was the World of Ruin, and it answered her call with a soft familiarity that made her long to return. She was not done with that place—not nearly.

But when she had conquered that world, then she would find more to make her own.

Light built around her, scaldingly bright and perfect.

The gray World of Ruin closed back around her, embracing her like Mask's old leather. It was a comforting feeling, this familiarity. It felt not unlike the comforting weight of a thick blanket that enwrapped her, sheltering and also stifling. Her body felt heavy indeed, the lightness she had known in the space between worlds crushed down beneath too much suffering and pain. And yet, Semana retained some of that lightness—a sense of purpose in a dark world teetering on the precipice.

She knew exactly what to do. What she was *meant* to do.

Breathing slowly in and out, Semana lay on her back and wondered why she hadn't died. There was so much blood pooled beneath her, black and frozen in the chill atop the mountain. The wind howled as night approached, and the temperature dropped so fast even she could feel it. Perhaps the cold had stopped the bleeding, even if her Frostfire kept the chill from harming her directly. She did not know the full extent of its power. Regardless, Semana couldn't feel her bloodless left leg below the thigh, and a thousand unseen needles pricked at the rest of her body as it slowly awoke from the cold. Her arms seemed almost too heavy to lift, but she knew she had to move. She had to get up.

She was the Blood of rulers and killers, of fleshborn gods and the most daring of mortals.

She could do this.

A thin rime of ice crinkled as Semana levered herself into a sitting position. Her left leg started hurting as soon as she moved it even slightly, filling her body with vice-like pain that threatened to knock her back into the darkness, this time to stay. Despite herself, she hissed at the hurt, and her breath came out in a cold stream of mist between her pale lips. For now, that felt like all she had—her breath—but it would have to be enough.

Semana trembled, and it took her a moment to realize that the movement came not from herself, but the stone beneath her. She held her breath for two heartbeats, and the ground shifted once more, dislodging several smaller rocks to skitter down into the bowl of the mountain's summit. A wide stretch of the pitted and scored slope to Semana's left folded in upon itself, retracting into a single long wedge that rustled gently against the stone. It was only when she saw the massive claws that extended from the tip of that wedge and from the corner of the slope that Semana understood what she was seeing.

She lay upon one of the silver dragon's wings.

How the beast had managed to land unobserved near the center of the moot and camouflage itself there without being discovered, she did not know. It lay prostrate and worshipful toward the summit of Iseldra's Folly, pressing itself against the slope of the sacred mountain like a child clinging to its mother, only recently disturbed by the fighting. Its head came into view, unfolding from around the natural tower where Darak had stabbed Afferath. Its face and neck bore the damage she'd inflicted upon it with her Plaguefire, but there was no anger in its eyes—only an unfathomable sorrow that threatened to draw Semana in and swallow her whole.

They were the same, she and the dragon: noble, beautiful creatures scarred and betrayed by a world that tolerated neither nobility nor beauty.

Semana held up her hands to the dragon to signal peace, and the beast seemed to understand. It furled the wing upon which she sat, sliding her over toward its outstretched arms. Semana laid her hand gently on the dragon's arm, feeling powerful muscles ripple below its scales in response. The beast shivered at first, then relaxed under her touch. Something in her called to something in it. The Frostfire, she knew, but also something more.

From the intelligence she saw in its great eyes, she knew without a doubt that the dragon recognized and remembered her. It had sought her out more than once, and she had proven a match for it on both occasions. She did not feel like prey—not any more. More like...*pack.*

That realization shook her to her very moorings.

An arm seemingly sculpted of obsidian appeared above her, an open hand extended down in her direction. The Deathless Gilt stood over Semana, the mountain wind sweeping his black cloak out to billow behind him like his own draconic wings. He was as dark as the dragon was light, night to the beast's day, and yet they seemed to understand each other in a way Semana couldn't fathom.

"Come away," Gilt said. "There is still time, before the pass closes tonight."

Part of Semana wanted to. Wanted very badly to go with him.

But she had seen that space between worlds. Glimpsed those windows into other realities. Understood her destiny and what awaited her. She could not run from it.

She didn't have to say anything. He read all that in her face. His expression darkened, but he nodded in understanding.

Then, slowly, he dropped to one knee at her side.

Today was a day of celebration and revelry.

Bodies coursed and writhed in the clearing at the summit of Iseldra's Folly: barbarians clashing and bending in one another's bodies in the wake of yet another Grand Moot. The Circle had seen its first death in over a decade, and soon a new druid would stand among the Circle. For the first time in the history of the High Druids, the new member of the Circle would be a man, and that unbalanced the ritualized orgy. Men had issued challenges in moots past, but they had always met with quick and efficient doom, reinforcing the dominance of the feminine. The victory of Darak, however, emboldened them to seize some measure of worth and strength, and they took greater risks and pushed harder during the revelry, which became equal parts wrestling and lovemaking.

Perhaps it was this that brought the High Druids' displeasure, casting a pall across their faces as they stood beneath their trees. Surely none of them had held much love for Afferath, but they recognized the challenge to their power. Carr the Axe glared murderously at Darak, as did Fellis the Night

Wolf—neither would soon forgive him his audacity in tainting their great circle. Mayel the Even-Handed wore an expression that seemed indifferent, but contained a world of disapproval for those who knew her well. Naor the Raging Flame seemed to have accepted this course of events, albeit grudgingly, but she kept looking for guidance to Erethar the Unmoving. The Grand Druid stood vigil over the chaotic revelry, expressing nothing overt but painted with a far away darkness.

Darak stood above it all, beaming bright and glorious. All his plans had come to fruition, and he was right to bask in victory. Nothing could touch him. Nothing could disrupt his rise. He clasped the bloody necklace and raised it to his nose and lips to inhale Afferath's scent.

Erethar raised her arms for silence and stillness, which were given her readily. All eyes turned upon her, and those of lower station bowed their heads or offered their necks in submission. Mayel stepped forward and opened her mouth, ready to speak for the Grand Druid, but Erethar cut her off with a single swipe of her hand. Face darkening in surprise and embarrassment, Mayel stepped back toward her tree, checking herself to stay composed. The barbarians gathered in the clearing looked in awe at the Grand Druid, overwhelmed with anticipation of hearing her voice.

It was such a pretty picture, she almost felt guilty spoiling it.

"Hold."

Mask stepped into the clearing from among the trees, shrouded by swirling silver-white magic. Frosted black leather wrapped her slender limbs and power leaked from her many relics: her silver glove, her helmet, her breastplate. She stank of blood, which coated her like wet paint. She floated slightly above the ground, so that none would know of her injured leg. She burned on full power and her Frostfire boiled around her like a shroud of ravenous death.

"Anathema!" shouted one of the High Druids, who rose up and pointed her hands at Mask.

Worldfire surged through the Circle, seeking to drain away Mask's relics. Another day, she might have tried to slay the druid before she could complete the counterspell, but not this day. Mask let the spell run its course, sapping the energy from her relics and dispersing it into the natural world. It made no great difference to the sorcerer. The magic shrouding her helm, glove, and breastplate only burned hotter, and she lost not a single inch as she levitated. The Worldfire drank and drank of her magic, and Mask always had more to give. No mortal body could hold that much power. But what was its source?

That was when the dragon appeared behind Mask, its head reaching through the trees and rising up over her shoulder. Its wings pushed through the forest and spread out around the clearing, enclosing all the druids in a dome of silver scales that blotted out the moon and stars.

The looks of terror and confusion around the clearing almost made her smile in the depths of her mask. To see the Angel of Ruin come among them—surging with power and impossible to slow or weaken—drove the barbarians not a little out of their minds. And when the dragon appeared, they lost their grip on reality entirely. Some shouted and screamed. Some brandished weapons and issued hollow threats. Some prostrated themselves on the ground and worshiped her. Still others stared as if the coming of a goddess had struck them deaf and dumb and unable to look away.

The rest of the Circle was on its feet now, bearing silent, angry witness to the spectacle. Fellis had drawn two arrows back to her cheek, and Carr held her axe at the ready. Other Druids she did not know had also drawn weapons or were in the process of summoning magic. Thorny vines curled around a green-haired Druid, whipping back and forth like a sentient weapon. Every one of them made ready for battle, in preparation for a challenge. It was the first time Mask had seen fear among them.

Erethar swept up a hand and turned to Mask. "What will you, Blood Angel?"

"Not an angel but a mask," she said. "And beneath, a queen."

Mask reached up and removed her helmet, allowing her pale hair to sweep around her shoulders.

"I am Semana Denerre nô Ravalis," she said. "And I am Blood Queen of Tar Vangr and all the northern reaches of Calatan, a title I am owed by birth and by right. I am one of you, by power and by deed." She pointed around at the members of the Circle. "I bested three of you. I should be among you."

A hush fell through the clearing, as the barbarians looked around at one another in confusion and unease. Whispers permeated the assemblage. This was not how things were done. A challenge had to be issued, and an acolyte could only ascend to the seat of the druid slain. Twelve High Druids stood in the Circle, and there was no room for a thirteenth.

"No." The druid who had challenged Semana at first stepped forward, thrusting her chest boldly like an ape challenged for dominance. Whether from age or weather, her pitted face and body resembled the flesh of an old tree. "I am Saegel of the Rotting Leaves, and I say no. You are a child with no respect for our ways or customs. If you had, you would know the Circle cannot have thirteen." Worldfire flared around her. "Whatever power you claim, you do not deserve a place among us. Leave now or die."

Mask opened her mouth to speak, but a strangled gasp of pain emerged in place of words. Her insides locked up in sudden agony, her bones grinding together and her lungs filling with fluid. It seemed Saegel wasn't going to give her that choice after all. Was this what Plaguefire felt like to its victims?

It took all of Mask's power and grit to stay upright. She held herself up with her glove's magic, knowing that to stumble or fall would be to concede defeat. It was not enough to survive—she had to endure. She had to prove to the assembled Circle and the most powerful of the Children of Ruin that she deserved this. Saegel's power rotted her innards and played havoc with her body, but she would see it through. She pulled more Frostfire from the dragon, fueling herself until the pain eased and she could breathe normally. Her thoughts were giddy and distracted.

"Twelve," she said. "I see only eleven, unless you will allow my brother to take the vacant seat. Is he the one you truly prefer? Or do you favor the strongest?"

Darak stared up at her, his whole body trembling. His dark complexion had gone almost sallow with fear, and Mask found herself enjoying every drop of it.

The words put enough doubt into Saegel to disrupt her focus, and the pain in Mask's body eased. She pushed through the haze and latched onto the High Druid's blood, seizing it in her greedy hands like the reins of a horse. Saegel stood suddenly taut, upright with her eyes wide, and stared at Mask. Her mouth moved but no words emerged. She and Mask locked into silent combat, even as their words filled the clearing. The barbarians might not have known what transpired, but the High Druids were not fooled. They remained silent and impassive, watching the unfolding duel between Mask and Saegel. Both had acted outside the established rules and customs of the moot, and that made their challenge acceptable.

Mask's eyes watered and she tasted blood and bile. She had to devote all her power just to stay standing, but perhaps she could delay Saegel long enough…

"Admit me," Mask said, words quavering. "Admit me among you, for your own survival. For if I do not stand among you, then I will stand above you. Above *all* of you."

The shadows parted beside Saegel, and a man seemingly made of obsidian fell upon her, reaching out with hands made of darkness. Only Mask and Saegel saw him, the former because she knew to look, and the latter because Gilt wanted her to see him. He did not strike her—did not so much as touch her—but his appearance was enough to distract her as though someone had screamed in her ear. Instantly, her magic fell away, and Mask had to fight to keep from gasping in relief. She drew the last of the dragon's Frostfire to edify herself and looked upon the Circle with cool confidence.

Erethar nodded at length, then gestured to her mouthpiece. Mayel stepped forward and surveyed the clearing, looking in the faces of the acolytes, High Druids, and finally Mask and the dragon.

"A Circle of Twelve," Mayel said. "But I see only eleven worthy."

Saegel's eyes gleamed at Mask, murderous and triumphant. "You are not worthy," she said.

Then metal whined through the air as an axe spun end over end. It cleaved into the Saegel's chest, knocking the High Druid back with the force of a battering ram. Gilt vanished from her side as though he had never stood there.

"Ruin favors strength," Carr the Axe said. "Deeds, not words. And power."

Mask stiffened slightly at the suddenness of the strike, then let out a breath.

Erethar turned to Mask and smiled.

"Welcome," she said. "Mask of the Blood Queen."

EPILOGUE

SEASONS PASSED AND THE white receded from the lowlands of the north. Ice turned to water, snow to sludge, and green started to come back into the world. The skies to the south and west brightened and colors returned to the land. Summer had arrived at last, and on Midsummer's day, it almost felt warm. The heat and vitality lasted too short a time, and the season started to move toward autumn within days.

Atop the Narkggr Wound, the farthest north and east any mortal had ever traveled, the world remained much the same year round. The snows dug in deep, losing only a little of their pack at the height of summer. The World of Ruin turned, but the lands of the dead remained constant.

Game was sparse in this place, consisting of snowy white rabbits adapted to dwell in the harsh climes, and far more dangerous creatures that descended from abominations twisted by the deadly magic that had infected Necthana. Winter wolves with two or three heads, massive serpents that burned with an inner fire, and four-winged birds of prey that stalked the mountaintops seeking easy meals. Deadly as they were, all learned to fear the man with the sword made of ice.

He built a cabin of sorts—a small shelter from the worst of the elements. He hunted and cooked and waited. He skinned white-furred deer and mended his clothes and waited. He started a hundred pieces of whittling but never finished them. His mind could neither focus nor rest but lingered, unbalanced.

He did as much as he needed to maintain himself. No more, and no less. For he knew, deep in the darkest pits of his frozen heart, that he would yet be needed.

He spoke with shades of those he had loved and lost. He ignored the presence of those he could not bear to see again. He carried on conversations with himself.

Every night, he watched Iseldra's Folly, and every morn he awoke to look at it again. Some nights, bright magic would flare above the broken mountains, but most nights it would not. Great events were transpiring, and he had no way to intervene.

He could only wait and watch.

When they found him, the Lord of Tears sat at the summit of the Narkggr Wound, staring out around the sweeping panorama of the World of Ruin. His rime-frosted cloak swayed slowly in the wind, making a soft crackling noise. His ice-choked face was turned toward the distant Iseldra's Folly, his ice blue eyes all but frozen as they stared. How long he had sat there watching, no one could say—not even him. A plume of smoke marked his campsite, where he kept his eternal vigil over the lands of ice, but even the fire seemed cold and dead.

He seemed almost a part of the landscape—a natural, frozen outgrowth of the stone below.

"Regel?" came a voice from behind him.

He turned his face slightly, ice crinkling in the hollows around his eyes. There she stood, a woman seemingly made of fire for how vividly she stood out against the white landscape. A thick winter coat of crimson fabric with touches of golden fur cloaked her strong body and swelling belly, and her hair streamed out behind her like the sun. Over her eyes she wore a bright red blindfold, and Regel could see faint scars around its edges—the result of reaving magic that had stolen her sight.

"Regel," Ovelia said again. "It's me."

He'd heard such things before. He looked back toward the distant mountain.

"Let me try."

A figure all in black stepped around to stand before him, snow spattering her voluminous robes like blood from a wound. Her voice came forth ragged but strong. She extended one velvet-wrapped hand and touched his frozen face, then pulled away in surprise.

"He's cold as death," the woman said.

Regel looked up at her, curious. He'd never seen this particular specter before, but she resembled other figures he'd seen. She was Mask and she was Rose and she was...someone else as well, but that could not be. The Deathless wore black as a matter of course, but rarely did they cover themselves fully. He sensed a certain physical fragility to this woman, but a force of will so deep and powerful he had rarely met its match.

"Who are you?" he asked, his voice hoarse and guttural from disuse.

"I am Lady Shard," she said. "And I need you to get up. Right now."

Accustomed to command. Ordering him about without question.

And warm.

So warm.

Regel stood, shaking off the rimefrost that had frozen him to the earth. In the process, his cloak swayed open, and the gleam of Frostburn's blue mage-glass blade rippled across the snow.

In a heartbeat, Ovelia stood between him and the black-swaddled Lady Shard, *Draca* drawn and pointed at his face. The shadows burned around the sword, painting images of a furious duel and blood to be shed. Awakened from its torpor, Frostburn screamed in his head for their blood to soothe its gnawing hunger.

"Regel," Ovelia said. "Stand. Down."

He considered. The old Ovelia—rival, friend, lover—would not kill him, no matter how he threatened her, and he had given her plenty of cause and opportunity. It was not in her nature. This new Ovelia, however…She, he did not know. He recognized her determination, but what had happened to her over much of a year to instill in her the deadly assurance he saw on her face? She would kill him in a heartbeat if he so much as took a threatening step toward this Lady Shard. Never had he seen her so protective, except when she stood between a foe and Semana.

Slowly, he lowered Frostburn and stuck its point in the snow at his feet.

Ovelia took his gesture as a sign of peace. That, and the shadows around Draca had subsided. They both knew Regel meant them no harm.

"Yes," Lady Shard said. "Now that our respective egos have been assuaged, we should make haste back to Hecatomb. We have much to discuss."

Below them, five hundred paces down the slope, a sleek silver skyship rocked uneasily on the snow. It looked not unlike the dragon he and Semana had encountered before the Ruined Cauldron, but folded and angled like a lance toward a foe. Regel had never seen anything so bright and new in all his years in the World of Ruin.

Lady Shard walked on ahead toward the ship, her movements a touch awkward as though from long ago injuries. She reminded him so much of Mask at that moment, he almost thought he had lost his mind entirely and would find only gentle death waiting if he followed her. Ovelia's warm hand, however, as she took Regel's, was real enough. He clung to it as though to his only lifeline.

Regel watched her curiously, his brows furrowing. "Who is that?" he asked.

Ovelia caught her breath, and her face looked pale. She smiled slightly, the corners of her lips crinkling upward in the first genuine display of pleasure he'd seen in what seemed like forever.

"Hope," was all she said.

Regel nodded. He didn't understand, but nor did he argue. Hope was something he had all but abandoned long ago. Ovelia had found her hope in Lady Shard, and he had some yet as well.

And something about her silhouette caught his attention. He only consciously noted it when she touched her belly. "You are with child," he said. "How—?"

Without her eyes, Ovelia turned pointedly away from Regel. He understood the implication: it was a tale for another time.

"Where is—?" Ovelia caught herself. "Semana. Where is she?"

"Gone," Regel said. "Lost. I tried to stop her, and I should not have."

"What does that mean?" Ovelia asked. "Where is she, Regel?"

A tear leaked out of Regel's eye and froze on his cheek, to match the black one inked by its side.

"She has chosen her path," he said. "And we must walk ours."

THE NAMED AND MARKED OF RUIN

Ravalis, the Blood of Summer

"Summer Lasts a Day"
Outlander Rulers of Tar Vangr, City of Winter

Cassian Ravalis (892–961): Last King of Luether (City of Summer), elder brother to Demetrus, father to Garin, perished in fall of Luether.
Demetrus Ravalis (894–981): Former King of Tar Vangr, younger brother to Cassian, father to Strevon, Paeter, Alistra, Lan and others. Slain Ruin's Night before 982 in Tar Vangr.
Ansa Ravalis nô Dorane (889–938): Wife to Demetrus Ravalis, perished birthing daughter Alistra.
Anthien Ravalis nô Vultara (916–961): Mistress and eventually second wife to Demetrus Ravalis, perished in the fall of Luether.
Toblius Ravalis (910–present): Younger half-brother to Cassian and Demetrus, husband to Alcha Varas.
Strevon Ravalis (930–961): The Hawk of Luether, first son of Demetrus, perished in the fall of Luether.
Paeter Ravalis (933–976): The Jackal of Luether, second son of Demetrus, husband to Lenalin Denerre, father to Darak and Semana, slain under mysterious circumstances.
Nameless (935–937): Third son of Demetrus, perished nameless.
Alistra (938–present?): The Spider of Luether, only daughter of Demetrus, imprisoned in the tunnels for unknown crimes.
Dorian Ravalis (940–961): The Wolf of Luether, son to Demetrus, perished in the fall of Luether.
Garin Ravalis (943–present): The Fox of Luether, former crown-prince of Luether, only son of Cassian.
Alcarin Summer (954–present): Smallborn squire to Garin.
King Lan Ravalis (944–present): King of Tar Vangr, the Eunuch King, the Bear of Luether, son of Demetrus, husband to Laegra.
Laegra Ravalis nô Vargaen (940–present): Daughter of house Vargaen, neglected wife to Lan.
Alcha Ravalis nô Varas (930–present): Wife to Toblius, wed after Fall of Luether.

Boulis Ravalis (948–present): The Hound of Luether, son of Toblius.
Tolus Ravalis (951–present): The Falcon of Luether, son of Toblius.
Vhaerynn the Necromancer (unknown–present): Blood sorcerer and vizier to Demetrus.

Denerre, the Blood of Winter

Justice In the Storm
Former Rulers of Tar Vangr, all but extinct

Aritana Denerre (885–932): Former ruler of Tar Vangr (910-932), youngest ruler of Tar Vangr in centuries, mother to Mortiun and Orbrin.
Moritun Denerre (911–936): Former ruler of Tar Vangr (932-936), elder brother to Orbrin, perished suddenly and unexpectedly in battle.
Orbrin Denerre (916–976): The Winter King, former ruler of Tar Vangr (r. 936-976), father to Althar and Lenalin and a third nameless child, perished at the hands of Ovelia the Bloodbreaker.
Matir Thorass (914–961): Wife to Moritun, political bond to Orbrin, mother to Althar and Lenalin and a third nameless child, perished in the fall of Luether.
Althar Denerre (937–955): Former Crown Prince of Denerre, perished in a duel.
Nameless (938–942): Second son of Denerre, perished in the cradle without a name.
Lenalin Denerre (940–966): Wife to Lan Ravalis, perished under mysterious circumstances.
Darak Ravalis nô Denerre (961–971): Son to Lan Ravalis and Lenalin Denerre, exiled to Ruin for treason at a young age, presumed dead.
Semana Denerre nô Ravalis (963–present): Last Heir of Winter, daughter to Lan and Lenalin, master to Tithian. Faked death in 976 and took up the mantle of Mask.
Tithian Davargorn (963–present): Smallborn winterborn pageboy, then squire to Semana. Faked death in 976 and became loyal servant of Semana.

Dracaris, the Blood of the Dragon

Eternal, Unyielding
Treacherous Sworn Shields to Denerre

Norlest Dracaris (917–961): Sworn Shield to Orbrin, father to Ovelia, perished in the fall of Luether.
Aniset Winter (922–942): Smallborn mother to Ovelia, perished in childbirth.

Ovelia Dracaris the Bloodbreaker (942–present): Sworn Shield to Lenalin, slew the Winter King in 976, mortally injured in the assault on the Summer King Demetrus in 981.
The Circle of Tears ("Ever Weep, Ever Watch"): A consortium of Spies in Tar Vangr
Regel Winter the Oathbreaker (936–present): The Lord of Tears, formerly the Frostburn, Shadow of the Winter King, sworn slayer in service to Orbrin Denerre, current spymaster of the Circle of Tears.
Serris (960–981): Smallborn squire to Regel, First of Tears. Slain Ruin's Night 981.
Erim (961–present): Smallborn thief, occasional lover to Serris, bastard son of a Dolvrath noble.
Vidia (946–present): Smallborn baker.
Nacacia (957–present): Smallborn warrior.
Daren (955–present): Smallborn warrior.
Krystir (955–present): Smallborn spy.
Meron (940–981): Soldier, bastard son of a Vortusk noble, slain by Ravalis soldiers.
Sarelle (979–present): Child of Serris.

Gardh

"The Wind Speaks for Us"
A frontier community long lost to Tar Vangr

Phend (960–present): Protector of Gardh, a hunter.
Jeht (942–979): Former Protector of Gardh, deceased.
Tsarn (938–present): Smallborn merchant of Gardh
Nys (936–present): Smallborn warrior of Gardh
Hiesk (937–present): Smallborn warrior of Gardh

Circle of Druids

"Ours is the Power, Ours the World"
The rulers of the barbaric Children of Ruin

Erethar, the Unmoving (unknown–present): Grand druid, female.
Mayel, the Even-Handed (930–present): High druid, female.
Carr, the Axe (943–present): High druid, female.
Naor, the Raging Flame (945–present): High druid, female.
Afferath, Mistress of the Rain (950–present): High druid, female.
Fellis, the Night Wolf (948–present): High druid, female.
Saegel, the Rotting Leaves (927–present): High druid, female.

Children of Ruin

Barbarians warped by the broken magic of the World of Ruin

Dar-Karsk (961–present): Rotpriest, former squire to Afferath, male.
Kalik (950–present): Servant to Dar-Karsk, female.
Bellows in the Deep (955–present): Warrior sworn to Dar-Karsk, male.
Rending Gash (963–present): Warrior sworn to Dar-Karsk, female.
Crown of Fire (960–present): Warrior sworn to Dar-Karsk, male.
Fierce Wind (957–present): Warrior sworn to Dar-Karsk, female.
Mountain's Rage (952–present): Bodyguard to Afferath, male.
"Right" and "Left" (956–present): Bodyguards to Afferath, male brothers.
Breaker of Frost and Ice (953–present): Bodyguard to Afferath, female.

Necthana, City of the Deathless

"Eternity without Death"
The Deathless Fae of Legend

Rose (540–500 SA): Queen of Necthana, female after death.
Gilt (912–952): Warder, male.
Blood (952–980): Sentry of Necthana, fae.
Dawn (954–980): Sentry of Necthana, male after death.
Silver (914–946): Sentry of Necthana, fae.
Dew (897–930): Sentry of Necthana, fae.
Summit (287–340): Explorer, male after death

ABOUT THE AUTHOR

Erik Scott de Bie (tip: "de Bie or not de Bie, that is the question") grew up in the smoggy central valley and verdant mountains of California. He has been writing fantasy and scifi novels since before he could drive, and has been published since before he got his degree from Willamette University. He lives in Seattle with his wife Shelley and a menagerie of cuddly dire animals.

Erik's work has also appeared in the Forgotten Realms D&D setting, Pathfinder's Golarion, the Iron Kingdoms of Warmachine, several settings with Onder Librum including the fantastic Stormtalons, unnerving Hellmaw, and stellar Lost Princesses of Mars, plus countless anthologies, both shared world and original. He is also the author of the multi-media Justice/Vengeance superhero series.

Check out World of Ruin updates, lore, deleted scenes, and behind-the-scenes features on erikscottdebie.com, as well as Erik's ever-growing bibliography. Find him on Facebook at www.facebook.com/erik.s.debie or on Twitter: @erikscottdebie.

www.ingramcontent.com/pod-product-compliance
Lightning Source LLC
Chambersburg PA
CBHW031102260626
47172CB00001B/182